HEADLAND

A BILL MURDOCH MYSTERY

HEADLAND

GED
GILLMORE

 deGrevilo
Publishing

Cataloguing in Publication details are available from the National Library of Australia www.trove.nla.gov.au

Creator: Gillmore, Ged

Title: Headland : A Bill Murdoch Mystery / Ged Gillmore.

ISBN: 9780994178695 (paperback)
ISBN: 9780994178657 (ebook)

Subjects: Drug dealers—Australia—Fiction.
          Detective and mystery stories, Australian.
          Suspense fiction, Australian.

Editing: Bernadette Kearns, Book Nanny Writing and Editing Services
          Kate O'Donnell, Line Creative Services
Additional Proofreading: Ashley Casey
Typesetting: Oliver Sands
Cover design: Luke Causby @ Blue Cork
Cover photograph: Matt Mason

Set in Adobe Garamond Pro 10.5pt
10 9 8 7 6 5 4 3 2 1

For more information on Ged Gillmore and his books, see his website at:
www.gedgillmore.com

For OS, who makes everything possible

She came for Murdoch on a Tuesday night, like maybe she knew it was the night he sorted his stock. Later, of course, there was no maybe about it. She knew all right, the same way she knew not to use the lift or bring fewer than six big men.

Murdoch had just turned on the light when they came through his door. Before that he'd stood in darkness, staring out his grubby window to study life in the units across the wasteland. He'd always thought it weird how Australians called them 'units', but then maybe it was weird how you called them 'flats' back home. Turned out both descriptions were right. In the block across the way, he could watch as many flat units of life as chose not to close their curtains. Couples fighting, children chasing in and out of view, women walking around in towels. He did it too often, he knew, staring down at people most nights while the oven warmed his food and heated the bare rooftop shack around him. He'd thought once or twice of breaking in over there, hiding microphones so he could hear what good citizens talked about, understand what made them tick. He wouldn't do it, of course, he wasn't mental and there was a rule about avoiding unnecessary risks. But it would be interesting to know what normal people worried about, what they wanted from life.

On this mid-winter Tuesday night, as a plastic lasagne thawed in the oven, Murdoch watched across the darkness as a young Asian man on the other side moved about his kitchen, choosing, chopping, frying in bursts of steam. A dark-haired woman came into view and said something that made the man laugh, made him reach for her until she danced out of the way. The smell of Murdoch's own dinner demanded his attention, but he didn't want to break the spell of the darkness. He wanted to know if the Chinese guy would stop his cooking and go after the girl – maybe they'd leave the curtains open for that too. But then rain spattered against his window, reality determined to get his attention, so he turned with a sigh, crossed to the light switch and flicked it on. Above him, the fluorescents hummed and thought about it, before stuttering the breezeblock shack into brightness.

No one could see into Murdoch's place – the warehouse roof was higher than any of the units across the way – but always when he turned on the light, he thought about what they would see if they could. A scarred and wiry man, too old for his years, red hair shorn short, dark eyes that unnerved people, he didn't know why. A man alone in an empty room – a *nearly* empty room. Apart from the oven, there was only his flimsy camp bed, a small folding table and a chair. The only thing on the walls was his noticeboard, a riot of colour against the breezeblocks. Here, creased facades of comfortable houses struggled with overlapping gardens while badly folded living rooms fought sleek kitchens. Seeing the mess of pictures now, Murdoch remembered a page he'd torn from a magazine earlier in the day. He pulled it from his pocket, unfolded it, and stared at its picture: a pair of matching sofas in front of broad French doors open to a garden. He was pinning it up with the others when he heard the door being kicked in.

Cynthia always told Murdoch he was built like a cattle dog, all prick and sinew, and not an ounce of fat. He said, yeah, well, most big blokes were all intimidation and slow punches – he'd rather be quick, and a smaller target, any time.

'You get too big,' he told her, 'and some bastard's always got to prove he's bigger.'

Most of the guys he'd put down hadn't seen it coming: they'd thought he was just another runt they could kick out of the way. That was before he got a reputation; after that, people avoided him. But the guys who came into his place that night were not most big blokes. Murdoch had made it less than halfway to his flimsy camp bed – and, more to the point, the Beretta beneath it – before they had him down, one on each limb. They were very professional, none of them firmer than they needed to be. Murdoch swore at them, told them they'd got the wrong man, he'd not done nothing wrong. In reply, they pressed him gently against the cold concrete until, at last, he heard himself – heard his noise was the only noise there was, and heard it wasn't helping. He stopped then. Listened to his breath instead, heavy and liquid against the hard, grey floor. Closed his eyes and tried to think.

This, it seemed, was what they were waiting for. The guy on his right arm – the only one of the four he could see: a huge Islander all neck and tattoos and perfect teeth, drops of rain glistening on his face – shouted to someone outside the door.

'Down!'

The message was repeated across the warehouse roof so that now there were at least six of them and Murdoch was scared. A second later and he heard the huge goods lift moving toward the ground floor.

'It's all right,' said the Islander, smiling down at him. 'No need to worry.'

Murdoch knew what he must look like. A dog after losing a fight, eyes wild, but nothing much else able to move. 'He's right,' said the others, heavy men he couldn't see. 'We're not here to hurt you,' and 'It'll be fine, mate.'

'Get off me, then!'

He'd wanted to keep the fear from his voice and it came out as aggression.

'Soon,' said the Islander. 'Soon, buddy.'

Murdoch listened to the lift working its way up the warehouse floors. Then he felt the concrete beneath him vibrate as it shuddered to a halt, the rumble of cables replaced by a shriek of heavy metal doors. After that there was no sound but the rain until the broken door of the shack whined on its hinges and firm footsteps entered the room. They brought black and business-like shoes around the crouching Islander to stop close to Murdoch's face. His gaze travelled up the pinstriped trouser legs above them, but he could see no higher.

'I'm very sorry to do it like this, Bill, really I am.'

A woman's voice: well-spoken, but so husky it croaked, like she'd started smoking in the womb. Then silence again. She was waiting for him to speak.

'What do you want?'

'I want to talk to you, my dear. I want to make you an offer.'

'Who are you?'

'We'll get to that.'

'Get these bastards off me.'

The shoes adjusted and the pinstripes bent at the knee until she was squatting above him: a big woman with thick hair and strong features. Straight nose, clear skin, bright blue eyes under delicate eyebrows. She leaned her head to one side and examined him – should she put the dog down or spend the money on a vet? – unbuttoned her pinstriped jacket and held it open to reveal a Glock 26, snug in its Serpa.

'Now,' she said. 'You know there's a round in the chamber. Are you sure I can get them off you?'

This was when you were supposed to give in. Sigh, cry, look at the floor and promise them the world. Murdoch held the woman's eye and nodded slowly.

The heavies picked him up, sat him on the chair and – boys in a doll's house they'd promised not to break – carried the table towards the oven. There they stood around it, playing cards they'd produced from somewhere. Murdoch recognised one of them as the big pink guy he did business with most Saturdays, face like a butcher in an ad on the telly. The woman stood apart from them, closer to Murdoch, as she introduced herself as Maria Dinos; apologies again for doing things this way. She smiled and leaned against the wall beside her until she realised it was leaving grey dust on her suit. Brushing it off, she kept a careful eye on Murdoch, but at no point did she look worried about him.

'First of all,' she said, 'I need to reiterate, we are not here to harm you. I'm going to make you an offer. If you refuse we will leave again and none of this happened. You won't see Tommy here,' – she indicated towards the pink-faced man – 'on a Saturday night. If you see any of us again, we will not recognise you, and you will not recognise us. Do I make myself clear, my dear?'

Murdoch held her eye, but said nothing. He could smell his dinner burning, was surprised none of them could smell it too.

Maria smiled. 'That's smart, Bill, letting me do the talking. I like that. It's an example of why we'd like you to work with us. Put that *down!*'

Murdoch followed her glare to the shortest of the heavies – a cube of a man with dreadlocks and a bulbous nose – who had picked up a beer bottle from the work surface next to the oven. The cube blushed and apologised, said he was just moving it out the way of his elbow, boss, then watched shamefaced as the Islander with the tattoos reached past him with gloved hands, wiped the bottle down on his T-shirt and put it back in its original position.

'Oven's on, boss,' said the Islander. 'Something burning in there.'

Maria Dinos told him to bloody well turn it off, then and watched him do it before turning back to Murdoch. 'We will touch nothing else in your home …'

She looked around and seemed to notice for the first time there was nothing much else to touch. Her eyes stopped on the noticeboard and she wandered over to it, not touching as per her promise, but surveying its contents closely before turning back to him.

'I'm guessing you'd like me to cut the bullshit and get on with it?'

Still he just sat and looked at her, the only noise the slap of the cards on the table.

Maria smiled, a little less easily than before, and continued. 'The thing is, Bill, I'm here to offer you a job.'

Part One

CBD

Murdoch checked his watch, gave the waitress his best smile, and ordered a coffee he didn't want. It was forty minutes before he had to be in the George Street office, but it was too hot to hang about on the street, especially in a suit. The summer had been relentless and now, at the end of February, even he was sick of it. He told himself he should have brought a newspaper – he could have sat fiddling with his pen above the cryptic crossword like he knew how to work one out. He'd seen a bloke do this just a week before: alone at a table for over an hour after he'd finished eating, inconspicuous because of a newspaper.

Eighteen months now he'd been doing the job and still he felt out of place. It was the clothes that bothered him most: suits, shirts, ties, shoes that cost more than his first car. He'd always liked the idea of being a spiv and, stupid as it was, it had been one of the reasons he'd taken Maria up on her offer. He'd had no idea how uncomfortable it would be. How your tie was either too tight or too loose; how your jacket pulled and restricted you whenever you sat down. The guy he had seen the previous week, the one with the cryptic crossword, had hung his jacket around his shoulders like it was a cape, but Murdoch had never seen anyone else do that. Here, in this restaurant, all the blokes kept their jackets on all the way through the meal, so Murdoch did the same.

With nothing else to look at, he studied these men in their jackets and their suntans, leaning forward to share secrets before pushing back against the table and laughing loudly, either at what they'd heard or, more likely he reckoned, at what they'd just said themselves. As he watched, a few tables away, a well-maintained brunette turned and caught his eye. She held it for a less than a second before deciding no, nothing of interest. Right next to him, two well-fed bankers were talking loudly, whole sentences in a foreign language.

'They're running the PSG like a PWG and, if they don't sign off before the end of the financial year, our NPV calcs are blown.'

Murdoch saw the waitress returning with his coffee and checked his watch again.

'Scuse me, boys,' he interrupted the men beside him. 'Mind if I have a squiz at your paper?'

They turned and looked at him like the wall had spoken. Then the older of the two, a man who'd probably been born in a suit, realised there was a *Sydney Morning Herald* under his elbow.

'Oh,' he said, 'I don't see why not.'

He handed it over and there Murdoch was, struggling with the crossword, when the waitress arrived with his coffee. He barely looked up when she set it down beside his paper. Seeing her hovering out of the corner of his eye, he ignored her until, eventually, she disappeared without asking if he wanted the bill.

The office in George Street had a long-legged receptionist, who went out for a chai latte every day between two thirty and three o'clock. Murdoch could tell she wasn't supposed to. She'd cross the huge marble lobby as fast as her clicking heels would allow, barely squeezing out a tight smile for the security guards before dodging the traffic on George Street, no time to wait for a gap. Then she'd stand beside the Daily Grind coffee cart, smoking a thin cigarette while she waited for her drink. She was a good-looking girl: long legs in a short skirt, nice eyes, blonde hair done up in a way that was meant to fall down again. She ignored the looks she got, grabbed her chai as soon as it was ready – another tight smile – dropped her cigarette and repeated the process in reverse, even breaking into a trot across the echoing lobby if she thought she could make an open lift. Every weekday, regular as clockwork, six- to nine-minute turnaround.

Murdoch left the restaurant at exactly twenty-five past two, the humidity a shock after the crisp air conditioning, and walked up George Street as slowly as he could. He stood on the corner of King Street, hating his jacket and arching his back to keep his shirt off the sweat slowly forming there. Cars and delivery vans roared past, their noise contributing to the heat somehow. Then the receptionist appeared on the pavement not two metres away from him. As she started to cross the road, he turned and ducked into the building she had just left, crossing the lobby and taking the first empty lift to the tenth floor.

It still surprised him that in the right suit you could walk into most buildings in the Central Business District. Surely the whole point of security guards was to keep people like him out? But even if one of the guards ever did look up, all he needed to do was smile and they'd call him 'sir' and watch

4

him walk past. Not everywhere, it was true; not any more. Some of his meetings were in buildings where you had to be scanned through a barrier. But, even there, all he needed was the name of the person he was visiting and he was given a magical swipe card and told where to go. Like no one in the world had ever done anything bad in a suit.

Murdoch wasn't complaining. He liked being part of this system of trust, this assumption that everyone is all right and not out to do you any harm. So what if he was still dealing poison the same way he'd always done? Or, on bad days like today, protecting the Club's patch? At least he wasn't doing it with the normal scum: animals with no interest in getting to the other side.

The previous time he'd been to the tenth floor – on his rehearsal run – he'd leaned across the empty reception desk and stolen some paper with the serviced office's letterhead. He'd scribbled a note on it, written like he was in a hurry:

Couldn't find anyone here. Have gone into the Waratah Room as per our telephone conversation. Under no circumstances to be disturbed until Mr Chaplin arrives.

Regards, J Smith.

He walked around the desk and laid the note on the receptionist's red office chair. The seat was still warm and he left his hand there a second, thinking of those legs. Then he hurried down the corridor.

The Waratah Room was furthest from the reception desk, next to the Gymea Studio and opposite the Banksia Boardroom. It was the smallest office on the floor, but still big enough to hold a solid desk in front of a standard-issue leather executive chair and, closer to the door near a frosted sash window, a small meeting table with four padded chairs. Heavy, inoffensive furniture.

Murdoch set his briefcase on the table and stood listening, eyes fixed on his watch. Chaplin, of course, would be late. His type always was. He'd arrive in a rush and not apologise, ignoring any comment you might make about it. Or worse, he'd swear, tell you to deal with someone else if you didn't like it, and threaten you for wasting his time.

5

After five minutes, Murdoch thought he heard the lift doors, but sound travelled badly up here: that was half the point. Another five minutes, still undisturbed, and he told himself to relax. He took off his jacket and hung it on the back of the leather chair, the way his buyers did in their offices. Walked over to the meeting table and, pushing one of the chairs aside, checked the sash window still ran smooth. He left the window a little open, like he wanted to let some air in. Thought about taking off his tie, but decided against it. Instead, he took off his belt and put it in his pocket.

With his waistband looser, he realised how uncomfortable he'd been since leaving the restaurant. It wasn't just the weight of his lunch or the coffee he'd drunk despite himself. These enforcement jobs always got him in the stomach and this one was going to be the worst yet: a man who'd run out of warnings. Murdoch looked at the phone on the desk and wondered if maybe it wasn't too late to call Maria and tell her he wasn't willing to do it. He frowned at the idea and pushed it away: a stranger's cigarette smoke on the street. Returning to the window with renewed determination, he opened the sash fully and leaned out to look up at the heavy grey sky, then all the way down, ten storeys to the bottom of the lightwell, where an air conditioning unit sat in a pool of dirt.

He was still there, looking out the window and thinking about school, the first time he got into real trouble, when the phone on the desk rang. He walked over and punched the speakerphone button the way he'd seen his clients do – too important to pick up a receiver.

'Smith.'

'Hello, Mr Smith, sorry for not being here when you arrived. I have Mr Chaplin for you.'

She had a voice like a secretary in a black-and-white movie, a suggestive smile under everything she said. Murdoch wondered if she always spoke like that, or if it was just part of the job – how she'd act if they ever met face-to-face. He thanked her and asked her to send Mr Chaplin through. Hit the button on the phone again and picked up his briefcase, took out a pair of handcuffs and put them in his other trouser pocket. For a second or two, he perched on the edge of the desk, but then – a better idea – ran behind it, the fat leather chair creaking in protest as he lowered himself.

Before he'd gone inside Murdoch had looked young for his age. It was the red hair, the thin and sickly frame, all those fucking freckles. He'd

6

resented it a lot of the time, but the rest of the time he'd used it, had made the clueless little schoolboy act – 'he seemed so innocent, officer' – his speciality. Not that his baby-face had helped when the big job went wrong. They'd done it five days past his eighteenth birthday and, all of a sudden, his round face and wide eyes had been useless. Twelve years down the drain, thank you very much.

Murdoch didn't generally let himself think this way – everything in his life was about the future now – but as soon as Paul Chaplin walked into the room, a whole crowd of memories rushed him at once, like they'd been gathering their numbers out of sight waiting for the right moment.

'You all right, mate?' said Chaplin. 'You look like you've seen a ghost.'

Murdoch told him he was fine and within a few seconds he was. 'Close the door,' he said. 'Sit down. Hope you don't mind me asking, mate, but how old are you?'

Chaplin grabbed a chair from the meeting table, dragged it noisily towards the desk and slouched into it. 'Aw, don't. I get this all the time. I'm older than I look. Old enough to get a drink in a pub. Old enough to be doing business with you. Jason, is it? You said Benny James gave you my name?'

A precarious ginger quiff wobbled above Chaplin's freckles as he spoke, the kid repeatedly putting up a hand to check it was still there. The bag on the floor beside him was the same type of Adidas satchel Murdoch had had as a kid.

Murdoch shook his head slowly, closed his eyes and ran a hand across his own close-cropped scalp. This wasn't going to be easy. He heard Chaplin talking again and opened his eyes to find the skinny kid leaning in over the huge desk – a little boy playing grown-ups.

'Mate, you sure you're all right? You crook or something? You know, I'm a bit busy, so if we can get on with it?'

Murdoch gave him a level stare. 'Maybe we wouldn't be in such a rush if you hadn't been late.'

'Excuse me?'

'You heard.'

'Look, Mr Pommie Smith or whatever your name is, you buying or not? Two more minutes of this and I'm out of here.'

Murdoch sighed and nodded slowly. He stood and walked around the desk, rested against it and looked down at his former self. 'OK, Chaplin, what you got?'

'Whatever you need, mate. Charlie, crack, pills, smack, G, P, ice or black. All of it cheaper than the competition and no messing. Just need a bit of notice for the bigger orders, no questions asked. What d'you need?'

'You don't mind Benny giving me your name?'

'Nah, why should I? A friend of Benny's is a friend of mine. Anyhoo, let's do this, shall we? I've got somewhere I need to be.'

'I wouldn't be too sure of that.'

Murdoch jabbed Chaplin twice hard on the nose, the second punch knocking the kid and his chair backwards onto the floor. Before he could get up, Murdoch was on him, sliding his belt around his neck, fastening it quickly, and pulling hard. Chaplin flailed in choking fury, his tiny fists everywhere until Murdoch gave him a few slaps and told him to calm down. The kid stared at him and turned his hands to his own throat, nails at the leather belt. Murdoch knelt beside him and adjusted it carefully – a man tuning a radio to a bout he wanted to hear – until Chaplin could breathe and gargle but couldn't shout. Once Murdoch had got it right, he stood, one foot on the restraint and one on Chaplin's chest. He undid his cufflinks and his watch and put them in his free pocket. Now he was ready to talk.

'Listen to me, you little arsewipe, you're out of this now, understand? You need to be either smart or tidy to survive in this game and you ain't neither. You let your clients give out your number to people what you don't know. You come to an office you can rent by the hour and sing like a canary to a bloke what you've never met before. You're late, you're rude and …'

The kid was trying to say something. Murdoch knelt and loosened the belt slightly.

'Fuck you,' said Chaplin.

Murdoch punched him hard in the stomach and, while the kid was still gasping, found a handkerchief and forced it into the boy's mouth. Then he pulled off his tie and used it to gag Chaplin tightly. The kid struggled again, kicking against the chair and punching anything he could find, but Murdoch avoided it easily enough. He only took his weight off the belt to push the kid away from the fallen chair, flip him over, catch his wrists like birds in a pet shop window and handcuff them behind his back. For a while this made Chaplin struggle even more, but then the kid was suddenly still, breathing heavily through his bloody nose, tears blotching his face. Murdoch sat him upright in the chair again – he was even lighter than he looked – and turned him to face the other side of the room. Chaplin hadn't got it. His eyes were wide, but, even handcuffed to a chair, there was no fear in them: someone was going to pay for this. Murdoch looked at him and shook his head. Pulled another of the chairs over from the meeting table and sat on it so his dark eyes were level with Chaplin's.

'Let me tell you something. My name is not Jason Smith. I am not an office worker what wants to buy drugs in a fake meeting. And you are not smart enough to deal in the CBD without the big boys noticing. You see this room? You want to know why I chose it? I booked the other ones near it too, by the way, so I know they're empty. We could be in one of them, but I chose this one because it has a handy little feature.'

He stood and moved the table and remaining chairs from between him and the sash window.

'The idea is I drop you ten floors to your certain death. It'll be a few days before anyone finds you, but, when they do, the news will get out to the right people soon enough. Then I can go back to meeting my sales targets without wasting my time on pest control until the next little arsewipe like you turns up. Except by then ...' But that was no one's business but his own.

Murdoch stopped rearranging the furniture and looked back at Chaplin. Now the kid had got it. He was breathing as heavily as he'd done on the floor, shaking the remains of his quiff violently left and right, shouting muffles through the gag of material in his mouth. Then he was crying. Great sobs shaking his pale frame so that the chair beneath him wobbled and threatened to topple over again. A dark patch spread across his lap.

Murdoch looked away and frowned, sat down and wiped his hand across his scalp again.

'As I was saying ...' But he said nothing else. Instead, he studied the vague white pattern in the carpet, staring at it and seeing nothing.

'Listen,' he said eventually. 'You have no idea what you're getting into here. You think you're just going to make more money than any of your mates and go and live it large on a beach somewhere. But it doesn't work like that, sunshine. You get caught with what you've got on you today and you'll go down for six to eight. And, mate, you're not a fighter, let's agree on that. They'll eat you up in there – they like boys with pasty pale arses. Next thing you know, you're out again and you've not got no way of making money without getting a bigger sentence and, then – bang – you're thirty-something, unemployable, and the only way to survive is by dealing with the scum of the world.'

Murdoch heard himself talking and stopped, no idea what the hell had got into him. The rule said no mercy – what wasn't clear about that? He forced himself up and dragged Chaplin – quiet now in some kind of daze – off his chair and over to the window. He had him halfway out before the kid came to life again.

Murdoch had seen a man shoot a horse once – the bloke had done a bad job of it, put three bullets into the beast before it would die – and when Chaplin started screaming behind his gag, he remembered the noises the horse had made: deep and high at the same time, everything it had coming out. Chaplin slammed a knee against the wall beneath the windowsill and cracked the plaster slightly, his other foot shooting out sidewards to catch Murdoch on the shin. It didn't hurt much, but Murdoch dropped him anyway. He watched Chaplin slide down the office wall and wriggle under the furniture crowded into the corner like it too was scared of the fall.

For long minutes, there was no noise but Chaplin's muted sobs and Murdoch's own breathing. Then, swearing at himself, Murdoch reached past the kid and picked up his briefcase from the floor. He took a length of cord from it and, struggling now, caught Chaplin's feet one by one, kneeling on them so he could tie them tightly together. He dragged the kid feet first to the other side of the desk, stood him, and pushed him down into the soft leather chair. Chaplin was quiet again, but he was still crying; more snot than blood from his nose now, a dirty bruise forming on his ashen forehead.

The Adidas bag sat undisturbed where Chaplin had left it on the floor, calm in the eye of the storm. Murdoch picked it up and went through it slowly, examining each of the packages before transferring them to his briefcase. He rolled down his sleeves, put his cufflinks back in, and picked up his jacket from the chair behind Chaplin. Then he crossed to the door, opened it slightly, stuck his ear to the crack and waited. Chaplin watched him in silence.

It was a good fifteen minutes before Murdoch heard the receptionist's heels on the tiles and the door to the bathroom swing. When he did, he pointed a stubby finger at Chaplin – 'You won't be this lucky again, you fuckwit,' – stepped into the corridor and let the door shut quietly behind him. Taking a deep breath, he swore at himself more vehemently than before and strode down the corridor towards the lifts. Within two minutes he was back on the sticky street, just another suit late for his next meeting.

Too late as it turned out. There was no way he could make it to Macquarie Street on time, not unless he ran all the way and arrived at the Club with a shirt more wet than dry. Checking his watch again, in case it had lied to him a minute before, Murdoch swore out loud and stopped so suddenly that another man bumped into him from behind. He was tall and sure of himself, this man, important enough to complain until he saw the kind of man Murdoch was. Watching him retreat, Murdoch was tempted to go after him; sometimes it was so difficult to remember who he wanted to be. He felt cool air on his back and, turning, found he was outside a café doorway, the business inside deserted but for a bored Vietnamese girl behind the counter. Murdoch walked in, dialling Maria Dinos's number.

'Maria, it's Bill. Listen, I'm running late. Can we move it to half past?'

'No, my dear, we can't. I've already got a four thirty and he's waiting outside. Can you do five fifteen? Or next week? You should have enough to get through the weekend, surely?'

There was a tightness in her husky voice and he wondered what he'd done wrong this time. 'Well, actually, today'd be better. I need some advice and it's getting kind of urgent.'

'Fine,' she said, 'five fifteen then.' Murdoch hung up and dialled Cynthia, ordering an iced tea from the Vietnamese girl, any excuse to stay in the air conditioning. Cynthia's phone rang out to voicemail so he hit redial.

'Hello, handsome,' she said when she answered at last. 'Everything all right?'

She was putting on a sexy voice for him and he realised the receptionist with the legs had been doing that too. No one spoke like that all the time. Murdoch told her he was going to be late.

'Oh Blackie, have you forgotten? I've got that thing on tonight. I did tell you. The girls are picking me up at nine.'

'I could get there at eight.'

She hesitated and he wondered if she had someone else there.

'Could you get here by seven, Blackie? If I promise to make it worth your while?'

'And how would you do that?'

'Well, I don't know, darl. I thought I'd just be lying on my bed in nothing but my knickers from seven o'clock onwards and you could work out the rest for me.'

He saw the girl behind the counter was listening, told Cynthia he'd see her at seven and hung up. Carried his tea to the back of the empty café and sat staring into space while his skin adjusted to the chill.

He'd met Cynthia on the platform at Redfern station. Despite her body, it was her hair he noticed first. Pitch-black and thick, there was something old-fashioned about it, like she'd just walked out of a movie. Or maybe it was the raincoat she had on, belted tight and unbuttoned, like she wasn't wearing anything underneath. She was compact and held herself well; anyone could see she was fit, even if these days it was the gym rather than nature holding gravity at bay. She'd caught him looking and asked him when the next express went and they'd chatted for a while, until next thing they knew, no one wanted to catch a train. They found a hotel nearby, neither of them pretending it was anything but what it was. They'd talked about how expensive Sydney was these days; how it cost so much just to have a good time. He'd wondered how much that was exactly and she'd said a hundred bucks, plus the hotel bill. And it was a good time: good enough to make it regular. They saw each other every Thursday night – most Thursday nights, sometimes she had something on. She let him go round to her place in Blacktown: two hundred bucks for a good time and a meal and he could stay through the night if he wanted. He never did – sometimes they didn't even do it – but he still figured he got his money's worth.

She called him Blackie because of his eyes. 'They're so frightening,' she'd said that first time in the stained hotel room in Redfern. Then later she changed her mind and told him they were frightened. Like there was someone hiding in there, backed up against the wall, terrified of what was going to happen next.

He watched the Vietnamese girl make her way down the café towards him, wiping tables that were already clean. She was tiny, four foot something, standing too long each day in high heels. She asked him if he wanted anything to eat and he said no thanks, the iced tea was fine. It was obvious she wanted to close the café but was too scared to ask him to leave. No sympathy for his black eyes there.

'It's all right, darlin',' he said, scraping his stool on the tiles so she jumped and scampered back to the counter. 'I know you want me gone.'

2.

The Club was in an old building in Macquarie Street, just tall enough to peer over the hospital and into the Botanic Gardens. Close enough to the law courts that you passed a few barristers on your way, gowns flapping black behind them like reminders you had to be careful. Every other building in the row was filled with doctors, the spaces around the doorbells crowded by brass adverts for dermatologists and oncologists and urologists. The Club building was the same. Stone steps ran up to its heavy wooden doors, standing open between the brass plaques to reveal a list of names and floor numbers inside. On many, letters were missing, so *Dr mith* shared with *Mr Pa el*. Fewer people visited this building than any other on the street, but it was no worse a front for that.

The glowering sky had grown darker through the afternoon, pressing its humidity onto the CBD until the towers tore at the clouds. Now, as Murdoch walked slowly up the steps of the Club, still trying to avoid a sweat, it started to rain, like the day was determined to get him damp one way or another. The huge waiting room on the top floor was stuffier than normal, its tall windows no protection from the heat outside. The fans that usually stood in each corner had been moved to face back towards the reception desk. The receptionist who sat there was new.

'Name?' he said as Murdoch approached, the fans ruffling his thick black hair: a gorilla in an open-top car.

'Afternoon,' said Murdoch.

'Name?'

'Fine, thanks. Bit hot out there. How are you?' Murdoch was still new enough to Australia to love this: the way they always asked each other how they were. None of them gave a shit, but it was nice all the same.

'Name?' said the gorilla for the third time. He was one of those blokes that need to shave every hour, his thick neck uncomfortable in its collar and tie, his dark features no better because of them. He ignored Murdoch's smile, sour eyes steady beneath bushy and unimpressed eyebrows.

'Murdoch.'

'Mr Murdoch?'

'Yeah, whatever. The doctor's expecting me.'

The gorilla sniffed, looked down at his desk, pushed aside an economics textbook and found the appointments register.

'Says you was supposed to be here at four.'

'Yeah, well, I called to say I was running late, didn't I? Rearranged for this time. If that's all right with you.'

The gorilla sniffed again. He could tell Murdoch was in a hurry. 'Well, Mr Whatever, seeing how yous's late, maybe the doctor can't see you at all.'

'Is someone else in with her?'

'No.'

'Well, let's see if your fat fingers can operate the phone. How about you buzz her and tell her I'm here?'

'How about you go fuck yourself?'

They looked at each other for a few seconds. *Any other time*, thought Murdoch, *you and me, sunshine*. But Cynthia was waiting in Blacktown.

'Listen,' he said, 'let's both stop wasting Maria's time, shall we? I'll be a good boy and you tell her Murdoch's here, how does that sound?'

He walked over to the windows and looked down at the street so the gorilla could do what he needed to, like it was his own choice. Outside the rain was heavier – it never rained lightly for long in this city – and Murdoch watched the traffic thicken. It was another ten minutes before Maria came out.

'You're here!' she said, striding across the room and grabbing his hand in the grip that always disturbed him. She was wearing a suit, of course – bespoke, of course – like she was off to buy something expensive: a football club or a ship.

'I was wondering where you were, my dear. Hussein, why didn't you tell me Murdoch was here?'

'Oh sorry,' said the gorilla. 'Did I forget to do that?'

The front ended at the door to Maria's office. This was no doctor's surgery. Thick rugs on dark floorboards, heavy furniture on little curved legs, satin on the walls that, according to Maria, had cost five hundred dollars a metre. There was hidden air conditioning, smooth as a breeze, the sole noise in the room the ticking of assorted clocks. Only the huge windows were the same as the waiting room, but even these were half-hidden by plush curtains, green velvet pooling in ripples where they hit the floor.

Maria's desk – the very desk at which General Somebody had planned the Battle of Something – was at the far end of the room. Murdoch rarely made it that far. Maria preferred to talk on the heavily studded leather sofas by the fireplace.

'What happened to Arnie?'

'Don't ask,' said Maria. 'Not my choice.'

'I've been out there for ten minutes, do you know that?'

'Don't let it bother you, my dear.'

'Do you know what, Maria? It does bother me. One of the main reasons I do this job is to avoid tossers like that.'

'Shut up, Bill!'

They stared at each other for a second, difficult to say who was more surprised. Maria had screeched at him, a higher-pitched tone than he'd ever heard from her. Murdoch smiled, thinking she'd apologise or something, but, instead, Maria sighed, got up and walked towards the windows, to a globe that opened out as a cocktail cabinet. She stood there with her broad back to him and asked if he wanted a drink.

'I'm fine, thanks.'

'Still a one-beer-a-day man, eh?'

'Something like that.'

She turned and looked at him, framed by the clouds outside.

'You still seeing that chick in Blacktown? Celia? It's not Celia, is it? Sonia? Sandra?'

He gave her a flat-eyed stare.

'Is nothing private?'

'No, my dear, nothing. I told you that when I hired you.'

'But you guys don't know who she is yet, do you?'

Maria didn't answer that. She came back to the sofas, sitting on the same one as him this time, whisky clinking in a chunky glass, her thighs spreading pinstripes across the leather.

'Did you sort out Chaplin?'

'Yeah.'

'How was it?'

'Yeah, fine. Not my favourite thing, you know that, but, yeah, job done. We won't see him again.'

Her face hid her amusement, but it came out in her husky voice. 'You didn't do it, did you, Bill?'

'What?'

'You didn't do it.'

'Didn't do what exactly?'

'Bill, look at me. You didn't knock him off, did you? Honestly, my dear, for a career criminal, you're a surprisingly bad liar. What's wrong? You going soft on me? What happened to "No-mess, No-mercy" Murdoch? All those rules you live by?'

'No mess is what happened. No need. He was an amateur. Trust me, I scared him; he won't be back.'

'Bet you a fiddy he will be. In fact, scrap that. I'll fine you a fiddy when he is, you hear me?'

She meant fifty grand and she wasn't joking, but she was trying to keep the tone light, trying to pretend she hadn't just lost it with him. Murdoch heard the carriage clock on the mantelpiece mark the half hour. Cynthia would be in the shower now, he should have left the building five minutes ago. He reached for his briefcase. 'Maybe we should get on with it?'

Maria said she supposed so, plonked her glass onto the coffee table and heaved herself wearily out of the sofa. Over at her desk, she clicked on a lamp – the sky outside darker by the minute – then leaned and opened a drawer as he read out his order. When she brought an assortment of plastic packages back to him, he threw them quickly into his briefcase: he'd be chopping and bagging all day tomorrow, care and attention could wait till then.

'Well, then …' He stood and rubbed his hand over his scalp.

'You said on the phone you needed some advice?'

'Oh yeah, it's fine. That can wait.'

'Sounded fairly urgent when you were on the phone, Bill. What you in such a rush for? You got someone more important to see?'

She walked back to the sofa – a few more lamps clicked into life on the way – and collapsed into its comfort again, patting the seat next to her. Murdoch sat down.

'I keep getting calls from some outfit what calls itself the ATO. Something to do with tax. I told them to get lost the first few times, but I think that made it worse.'

Maria rolled her eyes, sighed heavily, and asked him what his front was.

'My front?'

'What's your front? What's your shop?'

'Shop?'

'Bill, tell me you've got some way of explaining how you earn your money just in case anyone ever asks?'

'No one's ever asked. If I did I'd tell them to mind their—'

'Bill, this is the tax office. When they ask, you have to answer. You never heard of Al Capone? You need a front, my dear, a business. All those shops you see with no one ever in them, what do you think they're there for? For God's sake!'

She hadn't shouted again, but she wasn't far off it either. Murdoch looked at his hands, then over Maria's shoulder at the grandfather clock behind her. He could be half an hour late for Cyn, she wouldn't mind. They sat in silence for a minute or two until Maria said she was sorry.

'It's been a shit of a week, my dear. Hey, you sure you don't fancy a drink?'

'No, I'm fine. Listen, don't worry about the tax thing, I'll sort it out. I should let you go. I hope your week gets better …'

17

'The thing is, Bill, there's something I need to talk to you about too. There's been a bit of a … restructure. The Club's moved a few people around, so I've got a new boss. Regime change, you could call it. A change of strategy.'

Murdoch waited.

'The Club wants you to take on a bigger role than just dealing, something more similar to what I do. This fiddy-a-week stuff, well, the margins are good, but it's time-consuming and risky – too much traffic for too little profit. So, we're going to concentrate on the bigger stuff. They, that is, *we*, don't have many guys as dependable as you. You know, you present well, you're professional. No mess, no mercy, etcetera. So this small stuff isn't really making the best use of our prime resources. We need you to be the go-to guy for the deals with bigger distributors.'

'Prime resources?'

'Give me a break, Bill, that's how these people talk. They've all been to business school and shit. You should see the stuff they're asking me to do. Reports, spreadsheets. I was here till midnight last night.'

'No.'

'It's a great opportunity. Less running around, more free time.'

'No.'

Maria leaned back and gave him a look he hadn't seen on her before. Slowly he realised she was scared. He felt his stomach start up again, the belt of his trousers as snug as a noose.

'You know it's not what I want,' he said. 'We had a deal; another six months and I'm out of here.'

'To your little house by the sea?'

'What's so bleeding funny about that?!'

'Settle, petal; it's not funny. You know full well I think it's great that you've got an aim. It's …' she chose the word carefully '… *admirable*, Bill. But what if you could get there in three months?'

'Yeah, great idea, thanks. Except the last time someone told me there was a quick way out of the game, I was eighteen and got sent down for life. I was young and stupid then, Maria, but now I'm big and ugly. So thanks, but no thanks.'

She twirled what was left of her ice cubes, and he knew there was more to come. She nodded towards the waiting room.

'You know Arnie who's normally out on the desk?'

'What about him?'

'Seems the new management think I need a babysitter.'

'And Arnie?'

'Arnie was offered a different job out west somewhere. Arnie, twenty years in the Club, said thanks, but no thanks. He likes it here. Nice view of the Botanic Gardens.'

'And?'

She shrugged. 'His wife called me this morning asking if I knew where he was.'

They sat and looked at each other for a while.

'I could disappear,' he said.

'Disappear on the Club? Good luck with that.'

'Do they know much about me?'

'What could I tell them? I don't know much myself.'

'Right. Thank you.'

'Whatever. If you're going to do the disappearing act, Bill, you better do it fast.'

'What do you mean *fast*? We talking a week, a month?'

She shrugged and he rolled his eyes and swore. There was a rumble beyond the windows: thunder or a plane or a lorry in a pothole, impossible to tell. Then just the ticking of the clocks again, the clink of ice in Maria's glass as she took another slug.

'What about you?' Murdoch asked. 'What you going to do?'

Maria nearly cracked at this. A tiny tremor in her left eyelid, her top lip not as sure as it liked to be. Murdoch knew she had teenage daughters. She stood quickly and walked to the globe again. Asked if he was really sure about that drink.

Then she turned sooner than he'd thought and caught him scowling at his watch.

'Or you got somewhere better to be?'

'No,' he said. 'Not any more.'

3

The next day another waiting room. Shoddier this one and a lot busier: a constant stream of people walking in from the shops and hesitating over the machine before taking their ticket and hoping for the best. Murdoch watched the red numbers changing on the wall behind the counter: *A147*, *B12*, *A148*, then looked at everyone else watching them too. Someone had had a go at designing the space – zigzag seating in comforting colours, the same soft tones on the wall – but it was still a government office. He shifted in his seat for the third time in as many minutes and resisted rolling up his sleeves. On Maria's advice, he'd left his jacket and tie at home, but he wasn't any better off for it. The night's rain had hardly touched the humidity; what they needed was a real storm.

Maria had told him about the New South Wales Crime Commission and the government seizure of the proceeds of criminal activity, about legislation and guidelines on the minimum sentences for organised crime. Only then, when she'd seen he was listening, had she told him they could sort things out. Give him enough invoices to keep the ATO off his back forever.

'Tell them you're a psychoanalyst or a male prostitute,' she'd said. 'Anything to explain why people want to pay in cash. Porn merchant, pawn shop, psychic, pimp.' She laughed. 'Anything beginning with a "p".'

He'd said he was glad she found it funny and she'd told him to calm down.

'Tell them you're a cage fighter, Bill, on the unofficial street scene. They'll take one look at you and they'll believe it. They'll *want* to believe it; it'll be interesting. Something to tell the kids that night in suburbia. Guess who daddy met at work today?'

When he'd told her cage fighter didn't begin with a 'p', Maria had laughed again and said 'Pugilist does, my dear.' He'd had to go home and look it up. He'd hardly slept that night, had been up through the small hours researching on the internet, piecing together a story that someone might believe.

'William James Murdoch?'

A small pink mouse of a woman in dark trousers and a nondescript blouse had opened a door at the end of the line of counters. She stood blinking through her glasses and Murdoch could see that unless he answered quickly she was going to shout his name even louder. He hadn't heard his full name used since he'd last been sent down and couldn't see why this woman needed to use it now. He stood slowly and sauntered over. The mouse gave him the Minimum Polite Smile and said, 'This way, please,' before turning back the way she'd come, down an overlit corridor of identical green doors. Murdoch left the door to the waiting room open behind him and strolled after her, asking after a few steps if Mr Simms was too important to come and get people himself. The woman stopped and looked over her glasses and he saw that with a different personality – one that wore skirts and sexy shoes – she might turn your head. She had a good figure and thick blonde hair cut into a bob; it was her blonde eyelashes that made her look like a mouse.

'My name is Hannah Simms,' she said. 'I'm your tax inspector.'

She didn't seem to need a response to that and marched on, until, a few metres later, she stopped abruptly and opened a door on the left. Inside was a small white office. She gestured Murdoch through, offered him a metal chair, then squeezed past him and behind a grey metal desk. Reaching her own worn chair, she lowered herself into it so carefully that he wondered if it had let her down in the past.

'So, Mr Murdoch …'

'Please, call me Bill. Everyone calls me Bill.'

She sniffed at the idea and didn't comment, then gave him a sudden and uncomfortable smile. Like someone on a course somewhere had told her you should smile at the public. She reminded him of a prison counsellor he'd had, younger than him, when he was only twenty-three, terrified on her first week on the job. He'd made her life hell.

'It seems we had some difficulty contacting you?'

Maria had said he should apologise. Show humility, let them know they were in charge.

'I'm a busy man,' he said.

'Yes, we're all busy Mr … but all income has to be reviewed for taxation.'

Maria had said to agree to this vehemently. To say money for hospitals and roads didn't grow on trees. Murdoch said nothing.

Hannah Simms reached down and pulled a file from a drawer beneath her desk, then sat back carefully, testing the limits of her chair. She flipped the file open just out of his view.

'You have only one bank account in Australia?'

'Only one bank account anywhere.'

'In the name of William Murdoch?'

He found an imaginary thread to pull off the knee of his trousers. During the course of the previous night, he'd resigned himself to paying tax on the money banked in his own name. It was a protection racket, the same the world over, no reason the Australian government should be any different. But there were limits.

'What do you mean?' he said slowly.

'This one bank account, it's in the name of William Murdoch, I presume?'

'Oh. Yeah, course.'

'Yes, well, normally you see, Mr ... Bill ... normally we need your permission to look into your accounts. But as this case has been escalated due to your lack of responsiveness, I can now look into any bank account in Australia in that name and review the transactions at a daily level.'

Murdoch offered to give her the account number if that would make things easier and she tried her smile again and said, yes, it would. He dictated the numbers and they sat in silence for a while, Hannah Simms concentrating on her computer screen, Murdoch practising his breathing.

He watched Hannah Simms go through his bank account, printing off copies of the transactions, marking little asterisks next to certain lines with her pencil. She was younger than he'd thought at first, but in clothes designed for someone twice her age. Lamb dressed as mutton. Why would anyone do that? She had full lips, the top one floating as she read, and healthy skin that hadn't seen much disappointment. A tiny silver chain flashed into view as she bent forwards towards the computer screen and Murdoch bet himself five dollars it had a cross on the end of it. Behind her glasses were soft grey eyes. She looked up and caught him watching. Said, 'Sorry, just give me a second,' and pretended not to see his blush. It was another fifteen minutes before she was ready.

'So, Mr Murdoch.'

'Bill.'

'Yes, Bill. And you should call me Hannah, I suppose. So, tell me, for the past eighteen months you have clearly been earning an irregular but substantial cash income and not declaring any of it?'

'I had a lucky year. It won't be like this next year, trust me, so I thought if I can average it all out after a few years, then it'll be fine.'

'Really. I see here that you're an Australian citizen and yet we have no records of any tax being paid by you ever. How does that work?'

Steel in the grey now. Maria said don't resist them. Pretend to give them too much information, not too little.

'You tell me,' he said. 'You're the expert.'

Hannah Simms sighed and laid her pen down. She leaned forwards on her desk, looking at her hands as she spoke. 'I'm not sure if you're aware of this, Bill, but my job is to help you explain how you earn your money and why you don't pay tax on it. If I am unable to do that, you are facing at least a heavy fine and very possibly a jail sentence. Believe it or not, I don't want that to happen. What I would like to happen is for us to get along and explain what's going on, for you to pay your back taxes and for us both to get home on time.'

He believed her – maybe the mutton helped with that. Hannah Simms looked like she was tired with the job, not with him – as miserable in here as he was. He forced himself to apologise, easier than normal, and told her he wasn't used to this kind of thing. 'It's this whole place,' he said. 'It gives me the creeps. And' – no idea why he was sharing this – 'I'm told I have an issue with authority.'

'Yes, well, as for this place, try working here five days a week. And don't worry, I have a bit of an issue with authority myself.'

He doubted that, but it was nice of her to lie. He sat back in his chair and took another of her smiles – softer, more sincere this one. What the hell, he had to give her something. He explained he was only a few years out from England. Told her how his father had been Australian (no need to explain 'father' had never been more than a tiny word on his birth certificate) and how the smartest thing he, Murdoch, had ever done had been to get his citizenship sorted. Sensing he was on a roll – Hannah Simms nodding nicely and not taking notes – he fished out a business card, a new one from the machine at the station, and handed it over.

'A private detective?' she said, looking doubtful.

This, he knew, was where she'd ask to see his Commercial Agent and Private Inquiry licence, the minimum requirement, according to the internet, for private eyes in New South Wales. It was the biggest hole in his story. He could say he'd lost it and was waiting for a replacement, but he had no idea if the tax inspector had access to a central registry of all CAPI holders. He took a quiet breath and prepared his sweet and innocent face.

'Well,' she went on, 'it would explain why you're so cagey. Mind you, you must be good at it. Based on your income, you're clearly more Magnum than Marlowe. So, tell me, how does that work?'

He told himself not to look too relieved. Told her about the big corporate job, the case he couldn't talk about because it was still before the courts. She asked him how he'd got into that line of business and he wove in the elements of truth that make any lie work. How he hadn't done well at school, but knew he could do better than anything what he was qualified for. How he'd done manual labour, then some security, then through that met people who did investigations for a living. How he couldn't see himself surviving in an office job, no offence. Hannah Simms, genuinely interested it seemed, wanted details that couldn't have anything to do with tax.

'Do you ever get into any fights?' she asked. 'Lovers not wanting to be followed?'

'Sometimes, but I can handle myself. Course, it's always messy, but I get by.'

'Messy?'

'Yeah, you know.' She didn't. 'Well, when you see a fight in a film, it's all clean kicks and deflects, where in real life it's all grabbing and all over the place. You must have seen a fight?'

'No, never.'

'Come on, at school and stuff? Or in a pub on a Saturday night? You must have done.'

He watched her think about it, then shake her thick bob. She'd never been near anything like that. He raised his eyebrows and sat back in his chair, interested in her for the first time. 'Can I ask you a question, then?' he said. Then, when she nodded, 'You know when you was a kid, at school? After school, what'd you do?'

'In the evenings?'

24

'Yeah, when you'd finished school for the day, like. What did you do then?'

She looked at him guardedly, then seemed to decide he really wanted to know. Thought about it for a second, smiling at her memories.

'Oh, I don't know. Lots of stuff. I played a lot of netball, so I used to go to practice. Or swimming – my parents were swimmers and they wanted us girls to do it too, but I wasn't really into it. Homework, of course, always lots of homework. Round to friends' houses sometimes. Why do you ask?'

'No reason. And you never got into no trouble or nothing?'

'Oh, I wasn't a complete goody two-shoes. My dad caught me and my sister Sarah smoking cigarettes once when we were barely teenagers and I thought he was going to explode he was so angry. What? Why are you looking at me like that?'

'Nah, nothing.' He'd been shaking his head as he listened. 'Must have been nice. Did you go to the beach much?'

'I grew up on the beach! In a small town on the Central Coast. I don't think I could ever live away from it. I live in North Bondi now, go into the water every day.'

A small noise escaped him, a tiny grunt of jealousy. She asked him if he liked the ocean and he nodded and looked away. She looked down at her file and found his address.

'You live out west? Why don't you move closer to the beach? You could certainly afford it.'

'I'm saving,' he said, not wanting to tell her this. 'I've got this plan. I'm desperate for it. I've always wanted to live near the sea.'

'You and half of Australia.'

'There's these houses see, they're building these houses in Bronte, just back from the beach …'

'On Magdalen Road? They're going to be nice, I run past them sometimes. You're going for one of those? Well, I guess with your income you'll get a loan easily enough.'

He nodded, letting her believe that was the plan. Told her he'd put down a deposit – pointed to it coming out of the transaction account – and that he had six months to come up with the rest. Get a loan for the rest, he meant. He caught himself and got her to talk instead. Listened to her rattle on about all the Poms in Bronte, how it didn't seem fair somehow. Murdoch couldn't think of what to say to that and they sat in silence for a few seconds until Hannah Simms went back to her notes, trying to find something to ask him.

It wasn't difficult. There were questions about paperwork, a conversation about deductions, another about what he expected to earn next year. Maria had told him to keep the story simple and to this he had listened. He explained to Hannah Simms that he really shouldn't be telling her this, but a well-known Sydney club had a potential damages suit on their hands and they'd needed someone followed 24/7, full surveillance, indoors and out.

She asked him questions he hadn't prepared for and twice he nearly contradicted himself. Even on easier ground, her grey eyes never looked fully convinced. The tax inspector had a way of raising her eyebrows and waiting every time she asked a question. Like she was interested to see how long it would be before he tripped up. Or, like there was something she wasn't saying, was on the point of asking him about, but always held back. Out of nowhere she asked if he only worked in Sydney or sometimes took cases out of town. He told her he'd go wherever the work took him and wondered what in his bank account had made her ask that. He hadn't been out of Sydney since the day he'd arrived in Australia nearly two years earlier.

They were there for another hour – nothing but business now – a list of the paperwork he'd have to provide growing slowly between them. He hadn't a clue if she'd believed a word he'd said. They started on a new page of transactions and he found himself pulling his hands slowly down his face.

'You look tired,' she said.

She didn't. She looked as neatly ironed as when she'd first appeared in the doorway.

He told her he was fine. 'I'm just not very good with numbers. You can do them all in your head, I can tell. I'm a bit slower than you.'

'Well, everyone's clever at different things. Imagine me in a fight. Listen, you know above this building is the Westfield Tower, have you ever been up there? There's a rotating bar; it's nice. I think we've finished here for now. Would you object to me buying you a beer?'

Do what? Murdoch was momentarily lost for words. Then he asked, 'Are you allowed to buy clients beer?'

'You're a subject, not a client. And, anyway, it's ten past five. They don't pay me well enough to work any more than I have to. What do you reckon, beer or not?'

He looked at her differently as he followed her back along the corridor. Her arse firm in her trousers, the nape of her neck pale beneath the bob. He thought she'd be embarrassed to be seen leaving the office with him, but they didn't pass a soul.

'Ten past five in the public sector,' she said. 'No wonder people scoff.'

He didn't ask her what that meant.

In the hot and crowded lift, they were silent, strangers pressing them gently against each other, until his phone started ringing. When he fished it out to kill the call, Hannah didn't hide her study of its screen.

'Who's Maria?' she asked. Then, looking up at him, 'You want to tell me to mind my own business, don't you?'

'Not in front of a bunch of strangers.'

The man behind Hannah looked up at the remark and smirked. Catching Murdoch's eye, he left his smirk behind, rubbed his nose and looked quickly down again.

Murdoch had been up the tower before, but never at that time of day. Out east, the horizon was still clear – light blue separate from the darker sea – but to their right, thirty clicks across the city, night was creeping up from behind the mountains, the edge of the sky darkening like paper about to burn. Hannah Simms said it was a shame; she'd hoped there'd be a sunset.

'It's not the same as seeing it set over the ocean, but sometimes you can come up here and watch the sky turn all sorts of pink and orange. And there's supposed to be a storm on the way, thank God. I thought we might see something of it.'

Murdoch told her he'd never seen a sunset over the sea and he didn't know you could see storms coming. She gave him a strange look, like he might be joking, then told him to go and wait by the window, she'd find him when she'd got the drinks.

It took her longer than he expected – the bar busier by the dozen every time the lift doors opened – and he had time to pinpoint the part of the town where they were building his house. He walked slowly against the turn of the room to keep it fixed in his sights, began to think maybe Hannah Simms was fussing in the bathroom until she pushed through the crowd looking just the same: no extra lipstick, glasses still halfway down her nose.

'Listen,' she said, passing him a beer, 'I'm feeling a bit stupid.'

They both heard his phone ring again. He ignored it and asked her why she felt stupid, but she just nodded at his trouser pocket and asked him if he was going to answer that. He sighed and pulled out the phone. It vibrated in his hand like a frightened bird.

'Maria again?' Hannah was delighted. 'Goodness, she's persistent.'

'She's a colleague.'

'I thought you worked alone?'

That look again, the little raise of the eyebrows. Music started up, Latin beats two notches too loud, and he had to raise his voice. 'She's someone I often use for stuff. Surveillance, that kind of thing. Are you still inspecting me or is this a social drink?'

'Talk to her,' she said, walking over to the window to study the dying sky. He looked at his phone again – Maria didn't ring unless she had to – until suddenly it fell silent in his hand. He knew he should call back, find out what was wrong, but Hannah Simms hadn't answered his question. He joined her at the view and asked her why she felt stupid.

'It's embarrassing either way. I mean, I may be making all of this up – or not – so I'll just say it. I asked you out for a drink and then came up here talking about sunsets and I'm worried I've given you the wrong impression. I'm not remotely interested in you from a ... well, this isn't supposed to be a romantic thing. Not a date or anything.'

'Oh.'

'Did you think it was?'

'I wasn't sure.'

Not the right answer apparently. Hannah Simms took a sip from her huge white wine and frowned over the rim of the glass. 'Couldn't you try and look a little disappointed?'

'Do you want me to be disappointed? Maybe that's the point of the drink?'

'No! I'm just ... you're not making this very easy, you know.'

She'd adopted the mutton tone again, a little colour in her cheeks this time. It was his fault he hadn't got the wrong end of the stick and now matron was being made to suffer.

'All right,' he said, 'I'll admit I'm curious.'

'Curious?'

'Well, I'm the subject of one of these investigations of yours. You're clearly very professional. You've brought me up here for a drink, but it's not a date. So, what is it? Part of the investigation, then?'

They'd stopped walking against the turn of the room and the view of Bronte was drifting slowly out of sight. Hannah suggested they sit down, maybe somewhere a little quieter. Further around the bar they found some stools, where the tax inspector sat fidgeting for a full flat minute before she spoke again. She asked him if he'd ever heard of Georgie Walker. She had to repeat the name twice through the noise of the music before he shook his head.

'It was in all the papers, although not for long, of course. Some drunk football star was soon judged far more deserving of attention. Georgie was – she is – my niece. She lives where I grew up, on the Central Coast. At least, she did. Then she disappeared. Lovely girl, very pretty, very timid and shy. They put her picture on the front pages and everything. She was an angel. But I suppose they always are, aren't they?'

'They?'

'These kids who disappear. The papers always describe them as if they're lovely, although in my experience most teenagers are absolute brats. But Georgie, she really was great, a really good girl. Her mum – my sister, Sarah – had died in a hit-and-run a few years earlier, when Georgie was fourteen, a terrible age to lose a parent. Georgie never got over it – refused to even discuss it. She had always been quiet but after that she just withdrew into herself. Still, we were close. I tried to be there for her as much as I could. Then, when she was seventeen, well …'

Murdoch couldn't see where Hannah Simms's story was going. He was more interested in why Maria was calling him on a Friday night.

'Sorry, love, what happened when your niece was seventeen?'

If he remembered too late to give the question a frown, to look like he really cared, Hannah Simms didn't seem to notice. She thought carefully before coming to the point of her story, to the reason why they were here, chatting in a bar, when Murdoch should be calling Maria. He forced himself to concentrate, to lean in and listen closely, like Hannah's words could drown out his worries.

'No one knows what happened,' she said. 'One day Georgie just didn't come home. Gone. Not a clue. The police investigated and came up with exactly nothing.' Hannah bit her lip, took another sip of wine. 'Don't worry, I'm not going to cry or anything. I've done all my crying and, anyway, it's not really my style. I have a favour to ask.'

Murdoch's phone was vibrating in his pocket again. If Maria had given him some bad gear he was going to have to make a lot of calls very fast. There was no way around it: he was going to have to answer. But the phone stopped as soon as he'd got it out of his pocket, like it had only been teasing, any reaction enough. He frowned at it, then stared vaguely across the bar, wondering what to do. The sky outside the windows was black now, the view replaced by reflections of the crowd inside. He saw himself and Hannah Simms, seated at a bar like a normal couple, out for fun on a Friday night. Saw that she was talking to him and knew he should listen. Turned towards her and found her waiting for an answer.

'Sorry, darlin',' he said, 'I'm not sure I understand. You want me to what?'

She leaned closer to him and shouted. 'It is loud in here, isn't it? I'm giving you a case, Bill. You said now that big corporate job was finished, you had nothing else on until the club surveillance starts. And you said you'd travel to wherever the work is. So I'm offering you this case. I want you to find out what happened to my niece, Georgie.'

4.

The storm came ashore just after eleven. The radio had hyped it up, warning people to get home on time: the end of the world was nigh. In the event, it was just rain. A lot of it – by midnight so heavy you couldn't see much else – but just rain.

Macquarie Street was drowned. When the lights changed down by the park – blurs of red to blurs of green – the odd taxi splashed slowly past, but otherwise all was quiet. The sparse street lights jaundiced the rain-shot pavements, the flowing gutters and, here and there, a drain bubbling like a broken pipe. Any cars parked away from the lights sat in virtual darkness, the colour of their paintwork indistinguishable, anyone inside no more than a shadow.

Murdoch opened his window a crack and smoked another cigarette. Maria had stopped calling him while he was still in the bar, but then a text had arrived asking him to come to the office for twelve thirty. This wasn't a strange time for her – Maria worked all hours – but she'd written: *please, mate.* He couldn't remember if he'd ever heard Maria call anyone 'mate'.

There had been a voicemail too. 'Bill …' her voice breathless, or whispering, it was hard to tell, '… don't …' And that was it.

He'd listened to it four times in the lift down from the bar, Hannah Simms pretending not to be curious, just asking once they were out on Market Street if everything was OK. It was still rush hour, waves of black-clad corporates looming up and dodging them at the last minute, and he'd forced himself to smile and tell her everything was fine.

'So, you'll take the case then?' she'd asked. Hopeful, not suspicious now, least not as far as he could tell. He told her he couldn't think of a good reason why not, which was true enough, even if he'd work one out soon enough. Hannah told him she knew what his rates were and refused any talk of a discount; something about a conflict of interest. Then she shook his hand, like that was the normal thing to do, and threw herself into the throng of people hurrying home for dinner.

He had stood there, an obstacle in the evening, wondering vaguely how he was going to talk his way out of that one, then listened to the voicemail again. 'Bill … don't …' Looked at the text again: *Please come, please, mate.* No answers to his calls or texts since then.

It seemed unlikely, but with the car window open, he could smell the park down the road, wet earth and tree-smells mingling with his cigarette in the night. In his mirror, he watched a hand-holding couple walk up from that direction, umbrellaed silhouettes growing bigger until they were in his blind spot. He held himself still and watched them pass, the man spotting Murdoch's lit cigarette at the last minute, looking back over his shoulder at the car, but not slowing his pace. Within a minute, the couple was out of sight again, beyond the thick curtain of rain. Murdoch noticed the tension in his shoulders, swore at himself and tried to relax.

The problem with Hannah Simms was one of timing: how soon he could claim another case. It would be easy enough to say the fictional surveillance job had started up sooner than he'd thought, but the way to really get her off his back would be to make a start on her job. Drive up to the sticks like she'd suggested, hang around, find out nothing, then get the hell out of there. He'd heard of the Central Coast, knew it wasn't far. Maria was always up there for business and he remembered thinking a 'central coast' sounded like a contradiction in terms.

'There's a place you can stay for free,' Hannah Simms had said. Selling it to him by then, or giving him less of a way out – who knew? 'My parents left years ago, but I've got a little house up there. Cute little thing on stilts – lovely view over the lagoon – and you can stay there while you're on the case. That would save on expenses, I guess?'

He'd nodded at this too soon. A big hotel allowance might have been a way out of it. She'd said as far as she was concerned he could start right away – she'd just phone someone and get Murdoch the keys – and he'd said he'd have to see. Then, under the gaze of those grey eyes again, he said that shouldn't be a problem, but he'd let her know for sure in the morning. Because Maria would know what to do. She'd slag him off, but she'd know what to do. He swore under his breath and rolled up his window again, watching a rat run between two cars before disappearing into new shadows. He looked up at Maria's office window and wondered what it meant that he could still see no light on in there.

His phone rang three times before he knew what it was and realised he'd been asleep. He grabbed at it half-awake, hit the wrong button, swore out loud and tried again.

'Hello?'

Nothing.

'Maria?'

There was a loud tap on the window next to him, gold heavy on the glass. Attached to it was Hussein from reception, under a golf umbrella, Maria's phone in his hand and a fat smile on his face. A large car idled behind him. Murdoch punched his own phone quiet and rolled down the window.

'Nice one, Einstein,' he said. 'You do know you're supposed to speak into the mouthpiece, not carry it to the person you're calling?'

'Sorry, pussyboy, did I wake you? Your boss wants to talk to you.'

Hussein nodded to the car behind him, a black Audi with black windows, its motor humming steadily under the rain.

'Funny,' said Murdoch. 'Last time I looked I didn't have a boss.'

Hussein shook his head. He put Maria's phone into his trouser pocket then opened his jacket to reveal a holster and the handle of a heavy revolver. No smile on his face now.

'How's about you come and see what it's like in a big boy's car?'

An old lag in Belmarsh had told Murdoch this: most blokes what got pulled over by the cops was in a car what was either too beat up or too flashy by half. You drive something twenty years old with all its hubcaps missing, the law's going to keep an eye on you. Drive a Porsche or a Ferrari before you're white and sixty, they're going to do the same. And what did the rule say? The rule said Don't Get Noticed. So when Maria had told Murdoch he needed a car, he'd googled to see what was most popular and bought himself a Mazda 3, one year old.

'Bloody hell, my dear.' Maria had laughed when she'd seen it. 'It looks like something a suburban dad would drive!'

Like that wasn't the whole point? She told him he should spoil himself and he'd told her that could wait.

'When I've got my house, then I'll get a proper one,' he'd said. 'Then I'll get a deckchair and sit on the other side of the road.' They'd been standing on the steps of Macquarie Street, winter sunlight bouncing off the new car. 'I'll sit there all afternoon looking at my house and my car. At six o'clock, I'll have my beer and I'll be there with a beer and a house and car and I'll have made it. Until then, this will do.' 'This' meaning not just the car but the whole business: Macquarie Street, the whole CBD. She'd asked him what kind of car he'd get and he said he didn't know. Something what looked expensive and was silent when you drove it. Something what smelled good.

He thought of this now as he opened the heavy door to the Audi and the scent of new leather filled his nose. Hussein had moved round to the driver's side, taking the umbrella with him, standing with one hand on the door handle waiting for Murdoch to get in. Maybe he wasn't so dumb, after all.

33

On the broad backseat of the car sat a well-tanned and broad-shouldered man with salt-and-pepper hair and a generous smile. He reminded Murdoch of one of his regular buyers, a guy high up enough in insurance to have his own office and two secretaries. The man in the car reached over to shake hands as Murdoch slid in next to him, then returned to his relaxed pose, one arm on the armrest in the door, the other along the back of the seat, his silk tie loosened, his top button undone. He had dark circles under his soft brown eyes. *I might own the world, but it's been a long day.*

'Bill, pleasure to meet you. I've heard all about you.'

'Can't say the same,' said Murdoch. 'You are?'

The man apologised, a little too profusely, and introduced himself as Harris. No first name, apparently. He was a big unit, an athlete gone to seed, perfect teeth flashing as he hoped Murdoch understood the need for the cloak-and-dagger stuff; hoped it wasn't too late a meeting time; hoped he'd had a productive day. Murdoch asked again who he was.

'I'm the new Exec for New South Wales Metro. No doubt you've heard there's been a shake-up?'

'I didn't catch the name of the company you work for?'

'Ah Bill, very wise, very cautious. That's what we like about you; you're a pro. Don't worry, mate, we're all on the same side. I'm with the Club; I work with Maria Dinos. You could say I'm her new boss.'

Murdoch didn't want to talk about who was boss to who. Hussein had no sooner squeezed himself behind the steering wheel than he'd started the engine. Now they were driving fast, all doors safely locked from the front, down to the Cross City Tunnel and out past the Fish Market.

'Tell me a bit about yourself, Bill. Actually, before you do that, tell me what you'd like to drink.'

Harris opened the armrest between them to reveal heavy glasses and small bottles softly lit from below. As they turned yet another corner, everything clinked and sparkled, like a Christmas tree on a ship in rough seas. Murdoch asked for a water and Harris, passing no judgement, gave him some from a bottle with Italian writing before helping himself to a whisky.

'Doctor says I shouldn't,' he said, raising the glass like this was a toast. 'But then he gives me these fantastic pills which means I can. They don't help with the stress, but they stop it killing me too soon.'

Harris found a brown bottle from somewhere beside him and threw three tiny tablets down his throat with a glug of the whisky.

'So, Bill, tell me about yourself.'

'I'm curious about where Maria is. And why your gorilla has her phone.'

Harris waited. If he was disappointed when Murdoch had nothing else to say, it didn't show in his smile. 'Your loyalty is … noted. You'll see Maria very soon. How far away are we, Hussein? Less than five minutes, I'd say. Which really gives us very little time to get acquainted. Here, I'll go first. Twelve years with the Club; originally from Wagga Wagga; three kids; very happy to be back in Sydney after too long down in Victoria. Now, your turn. You're English?'

'Yeah.'

'I hear you chose this life fairly early on, is that right?'

'I don't remember choosing it at all.'

'Got on the wrong train too early and couldn't make it back home? Yes, well, tell me about it, mate. Still, the way I look at it, if that's the train you're on, you may as well get a first-class ticket, eh?'

The cream leather squeaked as Harris turned himself towards Murdoch and established eye contact. 'Look, Bill, I know you're wondering what the hell's going on, but trust me, we're on the same side. Hussein's presence here should be proof enough of that. Why don't you relax? Soon the mystery will all become clear. Now tell me, did Maria talk to you about the plans we've got for your career? The Club is a big organisation, you know, practically no limits for someone who's professional and ambitious.'

They were off the main road now, plashing through the rain along dark and quiet streets, none of them recognisable. So close to the CBD and yet Murdoch might as well have been in Africa.

'Who says I'm ambitious?'

'We're all ambitious, mate. Just ambitious for different things. Me, I like to find out what people's ambitions are and then I like to see how I can help them succeed. For example, you are clearly a saver, so I bet your ambition involves a certain amount of money. Or maybe something a certain amount of money can buy?'

'A saver?'

'Yes. All those accounts in different names with all that money in them. Most of our distributors struggle with gambling or, inevitably, substance abuse. It's rare to find someone with the self-discipline to save ...' he pulled a note from his jacket pocket, '... over three hundred thousand dollars in an account in your own name and, bloody hell, Bill, almost two million in five other accounts. What you saving that up for then?'

Murdoch could taste his last cigarette. He wrapped his hands firmly around his glass, coughed to get the croak out of his voice. 'What d'you know about that?'

'Come on, mate. It's my job to know this stuff. Anyone in the Club should know this kind of detail about her or his employees. You were born in a part of London called Peckham, or found there, should I say? First nine years in orphanages – it seems you proved resolutely unadoptable – and then a few spells in young offenders' places, mostly one called Cookham Wood. Then the big-boys' jail. Oh, sorry, don't you like talking about this stuff?'

That was an understatement. Murdoch didn't discuss his history with anyone. He'd read somewhere it was healthy to talk about your past, but maybe that was for people who could bear to hear it repeated. Harris was still talking.

'You see, Bill, you might not be very good at talking about yourself, but we are very good at finding out what we need to know. Or at least some of us are. Maria, for example, Maria is not very good and there's no excuse for that. You see, with our contacts in the banks and the rating agencies, and a little spyware to see what websites you visit, it took my guys all of three days to find this stuff out.' He refolded the paper, returned it to his jacket pocket and wagged a thick finger in Murdoch's direction. 'Unless you've got a few more little stashes we haven't found yet, you naughty boy.'

This was why he never carried a gun.

'I earned that money.'

'Yes, yes, it's yours, mate, I don't want it. But I need to keep tabs on my employees. Need to know where they are at any time. You ever touch any of that money and we'll be able to see immediately. That's fair enough, isn't it? Oh look, we've arrived. Let's get a little fresh air – you look like you could use it. Get carsick, do you?'

They'd driven through a low, burned-out factory and were on a flat wasteland, grass-cracked concrete spreading wet in each direction. The space was hemmed in on all sides: the factory's remaining wall surprisingly far behind them, high mesh fences left and right, the thick black harbour close and slapping in front. Hussein was out of the car as soon as it was still, Harris waiting until his door was opened and an umbrella held above him. He reached to the shelf behind him, grabbed a thick black walking stick and used it to get himself out of the car. Once there, he leaned down and looked in at Murdoch.

'Please, Bill. I have something to show you.'

Murdoch followed him out. The rain was lighter than it had been on Macquarie Street, but he accepted the furled umbrella Hussein passed to him. He had no other weapon.

'I love this city,' said Harris, breathing in the air like they were on a hilltop. 'Been trying to get back here for years – still can't really believe I've made it.'

'Most people prefer the beach.'

Murdoch said it just to say something: to show he wasn't scared; wasn't wondering where Hussein was going with that fat old revolver of his. He watched the gorilla circle to the back of the car and, after looking at Harris for confirmation, use the remote to open the boot.

'Go on,' said Harris with an encouraging smile. 'Go and have a look.'

Maria was the worse for wear. Her big hair covered half her face, sticking in strands to damp bruises. Her hands were tied behind her back and silver duct tape covered her mouth. She'd struggled for air in the boot and now lay sucking it in sharply through her nostrils. Her eyes were wild, unable to tell Murdoch a thing.

Hussein put his umbrella on the ground, where it rolled back and forth before blowing away across the concrete. The gorilla swore but let it go; instead, he reached down into the boot and swung Maria's feet out of the car. Then, already soaked, he reached forwards, grabbed her under the armpits and struggled with her until she was half-standing, half-leaning against the Audi. Harris was beside Murdoch now, the rims of their umbrellas bouncing against each other, a firm hand on Murdoch's shoulder, his voice quiet in his ear.

'You see, mate, unlike you, Maria is not a model employee. She seems to think she knows better ways to run her team than we, as an organisation, have decided upon.'

Now Murdoch regretted his lack of a gun. He watched Hussein stand Maria fully upright and push her towards the water. Two steps and he pushed her again. She stumbled forwards, then stopped and bent to the left. Murdoch could see what was coming and if Hussein had been half a fighter he'd have seen it too. Harris shouted 'Watch!' But he shouted it too late. Maria raised her right leg in a swift hook that swung Hussein's face around towards them. The gorilla hit the ground heavily, was up again within a second, but Maria had repositioned to give him a donkey kick in the stomach, her full weight behind it. Hussein fell again, rolling this time through brown puddles and gasping like all the wet air around them wasn't enough for his lungs. Murdoch took a step forward, but Harris's left hand was still on his shoulder, while his right hand had dropped the cane and dipped inside his jacket. Then there was nothing but noise: two huge blasts filling the night, bouncing off the concrete and the car and the factory wall, bigger than the black water in the harbour. Murdoch's ears rang as he watched Maria spin and fall in strange angles to the ground, the space she occupied in the world a fraction of what it had been a moment before. He shook Harris's hand off his shoulder and walked over.

Squatting beside her, he felt for Maria's pulse, like he couldn't see the huge exit wound where her heart had been. Through the ringing in his ears, Harris's cane came tapping at the concrete; then the man's brogues appeared beside Maria's hair.

'You see, Bill, you can run around in a fancy suit all you want, but at the end of the day it's a nasty business. Always has been, always will be. You forget that … well, you end up like Maria here. By the way, mate, congratulations, you're hereby promoted. Your first office job. You start first thing in the morning.'

5

They left Murdoch back in Macquarie Street, the rain still hammering, the gutters flowing like rivers. He must have driven himself home from there – although he didn't remember the journey – must have showered at some point, his wet head too warm for it to be from the rain. At one point, he found himself cleaning his rooftop shack. Changing the bed linen, sweeping out under the bed like he was back inside. Next, he was staring at the ceiling, all his blankets on him and unable to get warm. He might have slept; he had no idea. He watched his alarm clock ring for five minutes before turning it off.

When he arrived back at the office a few hours later, Murdoch expected to find Hussein there – weekends meant nothing to the Club – but he arrived to a cold and mournful building. Using keys Harris had thrown into his lap the night before, he unlocked one door after another. He sat at Maria's huge desk and stared at all the furniture in the room, tried the smaller keys on it, found hard drives and expensive glassware, old books that looked like they were worth something. He opened the globe under the window and smelled the whisky, stood a while with his hand on the wallpaper, wondering what made it so expensive. Outside the weekend traffic was starting up, the sky properly blue for the first time in a week.

At eight he phoned Harris. 'I need a computer guy to come and get into some of these files,' he said. 'The passwords you gave me don't work for all of them. And I need Maria's appointments book.'

Harris was amused or, more likely, pleased with himself. 'Bill, I underestimated you. Straight into it, that's what I like to see. And you've underestimated me, but you'll learn not to do that.' He gave Murdoch the combination to the safe, told him the hackers were working on the files as they spoke. 'As for the appointments, well, we've bumped everything back by a few days. Give you a little time to get the lay of the land. I thought I'd swing by this morning and we could discuss targets.'

Murdoch rubbed his palm across his tiny spikes of his hair and looked down at what his feet could feel under the desk. Maria's shoes, lying on their side, one half-crushed with the heel broken.

'Bill?'

'Good idea. But listen, I need to wrap some of my old stuff up first. I had meetings for this morning. It's taken me eighteen months to build up that client base and it's too good to lose. Who's replacing me by the way?'

'Can we talk about this when I'm there?'

'Fine. But can you make it this afternoon? Let me wrap up today's business, make arrangements for next week, so it's a neat handover.'

Harris congratulated himself again, told Murdoch it would be midday and hung up without saying goodbye. Murdoch ran down to his car – Hussein still nowhere to be seen – and pulled out one of his bags from the boot, the only one with any room in it.

Back upstairs, he locked the office door behind him and walked to the safe, quickly counting the money he found there. Twenty-three thousand, four hundred and fifty dollars; it would have to do. In the desk, he found a few hundred more, nothing anywhere else. Checking the waiting room was still empty, he returned to the safe and took the rest of its contents: three or four kilos of uncut cocaine in tidy plastic packaging. He put the coke in the bottom drawer of the reception desk – the only one with a key in it – locked it and took the key with him.

The traffic had clotted by the time he left the office and it took him forty minutes to reach Strathfield station. He walked with his bags towards the heaving traffic of the Parramatta Road, then along it – a kilometre or more through one car yard after another – until he found a VW Golf in the right condition. It took him less than fifteen minutes to persuade the dealer to sell it for cash, no questions asked. Another hour after that, driving around streets he didn't know, until he was convinced he hadn't been followed.

He found a McDonald's and forced himself to eat while he wrote down all the numbers from his phone. Bought a map at a petrol station and weaved his way north under a brightening sky: suburbs he'd heard of and suburbs he hadn't, Saturday traffic getting worse by the minute. A while later he stopped again, looked up the number for the *Telegraph* and dialled it. Changed his mind and made the call from a filling station payphone instead, the smell of petrol mixing with his fear and his McDonald's to produce a nausea that threatened to spew.

He said he wanted to speak to someone who wanted a good story. This wasn't against the rules: talking to a journalist was nothing like talking to the law. The receptionist put him through to the news desk and – after a few minutes of pre-recorded news talk – a voice that had heard it all before came on the line: 'Harvey Clarke at your service.' Murdoch checked he was talking to a journalist, refused to give his name, but gave Clarke everything else, listening to the change in the journalist's voice as the details became more interesting.

'Take the cops with you,' Murdoch told him, 'or you won't be heard of again. Tell them to look in the bottom drawer of the reception desk. Tell them it's the same guys what knocked off Maria Dinos last night.'

He spelled out the name: no idea if it was real or not. They'd left Maria lying where she'd died. Someone would have found her by now. Clarke asked Murdoch to come in and talk some more, said there could be serious money in it for him. Murdoch hung up and drove on again, trying to work out which way he should head. Before he'd decided, his mobile rang. Harris.

'Murdoch, we had an appointment. Where are you? Hussein says you haven't been in since he got here.'

'Hussein gets in too late in the mornings. You should fire him.'

'Stop arsing around and get up here now.'

'I'll be there as soon as I can. One of my clients was late and I'm backed up. Thirty minutes, max.'

He hung up before Harris had a chance to respond and drove on, wondering what the hell he was supposed to do now. The house in Magdalen Road was gone, he accepted that. It had always been too good to be true: blokes like him didn't end up in nice houses near the sea. But the money in the bank was his. As soon as the story hit the papers and he could be sure the Club's attention was focused on sorting that mess out, he'd access the cash and disappear again. But in the meantime?

He thought of the Club's operations centres: Blacktown, the Canberra run, something big on the Central Coast. They'd expect him to run inland, disappear into the bush and then the desert. He'd heard the outback was full of people who'd escaped from life, but he doubted that would stop the Club from finding him there. He tried to think of what they'd least expect. He couldn't exactly hide in the basement of Macquarie Street, but there were other places they wouldn't think to look.

He found Hannah Simms's number and a petrol station with another payphone – who knew so many still existed? The tax inspector sounded surprised when he confirmed he was taking her case. But, after a small hesitation, she gave him precise directions and told him the local real estate agent, a friend of hers called Davie, would meet him up there.

It was another twenty minutes before Murdoch's phone rang again. He was on the freeway by then, three lanes of traffic rushing down to the Hawkesbury: the weekend world on the move. As he approached the bridge, Murdoch slowed to look at the river. From the map, he'd not expected it to be so wide – there were islands out to his right, boats made tiny by so much water. When Harris's number flashed on his phone, Murdoch buzzed down the passenger window before answering.

'You're a dead man,' said Harris, out of breath and whispering. 'I hope you know that. There is nowhere in the world I will not find you.'

'Can't wait, mate. I *seriously* cannot wait.'

Murdoch allowed himself a smile – no idea where it had come from – and unfurled his left arm in a toss that sent the phone flying through the open window, over the balustrade and, tiny in his wing mirror, down to the waters of the majestic Hawkesbury.

Part Two

MONTAUBAN

6

Davie woke earlier than he meant to and, for once, he stayed awake. Whatever had woken him was happening still and he lay there lazily, waiting to work out what it was. It wasn't the sunlight pushing through the yellow of the curtain: that would wake him every morning if he let it – at six o'clock at this time of year. The idea of there being a six a.m. weighed on his eyelids and threatened to drag him back down. Except there was that thing: the thing that had woken him.

He rolled over to check his watch, not only for the time, but also for the three little letters confirming it was Sunday and he could lie in as late as he wanted. Sunday it was and yet here he was, awake at ten past midday. Stretching out a foot, he grabbed the flimsy yellow curtain between two toes and tugged it to the right, his bedroom brightening white. Still he lay there, blinking for a while, studying his feet in the sunlight, the rest of his nakedness in relative shade. Not too bad for a bloke past thirty, he thought; still blond all over, nothing you could call flabby yet. Muscles which, when he rolled into the right angle of the light, looked toned enough. His stomach could be flatter, but, hell, whose couldn't? Further down, his semi-erect penis looked back up at him forlornly, a dog hoping for a walk. Davie thought about it, decided no, got up instead and padded through to the bathroom. Then back to the kitchen, where he flicked on the kettle.

There had been a time, not too long before, when Davie's Sundays had been full of self-recrimination. If he got up too late, which he did every Sunday, he'd ask himself where the day had gone, what he'd achieved by lying in bed. This, inevitably, led to the question of where the last ten years had gone, what he'd achieved by staying in his stupid job, living in this stupid house. The 'stupid house' part had never worked. Even on those what-am-I-doing-with-my-life Sundays, the phrase had rung false in his head. He loved his place. Natalie always told him it was a hovel, but it was *his* hovel – not legally perhaps, but by now it was hollowed out to suit his shape.

The house. There was something about not leaving the house. Something about today and not leaving the house. Was it worrying about that that had woken him? Davie thought about it as he sniffed at the last of the milk – more optimism than wisdom – then scowled and threw the carton in the rubbish. Some milk splashed against the wall next to the bin and, as he watched it dribble down to dry among other dried dribbles, he forced himself to try and remember. Had someone told him something that had made him not want to leave the house? He walked absent-mindedly back into the living room, breaking away from his fuzzy thoughts only at the sound of a voice outside his front door. A faint male voice.

The house stood on stilts at the top of a steep grass driveway; there shouldn't be a voice nearby unless it was on its way to visit him. Davie stood and listened carefully. Whoever it was, they were at the bottom of the steps, down on the driveway itself, or maybe on the rough wall that climbed the other side of the grass. Great. Now, if he wanted to go and get a coffee, he'd come face-to-face with whoever it was. And, of course, it would be some kid, mucking about or having a smoke. Davie would have to tell him to get lost or, at best, ask him politely to get lost. Neither would do any good. To stop the kid coming back, with mates and a bong next time, he'd have to yell at him, listen to him yelling obscenities back, chase him threateningly out of sight and worry for the next week about the house getting egged.

Or, worse, it would be a neighbour: someone with nothing to do but chat – asking Davie what he was up to, telling him what he should be doing with the beautiful day, asking himself in for a cuppa and settling comfortably into Davie's sofa. Davie groaned out loud, walked back into the bedroom and flopped onto the bed. Almost immediately, the kettle started bubbling, mocking his lack of milk and – if he could be bothered walking back to the kitchen – his likely lack of coffee too.

It was only when he found his phone, and the text from his ex-wife, that Davie remembered anything of the night before. *Bill Murdoch* said the message on his screen. *Don't forget.* Davie stared at it. Where had he even been last night? It took him a worryingly long time to remember the surf club. Someone's birthday, an open bar, Anne Lincoln singing; the rest a blur. He'd got home late and, that's right, She Who Must Be Avoided had called and the beer had tricked him into answering. They'd argued, of course, but before that there had been something. A piece of information he'd assured her he was capable of retaining, if only she could be less patronising about it. Something about the house. He lay back, staring at the ceiling, willing himself to remember. Soon, he fell asleep.

7

Murdoch had arrived before the agreed time, the dot on the map that was Montauban easy enough to find. It was at the end of a long and winding stretch called Crown Road, probably because it ran along the crown of the hills before dropping down to the sea when it reached the town. He'd planned to drive around first to check the place out – like he knew what that meant – but Montauban turned out to be tiny: a couple of hundred houses littering the northern side of a bay, Crown Road the only way in or out; almost everything in town facing the sea, its horizon dotted with tanker ships.

Apart from the mismatched houses and a hulking surf club on the beach, the only thing in town was a strip mall of six shops. It sat across the tarmac from the sand: two tatty storeys of ugly pink brick. The first shop – the one closest to the little roundabout that split the road into town left and right along the beach – was empty, nothing in its windows but faded *For Lease* signs. Past that was some sort of general store, then an estate agent's – locked – a shoddy café, a bakery and, last of all, a pungent chip shop.

The pavement outside the shops was busy enough, people grabbing coffees and shouting at their kids, or sitting around looking smug. Across the road was a wooden viewing platform – the sand below deserted compared to any of the beaches in Sydney – where Murdoch read signs about whale watching and the importance of replanting the shore front. He wandered down a sandy path between overgrown dunes and slowly along the beach until it narrowed between the waves and a lake. So close to the constantly shifting sea, the green lake water looked out of place, pushing placidly back into the land. Around it, and further along the sand, more houses were scattered here and there amongst scruffy trees. Five hundred metres on, at the far end of the beach, was another headland, mirroring the one that closed the northern end of the bay.

The house Murdoch wanted was on Montagne Road, the same road as the strip of shops, after it had turned from the beach and – greenery shadowing it on both sides – started curving around the lake he'd seen from the shore. Number ninety-seven was a tiny house in the sky. Most of its paint, once white, had peeled away to leave mottled patches of grey, like a sick animal losing its skin. The house sat on tall and frail stilts which, in turn, sat at the top of a steep grass driveway. To get to its front door, you had to climb a dry wooden staircase. It wasn't really a house at all, thought Murdoch, more like someone had lifted a room off the hill and added bits onto it. You could see from down here where the kitchen was. It made him think of his place on the warehouse roof and he spat bitterly at the grass between his feet.

Parking under the wooden stairs, he strolled across the driveway to a wall of rocks, climbed onto it, and sat smoking in the sunlight. Beyond the road below him, the lake sent up sparks of sunlight through thick green shrubs that moved with the breeze. Behind him, gigantic trees creaked to the same rhythm, whistled at by birds he couldn't see.

After half an hour or so, the road began to show signs of life. Kids slouching past in soccer kits, an occasional mum with a pushchair, older people in sensible clothes on the way back from the shops. Murdoch would see them a hundred yards away, where a bulge of hill forced the road out towards the lake. Then they'd disappear behind the curve of the land until they were suddenly passing the bottom of the driveway below him. Every one of them acknowledged his presence, smiled up or said it was a beautiful day; wasn't it a great day; g'day. Murdoch nodded at the first few, even raised a lit cigarette. Then he phoned Cynthia as an excuse not to respond.

'Oh, it's you,' she said on his fourth attempt. 'I didn't recognise the number. You got a new phone?'

'Yeah. Don't save it, though, I'll change it again soon enough. How you doing?'

'Ooh, what's wrong, Blackie?'

'Who says anything's wrong?'

'You didn't show up on Thursday, you've got a new number that might not last, you've got a weird tremble in your voice, you phoned three times before I answered. You all right, what's happened to you?'

'I always phone three times before you answer. I'm fine. Just got into a little trouble, that's all. I'm out of town for a bit while it blows over.'

'Where are you?'

'Nowhere.'

'Go on, where?'

'Timbuktu. Miles away.'

She laughed and he thought he could hear her hiding the relief. He wasn't looking for a place to stay. She asked him how long it would be before they saw each other again, like they were a young couple in love or something.

'I don't know, darlin'. These people, they've got something of mine and I need to distract them a bit so I can get it back. I might already have done that; I can't tell. So I'm taking a little holiday, waiting for my moment.'

'Ooh, a holiday. Wish you'd taken me with you. Bet you're staying somewhere nice?'

He looked up at the stilt house, the empty road below him, spat silently onto the grass again. 'It's quiet,' he said. 'I'm waiting for the estate agent. Some bloke called Davie, what's going to turn up here and gimme the key. Ever heard of a grown man calling himself Davie?'

'Well, Blackie, just you remember you're on holiday. Try and have some fun.'

'I just want to get inside and close my eyes. Get my shit together, know what I mean?'

'You relax, darl. And don't worry. Whatever it is you're up to, you're a smart bloke, you'll work it out.'

She was good at this. Giving advice without knowing what she was talking about. Early on she'd suggested they come up with little lies so they could talk about stuff. Like the house he was going to buy in Katoomba or his job with the chemical company. She was in professional services. A language that allowed them to talk without mentioning the things they were talking about.

'It's good to hear your voice, Cyn.'

'It's good to talk to you too, darl. You make sure you keep in touch. Let me know when I can come and join that hard, little body on holiday.'

He let her talk like that for a while more, lying down on the wall as he listened, the sun blood-orange on his eyelids.

The estate agent was five minutes late when a young woman in a T-shirt and jeans rounded the curve from the beach and the shops. She was carrying a sports bag and, even from this distance, Murdoch could see how its strap pressed the cotton of the T-shirt against her. He sat up and watched until she disappeared into the curve of the hill beside him, thinking about how to respond when she said hello. Five, four, three, two, one; he flicked his cigarette nonchalantly at the stone wall and checked his nails like Marlon Brando.

'Where do you think that's going to go?' The woman was at the bottom of the driveway, arms crossed and frowning.

''Scuse me, darlin'?'

'Your cigarette butt. Where do you think it's going to go now?'

Murdoch looked at her blankly. Either it was a trick question or he'd done something wrong. As the young woman shifted the strap across her chest – it was too hot a day to be carrying so much weight – it pulled up her T-shirt, revealing a flat and tanned stomach.

'I'll tell you, will I?' she said. 'It's going to get washed into a storm drain and then, about two minutes later, into the lagoon there. And then a fish will eat it and probably die.'

Murdoch climbed slowly off the wall, crouched down and searched in the dirt until he found the butt. He picked it up and put it in his pocket, then turned with his best smile. 'What's a lagoon, then?'

It took him a while to soften her up, but he got there in the end. Questions, apologies, wide-eyed ignorance. Her accent was different from the ones he'd heard in Sydney, more like what he thought an Australian accent should be. Not a beer ad exactly, but a step in that direction. She asked if he was a Pom, said she'd been over there herself, spent some time in London. He asked her how she'd liked it.

'Look around you,' she said. 'I grew up here. How do you think I liked it?'

He made a show of looking up to the trees that towered above them, squinting through the greenery, listening to the ocean booming around the corner. He walked down the grass driveway and joined her on the road, asked her if she knew what kind of trees these were, scrutinising her as he pretended to listen to her answer. Her face wasn't bad: small nose, fine eyebrows, great lips. She had big green eyes and good skin. The chin was a little strong, but that was probably the attitude. It was her uncertain smile that made her less than beautiful – that and her awkward way with her hands. Realising she had stopped talking, he told her he was a city boy and was still getting used to the quiet.

'So, what you doing up here then, city boy? You take a wrong turn on the Pacific Highway?'

'Needed a holiday, didn't I? Thought I'd come up here and chill out for a bit. Bit of R&R, know what I mean?'

'An escape from the urban jungle?'

'That kind of thing. Bit of time off, at least. I'm supposed to be working, but we'll see. I think a bit of dossing about might be just what the doctor ordered. You ever go down the urban jungle yourself?'

She laughed and shook her head, gave him little sparks of eye contact and he knew she fancied him back. Now he could ask her name. She asked him his first, but when he opened his mouth to answer, someone else did it for him.

'Murdoch! Yo, man, you Murdoch?'

They both looked up towards the stilt house. On the sagging balcony that ran along its front stood a man wearing nothing but a towel. He was unshaven, blond, clearly just out of bed. Murdoch stared up at him. He hadn't thought someone might be inside the place and felt a flush of rage at himself for not bothering to find out. He raised a hand and said he'd be up in a second. Turned back to find the girl had started walking away.

'Hey,' he said. 'See you around?'

'Oh yes, Bill Murdoch,' she virtually spat it, like she didn't like the taste of his name in her mouth. 'You'll definitely see me around.'

8.

The bloke in the towel opened the front door before Murdoch was halfway up the creaking stairs. He said his name was Davie Simms and stood there, grinning like a fool, slouching half-naked like no one had ever told him he had a gut. Murdoch scowled up at him.

'You're Davie?'

'Yep'

'I thought you was an estate agent. What you done, moved in?'

The man called Davie didn't have a response to that so Murdoch carried on up the front steps, ignoring the other man's proffered hand and pushing past him into the house.

The place was no bigger than it looked from down near the road. The front door opened onto a room, half-kitchen half-lounge, where dark wooden floors ate the light. Over by the balcony, it was brighter: double glass doors framing the view, the lake that was now a lagoon right there at your feet, the beach, and even the ship-dotted horizon, surprisingly close. It smelled damp, smelled like a small space where a man ate and slept. Looked that way too.

'Don't worry,' said Davie. 'It isn't always this bad. Well, that's not true, but I've been wanting an excuse to tidy up, so you can be it. It's just that Hannah didn't give me much notice. Fancy a beer?'

'No thanks.'

'You don't want a beer?'

'I don't want a beer.'

'Please tell me you drink.'

'I don't want a beer, all right? Like I said, I thought you was supposed to be an estate agent. Thought you was going to meet me outside. What you doing in here?'

Davie looked at him for a second, furrowing his blond eyebrows and then, out of nowhere, burst into laughter. 'Hang on,' he said. 'I know what happened. Hannah said you could stay here and said I was an estate agent and I'd meet you and give you the key. Right?'

'Something like that.'

'Ha! Well, I am an estate agent. But I bet she didn't mention that I live here too? That woman! I'm her ex-husband. Bet she didn't tell you that either, did she? Typical. Got to laugh though, haven't you?'

Murdoch took a deep breath and clenched and relaxed his fists behind his back. He pictured Davie bleeding on the driveway below the balcony, wondered how funny he'd find it then. Another deep breath and he heard himself asking if he had a room of his own at least? Davie padded past him, still wearing his stupid grin, and opened a door to a large white room with a view of the beach.

'I'm in here,' he said. 'And you're back there, near the bathroom.'

It was a dingy little room half-buried in the hillside, a single bed and three ugly drawers struggling for space, a small window with bars on it.

'Local kids kept breaking in,' explained Davie, standing too close to him in the doorway. 'That's the only window you can get to from outside without a ladder – trust the little bastards to work that one out. The room's quiet, though, unless someone's in the bathroom.'

'There's no other room?'

'Fraid not.'

'You out much?'

Davie looked at him. 'Dude, I'd prefer not to share either. But I seem to remember from Hannah that you're living here for free, which I am not. So, if either of us has a reason to complain, it's me. Oh ...' He turned back into the living room and hunted among the junk on the coffee table, until, with a whoop, he produced a piece of paper which he thrust at Murdoch. 'Hannah asked me to give you this. I think it's people she wants you to talk to.'

Murdoch snatched the paper roughly and stared at it. It was a list of names badly scrawled in blunt pencil:

PAUL WALKER, TOM WALKER, ANNE LINCOLN

TROY MCLAREN

MARGARET HARPER, ALYCIA THORNTON

He folded it roughly and shoved it into his pocket, no intention of wasting his time on Hannah Simms's case. It was going to take all his mental energy to get at his money, then he'd do a runner the same way the tax inspector's niece had done.

'How long you around for anyway?' Davie asked him. 'Hannah was very vague on that.'

'Two weeks max. Any more than that and I think I'd go mental.'

'Yeah, well, let's keep ourselves to ourselves until then, eh?' The estate agent pushed a hand through his floppy blond hair. 'Not that I imagine you'll be here much, what with you out detecting the whole time.'

Feeling his fingernails in the palms of his hands, Murdoch took a deep breath and turned away into the bedroom. He heard Davie's voice behind him, an attempt at conciliation.

'Are you not used to sharing?'

'No.' Murdoch closed the door between them. 'That's the bleeding opposite of the problem.'

9

A southerly rolled in that night, rattling twigs and leaves onto the roof of the stilt house and shattering any chances of sleep. The next morning the beach was a mess, the sea boiling white, the sand littered with seaweed and a dead bird or two. Across the road from the beach, at the shops, the wind was scouring and inescapable. Murdoch swore for the fourth time in as many minutes and wondered why he hadn't driven the two hundred yards from the house. Only the general store was open. Sweets, take-away coffee, flip-flops, scuba masks, milk, pasta, boogie boards, pies; there didn't seem to be much the place didn't sell.

'You're the private detective,' said the woman behind the counter as soon as he walked in.

'Am I?'

'Yes, you are. Ha, ha! Maybe I should be the detective for knowing that!'

She gave him a wink she was thirty years too old for and laughed again. She was a large woman, unevenly blonde, with huge jewellery that rattled as she laughed, her teeth spotted with lipstick. Murdoch asked her for a flat white and walked over to the piles of newspapers.

'I hope you find something out,' she called through the steam of the coffee machine. 'She was a lovely girl, that Georgie Walker. Ooh, I shouldn't say "was" should I? Should say "is". But I can't believe she ran off; not her, she'd be too frightened. Little mouse of a thing she was and, besides, she'd never leave Tom all on his own. How long are you giving yourself?'

'What for?'

'How long you in town for? You're staying with Davie Wonder, aren't ya?'

Murdoch scowled. 'It's a bit early in the morning to be talking business, innit? Especially when it's none of yours. Just the coffee and the papers, thanks.'

It took her a minute to get that. She started to say something else, but changed her mind. Plonked his coffee on the counter without a lid or a smile and told him it was three dollars, unless there was anything else he wanted.

So now Murdoch had to get sandblasted outside while he waited for the bakery to open: the wind off the ocean cutting him like he was naked. He huddled in a doorway between the bakery and the chip shop watching a cat inside the glass door. The cat pressed itself against the glass, stared up at him, then lifted a back leg and started licking its arse. Murdoch swore and spat without thinking, then swore again as the coffee-brown gob blew into the leg of his jeans.

Six people said good morning to him before he could get inside. All of them said something about the wind, like no one else might have noticed. It was a southerly; a southerly buster, straight up from the Antarctic; isn't it cold? The last of them was Davie, juddering up to the kerb in a horrible little Hyundai Excel, its paintwork the colour of genitalia.

'Dude, what the hell are you doing out in this weather? It's horrible. Want a lift home?'

Murdoch shook his head. 'What time does this bleeding bakery open? It says six thirty on the door, but I reckon that was over an hour ago.'

Davie laughed, struggling to close his car door in the wind. 'Whoa, city boy. You're on Montie time now. Six thirty-*ish* it should say. She normally gets here before nine.'

'You're kidding me.'

'Yeah, I am. You're surprisingly gullible for a detective. She'll be along any minute.'

Davie gave a smug grin and disappeared into the general store as another car drew up and parked beside the Hyundai. A young Indian woman in a tracksuit got out, her shoulders hunched against the weather as she walked up to the bakery door, jangling a bunch of keys.

'You're keen,' she said, as Murdoch helped her lift the metal grating. 'You're the detective, aren't you? What you doing, looking for clues?'

Back in his room, Murdoch wrapped himself cross-legged in the duvet. Using his now-cold coffee to swill down a blueberry muffin that had never seen a blueberry, he spread the papers on the bed. He'd hoped for a front page. Knew it was too much to ask for, but had hoped for it all the same. Instead there was some sports star battling with drugs, beneath it a special offer on school books. He made himself turn the pages slowly, trying to remember the journalist's name. But there was nothing. No mention of any raid in Macquarie Street, no mention of Maria Dinos or any other murdered woman. No article by anyone called Harvey. He went through the pages twice, found himself searching in the sports section before he gave up.

He told himself it didn't matter. Told himself the journalist would be gathering extra evidence, investigating to get a bigger story. So Murdoch's window of opportunity would start a bit later – so what? He could wait. As soon as the shit hit the fan, as soon as the headlines started and Harris was spending twenty-four-seven getting it out of the papers, he'd take his money and run. He couldn't imagine the Club tolerating that kind of noise.

The next morning, he was outside the paper shop at 7.20 a.m. No coffee. No wind or cold either, the storm had blown through as quickly as it had arrived. And nothing in the paper. Nor the next day. Nor the two days after that.

10.

Thursday, Murdoch drove to the Blue Mountains. He figured if the Club heard he'd been to a bank south of Sydney, they'd know he'd really gone north, so he decided to go west and keep them guessing.

The drive to Katoomba should have calmed him: glimpses of forest stretching to the horizon, no limits to where you could hide. But the winding road away from the coast felt like a backward step. He parked in Blackheath and caught the train back to Katoomba – no idea if it made things any safer. The grey haze of a bush fire hung in the air, a bonfire smell no one could escape. On the train, there was a flush-faced man determined to chat, no matter how little Murdoch responded. 'It's always bush fires or downpours up here,' he said. 'If it doesn't kill you one way, it'll try another.'

The bank in Katoomba was next to the police station and this, at least, made Murdoch laugh. The next building along was probably the local chapter of the Club or the law courts or the local clink. He considered changing plans, finding the next town down the train line and going there instead. But a bigger branch would have more cash, so he told himself he was just being paranoid and forced himself inside.

The branch had been recently refurbished, some designer's idea of what a bank should look like: desks you couldn't talk at without being overheard and a minimum number of tellers. He stood in line tapping his car key against his thigh, the automatic doors hissing open and shut behind him.

'You go first, dear,' said the old woman ahead of him in the queue. 'I like to see my regular gentleman.'

At the counter, a young girl in a headscarf caught the eye of the teller the old woman wanted to see: a pale teenager in a V-neck jumper.

'Won't be long, Mrs Dempsey,' the young man called past the customer he was serving. 'Unless Fatima can help you, maybe?'

Murdoch forced himself forwards. It had been a teller who had got him sent down for life five days past his eighteenth birthday. It was a lie they didn't care about the cash they looked after. This one had grabbed the barrel of his sawn-off with one hand and pressed a button somewhere with the other. He hadn't meant for the gun to go off. Now, he told the girl behind the counter he wanted to withdraw fifty thousand dollars and gave her his card, passport and driver's licence before she could ask. As she started typing numbers into the screen, he checked his watch. No reason he shouldn't be out of here in eight minutes.

'Thank you, Mr Murdoch. Now I am seeing here you have a lot of funds in a standard transaction account. Can I interest you in a term deposit at all? It would attract a much more favourable rate of interest.'

'Just the cash, thanks.'

'Well, if you do—'

'Just the cash!'

The teller in the V-neck jumper and the old woman he was now serving both looked over. 'Sorry,' Murdoch said to no one in particular. 'I'm in a bit of a hurry.'

The girl in the headscarf smiled nervously, careful not to catch her colleague's eye this time and frowned at the screen.

'That's strange,' she said and started typing again. Behind Murdoch, there was a sudden and violent noise. Then, as the doors to the branch slid open, it grew louder still. Murdoch swung around, eyes wide until he realised it was a pneumatic drill out on the street, men working on the road. He turned back to find the teller staring at him.

'The noise,' he said. 'It made me jump.'

She smiled less certainly still. Looked away from him too quickly, concentrating on the keyboard as she spoke. 'There's a note on your account, Mr Murdoch. I need to make a quick call, I won't be a moment.'

'Why?'

'Excuse me?'

'Why do you need to make a call? I just want my money.'

A short, middle-aged woman in the same uniform as the teller appeared at Murdoch's elbow, dumpy with authority.

'Is everything all right?' she said.

'No, it's not. I want my money and your colleague here is telling me she needs to make a phone call first.'

'Fatima?'

'There's a note on the system, Sandra. I've not seen one like it before and—'

The shorter woman told her to wait, she'd come round. Murdoch watched her waddle to the end of the counters, enter a security code and disappear through a door. Then he turned and stared at the old woman and the young teller beside him until they remembered they weren't here for the show. The woman called Sandra reappeared behind the counter and made her way to Fatima's screen.

'That's strange,' she said. 'I'm very sorry, sir, but we are going to have to make a call.'

'Fine,' Murdoch made himself say. 'Do us a favour though. Give me my card and my passport and stuff. I'll go to the post office and come back in ten minutes.'

And slowly, slowly, slowly he walked out of the bank.

The next morning there was still no story in the newspaper. Murdoch had slept badly, exhaustion battling with nightmares and empty hours of thinking. The humidity had returned and he lay there sweating, determined to sleep until, as the light seeped in, he decided he might as well get up. Then he opened his eyes and it was nine o'clock, bedclothes on the floor like a covered corpse, the bed beneath him damp.

Out on the street, hordes of flies had arrived. They buzzed stubbornly, dodging his swats and mocking him in lazy corners. They'd be gone the next day; he'd seen the phenomenon in Sydney, but that didn't make them any more bearable. He trudged through the heat to the shops – the woman in the general store barely acknowledging him other than to take his money – and shook the flies off his paper, scouring the headlines all the way back to the house, not looking up until he was at the bottom of the steps. Above him, the front door was swinging open on its hinges.

Murdoch took the steps two at a time, paused in the main room only to grab a heavy ashtray, then kicked open the other doors one by one. In his own room, he banged his knee brutally as he dropped to the floor and scrabbled under the bed. The brown briefcase from Macquarie Street was there, untouched, cash packed around his Beretta. He sat back against the bed and held it in his arms like a child he'd thought he'd lost.

That afternoon he drove to Crosley, twenty clicks along the Crown Road, borders thick with undergrowth eager to reclaim the land. He drove with the windows open, the only way to cool the car, the brown briefcase of cash belted into the passenger seat beside him. He'd left the Beretta back in the shack – the mood he was in, it was the safest place for it.

Davie, behind his desk in the estate agent's, had been unmoved by the story of the open front door.

'Oh yeah, it does that. I think it's the humidity, warps the wood or something.'

'Isn't there a lock?'

'No need, nothing to steal.'

'I thought you said kids used to break in?'

'Yeah, to smoke joints and hang out when no one lived there. Not to flog anything. Why, is something missing?'

Murdoch had shared enough space with blokes to resist telling Davie what he thought was missing. Instead, he asked where the nearest real town was.

'Crosley,' Davie told him. 'I warn you though, it's a hole. Malled to death. As soon as they opened up Bell Fair, all the shops moved over there and the zombies took over the town centre.'

He wasn't wrong. On the map, Crosley had it all. Curving around the edges of an ocean inlet called Broadwater, it was surrounded inland by undeveloped green. In the flesh, Crosley was less appealing. Macquarie

Road, the town's high street, held concrete car parks squatting half-empty between discount stores with metal bars on the windows. Litter filled the gutters, and the few people Murdoch could see – the zombies Davie had told him about – looked drunk and, if not homeless, then not far off it.

Murdoch pulled up next to a bank of payphones. Across the road, two women were hurling abuse at each other as a three-legged dog skipped around them barking for a fight. Murdoch took the briefcase of cash into a shop that smelled of damp, bought a cheap phonecard and returned to the payphones. Three tracksuited youths, who'd ambled over to look at his car, caught him looking, snarled, and walked away again.

The phones actually worked, all of them, but only the last one he tried was free of chewing gum or what looked like dried tobacco. He stood the briefcase between his feet, picked his trousers, damp with sweat, off the back of his legs, and dialled: first the phonecard numbers and PIN, then the number for the *Telegraph*. He had no idea if using the phonecard would make it more difficult to trace the call, but it was worth a try. A receptionist answered on the first ring and he asked to be put through to the news desk.

'Anyone in particular?'

'Someone Harvey? I spoke to him before. Older bloke, by the sound of it.'

'Harvey Clarke. Who can I say's calling?'

'Tell him it's the bloke what called him about the Club, he'll know.'

'About a club?'

'That's what I said.'

She took her time about it – four minutes by Murdoch's watch – news blabbing in his ear while he watched the street and tried not to smell the phone in his hand. The more he stared at the scene around him, the more zombies he saw. They held up the buildings in twos and threes, sat smoking in the bus shelters or squatting in shady corners, more tattoos than clothes. Smack, he reckoned; there'd be a meth clinic nearby about to open. At least he'd managed to avoid that. Mind you, twenty-odd years in prison cells – how exactly had that been any better?

He was moving the phone from ear to ear, swatting at flies, when a voice interrupted the adverts. Its owner was out of breath, had run from somewhere to take the call.

'Harvey Clarke speaking!'

'Hello, Harvey.'

'Is that Deep Throat?'

'You what?'

'Never mind, bad joke. I'm glad you called me back, mate, I've been wanting to talk to you some more.'

'Yeah, well, I kind of noticed the lack of progress.'

'Lack of progress? No, not at all. This thing's bigger than I thought. The police have closed ranks and that's always a good sign, trust me. I'm telling you, if we can develop this thing properly—'

'What do you mean develop it properly? I gave you a tip—'

'Yes, you did, mate – tip of the iceberg. This has got the potential to be massive. You told me these people run Sydney and, if you're right, which I'm beginning to think you are, it means there's a political angle, police corruption, the works. I'm working with legal …'

Murdoch tried ignoring the flies on his sunglasses and the bridge of his nose; swatting only made it harder not to sweat. He turned his back to the sun and looked down at the briefcase between his feet.

'How long, Harvey?'

'What's that?'

'How long before you print the story?'

'Well, without your help, who knows? If you come in, talk to us in the strictest confidence, we could make it worth your whi—'

'I don't want your money, just print the bloody story!'

'It's not just about money – although it could be a tidy sum. We'll protect you too; with your full co-operation, we could get the story together in, what, eight or nine weeks?'

Murdoch gave up and swatted at a fly on his nose, missed and hit his sunglasses. One of the lenses flipped out and tumbled to the pavement where it snapped into three with a sharp little click like a wire being cut. He took a deep breath and hung up gently, resisting the urge to tear the receiver off the cord or use it to smash the phone to pieces. Knowing his anger was out of proportion didn't make it easier to control. It was like when he fought: the tunnel vision that made everything else invisible.

Throwing the remains of his sunglasses into the street, he walked back to the car and – the zombies watching in fascination – drove around the block at speed three or four times, until, at last, he had the sense to realise he was liable to kill someone. On his way into town, he'd passed a café near the train station. He'd thought at the time it was the kind of place you'd walk out of stinking of over-used cooking oil. Now he found it again, ordered a coffee and sat under a noisy fan, head in his hands, eyes shut, trying not to think about Harvey Clarke, but thinking about nothing else.

It took him an hour to come back out of it, to tell himself everything would be all right. He didn't need to believe it: he just needed to make himself say it. He had the vague impression that people had come and gone, sat opposite him and eaten, while the guy behind the counter – an ancient Greek man with a yellow moustache – had simply watched and left him alone. He probably thought Murdoch was another zombie, more dangerous than most from the look of him. *Well*, thought Murdoch, *that'd be right*.

Back at the car, he felt something was wrong before he saw it. Like a noise in the night you can't name, you just know it shouldn't be there. It was the way the light reflected on the passenger window, or rather the way it didn't. A strange feeling took hold of him as he got closer, like the humidity had suddenly doubled, working its way up from the tarmac and feasting on his skin, sucking the sweat out, pore by pore. There were shards of smashed glass on the road beside the car and now his skin wasn't big enough for his body, was stretching thin around his muscles and stinging with the effort of it all. Inside the car, on the passenger seat, much more glass, irregular beads of it in a halo around a rectangular patch where there was no glass at all.

Murdoch turned and ran back to the café, empty now but for the old man and his yellow moustache. Murdoch yelled at him.

'Did I have a bag with me when I came in here before?'

The old man was frightened, didn't understand.

'A bag,' Murdoch repeated, miming hurriedly with his hands. 'A small brown case. Like a briefcase? Did I have one here?'

He walked over to the table he'd been at and kicked the chairs from under it. The old man came up behind him, hands open wide, asking him to stop.

'No,' he said. 'No case. You have no case here. You had nothing.'

'It was in the car. I left the briefcase in my car.'

'Oh no.' Like everyone round there, the old man knew what that meant. 'It stolen? You not see the sign?'

He pointed to a faded poster above the table where Murdoch had sat. A cartoon thief with the words *Do Not Leave Valuables In Your Car* forming his red bag of loot. Two of the chairs Murdoch had kicked over lay on their sides at his feet. He said nothing, bent down and stood them upright. Pictured himself raising one and smashing it over the old man's head.

'Terrible here,' the old man was saying. 'Terrible people. You lose much?'

'Eighteen thousand dollars.'

The old man's eyes grew wide with fright. 'No? No! Terrible.' He shuffled back behind his counter, afraid to be tainted by such bad luck, or just afraid of anyone in that part of town with so much money to lose.

11.

With the curtains drawn, Murdoch's bedroom was so dark he could lie with his eyes open or closed and see no difference. It was like being buried alive, he thought, surprised by how comforting the idea was. He listened to Davie moving around, using the bathroom as loudly as possible, leaving the house three times before there was nothing else he could have forgotten.

Murdoch lay there for another hour at least after that, refusing to move, begging for sleep. He wondered why suicide was not an option, never had been. Unless he wondered if it would hurt, how long it would be before Davie summoned up the courage to knock on his door and discover his body. It would have to be pills, he thought, something gentle. He'd seen too many people die in pain to want to go like that.

It was the heat that got him up in the end: that and a final hope.

Hannah Simms answered on the first ring, hesitant and slightly breathless, as if she was dreading the call.

'Oh, it's you, Bill. I didn't recognise the number. Anything to report?'

'Thought I was a friend blowing you out?'

'Well, actually, yes. But you're not. Anything to report?'

'A date?'

'What?'

'You're going on a date tonight and you thought I was him changing his mind?'

She hesitated and Murdoch swore inside his head. He'd been trying to make friendly conversation. He commented hurriedly on the weather and she asked him for the third time if he had anything to report. He told her no, not yet, and bumbled clumsily towards the point. Listened to her voice turn from brusque and impatient to so cold it was surprising the phone didn't freeze.

'I'm sorry, Bill, you'll need to be clearer. What are you asking for exactly?'

'I need an advance. I've been expecting a payment what hasn't turned up and now I'm up here without enough money to buy food or fill up the car.'

Murdoch realised he was pacing around the living room. He took a deep breath and carried the call out onto the blinding balcony. It was no cooler than inside, the sky heavy, the trees silent, the horizon flat but for a tiny ship or two.

'You want money?'

'Is that a problem?'

'Well, no, of course not. Or at least it won't be when I can be convinced that I'm getting something in return.'

Murdoch rubbed his hand across his hair and told himself to be nice. 'You can't expect any progress yet, sweetheart.'

'Progress in outcomes, no, but in terms of input, yes. I asked Davie to pass you on a list of people to talk to. How are you going with that?'

Shit. 'Well, don't worry, talking to the locals is one of the avenues I'll follow.'

'And the others? Are drinking coffee and reading the paper among them? Is that how you hope to find Georgie?'

The outside stairs creaked, the front door slammed and then Davie was at the balcony door. 'Dude! Want to come for a surf?'

Murdoch shook his head and mouthed that he was talking to Hannah. Davie made a horror face, shook his fingers like he'd just been stung and disappeared into the house. Murdoch whispered harshly into the phone. 'Do you have people spying on me now?' Davie telling you what I'm up to, is he?'

'Davie and I speak to each other as little as we possibly can, trust me, but I do have other friends up there. Montie is a small town, Bill, everyone spies on everyone. I don't have to ask and I know from gossip what you're up to. You purport to be a private detective. All I want is to see some evidence of that. I am paying you, after all.'

'Not yet, you're not.'

'No, but you're not being a detective yet either.'

The front door slammed again, the stairs creaked again; Davie came into view down on the driveway. He was carrying a surfboard and a towel Murdoch had last seen on the bathroom floor. When Davie turned and waved the towel up at him as a goodbye, Murdoch stepped back out of view.

'Listen,' he told Hannah, 'I do normally ask for a retainer, you know.'

'So why didn't you?'

They were quiet for a minute, then Hannah sighed.

'Look, maybe this whole thing was a mistake; maybe we should forget about it and you should come back to Sydney. We just need to meet a few more times to review your file and then we can say goodbye.'

'No.'

He tried to take the urgency out of his voice, squatted down on his haunches, ran his hand across his hair again. 'Listen, I can understand why it looks like I've not done nothing. I've been getting the lie of the land, finding out how things work around here. Let's wait a few days. Then, when you've seen the progress I've made, maybe you'll feel better about sending some money my way. It's not like I want to ask, but someone has let me down badly.'

'What about all that money in your bank account?'

'Well, some bills had to be paid and the rest is committed to other stuff coming in. I have ...' he searched for the word '... overheads. Like I said, I wasn't expecting this trouble.' He was picking at a thread in the carpet, pulling at it so hard that his fingers hurt. 'What do you think?'

There was a long silence, the sound of her breathing the only evidence she hadn't hung up on him.

'We'll see,' she said at last.

Murdoch thanked her, apologised again and hung up. He was still there, picking at the carpet, when Davie arrived home hours later to tell him how perfect the ocean was.

12.

On his first visit to the beach that morning, Davie had discovered that the forecasts had got it wrong. All week the waves had been teasing him: trapped as he was behind the window of Deutsch & Bowler, stuck in a shirt and tie when he should be wearing boardies and a rashie. Worse, the online surf experts had all agreed that Friday afternoon the swell would die down and turn. Davie had reminded himself, day after day, that at the weekend – his first Saturday off in weeks – he'd have to make do with a swim.

But, down at the beach, he found the waves were as perfect as they'd been all week. Even better, out at the point, it was pumping. He ran all the way home to grab his board – more than happy to leave Bill on the phone to Hannah – and all the way back to the beach, surfing off the headland for over two hours. Then, at lunchtime, when the tide and the forecast lull began to suck in at last, he went home again to swap his fish for his longboard. As a result, he also managed to squeeze half an afternoon's fun from the waves before they finally disappeared. By four o'clock, exhausted and tingling with burny tan, he was thinking he'd had the perfect Saturday, no idea it was about to get more exciting.

'I'm cooking you dinner,' he told Bill, back at the house once again, this time from the shops. 'Spag bol, my speciality.'

'No thanks.'

The Englishman barely looked up from his reading. As far as Davie could tell, Bill hadn't left the shack all day other than to buy his newspapers. No wonder he was so pasty.

'Aw, come on,' Davie said. 'I've been to the general store, bought the ingredients and everything. And I've got to use the mince in the fridge, else it'll go past its use-by date.'

This wasn't strictly true. The mince was already past its use-by date, but Davie had sniffed it carefully and was pretty sure it wouldn't poison them. Still, the Englishman didn't look up. Instead, he turned a page of his *Telegraph* and continued reading carefully, as if looking for something specific.

Davie rolled his eyes. Wait until his housemate smelled the garlic sizzling in the olive oil, the irresistible scent of cooking meat wafting through the shack, then he'd see who wanted to be a grumpy-pants.

'I normally open the balcony door when I cook,' Davie told him. 'I hate cooking with it closed – it gets so hot in here. I should get a barbie on the balcony really. Anyway, the mozzies get in, but they don't bother me much. You're pale though, so I bet they love you. Do you want me to keep it closed?'

Bill looked up at last. He seemed exhausted, as if he'd been the one doing hours of exercise, not lounging around indoors all day. When he spoke, it sounded to Davie as if the effort of pushing out the single syllable was almost more than he could bear.

'What?'

'I said do you want me to keep the door closed against the mosquitoes?'

'You said it gets too hot in the kitchen.'

'Well, it will. But I can put up with that if the mozzies are going to bother you. I'm sure you'd do the same for me.'

Bill peered at him, as if confused by what he had said, or unsure whether to trust in it. The man was like a stray dog, thought Davie, constantly scared you were going to kick it, but wanting to sniff you all the same.

'It's fine,' Bill said at last.

'Mozzies don't bother you?'

'Yeah, they do, actually. Bleeding golf ball under the skin every time I get bitten.'

'Fine, I'll leave it closed then.' Davie walked back to the corner kitchen and started unpacking the shopping. When he looked up again across the counter into the lounge room, Bill was still studying him.

'Change your mind?' said Davie. 'You hungry after all?'

Another strange look, as if the Englishman was struggling to understand.

'Yeah, I am actually,' he said slowly. 'Spag bol would be all right. Very ... considerate of you. Nice, I mean. Thanks.'

Davie had been told his whole life he talked too much, but, in his opinion, quiet people liked to listen. Bill Murdoch was no exception. As Davie told him over dinner and beers about the day's surfing, his job at D&B, how long he'd lived in the shack, Bill barely said a word. The trouble was, when Davie asked him what life was like as a private detective, he barely said a word about that either.

'Aw, come on,' said Davie. 'There must be loads of exciting stories.'

'Nah.'

'No mysteries you managed to solve through hours of painstaking work?'

'Not really.'

'What about ...'

'Tell me about Georgie Walker,' Bill interrupted. 'She must have been your niece too when you was married to Hannah. What d'you reckon happened to her then?'

It was a blatant change of subject, but Davie rode with it. There was something so edgy about his new housemate – the wiry little man so *angry* all the time – that he couldn't help but try and appease him. If Bill wanted to talk about Georgie, they'd talk about Georgie. Besides, he'd been waiting all week for the mysterious private detective to ask him about the case that had brought him to town. Trouble was, Davie didn't have anything to tell him.

'I don't know,' he said. 'I guess she ran away.'

'Course she did. But where to?

Davie shrugged his shoulders. 'No idea. I didn't really know her very well. She was still a toddler when I went to ... work overseas. That was when Hannah and I began to break up. Hannah wanted to stay here with her family, which really meant her sister Sarah and her kids. If you ask me, Hannah probably didn't trust Sarah to raise Georgie and Tom right. She wasn't strict enough for Hannah's liking.'

'And what happened to her then?'

'Who, Sarah? Hit-and-run. Some bastard knocked her down and left her dead in the street over in Taradale. She was lovely, Sarah, nothing like Hannah. I definitely married the wrong one. Sarah was up for anything, a real laugh. Her poor husband Paul – you know, Georgie's dad? – the police grilled him like crazy. And get this, Hannah told them she thought Sarah was too good for him and probably wanted to leave him. I've no idea where she got that idea from, but it meant Paul became suspect number one, despite the fact he could prove he was in Port Macquarie with the kids at the time. Then, three years later, Georgie goes missing and the opposite happens. Try as he might, Paul can't get the police to pay him any attention. He's really been through it. If that was me, I'd go postal. Shoot up Crosley police station and end up with a three-dot tattoo.'

'A three-dot tattoo?'

'Or something like that. You have to join a gang when you go to prison, you know, or you don't survive. You have to wear the gang tattoo and everything.'

'That's bollocks. You ca—'

'No, I saw it on TV. You have to join a gang or they kill you in the first week.' Davie caught the look on Bill's face. 'Really, that's what they said.'

'It's bullshit.'

'How do you know?'

The Englishman seemed to shrink, his frame retracting into itself. He scowled and looked away to the balcony door, as if he was studying the view outside; as if that was possible through the steam and the black reflections.

'I just do.'

'Oh my God,' said Davie. 'Were you in prison? In England?!'

'No.'

'You were, weren't you! Wow! And I thought sharing a house with a private detective was exciting enough! Should I lock my door at night? What did you go inside for? How long were you in there?'

Eventually Davie realised he should stop – about four sentences too late, as ever. The small man opposite him had clenched his fists and was sitting rigidly, the tendons in his neck like guy ropes, his black eyes focused on his empty plate. A man turned to stone.

'Oh, I'm really sorry,' Davie garbled. 'That was really insensitive of me. Listen, er, have another beer and I'll tell you everything I know about Georgie. She was seventeen when she went missi—'

'Don't tell no one.' Bill was still looking at his plate, staring so hard Davie half expected the crockery to break in two. 'I don't like people knowing. You wouldn't understand it, but nice little town like this – normal people what've never seen nothing nasty – they look at you different when they know you was inside. And, yeah, I did some bad shit, but that was years ago. I'm not like that no more and I don't want people thinking I am. So, don't say nothing. Right?'

The Englishman looked up, his black eyes pleading. Davie wondered if his normal gruff manner – his preference for monosyllables – was a front to hide his fragility. If what he'd thought was anger, or tiredness, was in fact a heavy sadness weighing the man down?

'Of course I won't tell anyone!' Davie said vehemently. He was, after all, a man who knew what it was to live in the shadow of your past. 'It's nobody's business, is it? I won't even tell Natalie if you don't want me to. Promise.'

Bill nodded and looked down at his hands again. Then, looking up with his normal severe frown, he asked, 'Natalie? Who the hell's Natalie?'

13.

Paul Walker was the first name on Hannah's list. There was something about him that reminded Murdoch of Harris, the Club exec, but he had no idea what it was. Walker was tall – six four, at least – and held himself to his full height, unafraid of the world. He had an energetic walk that said he was the kind of bloke who got things done and didn't moan about it. He had a good tan and expensive sunglasses, the frames barely there, well-made clothes that looked comfortable on him. It was his face that gave away what he'd been through. It hung thick and loose on his cheekbones, taut only around his eyes and the corners of his mouth. His smile was uncertain or, at best, an effort, like he wanted to smile more but kept forgetting. Murdoch thought he looked like a middle-aged man dressed up like an old one: an actor on the telly when they'd overdone the ageing. Or maybe just like a bloke who'd had bad things happen to him. God knows, he'd seen enough of them.

Walker sat him in an armchair in the living room and went off to the kitchen to make them both a pot of tea. As soon as he was alone, Murdoch was on his feet again, examining the furniture, running his hands over all the curved edges, the fireplace, the sofas, the drinks cabinet – all of it quality stuff. He flipped through the heavy books on the coffee table, one of them a retrospective of buildings Walker had designed, a letter from the Premier folded inside. Murdoch tried each of the seats – a regular little Goldilocks – then walked over to the French doors and looked out across a well-swept patio to a garden which ran into the lagoon.

'Do you have a garden, Bill?'

Walker sat the tray of tea carefully onto the coffee table before joining him at the door. Murdoch heard himself saying he'd love a garden, like he'd even thought of it before.

'It's constant work,' said Walker. 'It's like being at uni; you never rest without feeling guilty – there's always something you should be working on.'

He opened the doors and they walked out onto the patio, the sun still strong but lower now, the shadows of the trees stretched thin across the lawn below them. For the lack of anything else to say, Murdoch asked what some of the plants were. Walker pointed at them slowly: a hedge beginning with 'V' that needed trimming; young trees he ought to feed; a bed of red robin that he really should move, except it went in before Georgie disappeared, and he wanted everything to stay the same for when she came back. It was the first time either of them had mentioned the missing girl's name and it hung awkwardly between them, until Walker said their tea was getting cold.

They talked about his wife, Sarah, at first. How her death had rocked the whole family. Then about Hannah. How close she and Georgie had been; how frustrated Hannah had been with the police investigation into Georgie's disappearance. Murdoch suspected Walker needed to get to the subject of his daughter slowly and so he let the man talk, more interested in the reflection of himself in Walker's sunglasses. Bill Murdoch in a beautiful room drinking tea from a china cup. He tuned in again as Walker paused, sipping deliberately at his tea, not knowing how to phrase what he wanted to say next, then letting it blurt out too quickly.

'Do you really think you can find her, Bill? I mean, I know you people can do things the police can't do but ...Well, DC Conquest was very good and very thorough. I just wonder what else you can do?'

Murdoch asked Walker if he'd rather he didn't investigate. If they should tell Hannah this wasn't such a good idea?

'No, no, not at all. I really want you to do this. God, of course I do. It's just ... well, it's my son, Tom. I don't want to get his hopes up unless there's a real chance. This hit him so hard – he and Georgina were as thick as thieves – and he only now seems to be coming out the other end of it. I couldn't bear for him to think you're going to find her and then for it not to happen.'

Murdoch sat back in his chair and said nothing. Eventually, Walker confessed – yes, he was scared of getting his own hopes up too. Then a bell rang out in the hallway and the man gave a tired smile.

'Perfect timing,' he said, pulling his huge frame off the sofa. 'I hope you don't mind, but I asked DC Conquest to join us. I thought it would make sense for you to get all the details up front.'

Murdoch didn't have time to mind or not: Walker was already gone into the hallway. He heard voices, then Walker returned to the living room with a puzzled frown.

'I didn't realise you two had already met,' he said.

'Not officially,' said the woman behind him.

Her sports bag had been replaced by a leather satchel, but her chin was strong with attitude again, her green eyes frowning like when they'd first met outside Davie's house. She held out her hand as she walked up to him.

'How are you, Bill? I'm DC Natalie Conquest. How's the dossing and the R&R going?'

14

They sat in opposite sofas, Murdoch with his back to the garden facing Walker and DC Conquest across the tray of cooling tea. Murdoch had fronted enough coppers in his life not to be to be intimidated by the Detective Constable's scowls, knew the exact smiles that would wind her up.

'Georgina was always such a good girl,' Paul Walker was telling him. 'Always. Losing her mum when she was so young, she had to grow up quickly. Tom was still a baby and, inevitably, Georgina ended up taking care of him. But she never complained. Then, later, when other girls started messing around with boys or getting into trouble – Georgina went to the best school in the area, but nowhere's perfect – she missed out on all of that. She was a very quiet girl, used to come home and do her homework and, if I was working late, she'd cook. It's how I know she hasn't run away, you see; she wouldn't do that to me and Tom. I'm sure that's what all parents say; I'm sure you hear it all the time. But she just wouldn't.'

The man's voice was flat, as if any emotion left in the story was merely a memory of something he'd once felt. Murdoch noticed DC Conquest start to reach out to him a few times, but then hold herself back, and he wondered how close they were. Only once she was sure Walker had finished, did the policewoman cough and start to talk herself.

'Is that right, Bill? Do you hear that all the time?' She wasn't really looking for an answer. 'I know I do. But I have to admit, in this case, even I find it difficult to believe that Georgie ran away. I live just round the corner and we knew each other a little. Not much, but she'd always say hello.'

'Right,' said Murdoch. 'And that was enough to make you think she wasn't one to run away, was it?'

Conquest flushed and gave him a flat-eyed stare. When she spoke again, her voice was louder than before.

'Listen, I've dealt with a lot of runaways in my time and I can tell you one thing. None of them were full of the joys of spring. Kids run away from home when they're unhappy, or bored, or scared of their parents. Georgie was none of those things.'

Walker placed a calming hand on the Detective Constable's forearm. 'Natalie was one of the few police officers who never doubted that,' he said. 'You could see with all the others they thought Georgie had hitched down to Sydney or something. They never said it, but you could tell. If it wasn't for Natalie, I'd have my doubts as to whether the police had investigated at all. I've asked Natalie to write out a summary of her findings for you. She can't share any official reports with you, of course, but I know she's eager to help.'

Murdoch flashed Conquest a well-chosen smile. In return, she snatched some papers out of her satchel and shoved them over the coffee table towards him. Out in the hallway, the front door slammed and a boy's voice called out. Walker smiled and excused himself: he wouldn't be a minute. He looked relieved to leave them alone.

Murdoch chose a new smirk. 'Are you angry because you believed me about being here on holiday?'

'No, I'm angry because I still do believe you. I reckon you're on the make, up here for a little paid holiday, with Davie Wonder to sing you to sleep. I'd doubt you even had a CAPI licence if Hannah hadn't told me she'd confirmed it herself.'

She what? Unsettled by the statement, Murdoch lost the cool he'd managed until now.

'Or maybe,' he snapped at the Detective Constable, 'you're just pissed off that you couldn't solve the case and now I'm going to show you up.'

Conquest coloured again and stood, the evening sun bathing her face in light.

'Listen,' she said. 'This family's been through enough—'

She stopped as Walker re-entered the room, his hands on the shoulders of the young boy he was pushing gently ahead of him.

'Tom,' he said, 'you remember Natalie. And this is Bill Murdoch. He's going to see if he can find Georgina.'

Walker had said Tom was ten, but this kid looked years younger. Maybe it was his round face and his huge eyes, or, maybe, Murdoch thought, maybe that's what ten-year-olds look like in the nice part of town. Tom stuck out his hand and said, 'How you doing?' but he kept his eyes firmly on the floor. Murdoch shook the tiny hand – bones you could crush without thinking – but couldn't think of anything else to say. He smiled stiffly at Walker who told Tom to run along, the kid scampering away like he'd been let off with his life.

74

'What's wrong with him, then?' he asked.

'Nothing' said Conquest, before Walker could respond. 'He's just shy. Georgie was the same at that age, lots of kids are.'

Murdoch looked at her, thought of himself at ten, and said nothing.

Georgie's bedroom reminded Murdoch of the plants that Walker didn't want to move. It was like a room still lived in: the bed neatly made, a pink alarm clock on the bedside table. He didn't know enough about pop stars to recognise if the posters were out of date, but the calendar on the back of the door was two years old. He flipped through it like he knew what he was looking for, poked through the crowded noticeboard the same way, ignoring the memories it stoked of his shack on the warehouse roof. Concert tickets, shopping receipts, a *Far Side* cartoon. Next to the computer on the tiny desk, he found a pile of CDs.

'I thought it was all on your phone these days,' he said, self-conscious in the small room with the policewoman and Walker watching him. He picked up the CDs and looked through them, remembering something he'd seen on a TV show. 'Could I take some of these to listen to?'

Walker said 'No' at the same time as Conquest asked 'Why?' He told them it was all part of profile-building, discovering the personality of the person he was looking for.

'I don't know,' said Walker. 'It doesn't seem right. I know what you mean, I've listened to them all myself. But, it's just … they're Georgie's, you know. She always took good care of her stuff.'

Murdoch wasn't going to argue, but then DC Conquest spoke.

'Despite myself, I have to agree with him, Paul. As a methodology, profiling has been proven to be successful …' she glared at Murdoch, '… *if* you know what you're doing.'

'Tell you what,' said Murdoch. 'How about I take half of them and when I'm done with that lot, I'll bring them back and swap them for the rest? So there's always some here.'

Like that made sense. But Walker agreed, taking the pile from Murdoch and splitting it in two, giving him half back and placing the rest on the desk, tidying them neatly back into the exact position in which they'd originally stood. Murdoch asked for some photographs of Georgie, thinking Walker would find him some, but, once more, the Detective Constable was prepared. She fished for them in her satchel and, after a brief hesitation, handed them over.

There were half a dozen shots or more. Only two were formal poses, the rest showed a pretty blonde with her father's eyes, smiling warily, playing with her little brother, running on the beach. Murdoch had expected a fat child in a check school uniform, not this young woman: a real person something bad had happened to. For the first time, he understood the importance of what they thought he was here to do. Still, he couldn't resist reacting to the copper and her attitude. As soon as Walker had left the room, Murdoch took the half-pile of CDs from beside the computer and swapped them with the ones in his hand. DC Conquest watched him in silence until he gave her a leer and a wink. She rolled her eyes, told Murdoch he was a dag, and followed Walker out onto the landing.

Murdoch found Tom Walker at the bottom of the long garden, where it ran into the lagoon. He stood back, watching the kid from the shadows of a huge tree that stood in the middle of the sloping lawn. Tom was wearing a black cardboard hat with a skull-and-crossbones printed on one side. The hat was two sizes too big for him and it fell below his eyebrows, or sometimes off his head completely, when he walked to the target he'd hung from a twisted shrub at the water's edge, or bent to pick up his arrows. The little boy didn't seem to mind. Each time he'd pick the hat up again, or push it to the back of his head, all the while describing the savages Captain Tom Walker was fighting in his battle of the high seas. Murdoch knew he should interrupt: the kid would be embarrassed someone had caught him playing make-believe, but he didn't want to spoil the moment. The sun was warm on the back of his neck and there was a smell like nothing he'd known before. Sweet like a perfume but fresher, like walking past a flower shop. Imagine growing up in a place like this.

'Unhand her, you scoundrel!'

Tom's voice squeaked with the effort of misfiring another arrow. As if in response, a flock of raucous birds appeared over the roof of the house, flew low over the lawn and around the tree, then across the lagoon and into the greenery on the opposite side. Murdoch ducked, swore, and looked up to find Tom watching him.

'Hello.'

'Hello,' said Tom reluctantly. 'You said a bad word.'

'Oh, sorry about that. Them birds frightened me. Bit blooming loud, aren't they?'

'They're cockatoos.'

'Are they? See, I didn't know that.'

'Everyone knows cockatoos.'

'Well, everyone but me, maybe. What you playing at? Pirates?'

'Colonialism.'

'Right. I suppose everyone knows what that is too. I like your bow and arrow, mate, I always wanted one like that.'

Tom resisted for a second, then asked him why he hadn't had one then, which for some reason made Murdoch smile. Like a girly kid in a nice-smelling garden could begin to understand. He told Tom about the catapult he'd had as a kid, how him and his mates used to shoot rocks at buses. Tom laughed like it was naughty joke.

'Listen,' said Murdoch, 'your dad said I could ask you some questions.'

'What about?'

'About Georgie.'

No laughter now. Tom took a step back, looked at his shoes and shook his head.

'It's all right,' said Murdoch. 'It's not like you've done nothing wrong. I just need to know what kind of things she liked doing.'

'I don't know anything.'

'I haven't asked a question yet.'

'But I don't know anything. I don't, honestly.'

Tom was talking to his feet, so Murdoch sat and waited. He smelled the flowers again and listened to some ducks laughing at him from out on the water. It was a good minute before Tom looked up and, for the first time, Murdoch saw something in the garden he recognised.

'It's all right,' he said. 'There's nothing to be frightened of.'

For a second he thought Tom would trust him, lay down his bow and arrow and tell him something he didn't know. Something he could use to get some cash out of Hannah. Maybe Tom thought it too, but then another second passed and he was crying, shaking his head, and, before Murdoch could stop him, running past him up to the steps to the patio and into the house.

15

Down at the shops, the weekend was in full throttle. Cars were parked bumper to bumper, kids ran wet across the road and the scruffy café was full. Above the beach, at the top of the first path that ran down through the dunes, surfers and swimmers queued for the shower. Murdoch stood outside the general store, waiting ten minutes for a gap in the customers. Eventually, he gave up, took a deep breath and walked in. The old blonde with the jewellery was busy with a kid paying in small coins, but by the time Murdoch had picked up a Mars bar and put it on the counter, she had her hands on her hips and was glaring at him. They stood there for a few seconds, looking at each other over the shop counter.

'I want to say sorry,' said Murdoch, knowing full well he sounded anything but.

'What for?'

'For being rude to you that day when I first met you.'

'And?' She moved from one hip to the other, her jewellery rattling on her cleavage.

'Er?'

'For telling me to mind my own business.'

'I'm sorry I told you to mind your own business.'

Murdoch heard a stifled giggle and turned to see two small girls behind him, their wet swimsuits dripping sea water onto the floor. The woman behind the counter asked them what the hell they wanted.

'Snakes,' the smaller girl managed at last, her friend too terrified to speak.

'Two dollars fifty!'

The silent girl stepped forward and put the coins on the counter, took the plastic bag of sweets and ran out of the shop with her friend. Murdoch was tempted to follow.

'Is that all, then?'

'Is there something else I have to say sorry for?'

'I mean the Mars bar. That all?'

'And a coffee, thanks.'

It was the first time since his first visit that he'd given her reason to do more than snatch his newspaper money and bang the change down on the counter. The woman tutted and shuffled over to the coffee machine, banging the packed filter hard and loud. Murdoch leaned across the counter so he could see her.

'Funny thing is,' he said, 'I actually want you to do the opposite.'

'Meaning?'

'Meaning, I don't want you to mind your own business. I was wondering if I could ask you a few questions about Georgie Walker. Seeing as I'm investigating and all. And, well, I'm guessing you probably know everything what goes on in this town.'

She said nothing, concentrating instead on the steaming machine. By the time his coffee was ready, there was a queue of people behind him and the woman served them all before turning to him again.

'You've got a bloody nerve. You're lucky you're doing the job you're doing, else I wouldn't give you the time of day. But the police have given up on Georgie, that's for sure. And, although Hannah Simms and I might not see eye to eye on many things, I'll say one thing for her – she doesn't suffer fools. So, you're probably good at something, even if you are bloody rude, and Georgie was a lovely girl and her poor dad deserves to find out what happened to her. So, yes, OK, I can talk to you.'

She could talk all right. Murdoch stood there for over an hour, ticking off his questions about Georgie as she answered them without being asked, interrupting herself only to serve customers, sometimes not even then. Her name was Anne Lincoln, she'd had the store for over ten years and she'd known Georgie for all of that time. She'd seen her grow up: a sweet girl, very protective of her little brother; always polite, not like most teenagers, blah, blah, blah. Nothing Murdoch hadn't already heard from Hannah Simms or DC Conquest or anyone else he bumped into in the street. Everyone really did seem to care. He stood and scribbled illegibly as the store grew hotter around him, the sun reaching through the big front window and the coffee machine steaming regularly. Every few minutes, he had to adjust his position to keep his jeans from sticking to his legs.

'You need to get a pair of shorts, darl,' said Anne Lincoln over her shoulder. 'Grab some off the rack there – those bottom ones will fit you.'

He walked over and looked at the price. Made an excuse about having some at home. 'Anyway,' he said, 'I think we're all done. Unless there's anything else you can think of?'

Anne Lincoln made a face and nodded to the back of the shop, where three teenage boys were arguing half-heartedly about a tin of tuna. Only when they'd left did she come around the front of the counter to lay a heavily ringed hand on his forearm. It was a strangely intimate gesture, a gesture of trust. He felt like one of those con men that rip off old ladies for their life savings.

'Listen, darl,' she said quietly, 'just you watch yourself, is all. Not everyone around here's like me, you understand? I'm glad you're here, but not everyone will be. Watch out for them Harper boys is what I'm trying to say. You keep one eye open and be careful what questions you ask, you got it? And it's a dollar fifty for the Mars bar and three dollars for the coffee, thanks.'

16.

Monday. The sign outside the gates said Saint Cecilia's Grammar School for Girls had been serving the community since 1864. Murdoch didn't know they'd discovered Australia by 1864, but it was written on the sign, so it was probably true. The school itself – far enough north of Crosley not to be tainted by the town – sat hidden from the road, gates and hedges screening well-watered lawns and featureless red-brick buildings. The original schoolhouse was still there: all chimneys and windows, like an orphanage in a storybook, but it was dwarfed by modern sports halls and double-glazed dormitories.

Murdoch parked in the shadow of a windowless building and sat with his eyes closed. He'd toyed the day before with not checking the papers, had told himself the way to make the story appear was not to look for it. Except if that happened, he might miss his window of opportunity and, if the paper was going to break a big story, it might be more likely to do it on a Sunday. Harvey Clarke might have found something out, might have decided to put out a teaser to see what else came in, might this and might that, if, if, if, until Murdoch had bought the paper to put himself out of his misery. It hadn't worked.

He wound down the window and listened to the irregular shrieks of girls playing netball, opened his eyes and found he could see them a couple of hundred yards away: countless legs and ponytails, sports skirts chasing each other across the baking asphalt. He should take Harvey Clarke up on his offer of money. No one could protect him against the Club, but a handover of cash would be easy enough. It probably wasn't too late; it might even motivate the paper to get on and print the story.

'Excuse me, sir, can I help you?'

Murdoch flinched and swore, then turned to look through the open window beside him. A pale, bearded man was standing outside the car.

'I don't know. Can you?'

'Are you a parent?'

'Who's asking?'

'I was just wondering why you were sitting here watching the girls play netball?'

'Why, d'you think I'm a paedo or something?'

'I don't know who or what you are, sir. That's why I'm asking. All I know is you're sitting in your car watching thirteen-year-old girls play netball.'

Murdoch thought about this for a second. 'Fair enough. Does look a bit pervy.' He undid his seatbelt and got out of the car, the bearded man stepping out of the way. 'I'm looking for Troy McLaren. He's a teacher here, isn't he?'

'Who's asking?'

They were face-to-face now, Murdoch the taller man for once, but the bearded guy clearly unintimidated. He had wispy blond hair and the palest eyes Murdoch had ever seen, an unfinished sketch of a man.

'My name's Bill Murdoch. Mr McLaren's expecting me.'

The other man relaxed and laughed. 'Yes, I am,' he said, sticking out his hand. 'Nice to meet you, Bill.'

Troy McLaren's soft face, even framed by its thick beard, looked younger than it had to be. Unless, of course, the man had never seen anything bad in his life. Around here, who knew? Maybe that was possible.

'Call me Troy,' McLaren said. 'What are you doing out here? Why didn't you come into reception?'

Murdoch ran his hand across his head. What was he supposed to do? Explain he was staring into space trying to work out how to get his life back? 'Forgot my ID, didn't I?' he said. 'I was sitting there thinking about where I'd lost it. Sorry, they're just kids, I didn't even think ...'

'Don't worry about it. It happens to blokes all the time these days. You just have to smile at a kid and everyone starts screaming "stranger danger". Imagine what it's like when you're a teacher. But why did you think you need ID to get into a school?'

McLaren mumbled the end of the question, his soft voice trailing off, like he'd suddenly remembered something more important. He led Murdoch into the school reception hall. As they passed an empty desk and walked down a muted corridor with display cabinets full of trophies, Murdoch caught the teacher stealing curious glances at him. He himself was more interesting in the surroundings. He'd never been in a posh hotel – only mugs ever delivered to them – but he'd always imagined them looking like this. Huge flowers on the reception desk, framed landscapes the length of the corridor, venetian blinds and, in McLaren's office, leather seats.

'You were in juvenile detention,' McLaren said as soon as they sat down. 'Am I right?'

'You what?'

'I used to be an outreach worker. Well, I still am in a way. I work with a lot of the kids down at Bryanston – that's our local juvenile detention centre. And I'm one of those do-gooders who visit people in prison – always need my ID on me. So I'm guessing that you were in juvenile detention, am I right? That's why you thought you needed ID to come into a school.' McLaren beamed, pleased with himself, until he caught the expression on Murdoch's face. 'Oh shit, I'm not wrong, am I?'

Murdoch rubbed his hand across his scalp, caught himself doing it, and coughed.

'We're here to talk about Georgie Walker.'

'Of course.' McLaren blushed slightly. 'Of course, I'm sorry. That other stuff's your business. But can I say one thing? If Natalie Conquest doesn't know, you really need to tell her. It'll make things easier. It's always easier if you tell people.'

'When was the last time you saw her?'

'DC Conquest?'

'Georgie Walker.'

'Oh. Sorry ...'

McLaren rattled among the papers on his desk, swallowed by his blushes, until he found what he was looking for. He read out a list of dates, then launched into everything he could remember about the missing girl. Nothing unusual: no boyfriends, averagely popular at school. Murdoch struggled to listen. The leather of his chair was sucking at him. He remembered bare legs on hot seats in rooms with bars on the windows, a less friendly attitude behind the desk. He wanted to ask McLaren why it helped to tell people? What it was about him that still reeked of borstal? He asked if Georgie had been happy at school.

'Difficult to tell; she was so timid, I'm not sure she'd have told us if she wasn't. But I think she was. Happy at home, too, I thought. She was at that age, you know, where some kids look like they're beginning to realise their own potential. Like they could maybe run the country or be a surgeon or travel or, well, anything really. She was a hard worker, Georgie; not one of those girls who slouches around and thinks the world owes her a living. And she was beginning to lose some of her shyness, let her strength show through. People always think shy kids are weak, but Georgie had a bravery about her, you could see that. She stood up to people and recently she … well, you know, she was seventeen, full of the joys of life.'

'You was going to say something else?'

'No.'

'Yes, you was.'

McLaren looked him directly in the eye. 'No, really it was nothing.'

Murdoch let it go. Instead, he dragged the teacher through the questions he'd scribbled on a pad borrowed from the desk in Davie's living room. The way everyone in this town talked, he had to look like he was trying. After half an hour or so, McLaren leaned back in his chair, his fingers steepled on his chest, like they'd reached a silent agreement they were done. Murdoch readied himself to stand, then changed his mind.

'Before,' he said out of pure curiosity, 'you was going to say something. Something you're embarrassed and not sure about. Why don't you just say it and I'll tell you if it's all right or not?'

The teacher laughed and sat upright. 'Wow, you really are a detective, aren't you?'

'What was it you was going to say?'

'Well, there was something. I didn't want to tell the police this, didn't want to send them down the wrong track and, if I'm honest, I didn't want to give them the wrong idea about me.'

'But ...'

'But ... well, maybe it's just a stupid opinion. It's just that Georgie looked like ... well, you know, she was suddenly a bit more confident and adult, you know? Like she was ... well ...'

'Fucking?'

McLaren laughed again. 'That's not the word I'd have used. But, yes, like she was "a woman" all of a sudden. Hell, what a cliché; maybe I'm making it all up.'

Murdoch told McLaren it was all right; he could see why he wouldn't want to tell the cops something like that. 'I suppose you learn to spot that kind of thing, being around teenage girls all the time.'

'Well, I'm not sure about that. I mean, yes. No. I don't know.'

'Do you reckon any of her friends knew?' Murdoch pulled Hannah's list from his pocket. 'I'm talking to some girl called Alycia Thornton today – apparently, they was good mates?'

McLaren frowned, speaking more slowly again when he answered.

'They were, very close. Georgie was brave, like I said, but that also made her ... what's the word? Influenceable? Easily led? For a while we were worried; not sure what to do. Girls at that age can often react in the opposite way to how you want them to react. But, anyway, before we found out if Alycia was going to lead Georgie astray, Georgie went missing. And Alycia knew nothing about it. Didn't even seem all that upset about it, if you ask me; at least not for long. Then again, that probably says more about Alycia than anything else.'

'Meaning?'

He could see McLaren regretted his words. 'I shouldn't prejudice you. School doesn't bring out the best in some girls. You're going to talk to her; you form your own opinion.'

He refused to be drawn further, no matter how Murdoch asked, but they parted on friendly terms, McLaren insisting on walking Murdoch back to the car. When they said goodbye, the teacher trotted out the normal rubbish about how good it was to have someone looking at this again; how happy they all were he was there. McLaren's faith in him, the whole bleeding town's faith in him, made him uncomfortable. That wasn't the word. Awkward. Claustrophobic. Wrong. Murdoch barely listened as the teacher rattled on, thinking instead how he should really be working with Harvey Clarke. The journalist's advance would be far more than anything he could expect from Hannah Simms. But there were only two people left on his list, so what the hell, maybe he'd get Hannah's cash too and live more comfortably until he could get at some proper money. He shook McLaren's hand, then climbed quickly into the Golf, keen to escape the teacher's admiring smile. At least he'd learned something useful.

17.

The slow drive along the sun-dappled Crown Road didn't help Murdoch's feeling of being stuck: the idea that, if he didn't get a move on soon, he was going to be here forever. As he rolled down the hill into Montauban, he found himself staring at splashes in the bay, until he realised he was watching a pod of dolphins. *Jesus*, he thought as they swam out of view, *you lucky bastards.*

The scruffy café in the strip of shops opposite the beach was called Mon Tea Bon. 'Clever, isn't it?' Davie had asked gleefully, when telling him Margaret Harper worked there. 'Do you get it?'

Murdoch didn't get it, but he wasn't going to tell Davie that.

When he arrived, the café was empty apart from a harried-looking woman wiping down tables, wheezing as she bent to the far edges. At the sight of Murdoch, she stood bolt upright, made a hurried remark about being back in a minute and disappeared through a bead curtain. Its rattles were the only evidence she'd been there.

Murdoch took a seat in the huge front window and looked out at the empty street. The weekenders had gone back to the city and Montauban was so quiet he could hear the ocean hitting the shore. In his long trousers, he felt like an ant beneath a magnifying glass; the only man in Australia without a pair of shorts.

Soon, there were muffled voices from the kitchen, then the bead curtain rattled again and a gym-built bloke – mid-twenties, dorsal-fin hair, wide knees and a scowl – strode out. Murdoch, getting used to how the locals behaved, nodded hello and said g'day. The younger man ignored him and bulldogged out into the heat. As Murdoch watched through the dirty glass, he crossed the road, got into a ute and sat staring into the café from across the tarmac.

Another rattle and Murdoch realised the woman he'd first seen when he'd entered the café was standing beside his table. Up close, he could see her dress had known better days. Whatever colour it had once been, it was now yellow with a brown pattern which, on closer inspection, turned out to be a string of coffee stains. The woman herself hadn't fared much better. She was from an age before sunscreen and, what the sun hadn't got to, something else had. Alcohol, Murdoch reckoned. Maybe he was wrong; maybe she ate well and was in bed every night before nine; maybe it was a coincidence she smelled like a bottle of gin.

'You all right, love?' she said. 'Cup of tea?'

'I'm looking for Margaret Harper.'

'Oh.' The woman swallowed slowly. 'That's me.'

'Nice one. I wanted to talk to you about Georgie Walker. My name's Bill Murdoch, I'm a private detective.' He'd not said it before and it sounded ridiculous. 'Georgie used to work here, right?'

'That was a long time ago. She was very quiet. I don't remember much.'

'I thought it was only two years ago? I thought she was working here when she went missing?'

'Well, that's a long time, ain't it? Two years? I don't know anything. I've told the police everything. I can't talk to you.'

She wasn't talking to him. She was speaking words someone had told her to say. She glanced out of the window and, seeing he'd noticed, glanced quickly back down at him, opening and shutting her mouth silently until she managed to offer him a cup of tea again. Murdoch said sure, why not, a cuppa would be good. When Margaret Harper hurried behind the counter to make it, he stood, walked out of the café and across the tarmac. He was halfway to the ute before Scowlie started it up and pulled away, eight big cats purring slowly under the bonnet. Murdoch stood in the middle of the road and watched the ute roll to the end of the shops to turn left at the little roundabout. Then he listened to the cats roar up the hill and out of town.

Margaret Harper had left his tea on a table she hadn't finished wiping. It sat amongst crumbs and ring marks like the latest move in a difficult game. The woman herself was nowhere in sight. Murdoch called for her once, but he knew there was no point in calling again.

It was another half hour before the last person on Hannah's list arrived. Alycia Thornton was one of those girls you turn to look at without thinking: all hips and tits and a big toothy smile. She was wearing a long white shirt like a minidress, pulled tight with a broad leather belt, shoes that gave her an extra four inches. She arrived with a newspaper under one arm and spread it carefully on her seat before sitting down, careful not to lean on the table. When Murdoch asked her if she wanted a coffee, Alycia looked around and flicked her hair before wrinkling her nose.

'God no, not in here. Thanks, all the same.'

'You wanna go somewhere else?'

'In Montie, darling, where is there? No, this will have to do. We won't need long, will we?'

'You in a rush?'

She pulled off her oversized sunglasses and gave him a smouldering look. 'Bill, darling, this is *so* important, let's take our time over it. Do you have a list of questions? Fire away!'

Murdoch started off by confirming her age, thinking that might remind her not to call him 'darling' or pretend she wanted to flirt. It didn't work. Every question was a new excuse to bat her heavy lashes and linger on the eye contact. For the first time, he was genuinely interested in hearing about Georgie Walker: a little game to see if he could get Alycia to talk about anything but herself.

'Of course Georgie was happy at home,' she told him. 'Why wouldn't she be, with a swanky architect for a dad and living in that gorgeous house? You should see *my* parents and *our* place, seriously! You'd never believe me and mum and dad are related; sometimes I wonder if we really are. I think they must have found me somewhere. God, I can't wait to get away.' And, a little later, 'No, Georgie was always so *boring* about boys. She could have had them *flocking* around her, like I do. She was so pretty, not like me …' – a tiny pause that Murdoch didn't fill – '… and, in fact, I was *convinced* she'd started seeing someone, but Georgie wouldn't admit it. I wish I could be that discreet. As soon as I have a new boyfriend the whole *world* knows about it, makes me seem *terrible*.'

Hot behind the plate glass window, wasting his time with this self-obsessed fool, the frustration Murdoch had been feeling for days threatened to bubble over. He tried to focus on the conversation at hand; tried to imagine a girl as shy and polite as everyone said Georgie Walker was hanging around with the person opposite him. If Georgie was timid – half as timid as her brother, Tom – he could just imagine her being pushed around by the Alycia Thorntons of the world. He'd seen that kind of thing all his life. Alycia was doing her big-innocent-eyes act again.

'Trust me, Bill, I've wracked my brains about where Georgie could be and what might have happened to her. I'm sure it affected my exam results.'

'And what do you reckon happened to her?'

'Well, it's obvious, isn't it, darling? She ran away.'

'Really? And why would she do that, then?'

From Alycia, an extravagant and dramatic shrug. 'God knows. Maybe she did meet someone. Her dad's very strict; she probably knew he wouldn't like it. I'm planning on running away myself. There's this man I've started seeing—'

'I thought you said Georgie was too much of a good girl to do that. Why would a good girl, what wasn't interested in boys, run off?'

'Well, I don't know.'

'Nah, and you don't care neither.'

It took a second for Alycia to realise this wasn't a question. When it did, her youth appeared at last: eyes hurt and watery. 'I do! Of course, I care!'

'Really? You sound to me like you couldn't give a shit.'

It was out before he knew he was going to say it. Alycia stood suddenly and, without thinking, Murdoch grabbed her wrist. 'Sit down.'

'Ow! You're hurting me!'

She screamed it: the loudest noise in town. Pulled herself away with such force, that when he let her go, she fell backwards into her chair, banging harshly against the huge plate glass window between them and the street. Her newspaper clattered to the floor. Across the road, a teenage girl pushing a pram stopped to see what was happening and Margaret Harper appeared in a rattle of the bead curtain, hopping from foot to foot. Murdoch stood up and offered a hand to Alycia.

'I'm sorry, darlin',' he said. 'I didn't mean that to happen.'

Alycia had one hand against the glass window, tears across her face and her hair at odd angles. 'Leave me alone!' she screamed, somehow even louder than before. 'You're horrible!'

She stood, pushed past Murdoch, and ran from the café, leaving the young mother across the road and Margaret Harper to stare at him. He knew he should say something, knew he should tell them he'd not done nothing wrong. But, instead, he stared at Alycia's newspaper, spread across the floor in a wide, flat mess.

A small headline and the lines beneath it had caught his eye. He read them again and again, in case maybe he'd misunderstood: *Telegraph Journalist Dies in Freak Accident. Journalist Harvey Clarke killed in hit-and-run tragedy.*

18.

As Davie walked down from the road, he heard the streetlights clicking to life behind him. Soon they were shining around his shadow, casting a strange orange glow on the sand. The sun was long gone, but the sky above the ocean still had blue in it, the night half an hour away around the headland. Further along the beach, the gulls who'd gathered for the night were stepping nervously from foot to foot, turning their heads to keep an eye on the wiry little man sitting on the sand.

Even from this distance, Davie could see Bill's empties were set out in a perfect circle, twelve half-buried bottles black in the twilight. Bill himself was sitting cross-legged in the middle of them. He was wobbling, or maybe just shivering, Davie couldn't tell, even when he'd crossed the sand and was standing barely metres away. Bill's eyes were closed and, keen not to surprise him, Davie called out his greeting before approaching further.

'Please tell me you've got some beer left.'

Bill opened his eyes and looked up slowly, a man so full of liquid he had to concentrate not to spill any.

'Fuck off.'

'Give me a beer and then I'll fuck off.'

The Englishman tilted awkwardly to one side and Davie got ready to run, but Bill was just scrabbling around in the sand behind him. 'They're warm,' he said, as glass chinked against glass. Then, half a second of silence, and Davie felt something thud into the sand between his feet.

They sat in silence for a good twenty minutes, Davie feeling ridiculous on the beach in a suit, his work shoes full of sand. It was Bill who spoke first, nodding at the lights on the invisible horizon.

'Why's them ships always out there, then?'

'They're coal ships in and out of Newcastle. Take it all over the world. Sometimes they have to queue for days just to get in and load it up.'

'Right.'

Another ten minutes while the sky grew really black. Really cold too: both of them, chattering their teeth in the breeze off the waves. Then, 'Don't worry about Alycia,' Davie said to the darkness. 'She's a drama queen – everyone round here knows what she's like.'

'Yeah, thanks. That's not exactly the problem, though.'

'Anything I can help with?'

They listened to the rumble of a souped-up ute coming down the hill into town. Listened to its engine idle and then die outside the shops. That would be Jackson Harper, Davie thought.

'Listen,' Davie tried again. 'Do you need to borrow some money or something?'

Murdoch's laugh barked loud in the black air between them. 'Yeah, mate. You got two million bucks to spare?'

'I've got two *hundred* bucks I could spare. Plus, I sold a house today, how about that? Boss even gave me a new phone.'

He hated how pleased he sounded, but fished it out all the same, its screen bright between them.

'iPhones,' Bill said bitterly, his features ghoulish in the blue light from the phone. 'Could I have chosen a worse time to get put away? I come back out and the whole world needs a bleeding instruction booklet. Not that they even print them anymore.'

'Am I allowed to ask why you went to prison?'

From Murdoch a hesitation, then a new tone in his voice.

90

'Because, mate, surprising as it might seem, I did not have a nice childhood like everyone round here did. I didn't have your perfect little life, for example.'

'*My* perfect little life?'

'Yeah. Some of us was born in the shit. Some of us, as in me, had to fight every day since then to get what we wanted. What *I* wanted. Every. Fucking. Day. You have no idea how tiring that is. And then, just when I thought I'd got it; just then when it was *just* there …' he gestured wildly towards the ocean, '… it's gone! You wouldn't have a fucking clue.'

Davie put his phone away and they sat in darkness again. He heard Bill open two more beers, felt glass pressing clumsily against his leg until he took the bottle. Then he heard the Englishman taking a long drink before he started talking again, his voice less hoarse than before.

'Why do they call you Davie Wonder, then?'

'Who calls me that?'

'Ouch, easy Tiger. No one, everyone. What's that all about?'

'My perfect little life.'

'Go on then.'

Davie thought about it. 'Why were you in prison?'

'I asked first.'

'No, you didn't.'

'Suit yourself.'

Davie sighed. He'd never had to tell anyone about his past before. 'If I tell you about Davie Wonder, will you tell me about why you were in prison?'

'Sure. Don't worry, you can trust me. I'm a detective.'

Humour, thought Davie, was a good sign. He'd had images of Bill stumbling fully clothed into the waves. He didn't look like he could swim.

'When I was eighteen,' Davie said, 'I used to sing around here in pubs and clubs. Called myself Davie Wonder, just for a laugh, you know. Hannah and I were already married by then.'

'Jesus, you started young. I'd of thought Hannah was too sensible to do something like that.'

'Fair assumption. But she doesn't like being told what to do. Our parents said we couldn't get married, so as soon as we could, we ran off and did it. Half our friends already had kids, it didn't seem that rebellious.'

'And?'

'That's it.'

Bill belched loudly. 'You know what I'm good at, Davie? I'm good at knowing when there's more to what I'm being told. And?'

Davie sighed again. He'd never won a negotiation in his life. 'And I sent a tape to a few record companies and one day these A&R guys came to see me. And before you know it, I've got a record deal.' He took another slug of beer, a long one. Maybe Bill would interrupt him, change the subject.

'And?'

'And my first two songs both went to number one. So, then we went to the States and I had two songs in the top ten there. "Baby, Baby, Baby", you know that one? No, you wouldn't. Never sold anything in the UK, something to do with the lyrics. Got to number two in France and Italy though, something in Germany. And it was massive here. You know, you get any success in the States and the Aussies think you're the biggest thing since Captain Cook. Like you've just proven this country isn't just an island in the South Pacific. The album didn't do too badly, top twenty in the States for three weeks when I was touring there. That was fun ...'

He hoped Murdoch had fallen asleep, but here his voice came again, slurring in the darkness.

'You're kidding me, right?'

'Nope.'

'Bloody hell, what happened? How did you end up as an estate agent?'

'Nothing happened. People just stopped buying my records. No reason why, the next few weren't any worse than the ones that were big. I kept on at it for a while, kept partying for a while, thinking maybe the next one, maybe the one after that. Then next thing you know you're nearly thirty, no qualifications, no money left and all you're good for is selling houses to dickheads from Sydney. Just when you think you've got it made, the world at your feet, girls begging to sleep with you – not that I'd have done that, not with Hannah at home, but all the same ... Where was I? Oh yeah, you've got the world at your feet, everything you've ever dreamt of and then – boof! It's all gone. Not that I'd understand that, of course, not with my perfect little life.'

Bill loomed out of the dark, his face inches away, beery breath a match for the breeze. 'Are you fucking serious? You're famous?'

'I was famous.'

'You were a rock star.'

'I was a pop star. There's a big difference.'

'Jesus!'

Bill fell sideways, landing between the bottles and belching again.

'So then,' said Davie, 'tell me about prison.'

19.

It was properly dark when they ran out of booze, the stars clear and twinkling, the sea merged black into the air above it. Murdoch had thought he wanted to be alone, but somehow talking to Davie was better. Something to take his mind off things, stop him thinking stupid stuff like walking into the sea until it was all over at last. Drowning was a nice way to go, they said, but how could anyone know that?

He told Davie a few stories about life inside, then let him rattle on about life in Montauban. It sounded as nice as it looked and Murdoch wondered how long it would be before the Club found him there. He had no idea what time it was when Davie suggested they head home. There was more beer in the fridge, apparently.

The lamp posts above the beach didn't stretch much further than the shops. Within two minutes of leaving the strand, Murdoch and Davie were walking in a darkness punctuated only by the bright-edged curtains of the houses beside them. Then there were no houses: just the darkness of trees, thick in the breeze.

'Gives me the creeps at night this place,' said Murdoch. 'No pavements, no light, no— What's that noise?'

Davie, beside him, cocked his head to listen. 'It's the wind in the casuarinas. You know, those wispy trees by the lagoon? My mum calls them she-oaks. Nothing can survive underneath them, not even snakes or spiders. Apparently, the Aborigines used them like a nursery, because they knew nothing could eat the babies. Creepy isn't it, like a ghost or something? You only ever get it with casuarinas.'

Maybe Murdoch had meant that. He started walking again, slower now, listening hard to the unfamiliar night. In the distance, a real baby cried and he found that strangely comforting, like maybe it was that that he'd heard, or it was proof nothing could get at them either. He looked up at the stars, blurry in his beery vision, and told Davie for the third time that night that he'd like to learn their names: it was one of them things what everyone knew about apart from him. Then he stopped again and squinted down the dark road behind them.

'There's someone behind us,' he said.

'So?'

A gust of wind came through and the whispering of the casuarinas was lost to the rush of the huge gum trees overhead, twigs and buds rattling onto the tarmac around them. Murdoch stopped, closed his eyes and listened hard. Opened them again to find Davie had carried on along the road, twenty yards ahead and almost out of sight. He ran to catch him up.

'Someone's definitely behind us.'

'Yeah, dude, you said. Probably someone in front of us too. What's the matter, you feeling a bit scared away from the big city lights?'

The road had curved away from the lagoon into a dip where a thousand years of creek had cut into the hillside. Davie said in heavy rains it spilled over the road and Murdoch realised this was where anyone walking disappeared if you were watching them from the house. He found himself thinking of Natalie Conquest and how she'd looked that first time he'd seen her. They trudged on quietly, the banks of trees around them darker than the sky overhead, the only houses far from the road. Without discussing it, they were moving more quickly than before, each false step bumping them against each other.

'At least two of them,' said Murdoch. 'Can you hear?'

Davie stopped to listen, but Murdoch pulled him on. Around the next bend they'd see the lonely street lamp at the bottom of Davie's driveway.

'Dude, you're freaking me out. I walk this way every night; everything's fine.'

Murdoch said nothing. They climbed and rounded the bend, the street lamp further away than Murdoch had remembered, but the light from a house on their left showing the road that ran to it.

'Oh yeah!' said Davie. 'Now I can hear them. I reckon they're running.'

Murdoch turned, his breathing shallow, unwilling to admit any fear. But when two men came charging from the shadows, the larger of them holding a bicycle chain, he was ready.

20.

There was another side to Montauban. It lay north of Montauban Hill, the steep road that ran down into town and ended at the roundabout near the beach. Between Montauban Hill and the lagoon that formed its southern border, was the suburb Murdoch had seen so far. Here the land rose and fell slowly, any bit of high land, like the one where Davie's shack sat, soon ended by a new dip. Other than around the lagoon, big trees grew proud and apart from each other, flexing their branches against the sky.

North of Montauban Hill, things were different. Everything in this part of town was one long slope, up from the beach, to the ridge that pinned Montauban to the shore. Montagne Road, the road that ran around the entire suburb – beside the lagoon where Davie's shack sat and along the front of the beach - became a second-gear gradient north of the roundabout as it climbed to the top of broken cliffs. Each of the turnings running inland from it – like the one Murdoch now followed Davie down – was at a different height, the ground between them so sheer that every house was at least half on stilts. Even in the dark, Murdoch could see none of them would have a view. They were too crowded in by trees, even upstairs windows looking out into the canopy of giants growing further down the hill. The streets up here were even darker than those near the beach and Murdoch, completely lost, had to follow Davie closely. He had no idea where they were going and, given the state he was in, without Davie to guide him, he wouldn't make it back to the shack – let alone to wherever it was they were headed.

They turned to the left, the air around them so dark that Murdoch knew only from their footsteps that they were still on tarmac. Every time they had turned, it had been to the left and he felt like they were spiralling up the hillside, up and up into the dark, the crashing waves from the beach growing quieter below them.

Davie was walking fast, speed-walking in a dream. He wasn't going on about getting to a hospital any more, but he was still repeating his insistence that Murdoch get stitches – and that they had to hurry. Murdoch was in no mood to disagree. The wound in his forehead seemed to have stopped pumping, but he didn't trust it to stay closed. Fucking bicycle chains. Next time, he'd remember to duck before charging in and smashing a guy's face in.

Now they were climbing steps, with only a solitary lamp post halfway up being someone's idea of street lighting. Then another flat road; then they were climbing some more, all the steps in darkness this time. On the next street, at a house that looked like all the other dark houses they'd passed, Davie turned, crossed the little bridge that joined it to the hillside, and – before Murdoch could stop him – leant on the bell.

'Here, Davie mate. Who lives here, then?'

Davie turned and looked at him, one finger still on the buzzer. Even in the dark, Murdoch could see he was staring, talking to the wound in Murdoch's forehead.

'You need stitches,' Davie said mechanically. 'We have to hurry.'

Lights flicked on inside the house and – so quickly it made them both jump – its front door was yanked open, blinding them with brightness. It seemed to wake up the pain in Murdoch's wound and he winced against that too, focusing only slowly on the woman scowling in her overlit hallway. It was Detective Constable Natalie Conquest.

'It was horrible, Nat. There were two of them – they were trying to kill us, I know it. One of them had this chain thing and then ... Bill broke his arm; I heard it snap. Oh God, it was hideous. He was screaming – him or the other one. I thought Bill was going to kill them.'

Davie was talking too fast, brushing dirt from his trousers onto Natalie's living room carpet, no idea he was indoors now. Murdoch watched Natalie sit him down in the unlit room, bend over him and hold him tight.

'And you know how I hate blood, Nat. The one with the chain, his face was all cut up and his nose ...'

'He looks like he needs a drink,' said Murdoch, hovering in the doorway between the living room and the overlit hall. 'You got some whisky or something?'

Looking round, Natalie caught him examining her legs, stood quickly and pulled down the hem of her T-shirt.

'He's in shock, you idiot. Alcohol's the last thing he needs. Stay here, try and make him talk slower. I'll go and get a blanket.'

Murdoch watched her T-shirt rise again as she pushed past him out to the hall, her white knickers briefly on view as she ran up the stairs. He sat next to Davie and put his arm around him, told him it was all all right now, maybe he should stop being such a pussy. He studied the room around him, the IKEA furniture, the tasteful prints on the walls. There was a photo in a frame on the telly, but he couldn't make it out.

'You need stitches,' said Davie, turning to Murdoch like he'd just remembered.

'That's right, mate. But not at the hospital because they might call the law. Which is why we came here instead, to your friend what's a nurse. Oh no, my mistake, she's a bleeding copper.'

There were footsteps on the stairs then Natalie reappeared in the doorway, the hall light silhouetting her through the pale cotton of her T-shirt. Murdoch stood.

'I used to be a nurse,' she said. 'Here, Davie, put this round you.'

She unfolded a woollen blanket across his shoulders. Then she squatted and took his shoes off, pushed Murdoch out of the way and swung Davie's feet up, so now he was spreading dirt over her sofa too. She pressed her fingers gently over his scalp.

'He's not injured,' said Murdoch. 'Just took a tumble down the bank by the lagoon. He's fine.'

'And how did that happen?' Half-ignoring him, still pressing Davie all over.

'I pushed him. Didn't want him caught up in things, thought he'd be safer down there. Looks like I wasn't wrong.'

Natalie sat Murdoch on the side of the bath, found a clean flannel and washed off the blood until she found the wound. A two-centimetre gash just below his hairline, it began pumping again steadily as she cleaned around it.

'You clot easily.'

'Why thank you very much.'

'And you stink of beer.'

'Best anaesthingy on the market, innit? Was you really a nurse?'

She didn't answer this, just opened the cabinet and pulled out an impressive first-aid kit, rummaged through it and started threading a suture needle while she asked him what had happened.

'Beats me. Two blokes jumped us, one with a bike chain like Davie said. I didn't expect the twat to use it, I was too focused on his mate. Bloody hell, nasty piece of work he was. Looked like a knife-man.'

She asked him what that meant and Murdoch shrugged, said sometimes you could just tell. He could tell she wanted a proper answer, but he wasn't in the mood to elaborate. Instead, he watched her lay the threaded needle back on the sterile package it had come from before finding a small bottle of clear liquid and pouring it onto cotton wool.

'This is going to hurt,' she said.

'Yeah, I know. Listen, love, can I ask you a favour? Don't tell anyone about what happened tonight. Not a word, right?'

He looked up to check she'd understood, then nearly fell backwards into the bath when she pressed the alcohol against his head. He swore loudly and reached forwards, grabbing one of her legs to steady himself. Then he caught her eye and let the leg go.

'You all right?'

He nodded grimly.

'You're very pale.'

'I'll be fine; just get on with it will you?'

There was an open box of tampons on the toilet behind her and, every time the needle went in, he clenched his fists and concentrated on its logo. *Count to ten and it'll be fine – Libra 16 regular – don't ever let them see it hurts.* When it was done, six stitches that didn't look too bad in the mirror, they sat in the kitchen with tea. Natalie had put tracksuit trousers on; like she needed to worry the state he was in, the beer wearing off and everything starting to sting.

'Who were they?'

'No idea. Davie didn't know them neither, reckons they're not local. Thugs but not pros; no shortage of them about.'

'Did they say anything?'

'They said it was time for me to mind my own business. Don't know if they was going to say anything else after that. Here, you got anything stronger I can put in this?'

She reached up and pulled open the freezer unit above her fridge, tugged out a bottle of vodka and tipped a generous amount into his tea. Thought about it and took a quick swig for herself. She caught him grinning into his fortified tea.

'Bloody hell,' she said. 'Have fun tonight, did you?'

'Nah, not fun. That's not right. But you know there's this thing, when there's a few of them or they think they're bigger than you. This little moment when they suddenly realise they've got it wrong and it all shifts; it's like half a second, but it's all different and they know they've made a mistake. And it's … it's fantastic.'

'So you broke his arm?'

'Ha. I reckon he won't be swinging that chain for a while.'

'And split the other guy's nose, by the sound of it.'

'Yeah. And?'

'And would you say that's reasonable defence? Or would you think of that as more GBH?'

He put his tea down slowly. 'I don't know, darlin', I wasn't thinking of the niceties of the law when the two of them came at me with a chain. I was thinking about keeping Superman in there out of harm's way – and making sure they didn't come back for more. I let them run off, didn't I?'

'Oh how big of you.'

'And how fucking judgemental of you.' He stood suddenly, spilling his drink on the table. 'Thanks for the stitch-up job. Don't worry, I'll take them out myself.'

He bumped into Davie in the hallway – woken by the noise and bleary in his blanket.

'What's going on?'

'What's going on, mate, is you brought me to a copper's house and I was stupid enough to think she might be off-duty. Why don't you go back to your cot and ask the nursie to bring you a dummy?'

'Leave him alone, Bill.'

99

Natalie was in her kitchen doorway, looking like she wanted to say sorry but sounding like she wanted him to.

'Does this mean it's all over?' said Davie, a giant toddler woken in the night. 'Does this mean you're quitting?'

Murdoch found himself laughing. Pissed off, beaten up, hurt, but laughing. 'Jesus,' he said. 'You two don't know me at all, do you?'

21.

Once Davie had left for work, Murdoch lay listening to the noises left behind. In London or Sydney, it would be the rumble of traffic, sirens wailing in the distance. Here it was the ocean, screaming birds, trees rustling overhead. He decided to get up and cook some breakfast, buy the paper and make some plans. He closed his eyes to summon his strength and, next thing he knew, his phone was ringing and it was past midday. It was Hannah Simms, something close to concern in her voice.

'I hear you got beaten up?'

'Bleeding hell, darlin', that took you a whole fifteen hours to find out. What happened, telephones down?'

'Actually, I found out first thing this morning but I had a few meetings so I couldn't call. I'm presuming you're OK?'

'Your concern is touching.'

'Are you badly hurt?'

'No. I'm fine.'

'Well, then. Who do you think it was?'

'Don't know yet. Might just be someone what didn't like the look of me, but it wasn't no one local.'

'How do you know that?'

He could hear her typing, her attention on something else.

'Well, for one thing, Davie said so. And for another, given the way the grapevine works round here, if it was someone local, you'd of probably heard about it in advance and you could of called me to say they was coming.' There was a silence on the other end of the line and Murdoch wondered if Hannah even knew he was joking. 'Here,' he said, 'was Davie really a pop star?'

Now she laughed. 'Oh God, did he tell you about that? I thought he was over it. Personally, I found the whole thing really embarrassing; he's lucky to have landed on his feet back home, with the real estate thing.'

'You was already married by then, weren't you? You grew up together, right?'

'Is this relevant, Bill?'

Murdoch didn't answer that. 'Listen,' he said. 'Like I said the other day, cash is a bit tight at the moment. I've had to borrow some off Davie. Do you reckon you could get me some?'

That stopped her typing. He let her sit in the silence that followed.

'Sure,' she said at last. 'I'll put it into your account.'

'No! At least … No, you can't do that. Listen, Hannah, I can't tell you why but I've pissed off some nasty people. Pissed them off badly. They see any money going into that account and they'll come after you before they find me. How about you put it in Davie's account and I'll get it off him? Minus what I owe him, of course.'

'Intriguing. You're asking for your income to be paid via a third party's account. You know, that's the kind of thing that makes us tax inspectors very suspicious.'

'Well, tell you what, love. Why don't you interview yourself and see if you can find something out?'

Another tiny silence and she laughed again. The date had obviously gone well. She told him sure, but he needed to sort out a proper bank account soon or at least PayPal or something. Then they made awkward small talk for a minute or two: Murdoch pretending there was any real progress on the case, Hannah pretending to believe him.

Two hours later he was still in his underwear, lying on Davie's bed, and enjoying the last cigarette in the house. Out in the real world, it was a beautiful day: the sky blue and taut, the sun so high this was the only place in the house where it came through the windows. Murdoch hadn't been in Davie's room before and he examined the space slowly as he pulled on his fag. There was a row of books beside the bed with titles like *Feel the Fear and Do It Anyway* and *How to Make Friends and Influence People*. Above them, old photos were pinned frameless to the wall. Davie in a suit with a hot bird on each arm; with Hannah on a boat between two old people; at an awards ceremony somewhere. The hotter of the girls from the photo with the suit reappeared on the other walls, arms around Davie somewhere foreign, laughing in a bikini on a beach. Murdoch examined her close up, a real stunner, then lay back and closed his eyes, remembering his glimpse of Natalie Conquest's white underwear. Thought of a few other things and went to find his phone, brought it back to the sun-drenched room with his other hand now free of the cigarette. Cynthia answered on his third attempt.

'Hello, darl. Is my dark-eyed stranger back in town?'

'Not just yet.'

'Oh.' Then a silence, unusual for her. 'What a shame.'

'I'm working on it, darlin', trust me.'

Except he wasn't, of course. He was at a total loss, a warm and sunny dead end, every plan killing itself as soon as he thought it through. He asked Cyn what she was up to. Listened to her laugh and tell him she was doing the hoovering, nothing sexy at all. Not that she could talk for long, she added too fast, she was on her way out. Which probably meant someone was on the way in. He charmed her, told her how much he missed her, and in return got a funny story of what had happened over the weekend, full of little details – she knew how he liked them. Then she asked him where he was and he said 'nowhere' again, but told her about the night before, how he needed some TLC.

'Ooh, darl, you must be careful. Was it worth it?'

'Not exactly.'

'Well, maybe you should quit whatever it is you're trying to do, come on back to Sydney. Although, what is it they say? You know you're getting somewhere when it hurts?'

'Yeah, well, this hurts and I need a good nurse. What you wearing? Hang on, say that again.'

'Which bit?'

'You know you're getting somewhere when … What is it? It's not "when it hurts". It's when people start lying to you. "You know you're getting somewhere when people start lying to you." Who said that?'

'You did, darl. Why? Are people lying to you? You told me you can nearly always tell when people are lying to you.'

She was humouring him now: he could almost hear her looking at her watch. He took them back to familiar ground, flirtatious little in-jokes until he told her what hand he was holding the phone with. She played along, made a suggestion about what he should do with his other hand, was just getting into it, when a noise interrupted her.

'Oh Blackie, I'm so sorry, darl, I have to go.'

'You what? You're kidding me, right?'

'Sorry, darl, sorry!'

And he heard the little click that meant she'd gone.

He went back to his own bed and slept through the afternoon. Injuries always did this to him, made him sleep like nothing else, and he knew he'd heal quicker if he gave into it. He woke after five and lay there, looking at the ceiling and not getting up to make something to eat. He ran through the conversations of all the people he'd spoken to since the day he arrived in Montauban. Made himself pull up details and phrase them like a copper in a courtroom would. The witness denied all knowledge of this. The witness was not able to answer that. By the time Davie got home, complaining about the stench of cigarettes in the house, Murdoch reckoned he'd found two liars. If he got them to tell him the truth, maybe he could get some real cash out of Hannah Simms. Enough, at least, to buy himself some time. Besides, he admitted it to himself slowly, he was curious now.

22.

Alycia Thornton lived with her parents in Pacifico Road, about as far from the Pacific as you could get in Montauban. The street was high up in the bowl of the hill that formed the northern half of the suburb, the last tarmac before it gave way to bushland.

In daylight, this part of town felt no less different to the rest of Montauban than it had done in the dark. The tarmac was more likely to be broken up here, more overgrown at the edges by a mess of encroaching greenery. Bins were left on the street because there was nowhere else flat to put them, and they shared the trees' shadows with cars scruffier than those down near the beach.

The walk uphill in the afternoon heat was an effort. Murdoch had slept all morning again and felt no better for it, but he knew he had to get out of the house before tiredness turned into something worse. The ground between the roads he trod was even steeper than he'd imagined when wandering through the dark, everything below tumbling towards the ocean, everything above rising with the hill, and twice he had to use steps to climb between them.

Finding Pacifico Road at last, he stood outside number thirty-four, catching his breath and checking he hadn't sweated through his shirt. The house's front door was, like Natalie Conquest's, joined to the tarmac by a short wooden walkway over a slope that fell quickly away, scrubby plants and leaf litter emptying to dry earth under the house. Murdoch crossed, side-stepping a child's bike, and rang the doorbell. He put his hand to the stitches in his forehead and realised he should have covered them with a bandage. Not that he was nervous – the worst the Thorntons could do was chase him away – more that he remembered what he was to these people: a wounded enemy approaching the family home. In a few short days, he'd got used to people thinking better of him.

The woman who came to the door looked frazzled, like she'd been expecting him, and was dreading the visit. Her dark hair waved out in all directions; there were hints of darkness beneath her eyes. Murdoch introduced himself, holding himself back in case the door was slammed in his face. The woman smiled and put out her hand.

'Oh, you're the one who's trying to find out what happened to Georgie. Everyone's so glad you're here. She was such a lovely girl. The police …'

'Yeah' said Murdoch. 'I know.'

'Well, yes. I mean, won't you come in? Please mind the mess. Kids, eh? We've got five of them for our sins and every one's messier than the one before. Zac! Come and move this bike now!'

She ignored the muffled objection from somewhere upstairs and spoke to Murdoch over her shoulder as she led him down a corridor to the back of the house, apologising for the mess again, saying she needed to get something out of the oven before it burned the place down. The corridor opened into a kitchen with a huge dining table, it and every other surface hidden by toys, paperwork, sewing, tools.

'Go out on the deck,' said the woman. 'My husband's out there. John! This is …it's …'

'Bill Murdoch.'

'Sorry, love, I've got to get on with this. Go out on the deck, introduce yourself.'

A huge man with half a day's stubble was struggling out of a lounger when Murdoch stepped into the sunlight onto the deck; this far back from the road they were three storeys above the steep hillside. The man stuck out his hand and said 'John Thornton,' and sorry he hadn't heard what the missus had said, he was watching the cricket. He gestured at an ancient portable TV, deep in a cardboard box. As Murdoch looked, it produced a cheer, which made Thornton swear, reach into the box and turn it off.

'You following it?' he said.

'What's that?'

'The cricket. Thirty-nine for three, I don't know why the buggers bother. Sorry, mate, how can I help you?'

So Murdoch had to introduce himself again, thinking maybe now it would come. Maybe this guy could do more than just chase him off: maybe he could topple him over the railing to the dirty ground far below.

But Thornton beamed at him, one of his front teeth missing, shook his hand heavily and said he was pleased to meet him, everyone in town was so pleased he was there, the police, etc. He offered Murdoch a beer, refused to believe he didn't want something, whisked the television and its box onto the lounger and sat Murdoch at the table. Then he disappeared into the kitchen for a minute before returning with a tinkling glass of water. He sat himself at the table too, opened a beer – don't mind, do you? – and gave another gap-toothed grin. Murdoch asked him if he'd heard what had happened with Alycia.

'Yeah, sorry about that.' Thornton scratched the back of his neck. 'Aw shit, she didn't do that to you, did she?'

Murdoch touched his stitches again and mumbled something about falling down the stairs, Thornton continuing to listen for a few seconds after he'd finished. Then he said, 'Don't you worry about Alycia, mate. She's a right drama queen. Don't know where she gets it from – we certainly didn't bring her up to be like that. Can't wait till she's down in Sydney, to tell the truth.'

Thornton's wife came out from the kitchen over the end of this and she looked at him sharply. 'I didn't introduce myself,' she said, putting one hand out and running the other through her thick hair. 'Harriet, everyone calls me Hattie. Don't listen to Jonno, he's joking. Here, darl, you want something to eat?'

'I'm fine, thanks.'

'Sure? Suit yourself but you're more than welcome, there's plenty.' She perched next to the TV on the lounger and let out a weary sigh. 'I have to admit it though, Al is a handful. I'm so sorry. I heard she had one of her scenes.'

'It's no big deal,' said Murdoch. 'It was my fault, I probably came on a bit hard. I reckon she's upset about Georgie and all. I was thinking maybe I could apologise. Start over again.'

He shielded his eyes from the sun and looked at them hopefully. They nodded at him, smiling. A few seconds later they were still doing it.

'So,' said Murdoch. 'Is she around?'

'Alycia?'

'Yes. Alycia. Is she around?'

'Oh!' John now. 'Oh no, mate. I thought you knew, sorry. No, Alycia's gone away on the trip.'

The two of them beamed again, nodding in agreement, John struggling to keep down some gas from his beer.

'Trip?'

'The school trip, you know, the North Coast trip. Oh, maybe you don't know. Every summer the school organises this big camping trip up north, volunteering or something. Alycia wasn't going to go. Honestly, mate, for weeks it's been nothing round here but her saying she's not going, and her mum and me saying she should, and her refusing like we was ripping her away from something. Then, yesterday, it's all change. Like I said, a drama queen. We spent the whole day running around getting her stuff together. She could have done with a separate rucksack just for her bloody make-up. But she's gone, thank God, which is why I'm out here watching the cricket and not driving her to some rehearsal or workshop or whatever. It's like a little holiday, isn't it, Hat?'

Hat didn't look convinced. Murdoch asked how long Alycia would be gone.

'Two weeks,' John told him. 'You can ask at the school; they've got all the details. But I wouldn't worry yourself, not if it's just about apologising. Al upsets so many people she probably won't have even noticed.'

'I was hoping to ask her a few more questions.'

'Oh, of course.'

And they sat there, the two of them, nodding and beaming at him again.

23.

The trip down from Pacifico Road was no better than the walk up. The sun was lower but its heat was resilient and Murdoch still hadn't got round to buying any shorts. He'd given in to the Thorntons' offer of a beer and now he felt grubby and desperate for a fag. The sweat that had dried on his back and arms was flowing again and the wound in his head was pounding. He realised he could smell himself and decided to go home and shower before calling on his second liar. But the route down the hill took him past the Walker house and, when he rounded the corner, he saw Paul Walker in the driveway. He'd driven his huge BMW out of the garage and was leaning across it, waxing it carefully like he was applying sun cream to a good-looking girl.

Murdoch hung back in the shadows and studied the car glistening in the sunshine, the large house beyond, the perfectly placed plants and flowers. Looking up, Walker saw him, flashed his expensive smile and walked around the car. His T-shirt, socks and trainers were white; his khaki shorts were ironed.

'Bill! What are you doing back there?'

'Admiring your Beamer, mate. I'm embarrassed to be seen in the same street.'

Murdoch walked over, trying not to catch his reflection in the car's windscreen. Walker peered through his sunglasses at Murdoch's stitches.

'Wow. I heard that two guys had a go at you. What do you think it means? Sorry, that's really selfish of me. Are you OK?'

'I don't think it means nothing. At least, I don't think it's our best lead. Listen, Paul, I was wondering if maybe I could chat with Tom again?'

Walker leaned his lean frame against the car, pulled an uncomfortable face, and pushed his sunglasses up the bridge of his nose.

'Not for long,' said Murdoch. 'Just a few questions.'

'I don't know, Bill. He was pretty upset after you spoke at the weekend.'

'We only said a few words.'

'It's just, you know, this whole Georgie thing hit him hard. They were very close, she was very protective of him. It's hit us both hard, but he's a kid, and I think talking about it shook him up again. He wouldn't come out of his room after you left.'

'Do you think there's something he's not telling us?'

Walker thought about it. 'If I'm honest, I don't know. Actually, that's not true. If I'm honest, I don't think so. I think he's just upset and not as good at hiding it as I am, although if I wax this car any more I think I'll get through the paintwork.' He stood again and looked at the cloth in his hand.

'Maybe you could tell him he has to talk to me?' Murdoch, hating the whine in his voice, coughed it into a more serious tone. 'I think there's something he's not letting on. Will you tell him?'

Walker pulled an awkward smile. 'Look, Bill, no one is more desperate to find Georgie than me. But you know, I've just got Tom to a point where he's coping. He's fragile, you know.'

'What does that mean?'

'It means that if Tom doesn't want to talk to you, then I'm not going to force him to.'

'Even if it could help me find Georgie?'

They looked at each other a while. There was a hardness to Walker that Murdoch hadn't noticed before. Like he was nothing but the remains of the worst thing that could happen to a man: the cracks and corners of his bedrock worn smooth by the efforts of survival. Murdoch watched him turn and resume polishing his car, not looking up as he spoke through gritted teeth. 'I'm sorry. I've lost my wife, I've lost Georgie – I have to protect the one person I have left.'

Murdoch made some noises like he understood and got the hell out of there while his mouth was still under control.

Anne Lincoln gave him the shorts half-price. 'My little contribution to you finding that lovely kid,' she said, before telling him someone had attacked him and Natalie had given him stitches. Murdoch hadn't worn shorts in years. He felt weird walking down the street in them and, when he climbed onto the bonnet of his car, he had to sit carefully to avoid burning his calves.

It was muggy again, the late afternoon sweltering slowly as he sat and smoked and waited. Overhead, birds were fighting in the trees and he watched them, enjoying the sun on his legs, and wondering if he'd ever get used to good weather. After half an hour or so, earlier than he'd expected, he heard the bus roll down the hill into town. Another five minutes and the first schoolkids came into sight, rounding the curve towards him, just like Natalie Conquest had on that first day. He counted back twice, unable to believe it had only been eleven days ago, the thought giving him a glimmer of hope. Maybe he wasn't so far from his money after all. Then he swore as Natalie herself came into sight. She was carrying the same sports bag as on that first day, but, today, it was pressing a white shirt across her chest and her legs were long beneath cut-off denims. She disappeared from view and then reappeared two minutes later at the bottom of the driveway. Unable to abandon his lookout post, Murdoch was hoping she'd pass with no comment, so of course she stopped and called up to him, almost as sulky-mouthed as on that first day.

'Still here, then?'

'Looks like that way, don't it?'

'Still asking questions too, I hear.'

'Well, that's generally how it works, love.'

She sucked on that for a while, something in it softening her mouth. 'And how are the stitches?'

'Itchy.'

'Right. And what you up to?'

'Smoking.'

'Got a spare?'

She didn't wait for the answer, just lugged her sports bag up the grassy slope and climbed onto the bonnet beside him. If the hot metal burned the back of her legs, she didn't show it. Murdoch took a fag from his packet with his teeth, lit it and passed it over. Just to be clear who was in charge. Natalie took it without comment and made some noises about the weather. Then about Davie's shack, about how often she'd given up smoking. Easy openers even he couldn't resist, chit-chat to plaster over any hard feelings, or – more likely – to soften him up. Still, sitting in the sun with a pretty girl, nothing wrong with that. And it was difficult not to like her, even if she was a cop. Every time she leaned forwards to pull on her cigarette, her shirt curled apart and allowed a fleeting glimpse of the skin beneath. But it wasn't just that.

'So,' she said. 'What you doing then? You look like you're waiting for someone.'

He gestured with his cigarette to the trees above them. 'I'm watching the animals, aren't I? See them birds, they're right little bastards. One of them sees a different kind of bird, it starts squawking its head off until all its mates come; then they all start squawking and scare the other one away. They're only little but they'll pick on anything what comes near, even them big crows.'

Natalie told him the small birds were mynas, told him she liked the way they looked out for each other. 'You're right, they're tiny, but they thrive by sticking together. It's what communities are supposed to do. Maybe the other bird's the bastard, muscling in and threatening them?'

He turned and looked at her. Asked her which one he was then, threatening bastard or member of the community?

She frowned, waving away the smoke between them. 'Well, like the mynas, you're not a native. But, unlike them, I don't think you're too much of a threat to the local species. Maybe you'll even turn out to be a valuable member of the community.'

She smiled and he smiled back. Or smiled at the idea of being part of a community, maybe. He told her her hair was sticking out over her ears and she flustered at it, saying it was the humidity.

'I hear you saw Paul Walker yesterday,' she said quickly. 'He told me you wanted to see Tom again but he said no. I could talk to him, if you want? He's got a will of iron, but you just need to catch him in the right mood.'

'No thanks.'

'Wow, would you like to say that any quicker?'

'Thanks, nice thought, but no thanks.'

110

Three girls in gingham dresses walked past the bottom of the driveway, socks at random heights and bags too heavy for a hot afternoon. They waved up to Natalie and Murdoch, asked them how they were going and sloped on out of view.

'It's because I'm a policewoman, isn't it?'

Murdoch took a deep drag and thought about the chances of bullshitting her. Possible, probable even, if he could be arsed.

'Well, if I'm honest, yeah. I'm sorry, darlin', but where I come from there's a name for people what work with the police. But it's not just that. I just don't think I need your help. Thanks anyway.'

He looked her in the eye and flicked his cigarette butt down the driveway where it lay wisping to death. She looked at it for a second or two, then met his eye again.

'The school bus is in.'

'Yep.'

'And you're waiting for Tom to walk past so you can bump into him and ask a few simple questions.'

'You got a problem with that?'

She snorted and took a last drag before stubbing out her own cigarette slowly on the bottom of her shoe.

'You know what?' she said. 'I think you're really screwed up. You know full well I could help you, and you know full well you want to ask me. But you can't bring yourself to do it because of some weird little hang-up you've got about the police. And I think you like me, and I think you like it here, and I think if you got that chip off your shoulder, you might find other people like you too. And you know what else? Tom Walker has soccer practice on Thursday nights in East Crosley and then his dad picks him up on his way home from work. They'll be about another hour and a half. Except, of course, you've learned that from the police, so you'd better not use it or you'll be breaking your macho little code. So I could suggest you sit here on your bonnet and fry,' she jumped off like it was suddenly frying her, 'but I'm not going to. I'm going to suggest something else instead. I'm going to suggest you go round to the Walkers at ten o'clock on Saturday morning to pick up Tom. Because I've already persuaded Paul to let him talk to you.'

'Yeah, right.'

'Yes, Murdoch, it is right. Because that's how people behave around here. We look out for each other, like the mynas. I spoke to Paul because I was thinking maybe I was a bit harsh on you, thought I should offer an olive branch and we could work together. No, don't thank me.'

Until the last few words, she'd done a good job of keeping herself calm. Now her voice wobbled and she turned quickly, grabbing her sports bag from the dry ground. She walked down the driveway towards the road, pausing only to crouch, pick up his fag end, stub it out and put it in her pocket next to her own. Then she followed the schoolgirls out of sight.

24.

Saturday was March, the first day of autumn, and the weather changed like it could read the calendar. Grey skies raced over the coast, driven by a wind colder than Murdoch had felt in months. The ocean was a mess, yellow foam swirling full of sand, the water beneath it brown. It was another thing to annoy him, because he hadn't known the sea could get like that. Him, a man who'd grown up on an island.

Standing on the windblown beach, he shook his head hard, like he could deny the missed opportunities. It was no good. Every day he spent in this little town was another day of seeing what his life might have been like; how life was for kids on the other side. Beside him, Tom Walker tilted his little face up into the wind and gave him a strange look. Apart from the two of them, the beach was empty. Earlier there had been a father teaching his boys to fly a kite, standing behind them to help them pull the strings, but the wind had been too fierce and, like everyone else in Montauban, they had retreated indoors.

Murdoch hadn't really noticed it before, but there was something weird about Tom. He had thought the kid was just soft, a molly-coddled baby, but now he wondered if he wasn't a bit mental. He was terrified of everything, not just Murdoch. On the way to the beach, they'd passed a woman walking a small dog and Tom had hidden behind Murdoch's legs, whimpering on the edge of tears. And there was something about the way he held his hands, knuckles pulled back towards his elbows, each finger moving independently of the other. The kind of kid you pushed down the stairs at school.

'Where did this weather come from, eh, Tom?'

They were walking south into the wind, Tom twitching every time the water ran up towards them. Murdoch had his sunglasses on to keep the sand out of his eyes, but Tom was forced to look through his fingers.

'You want to turn around, mate? Have the sand blow into the back of your head instead?'

Tom shrugged and turned immediately, trudging back towards home at the same stubborn pace, his fingers still over his eyes. Murdoch watched him for a while, shaking his head again, before trotting to catch him up.

Of the dozen or so social workers he'd had as a kid, Murdoch could only name two he'd liked. The trouble with the rest of them was it felt like they were pretending. Like their little frowns and weird eye-contact and endless nods weren't real reactions, just tricks to make him talk. He'd never questioned his resentment of them: it was like a scar you were used to in the mirror. On the beach next to Tom, he wondered for the first time if the bad blood between him and them hadn't all been their fault.

The first social worker he'd liked had been Anna Mankin – funny that he could still remember her name. She was pretty, or at least she was young with an easy smile, more or less the same thing to a seven-year-old boy. She used to take him to the zoo, never asked him any questions unless it was about which animals he liked or if he wanted an ice cream. The other one, years later, had been called Henry something. Henry was short and tanned, sure of himself, didn't always see the need to be saying something. Henry was the kind of guy you could tell stuff to and he'd just nod and suck on his pipe, interested, but not like he was going to use it against you. It was Henry who'd advised him to make use of his birth certificate, his one bit of luck, and get an Australian passport. Murdoch had no idea what Henry would say to Tom right now. He looked down at the kid, shivering in the wind, reached out and put a hand on his shoulder. It felt fragile, something you might snap if you handled it too roughly. Tom looked up for a second, eyes wide, then down at his shoes again.

'Do you want an ice cream, mate?'

Another shrug and Murdoch thought he might pick the kid up and chuck him into the foaming waves, hold his head under until the bubbles stopped. Instead, he swore and turned inland, still holding Tom by the shoulder so the kid was forced to walk in front of him. When they reached the edge of the dunes, Murdoch told him to sit down, sat next to him, then lay back to look up at the tearing clouds, Tom Walker lost to his view.

'You don't have to do what you're told,' said Murdoch to the sky. 'Nothing like me when I was your age. I was a right tearaway. Do you know where I lived in those days?'

There was no reply and Murdoch imagined Tom shrugging and staring at his feet. Henry would have waited at this point. He remembered that, Henry always waiting, sucking on his pipe like it was none of his business whether you answered or not. He found a piece of grass sticking up through the sand and stuck it in his mouth, wiggled it between his teeth so it rolled in and out of view. Tom's voice was frail in the wind.

'England.'

'Yeah, but where in England? Not in a house.'

A longer pause this time.

'A church?'

'Ha! Jesus, no.'

'A unit?'

'Nope. One more guess.'

'Give me a clue.'

'It's where they put bad people.'

'Prison?'

'Correct.'

He heard Tom move next to him, turned to see the kid staring with those wide eyes.

'You were in prison when you were ten?'

'Well, they didn't call it prison. They called it borstal. Then they called it juvenile detention, then they called it a youth correction centre but, yeah, basically it was prison.'

'Why? What did you do?'

Murdoch's turn to pause. He'd planned on making something up but he knew Tom would know if he did. He'd have known at Tom's age. *What the hell.*

'Well, when I was nine, there was these lads at my school who thought it might be nice to pick on the new kid. I was always moving around, always the new kid, so I was kind of expecting it, and I was a good fighter, so it was normally all right. But these kids at this one school, they was right little bastards.'

Tom giggled at the word and Murdoch wanted to stop, but he remembered Henry. Remembered what it was like to be treated like an adult when you weren't one.

'Anyway, they dragged me up to the top of the school and hung me off the side. Three of 'em. One grabbed me by the belt and the others got my legs and they hung me upside-down. They told me if I didn't give them some money they'd bring me up there again and drop me off. I was so blooming scared I nearly wet myself.'

Tom shuffled closer, right into it, shrugs and feet forgotten. 'What did you do?'

'I did a bad thing.'

'What?'

'Well, I'm not proud of it. Or maybe I am. Anyway, they sent me away for it and I never really got out of the game again after that, not for long. Always in fights, always getting moved to worse and worse places. But I tell you what, those little bastards never hung anyone off that roof again.'

'What did you do?'

He was pleading now, laughing at Murdoch for teasing him like this, pressing the back of his funny hands to his face. Above him gulls shrieked sideways in the wind.

'Want me to tell you?'

'Yes!'

'OK, I'll tell you. But first I have to tell you something else. I need to tell you why I'm telling you this. Tom, I've spent my entire life surrounded by blokes what are really, *really* scared. You can see it in their eyes. They're like little mice, twitching around, trying to get back in the shadows as quick as they can before the cat comes and gets 'em. And that's you, mate. You're fu— You're terrified, I can see it. And you know what I reckon? I reckon someone's told you a bad thing's gonna happen if you tell anyone what you know. Like those kids on the roof told me. And you know what? If anyone ever tells you that, you should do to them what I did to that bastard fourteen-year-old what tried to frighten me.'

Tom was halfway to his feet, the wind whipping his hair as his head raised above the dunes. Murdoch pulled him back down by the sleeve of his jacket. 'Tom, I know Georgie had a boyfriend.'

The kid looked like Murdoch had held a knife to his throat, eyes wider than ever, his skin the same colour as the sand stretching away behind him.

'It's all right' said Murdoch. 'I'm not going to tell no one. I reckon this boyfriend told you that if you told anyone about him something bad would happen to you.'

Tom was shaking his head, tears in his eyes now, hands scrambling to push away from Murdoch's grasp on his jacket.

'Do you know what I did to that kid on the roof, Tom? Do you want to know?'

Tom was whimpering, still struggling, trying to get out of his jacket and run to freedom. Murdoch was thinking about whether he wanted to chase the kid up the beach and through the streets of Montauban – *Ex-Con Strips and Chases Child!* – when Tom collapsed into violent sobs, his hands over his face and a strange whining noise coming from deep in his throat. He fell into a foetal position, curled on the cold sand beside Murdoch, the sobs jerking his body. *Wait*, Murdoch told himself. *Wait like what Henry would have done.* But he'd forgotten what it was like to be a child, how long you can cry. Eventually he reached out and put a hand on Tom's shoulder again, more gently this time.

The kid slowed his noise and took a gulp of air. 'What?' he said through his hands.

'What what?'

'What did you do to those boys on the roof?'

'Oh. Well, you always have to go for the biggest one, see. As soon as they had me up again I kicked him in the balls. Unlucky for him, unlucky for me too really, he fell the wrong way and toppled off the edge. He hung on for a bit and, his mates having scarpered, I tried to pull him back up. But the fat bastard fell two floors. He broke both legs and a collarbone, fractured his skull and dislocated something. And some internal stuff too, I think, St Pancras or something.'

116

Tom was staring at him again, snot and tears sticking sand to one side of his face.

'And that's what'll happen to anyone what comes near you or your dad, you got that? Except I'll do it on purpose. So you've got nothing to be afraid of, mate. No matter what anyone's told you, no one's gonna lay a finger on you or your dad. You understand?'

Tom nodded.

'You believe me?'

Another nod.

'So who's this boyfriend what told you not to tell? Did he threaten you?'

Tom shook his head. 'No,' he said. 'It was Georgie.'

25.

The kid said he didn't mind who saw he'd been crying, but Murdoch told him he should. He started to explain to Tom the rule of never letting anyone see that you're hurting, then stopped halfway through. Maybe that rule didn't apply around here. Jesus, maybe none of them did. He frowned the idea away – too big a head-fuck to think of now – and made the kid wash his face at the edge of the waves, then dry his face on his jumper. Once done, Tom asked if he could have the ice cream Murdoch had offered earlier and this, for some reason, made Murdoch laugh. Then the kid asked again and Murdoch said of course he could. As long as he told him the rest of the story about Georgie.

As the wind blew them through the dunes and up towards the shops, Tom talked all the way. The wet hair around his face somehow made him look even younger and it was easy to believe he'd been waiting two years to tell his story.

'I used to follow Georgie all the time,' he said. 'Dad's always in the garden when he's not at work and if I go out there he makes me help him plant things and get dirty. I'm not allowed TV or iPad and reading's boring, so I used to follow her. It's easy, isn't it, following people when they don't know they're being followed?'

117

He looked up at Murdoch, his face full of expectation, like maybe this gave them something in common. Murdoch asked him where Georgie had gone.

'Well, mostly just down to the shops or to Alycia's, but then, one day, I followed her up to the big house. You know, through the bush on the headland? That was kind of difficult, because of the noise of the leaves, but kind of easy because I guessed where she was going. There's nowhere else up there to go, so I could stay a bit further away.'

'When was this?'

'Before she disappeared.'

'Yeah, I guessed that, mate.'

'Oh yeah, of course. I mean … it was summer holidays the first time. Just after Christmas – I had my new runners on and it was hot.'

'And how many times did you follow her up there?'

'Four.' No need to think about that. 'I was trying to get better at it. You know, like keeping close without her hearing me in the leaves, but she heard me in the end. I went round this big tree and she was waiting for me. It was really scary. She was, like, mad. Like she'd found me in her room or something. She yelled at me and she was crying loads. She said I mustn't tell dad or something really bad would happen like last time.'

'What d'you mean, like last time?'

'Oh,' Tom wiped his nose on his sleeve. 'That was before. Georgie was babysitting me one night and we had a fight and she hit me and she told me not to tell dad or else something bad would happen, but when Dad got home I did tell him, just to spite her and she got into ever so much trouble over it. Anyway, that was the night Mum got knocked down. Later, Georgie said it was nothing to do with me telling, but what if it was?' He looked up at Murdoch, tears in his eyes again. 'What if it was my fault?! I didn't want Dad to get knocked down too, so this time I didn't tell anyone. I didn't, I promise. Not till now, and still … But I didn't tell anyone else.'

Murdoch didn't want the kid to start bawling again so he put his hand out and ruffled his hair, no idea where the gesture came from. There was a part of him that wanted to squat down and hug the little boy, another that wanted to smack him around a bit.

'It's all right, mate. I know you didn't tell no one. And let's face it, it looks like something bad happened anyway, so you've done the right thing now. Was that the last time you followed her?'

'Of course! She made me promise not to, so I couldn't—' Tom stopped suddenly.

'What?' said Murdoch. 'What else?'

'Nothing. It's just I've broken my promise to her now, haven't I? Do you think something bad's going to happen to Dad? Do you think I should tell the police?'

'Jesus, no. Number one rule that, mate. Never tell the rozzers nothing. And listen, you make sure you don't tell no one else neither. Just me. That's really important.'

'Of course. Of course not!'

Murdoch asked Tom if he'd seen who Georgie was visiting.

'Not really. There are these gates and when she got close to them they'd open, so I reckon they could see her from inside. I never went out of the trees in case they saw me too. When she found me that time, I told her she had a boyfriend at the big house and I'd seen him and I knew everything and she went mad, so it was probably true. But I didn't really, I just made it up. And I didn't tell anyone ever till now.'

They were still ten yards short of the road, the hectic air full of sand, but Tom stopped, hair blowing across his face, his eyes fixed on Murdoch.

'You're going to find her, aren't you?'

'No promises, mate.'

'No, I know. But I think you are. I think you're a really good detective and I think you're going to find her.'

Before Murdoch could react, Tom jumped forwards and put his arms tight around him, his face in Murdoch's jumper again. Murdoch peeled the kid off and pushed him away, squatted so they were eye to eye.

'No promises, mate, I mean it. You hear me?'

He held a finger up to the boy's face so there could be no mistake. Tom held Murdoch's eye and nodded.

'But you might find her? Maybe?'

'Lots of things might happen. I don't want you getting your hopes up, OK?'

'OK.'

The kid turned and continued along the path, rabbiting now about what kind of ice cream he was going to get. Murdoch shook his head yet again, trying not to notice the little spring in Tom's step that hadn't been there before.

26.

Davie gasped when they came out of the trees and he saw what had been done to the big house. He and his sister, Jane, had played up here as kids – all the kids in Montie had done. The big house on the headland was where you went to prove you weren't a baby any more. It had been an all-day adventure, traipsing a kilometre along the beach, past the lagoon, past Mahon – the little town that mirrored Montie on the lagoon's far side – and up through the bush on the headland.

He remembered the smell you picked up on the way up through the trees: a mixture of dirt, sweat and broken leaves. Jane had once told him the big house was haunted and he remembered running through it screaming as the other kids hid, convinced he was going to die in there. To a small boy, the derelict wreck had been endless, gigantic rooms with holes in the walls, no end to the places a ghost could hide.

Even now, through adult eyes, the big house lived up to its name. Davie had heard, of course, that the place had been sold a few years ago – his regional manager berating him for not getting the deal for the agency – and he knew a lot of money had been spent on it since then, but he'd not been up for a look. Now, the broad bay windows that flanked the front door and, beside them, the symmetrical double-height sashes, all held glass: thirty-plus panes reflecting the day outside. The roof had been repaired and the brickwork had been pointed or, where necessary, repaired. But, he noticed sadly, only the house had been rescued. The old conservatory that sat at its northern end – where Davie had liked to imagine old ladies taking tea between exotic palms – was still a ruin, collapsed like the skeleton of some ancient animal strangled to death by weeds.

'Bougainvillea.' Davie said to Bill, as they surveyed the scene. 'Lantana.'

The two of them were standing like kids at a zoo, holding onto the bars and staring from a safe distance. Whoever had bought the house had spent money on a fence too: sturdy black railings, eight feet high, cutting off this tiny end of the headland, stopping only where they ran into steep scrub that fell away to clifftops. In line with the house's front door, black gates hung between two brick pillars, each with its own camera. Davie watched Bill walk back and forth in front of them; neither of the cameras moved.

'So, Bill. Are you going to tell me why we're here?'

'No.'

'Aw, go on.'

Bill said nothing, just spat into the rough grass at the base of the fence and started looking around on the ground for something. There would be no point in asking again. Bill only seemed interested in gathering information, never sharing it. He'd looked reluctant even asking Davie for the address of 'some big house on a headland'. When Davie had laughed and said he'd have to show him, Bill had needed convincing of that too. The drive in Davie's Excel up through the bush had helped. They'd tried four different dirt tracks before finding the one that climbed to the clearing in front of the house.

Bill seemed to have found what he was looking for. He squatted down, then stood with a stick in his hand. Whistled loudly and threw it over the fence. Then he whistled again, clapped his hands and waited. Davie forgot he'd decided not to ask any more questions.

'What are you doing?'

'Dogs,' said Bill.

'Dogs?'

'So you don't know who bought this place, then?

'Dude, I'd forgotten it even existed.'

'And there's no address for it?'

'Aw, there's probably an address. But you just ask anyone around here about the big house on the headland and they'll know it. You could probably put that on an envelope and it would get here.'

Bill nodded slowly like he was considering the idea. 'Right then,' he said. 'Let's go.'

Sick of his own whining, Davie was determined not to ask again what any of this had to do with Georgie Walker. On the bumping drive back to the road, then along the winding tarmac to Montie, he almost managed it, forgetting only once and feeling like an idiot when Bill answered him with silence.

Over dinner it was easy to remember not to ask again. Bill's furious attempts at cooking had left the kitchen like a slaughterhouse and the man himself red and taut. They ate in silence in front of the news. But then – after a muffled phone call with Hannah in his bedroom – Bill reappeared with a grim smile and an offer to tell him everything after all.

27.

On the phone to Hannah, whispering so Davie couldn't hear, Murdoch had realised he should have told Hannah earlier about Troy McLaren's suspicions. Maybe that would have been enough to generate some cash. Now, though, he had a problem.

'You know,' said Hannah, 'it's easy to say in hindsight, but I should have known she'd started seeing someone. I was always encouraging her to talk to me about boys; she was so pretty there must have been interest, but she never would. I wonder who it was?'

'No one nice, I reckon. I don't suppose you could use your work systems to find out who owns that house?'

'Bill, I could lose my job.'

'Yeah, well, if I have to go in there and snoop around I could lose my skin. They've got some serious security going on.'

'You will be careful,' Hannah was whispering too for some reason. 'I don't want you getting caught doing anything illegal while you're being paid by me. That could cost me my job too.'

'Yeah, well, once again, darlin', your concern is touching. By the way on the subject of jobs, as in being paid ...'

'You know, I'm amazed Georgie managed to keep the whole thing a secret. You know what Montie's like; everyone knows everything. How did she manage to have a love affair with no one finding out?'

The phrase surprised him. A 'love affair' sounded romantic, people in wigs a hundred years ago, too innocent for black railings and security cameras. He pictured a pretty girl picking her way nervously through the woods: Little Red Riding Hood scared of the wolf. He knew now that, around here, a seventeen-year-old would be little more than a kid.

'Listen,' he said, 'if I knew how to do anything in this town without everyone knowing about it, I'd be onto it, trust me. Oh yeah, that reminds me – don't talk to no one about this. I won't find out nothing if everyone in Montie's gossiping about what they know.'

'No, of course. I mean I don't anyway. So what are you going to do?'

'You really want to know? Let's just say I need some money for some tools. On top of that money you haven't sent me yet.'

'You're right, don't tell me. It's better that way. Just promise you'll be careful. Take a lookout or something.'

'Yeah, I'd better …'

Which was when he realised he had a problem. He said he'd think about it and promised to be careful. Had to mention money twice more before she agreed to transfer it straight away.

28.

That night a fat full moon heaved itself over the coast, glowing the ocean silver and darkening the shadows beneath the trees beyond their normal black. From where he stood, leaning against the Golf, Murdoch could see nothing. He was facing into woodland, lighting one cigarette off the other and trying not to listen to the sounds from the trees: a frog, a bird, something that couldn't be either. Even the wind was eerie, slow waves of sound racing across the hill, whispering in the distance, then huge and creaking overhead. Murdoch didn't even know what he was doing up here.

'Man, it's dark out here.'

Murdoch swore loudly and dropped his cigarette, toxic orange sparks tumbling down his front.

'Jesus, Davie, you scared the bleeding life out of me!'

'Whoa, take a pill. I thought you were a hardened criminal slash detective. You should be used to this stuff. It's me that should be nervous.'

'So where did you just go for twenty minutes?'

Davie laughed. 'Dude, I was gone two minutes max. I didn't want you to hear me peeing.'

'Very considerate. Well, at least you know how to move quietly; you're good for something.'

Davie took that for what it was worth and Murdoch felt him lean against the car.

'It's weird to think we might be about to discover what happened to Georgie.'

They lounged against the car in silence for a while until Davie asked Murdoch if he was nervous. Murdoch shrugged, then shook his head, forgetting he was invisible in the dark.

'You know, Bill, when someone like me, who talks a lot, asks you a question and you don't answer, it makes me feel like an idiot. It's really intimidating. I just thought you should know.'

Murdoch found another cigarette, lit it, and smoked in silence. In the trees behind them something broke a twig, rustled leaves, and moved on.

'You're all right,' said Murdoch. 'You're not an idiot; it's OK to talk. I mean, I like the way you always think something good's going to happen.'

The relief in Davie's voice was obvious. 'Not always. Imagine we were both going to get into a fight. I'd be terrified, whereas you'd be convinced you were going to win.'

Murdoch let out a plume of smoke. 'Yeah, but I'd know something bad was going to come out of me winning the fight. Like another five years or I'd find out the guy had died or something.'

'Well, maybe the lesson there is not to get into fights.'

'Yeah, like that's ever my choice. When was the last time you saw me picking trouble with anyone?'

The car creaked beneath him.

'Dude, are you joking? Every time you meet someone, you act like you're trying to pick a fight. Natalie, for example; you can't talk to her and not get into a blue.'

'I mean a fight, not an argument.'

'Same thing, isn't it? The only difference is the degree of aggression. Here's a challenge; next time you see Nat, try not fighting with her.'

124

The car shifted again and Murdoch knew Davie was standing, looking towards him with that oh-so-innocent face.

'Shut it, Davie. It's all right for you – you grew up in a world where nothing bad ever happened. I was inside; it was different.'

'It sounds to me like you're still in there. In your head, you are.'

'Oh fuck you. Look, we going to do this or not?'

Murdoch didn't wait for an answer. He spat onto the ground, lit his head torch, and stomped towards the big house.

Away from the tree cover, the ground was metallic with moonlight. Reaching the fence, Murdoch turned off his torch again and traced the path of the railings until he could feel the ground sloping beneath his feet. The headland was narrow here and Davie had told him if he carried on walking, pushing through the thick undergrowth now in front of him, he'd soon go over a cliff. Tempting as that was, Murdoch stepped up onto the small concrete wall that held the fence and walked sideways along it, bars hand-to-hand until they ran out. He squeezed himself between the last railing and a stubborn tree and – just like that – was on the inside.

He'd forgotten this feeling: the surprise at how easy it was; the thrill of doing something you knew wasn't a good idea. Halfway back to the gate, he found Davie not a million miles from the spot where he'd told him to wait. Through the fence, he asked him what the plan was.

'Really? Again? Haven't we done this like a hundred times?'

'What's the plan, Davie?'

From Davie, an exaggerated sigh. 'I stay here and do nothing. I don't make a noise or show any light. If anyone arrives, I call you on this walkie-talkie thing and get out of here. Otherwise, I wait at the car for you.'

He was petulant: the fat kid stuck in goal. Murdoch had had to snap at him earlier when he'd wanted to muck about with the radios. Now he told him to go and wait out of sight.

As soon as the cutting wheel connected his lines and the glass came away on the clamp, Murdoch began to worry. Nothing in life was this easy. The blade should have broken or the pane should have shattered as he started to pull it away. An alarm should have rung out or a snarling dog should have tried to bite him through the hole he'd cut. Instead there was nothing, just the tiny crunching of glass against glass, like the house was grinding its teeth. Of course, that didn't mean a thing. Maybe Crosley police already had an alarm screaming in the station, two dozen cop cars racing towards him. At least he'd had the sense to leave his Beretta back in Davie's shack: he wasn't risking a firearms charge.

The room he climbed into was furnished with dust, an undisturbed coat of it across the bare floor, his footprints soon clear in the grey light from the window. A second room was equally bare, echoing every sound, and he asked himself what he was doing there at all, breaking and entering at his age. Given his luck, he'd never get off with a caution, and even if he did, someone in the Club would hear about it soon enough. He should turn back now, trot back to the fence, and persuade Davie there was nothing to see. Get out while the going was good. Still though, Georgie.

An internal door gave way into a long hallway; no moonlight here: no light at all. He clicked his head torch back on – the noise huge in the silent space – and worked his way down to the front door, the beam wavering ahead of him like headlights on a country road. There were no pictures, no furniture, no carpet. He thought of Davie playing in here as a kid. Murdoch had rolled his eyes when Davie had told him the story, thinking, yeah, that made sense, he looked like he'd always been a pussy. Now he wasn't so sure he'd have been any braver. There *was* something frightening about the place, something wrong. Murdoch swore out loud, gave a smack to his two-day beard, and told himself to check every room.

He was halfway up the stairs before he realised what the wrong thing was. He went back through the empty spaces again, shone light on their identical magnolia walls and fake-floorboard lino, went upstairs, and found the same thing. Every room was square and empty, none of them a kitchen or a bathroom or a toilet. It was like a doll's house: like life could be lived between nothing but walls. In an upstairs room at the front of the house, he found a mattress, newish and barely stained. Beside it was a plastic bag with two empty Sprite cans and a sandwich wrapper. Something prompted him to check the walls and he found there were no light switches, no power points above the spaces where skirting-boards should be. He checked the little digital watch he'd bought and saw he'd been in there for no more than fifteen minutes. No need to hurry at all except, again, there was something wrong with this place, something that felt like a trap. Nothing that felt like a house.

Upstairs, the rooms at the back looked down on the ocean, waves visible only where the moonlight pulled across them like a luminous wake. There were coal ships in the distance: orange and red dots in the dark somewhere before the sea ended and the sky began. Nothing in any of the rooms, though; not until the last one where, standing guard in the dark, he found a sturdy wooden tripod in front of one of the windows. There was no telescope on top of it, but at the back of the room, there was a metal camera box. Inside, a pair of binoculars, expensively heavy in his hand. Murdoch walked to the window and looked through them, examining the ocean and its waves, the moon and its craters; nothing else to see. He was putting the glasses away again, balancing the metal box on one leg to get the clasp shut, when the radio on his side crackled to life, its static echoing through the house. Murdoch dropped the metal case and grabbed at the radio, furious with Davie. As the walkie-talkie came off his belt, he knew that the angle was wrong, but, before he could do anything about it, it had fallen from his grasp.

The radio dropped loudly onto the edge of the camera case and then, a crack of plastic replacing the static, skidded across the floor to lie silently in the dark. Murdoch walked over and picked it up. He jabbed at the buttons, but no red or green light appeared. Changing the angle of his torch, he checked the batteries as slowly as he could make himself move, then banged the thing at various angles on the heel of his hand. Nothing. Concentrating on his breathing, he squatted down, tidied the binoculars into the camera case and stowed it back where he'd found it. Out of the corner of his eye he saw a movement, looked again quickly, and saw it was his own shadow in the moonlight. Swearing viciously, he walked out onto the landing and started down the stairs. He was five steps from the bottom when he heard tyres on the gravel outside.

29

Stone Jimmy had been on the run from a stretch for GBH. The story went he'd used a forklift truck to crash through a prison wall and escape. Thirteen-year-old Billy Murdoch wasn't stupid enough to believe that, but he did believe someone's older brother had seen Jimmy coming and going from a house over on the estate. It was a half-derelict terrace – graffitied boards across the downstairs windows – and the game going around Cookham Wood was everyone was too chicken-shit to break out for the night, get inside that house and nick something. Stone Jimmy was their bogeyman: a fearful figure among boys who showed no fear of anyone. Just to say that you'd seen him from a distance, lumbering out of the pub or pushing a trolley along the street, raised your status.

So, of course, Murdoch decided to break into his house and – long story short – of course, he got caught. Maybe one of his mates dobbed him in; he never found out, but they'd probably done it for a laugh. Either way, Stone Jimmy was suddenly home and didn't feel like calling the cops. Murdoch got a broken arm and another note on his juvenile record for that. It was the last time he ever let anyone unnecessary know where he was going and maybe the first time he'd decided to get away from the animals.

He hadn't thought of this in years, hated all the childhood memories that were coming to him these days, but, breathing heavily in the empty big house, the scene played out vividly in his head. He could remember Stone Jimmy's breath. He swore silently and told himself to concentrate.

As soon as he'd heard the car outside, he'd retreated back up the stairs, realising too late what a stupid idea that was. Now he stood behind the door of the furthest room, trying hard to think what it meant that whoever had just driven up outside was smart enough not have their headlights on. Instead, as he listened to the creak of the front door, here he was remembering Stone Jimmy.

There were two voices, only one of them a man's. Whispering at first until the woman said, 'Oh fuck this, there's no one here,' and the man brusquely told her to get a move on and check every room. He said it like he thought he was in charge, but Murdoch could hear the cajoling in his voice.

'The system sent an alert for a reason, Rose, we need to check. You do that half; I'll go down here and we can head up the stairs together if you want.'

'I'm not scared. I can go upstairs myself, you know.'

'Whatever you want. But let's just do this properly, yeah?'

Murdoch thought they were in the downstairs hallway, but he had no way of being sure. The empty house echoed their voices so clearly they could have been in the room with him. He listened to the woman's light footsteps slowly climb the stairs, listened to her progress room by room towards him. She was simply walking around, he told himself, not looking properly at all. He was behind a door, he'd be fine, he himself had taken longer to study the rooms. Then suddenly she was there, no more than two metres away from him.

She was petite and wearing night-vision goggles, pushing them up onto her shaved head as he watched, the moonlight in this back room too bright for her. She blinked and rubbed her eyes, waiting for them to adjust. All she needed to do was turn to her left and she'd see him, but, when a low wolf whistle came up the stairs, she turned to her right and left the room. As she did so, the silver light from the window caught not only the automatic holstered to her right hip, but also the weapon strung across her back. A neatly compact Kalashnikov.

Murdoch listened to her footsteps descend the steps. The man had returned to whispering and Murdoch knew he'd found the cut-out window. It would only be minutes before one or both of them was back. He took off his shoes and padded over to the window. Pressed his hand against the glass to ensure it would break, then cupped his eyes and looked out. Trees and low bushes waved in the breeze. He took two steps back to summon the courage, but then thought, no, maybe not. Footsteps were at the bottom of the stairs again and, looking at the black window, he realised he wasn't ready and returned to his hiding place.

It was the man this time, he was almost certain: the steps heavier as they climbed, slower as they turned and went room to room. Downstairs he heard the untidy echo of someone doing the same, checking every room properly this time before moving on to the next. Figuring the stairs were uncovered, Murdoch forced himself out of his corner – a mouse trying to avoid the cat – around the door and onto the landing. The slow heavy footsteps on this level seemed to be coming from the left, the front of the house. There were three rooms there for the man to check, but Murdoch had no idea how far through them he'd already progressed. He walked slowly to the top of the stairs and started down them. On his way up, he had forgotten to take notice if any of them creaked – such a stupid basic thing to forget – and, cursing himself, took every second step, just in case.

His head was level with the floor of the landing when the woman appeared in the hallway below him. She stood inside the open front door, her right hand close to her side, heavy with the pistol. Murdoch froze, thinking he might be safe if still, but then he saw the woman's goggles turn towards him, their silhouette monstrous in the light through the door. She looked at him for half a second before raising the pistol and aiming it carefully. They looked at each other in silence, the only noise the distant searching of the man upstairs, and Murdoch slowly raised his hands. Not above his head, but to his head, as if to rest them on top. He switched on his head torch and shone it directly at her goggles, then dropped and tumbled down the stairs. The report of the pistol cracked the night like it was breaking the sky itself. The woman yelled through its massive echoes, calling a name and shouting instructions.

The words followed Murdoch as he raced through the front door and turned sharply to the left, firing all his energy into his legs, knowing he had only seconds to get to the corner of the house. He was nearly there, ignoring the scorching in his lungs, when a piece of plaster beside him exploded, its dust blowing into his cheek and half-blinding him. The surprise of it tripped him and he rolled, more by accident than good sense, as there was another explosion above him: a tiny corner of the house suddenly gone. Gravel sharp in his knees, Murdoch crawled the last two metres fast until he was safely around the corner and could stand and run again. He had to get under cover, somewhere no night glasses could find him, but he had misjudged the distance, forgotten the scruffy grass ran so far before meeting the scrub at the top of the cliffs. Heavy boots were racing along the front of the house after him: he wouldn't make it even halfway to the trees. He stuck close to the building instead, running in a crouch, until he found a doorway deep enough to hold him. Drawing breaths quietly was agony, his mouth wide in a silent howl, but as he reached up for his torch, he saw something beyond the fence that spurred him on – if only so he could kill Davie fucking Simms.

A second later and the heavy boots came charging around the corner where he had fallen. Murdoch let them approach, then stepped out and repeated what he'd done in the house, shining his head torch into the face that was no more than a few metres away. For some reason, the trick was less effective this time – the strongly built man in front of him barely flinched – but still, the third shot from his handheld went off towards the trees. Before he could get a fourth one off, Murdoch was on him, using both hands to snap the man's right arm over his own knee, pushing him backwards all the time.

The man cried out, a furious guttural sound, but he fell well, trying to bring Murdoch down with him. He half-managed it and they stumbled together, the pistol still in the man's right hand. Murdoch was up first and stamped on the broken arm; the gun dropped at last so he could bend and pick it up before stamping again. The other man cried out once more as he rolled away and tried to get the machine-gun from off his back. But his right arm was useless to him now: he looked like a contortionist failing to beat the clock. In the tumble, he'd lost his goggles and when Murdoch looked back from his weaving path to the end of the fence, he saw his opponent was down on one knee, his forehead in his good hand. Murdoch swung around the last railing without breaking his stride and ran to where Davie had parked the Golf. It looked different somehow and when a figure sat up in the driver's seat, Murdoch thought maybe he'd misunderstood. He took the safety catch off the pistol he'd taken from the man and held it in front of him as he circled the car, the air coming to him in loud gasps now no matter what he tried.

'Dude, it's me, don't shoot!' Davie's voice was high-pitched and desperate, the words rolled into one. 'Don't shoot me, don't shoot me, please.'

Murdoch tore the door open, got into the Golf, and watched past Davie as the man he'd fought with reacted to the noise of the car's engine. Murdoch couldn't speak – he was too busy sucking in air – but Davie needed no encouragement. They bounced furiously alongside the fence, the engine revving uncomfortably, both of them watching the man run lopsidedly beside them, back towards his own car. Then, as Davie steered them into the woods, Murdoch turned to keep his view. The moon was lower now, everything grey on black again, but until the steepness of the track came between them, he could see clearly enough. The man had reached his car, a huge black four-by-four, and was kicking the panel of its driver's door.

The first thing Murdoch said was, 'Kill the lights,' but that didn't work. There was no way they could follow the track without beams to guide them. He turned to see if they were being followed but soon realised there was no point to that either. If these people could see in the dark, they could probably drive in it too. He remembered their lack of headlights when they rolled up to the house and opened the window beside him, but he couldn't hear above the noise of the Golf, its engine revving unevenly as they dipped in and out of hollows. The four-by-four might be right behind them. He needed to remain calm but found himself shouting at Davie.

'As soon as we come to the next bend, stop the car and kill the engine. I need to listen.'

'No way, man, are you nuts? We've got to get the hell out of here right now.'

'Davie, they might be right behind us. They had these goggles on what let them see in the dark.'

Barely slowing the Golf, Davie reached into his pocket, fished something out and threw it into Murdoch's lap. A car key on a remote control.

'What's this?'

'Their car keys. I saw them go into the house and I thought, oh man, that can't be good. So I snuck up and let the air out of the tyres. Then I saw the keys and thought I'd take them too.'

'Davie, you muppet! What was the plan? We went through the bleeding plan!'

'Bill, in case you haven't noticed, we're sitting in a car with no one behind us. You got away. What was that noise – was it a gun? Did they shoot at you?'

Murdoch didn't respond. He looked down, wondering why his feet were hurting, and saw he'd left his shoes in the house. There was a taste of blood in his mouth and he rubbed his jaw, turning again and again to look into the blackness behind them. When they reached the road and Davie turned to the right, Murdoch asked him where they were going.

'Down this way, towards Kildare. The roads are quieter.'

'So?'

'Now Bill, I don't want you to be angry.'

'What else did you do, Davie?'

A tiny blue light in the wing mirror answered him. It flashed once, twice, before its noise reached them. The old wee-wah that always made his skin crawl.

'You didn't call the fucking police?'

'Dude, I thought they were going to shoot you. Or they were going to kidnap you or something; what the hell was I supposed to do?'

'How about Not Call The Police? I just did a fucking break-and-enter; I was the one what broke the law, they …'

Another police car approached from the direction they were heading, screaming as it passed them, and then glowing red in their mirrors as it braked where the track headed up to the house.

'How did you call them?'

'What do you mean?'

'I mean, how did you call them?'

'I used my work phone.'

'And you gave your name?'

'I'm not totally stupid. I gave a false name.'

'You are totally stupid, Davie. They've got your mobile number. Where's that phone?'

He saw Davie look towards the dashboard, saw the iPhone in the gap below the radio and snatched it before Davie could get to it; there was a flurry of arms: kids fighting over which station to listen to.

'What was the last call you made before the police?'

Murdoch was scanning through the recent calls, testing Davie rather than wanting information.

'I dunno. I called my mum this afternoon. That was it.'

'You called for a pizza at 5.45 p.m.'

'Oh yeah, and that.'

'Did you go and get it?'

'The pizza?'

'Yes, the pizza. Did you go and get it or did they deliver? This is important.'

'I went and got it.'

'OK. You left your phone in the pizza place, got it? You call up as soon as we get home and ask them if it's there. Then you cancel the account. What else? What else would you do if your phone got stolen?'

'Look up online to see where it is? There's this thing that lets you trace it. You're going to have to dump it.'

'OK, now you're thinking straight. I'll get rid of it. So, we were home all night playing video games. What game?'

'What?'

'What video game was we playing all night at home?'

'*Buzz.* No, *Call of Duty.*'

Murdoch watched Davie notice the speedometer and force himself to slow down. They were still twenty clicks over the speed limit, empty ill-lit streets tempting them faster.

'OK,' he said. 'We was home all night playing *Call of Duty*, you got it? You think you can stick to that plan, maybe?'

'Yes, Bill. And do you think you could maybe show the tiniest bit of gratitude to me for risking my life to save you from terrorists with guns and night-goggles and … things … and driving you away in the comfort of your own car?'

'Yeah, my car. My number plates, what the guys with the goggles could probably see and are now putting the word out for every villain this side of hell to look for.'

Davie told him to look at the bloody back seat. Murdoch turned and found his number plates lying flush against the left-hand door. That was why his car hadn't looked like his. He looked at Davie differently, then raised his eyebrows, but said nothing. Wound down his window, lit a cigarette, listened to distant sirens fading in the night. The moon was long gone and the sky above them was black.

'Good work,' he said at last. 'Thank you. Bleeding hell, you took a risk.'

'What was I supposed to do? Leave you there?'

'You wouldn't be the first.'

They drove in silence for a while, rolling up the kilometres between them and the trouble. When Davie spoke again he sounded excited, frightened, everything at once, like he was only now realising what he'd done. 'Wow, terrorists on the Central Coast. Did they sound foreign or anything? Do you think Georgie was one of them? Or maybe she spotted them and they kidnapped her! You know, white-slave trade kind of thing? I got their rego – SSU 638 – gave it to the police and everything.'

Murdoch tried to take the smile out of his voice. 'You got the rego?' A laugh escaping as he said it. Then he let it out properly, cackling in the speeding night like a madman. Davie said something, but plans were forming so fast Murdoch couldn't hear. He just looked over at his housemate and punched him hard in the shoulder. 'You got the rego! That's awesome. Dude.'

30.

Unlike the headland to the south of Montauban, the one closing off the north of the bay formed part of the suburb itself. This was where Montagne Road climbed steeply, the mansions on its ocean side teetering on increasingly high cliffs. The only thing above them was the Cook Lookout.

Someone in the seventies had thought the lookout would make a good tourist attraction: someone who'd convinced the council to put the world's ugliest obelisk in the middle of some scrub and fence it off from the cliff. There were safety warnings, plaques about what Cook had seen and how he'd named it; nothing about who'd lived here before then. Murdoch leaned on the fence and looked down at the ocean. There was a breeze in town that was a wind up here: the air full with seeds and fluff from the trees; empty crisp packets against the fence. Murdoch huddled over his lighter, took some deep drags and let the wind steal the smoke from his mouth. He'd smoked half the cigarette before he admitted what he wanted to do. He fished for his phone and dialled Cynthia's number. Four ring-outs before she answered.

'Hello?'

'Cyn, it's me.'

'Blackie!'

She almost shouted it. Like he'd caught her with someone else or surprised her doing something she shouldn't be doing. He could hear her breath as she moved around.

'You all right, Cyn?'

'Me? Good as gold.' She laughed in a way he hadn't heard before. 'Where are you, Blackie? You back in town?'

'I wish I was, darlin'. Then we could celebrate my good news.'

She didn't take the bait, just asked if he was coming back soon.

'Maybe. A light has definitely gone on at the end of the tunnel; put it that way. I wanted to tell you, cos there's no one else I can really share it with.'

'Tell me all about it, dearie.'

Dearie? Her voice had faded halfway through the sentence, like she was holding the phone away from her mouth.

'I wish you were here' he said.

'Me too. Why don't you tell me where you are and I'll come up.'

'OK. You got a pen?'

There was a fluster at the end of a line.

'Three minutes, is it?' he said.

'What's that Blackie?' The phone had moved again, her voice further away and struggling with its smile.

'You've got to keep me on the phone for three minutes, that right? Or is it quicker these days? Long enough for them to get a trace on the number without having to call me back?'

She gasped and then, for a while, he heard nothing. Fumbles maybe, strange echoing noises, life under a blanket, until her voice came on again.

'Ha ha, oh dear. I dropped the phone. What were you saying?'

Out on the ocean a tiny boat was making its way down the coastline, bumping between the whitecaps and the low grey sky. Seagulls hovered in and out of the overhang below him.

'Make sure they pay you, Cyn.'

'Who's that? I don't know what you're talking about. Why don't you tell me about your good news.'

Murdoch rubbed a hand across his scalp, eyes closed against the wind that was beginning to make them water.

'Take care of yourself, darlin',' he said. 'And don't worry, I understand. We was only ever a business arrangement.'

Maybe she said something else. If she did, he closed the phone on it. He wanted to throw the thing into the wind, but instead forced himself to take it apart, his cigarette clenched between his lips as he pulled out the SIM and bent it back and forth until it snapped. He huddled over, a half-hearted attempt to keep his ears out of the wind, and walked down towards the road, throwing his half-smoked cigarette at the bushfire sign.

At the bottom of the hill, where the surf club hulked on the beach near the little roundabout, someone called his name. He pretended not to hear – the last thing he needed just now – but then there she was, right behind him and calling again so he had to stop. Natalie Conquest on a bicycle, brown legs smoothing into Lycra, a stupid helmet on her head. She smiled awkwardly as she pulled up beside him. Not like she meant it, more like she couldn't think of anything better to do with her face. He forced a smile back, said he thought she caught the bus home.

'It's Sunday, I don't work all the time you know. Hannah tells me there's been some progress?'

Murdoch sighed loudly. 'What the fuck? How am I supposed to find stuff out if everyone keeps talking to each other, but not to me?'

Natalie rolled her eyes. 'Aw, suck it up, princess, she didn't tell me what the progress was. Wouldn't tell me anything, actually. Just said you were maybe getting somewhere. And don't worry, I'm not going to ask you either. I am still a *copper*, after all.'

He couldn't tell from her face if she was really annoyed or just teasing him. Bit of both by the looks of it, a hard sparkle in the green eyes.

'Listen,' she said. 'I want to ask you a question.'

'Really?'

'That a problem?'

'No,' he said. 'Go for it.'

'No, I mean, I want to talk to you about something. Have you got a few minutes?'

'So you can yell at me again? Nah, not really.'

'I won't yell at you again. I'll buy you a drink.'

She nodded at the surf club behind him, eyebrows raised in challenge. Maybe on another day he'd have said no, maybe the call with

Cynthia had weakened him. Or maybe it was the idea of a free cold beer while looking at those legs. Copper or no copper.

The surf club was packed. Locals watching the footy, forlorn weekenders blown off the beach, lifesavers in red-and-yellow uniforms, glum they had no one to save. Ruby, the Indian girl from the bakery, was at a table near the door and she grabbed Murdoch as he passed, saying she wanted to introduce him to her husband. A reedy guy, with the same dark skin and lilting accent as his wife, stood and shook Murdoch's hand.

'You're the detective.'

'So people keep telling me.'

'Well, I'm sure everyone also keeps telling you how happy we are you're here. Most of us.'

Murdoch ignored the nod towards his stitches. He said he should get going, gestured towards Natalie waiting for him.

'You're popular,' she said when he reached her at the bar. 'I got you a Coopers, but they wouldn't let me pay for it. Shall we sit outside?'

It was a good idea for a minute, but the sea spray and cold soon brought them back in. They found a table in the corner and Natalie made some rapid small talk out of the local gossip. Somebody reckoned they'd got food poisoning from the chip shop; a kid had swiped Davie's phone and made a crank call to the police. He could tell she was nervous, something he'd not seen on her before, and he asked her – nicely – to get to the point. There had been enough nasty surprises for the day. Natalie took a slug of beer before answering – a big one, like she needed help with the answer.

'Look, I accept I might have been a bit touchy the last few times we've met. And, if I'm honest, yeah, I'm bloody insulted by Hannah hiring a private detective. It's like she's so convinced someone else can find out more than we did about Georgie that she's willing to bet money on it. I mean, if private eyes are so good, why aren't they working for the police? Unless they're just in it for the money, of course.' She seemed to realise she'd gone off-track, took another slug of beer, and started again, slower this time. 'Anyway, my last performance review at work said I had a problem with my temper. Which is true, I guess. But I do really care about the Georgie Walker case and – from a professional point of view – I don't want my ... behaviour to hamper the investigation in any way. And, like you said the other night, I really don't know you at all. And I'm trying not to be prejudiced. Listen, what I'm trying to say is, I was wondering if we could let bygones be bygones and, you know, co-operate or something?'

'Yeah, OK.'

'What?' She narrowed her eyes at him over her next sip of beer. 'Are you serious? I thought you were allergic to coppers?'

He didn't ask her why she'd bothered asking then. 'Yeah, well, maybe I am. But right now, I need some help. See I've got a rego …'

'Why is that, by the way? Why do you hate us so much?'

It was his turn to drink: a third of his schooner while he waited for her to interrupt with another question. Then a slow look around the surf club, all the innocent faces, until he looked back and found her still waiting for an answer.

'Call it experience,' he said. 'I've had a few run-ins with the law and the result's not always been fair. You get bitten three times, you stop stroking dogs, know what I mean?'

Natalie barked out a humourless laugh, thanked him for the compliment, and asked him if he wanted another beer. She was halfway to the bar before he had a chance to answer.

'What I don't get,' she said on their third round of drinks 'is what made you choose to be a private investigator? I'd have thought, given the way you think about the police, you'd have made a good criminal.'

He looked around, conscious of the volume of her voice. 'Crims are not nice people,' he whispered fiercely. 'They're scum, animals.'

She challenged him on that – they were as human as him, surely? People who hadn't been lucky enough to have had the right guidance and opportunities.

'Nah,' he said. 'Not the ones I'm on about. They're animals, trust me. You know what I reckon is the difference between an animal and a human? A human sees someone what's suffering or struggling, they cross the road to help 'em. Like people round here do. An animal, out in Africa or the jungle or somewhere, they see another animal getting eaten, they just look the other way. They don't give a shit as long as they're all right. I saw it on the telly, zebras munching grass in a field whilst the lion's eating one of their mates. That's like the blokes I'm talking about; they don't give a shit for anyone but themselves. I've spent half my life trying …'

He heard himself and stopped. It was the beer that was making him talk like this, spilling his guts to a girl he hardly knew, a copper at that. He made an excuse about needing the lav and Natalie told him to get some more drinks in on the way back – it was his round.

She got him again on the next drink. Asked him what he wanted from life. Sober, he'd have deflected, got her to answer first and questioned her on the details. Maybe. Or maybe, he wanted to talk about it. Wanted to remind himself he had a future, one worth taking risks for. And besides, Natalie wasn't a bad listener. When he spoke, she took him seriously, made him feel like his answers were important.

'I want a nice house,' he told her. 'A good car and a quiet life. You know who I'm most jealous of? Paul Walker.'

Natalie gasped. 'You are joking, aren't you? The man's wife died and his daughter's gone missing. I don't think a big house and a car can make up for that.'

'Yeah, well, I've never had a wife or daughter but I reckon I'd give them up for that house.'

She slapped his arm and told him he was terrible, so he found a smile and pretended he'd been joking. 'You like Paul Walker, don't you?' he said. 'Were you two an item or something?'

'Mind your own business.' Natalie flushed red. 'I mean, no. Not really. Well, we went on a few dates once, a few years after his wife died, and he's very charming. But a bit old for me at the end of the day, old-fashioned ideas. Anyhow, then Georgie disappeared; so, like I said, mind your own business.'

She raised her eyebrows like that was the end of that. He told her it was a shame, she could be living in that lovely big house and she laughed despite herself and slapped his arm again.

He couldn't smoke inside so when Natalie went to the bathroom, he wove between the busy tables, slid open the doors, and stepped onto the deserted balcony. What daylight was left in the windblown sky was low in the distance, blurry stars out overhead, and he had a strange sense of having lost the afternoon, like he should have been outside or something. He heard the sliding door open and close behind him.

'Give us a drag,' said Natalie, shivering at his side.

He passed the cigarette over and thought of Hannah Simms, in trouble for smoking at school. 'I can't get over the stars here,' he said, just for something to say. 'I never really thought about 'em when I was … before I came down under, but people always said they was good. In Oz, I mean. And I always wondered why; because stars are just stars, innit? Nothing special. And then I come here and they're mental, like little lamps up there.'

She blew smoke out her nose. 'You're weird,' she said. 'You act the tough guy, stomping your muscly little body around under your macho frown. And then sometimes you're so innocent, like stars are *the most amazing thing.*'

He told her to fuck off and they stood there, passing the cigarette back and forth like it was a joint, silent until she asked him why he came to Australia. Like he'd not shared enough already that day. He shrugged his shoulders.

'Because I could. My dad was Australian apparently; they reckon I might even of been born here. Someone gave me the good advice to get a passport and as soon as I could I came. Got the fuck away from everything I'd known over there.'

She accepted that for an answer and he nearly told her how lucky she was to come from a place you believed was better than somewhere else. Instead, he stared up at the stars, wondering why beer always made them twinkle more.

They stumbled through the dark streets, the bicycle wobbling between them, a different route from the one he and Davie had taken.

'You really don't have to walk me home,' she said. 'I can look after myself.'

'Yeah, well, I can look after myself too and look what happened to me.'

She turned towards him, her feet slowing. It was too dark to see her face properly, but he knew she was going to ask another bloody question. 'Who do you reckon that was? It's so weird – I can't believe it happened in Montie. It's not like we're some outback place not used to strangers.'

'Beats me.'

She laughed at this until he did too. Then she pointed out a squat blue house and asked him if he knew who lived there.

'No idea. Oh yeah! Alycia Thornton. Jesus, I didn't know we'd come this far back. This isn't the way Davie and me came to your house before.'

'Shortcut.'

He shook his head. 'This town. It's tiny but it's like a maze.' Then, after a while, as they walked on again, 'What do you reckon to Alycia, then?'

'Nothing much. Maybe not as good a friend of Georgie's as she likes to pretend, but she's harmless enough. She puts on this big confident actress act, but underneath it all, she's just as confused and needy as all girls at that age.'

'Needy?'

'Yeah, very. She just wants everyone to like her. Why?'

'Nothing.'

'Bill!'

'No, really, nothing. I just didn't think she seemed needy, that's all. She seemed more like, you know, full of herself. Enjoying the drama of it all, flirting.'

'Maybe she fancied you?'

A flight of steps appeared in the verge beside them and they carried the bike down, passing through a single pool of yellow lamplight before emerging into the street he recognised as hers. Murdoch looked back the way they'd come.

'How can a shortcut have taken us to a street higher than yours?'

'I don't know.' Even in the dark he could see she was unsure about what she was going to say next. 'Maybe I was enjoying the walk.'

31.

News, horse racing, football, news. News, horse racing, football, news. Murdoch flipped through the channels, curtains drawn against the day, unable to escape the stench of himself. He knew he should shower, get the dried sweat and alcohol off, but anything that involved leaving the sofa wasn't going to happen. At ten o'clock, Davie came up the creaking stairs and burst through the front door full of the joys of the beach. Wet hair dripping dark patches down his T-shirt, cheeks full of colour, he was the anti-hangover on legs. Murdoch asked him why he wasn't at work.

'I worked yesterday. Got the day off. Want to do something? Check out that rego or something?'

'No.'

'Well, at least you're home safe. I was worried. When I got up and saw you weren't here, I thought maybe you'd got beaten up again or something.'

'I didn't get beaten up, Davie. I got injured beating them up, remember?'

'Oh dear, somebody's got a hangover. Good night? I heard you were out with Natalie.'

Murdoch looked at him sourly. 'How is it, exactly, that in this town everyone knows what everyone else is doing every minute of the bleeding day, but a seventeen-year-old girl can disappear into thin air and no one knows a fucking thing?'

'That's what you're here to tell us, Mr Detective. So where'd you go after the surf club?'

Murdoch flipped the channel again and pretended to watch the horses until Davie's board shorts blocked out the screen.

'Dude, you didn't?'

'Didn't I?'

Davie whooped and approached the sofa with his side of a high five. It wilted in the heat of Murdoch's stare. But Davie's enthusiasm, and his shorts in front of the TV screen, stayed where they were.

'Man, you are unbelievable. You know, when I said you should try not to fight with her …'

'Shut it, Davie.'

'I'm impressed and more than a little surprised by your powers of persuasion.'

'Davie …'

'Uh oh. I'm guessing things didn't go too well when you woke up in each other's loving arms this morning?'

That was an understatement. Natalie had been late for work and they'd both had bad headaches. She hadn't been willing to look up a car registration plate unless he told her why he wanted her to; he'd accused her of wanting credit for any progress on the case. A mug had been thrown.

'No, I mean it, Davie. Shut the fuck up.'

The horses became visible again, Davie taking his enthusiasm to the kitchen. 'You want eggs?'

'What kind?'

'Special magic kind for grumpy boys with hangovers. Oh, by the way, this'll cheer you up. Hannah phoned last night, asked if you'd call her.'

'Great.'

'And I just bumped into Tom Walker, who asked if he can come round and see you.'

Murdoch put a cushion over his face and pressed it hard. When he came up for air Davie was still talking.

'I thought maybe we could find out who that car rego belonged to and then follow up and see if there's any more clues?'

'We? What you talking about? You playing detective too now? Listen, Davie, this isn't a bleeding movie, that's not how it works. Thanks for your help on Saturday, but that's it, got it?'

Murdoch turned off the telly, pulled himself off the sofa and took his phone into the bedroom. Hannah answered on the first ring. Murdoch thought of Cynthia and a small knot formed in his stomach: indigestion or some bubble of hangover or something.

'Bill!'

Hannah said it like it was a quiz and she knew the right answer: the girl at the front of the class dislocating her shoulder to stick her hand up high enough.

'Davie said you returned my call. You could phone me directly you know.'

'I did – you didn't answer. Now listen, in your message you said there was progress. What happened?'

'Something significant. But Hannah, this is important. From now on, any conversation we have stays with us. No one else, got it? That includes Davie.'

'Is Davie a suspect?'

'Everyone's a suspect. Besides, I don't know who he talks to or what about, know what I mean?'

'Is this why you phoned me, Bill?'

'No. I have a car rego and I need to find out who it belongs to.'

'Maybe you should ask Natalie Conquest?'

He sat on the side of the bed and dabbed at his stitches with his free hand. His mouth tasted like an ashtray, but he'd left his glass of water in front of the telly.

'Yeah, I thought of that. I can't tell you the details, Hannah, but this thing's bigger than Georgie. If we involve the police, finding her won't be their priority. They'll get some big headlines and she'll never be seen again. I was thinking you might have access to systems what can tell us who a car is registered to? We'll let the police know in time, but, for now, I think it's better to go it alone.'

She said nothing. Said it for a long time, like she'd forgotten Murdoch knew that game too. He rummaged through his bedside drawer looking for painkillers. Found nothing, closed his eyes and waited. Hannah sighed and asked him to give her the registration number, read it back to him and asked him to hold. Tinny pop music came down the line, cheap lyrics about love and sunshine, three verses before Hannah came back with a name and an address.

32.

Davie had always hated the way some estate agents used the term 'architect-designed' to market the houses they were selling, as if that description wasn't true of every house. But, now, looking at Crosley Town Hall, he thought maybe the expression made sense. Maybe some buildings really were designed by people better suited to hairdressing or surgery. The Town Hall looked like a multi-storey car park with windows: a brown concrete monument to everything wrong with Crosley. Even on paper it couldn't have looked good.

The department he wanted was on the third floor, a dim low-ceilinged space where a sign in three languages told him to take a number and wait to be called. The walls were lined with brochures in neat wire racks – Drains, Tree Management, Assistance for the Vision Impaired. When he took his number, the girl behind the counter looked up and Davie gave her his best smile. She didn't smile back. Instead she returned to shuffling through papers before comparing them to her computer screen. Davie was beginning to wonder whether he ought to be doing this without telling Bill, when a buzzer sounded and his number appeared in dots above the counter. Still the girl didn't smile.

'Hi.'

'Yes?'

'My name's Davie Wonder and I was wondering if you could help me?'

'Yes?'

Not a blink of recognition, it wasn't even a name she *ought* to know. Close up she was no older than she looked: early twenties. Which made her maybe five years old when his last song came out – the one nobody bought.

'I'd like a permit for waterfront parking at Broadwater, please.'

'No worries. You got the rego papers?'

She was wearing a short-sleeved shirt with a retro garage logo on the breast pocket, low-slung jeans without a belt, hair cut short. Davie let the coast drift into his accent.

'Yeah, thing is I don't have 'em yet. Listen, I hate to sound like a dill, but I've not done this before. It's my first car. I don't even know what docs I'm supposed to get.'

The girl behind the counter tutted and sighed, rolled her eyes, but couldn't resist the opportunity to instruct. She told him there was a strict rule of only one permit per car, explained to him about the rego doc, the pink slip, the green slip, even told him to check for encumbrance, while he nodded and frowned like he was listening hard and not angling himself so he could see her screen. He borrowed a pen and wrote things down on a scrap of paper while she leaned on the counter with both forearms and read them upside down.

'So,' said Davie, not too bright, 'what if I get all the docs and he's already got a parking permit for the car?'

'Good point. Then you'll need to get him to sign that permit over to you so you can swap it for the one you want.'

'I bet he bloody has. Bet he's got one and not mentioned it.'

'Do you want me to check for you?'

'Can you do that?'

'Can if you know the rego.'

He made a show of searching for the right bit of paper. The girl was typing already, waiting for the number.

'Here you go. SSU 638. I bet he's got a permit.'

She tapped at the keyboard and grunted in satisfaction, not caring too much that he could see the screen. 'You're right, he has. The car's registered up in Bungaree, but he's got the parking permit for an address in West Crosley.' *124 Yalta Road* – Davie could read it easily enough.

'Bastard!' he said. 'So if I hadn't asked, he'd have kept his permit and I'd have been screwed.'

She shook her head; she'd seen it a thousand times. Davie forced himself to frown and keep playing dumb all the way down the stairs and out of the ugly building.

33.

Meanwhile, Murdoch had driven to the address Hannah had given him. His head was still hurting and his breath would put him over the limit, but a drink-driving charge was preferable to Tom Walker's hopeful face. He drove through Crosley and took the quiet highway north, the cloudless sky mocking the millions back at work. Bungaree was one exit away, fifteen minutes of driving, and when Murdoch found the street easily enough he thought it was probably too good to be true.

Bungaree Light Industrial Estate: a grid of treeless roads between low reflective buildings, cracked car spaces smelling of petrol. Jobsons Boat Mechanics, Patterson Precision Cardboards, ATL Ducting Systems. A sign outside a red-brick block advertised sandwiches and hot drinks. It was surrounded by plastic garden furniture lying on its sides, but the café door was open and a smell of hot chip fat was drifting outside. Murdoch ordered tea from a woman who had once, a hundred years before, been told she looked good in a sleeveless top.

'This is Brintons Road all right,' she said. 'But I don't think there's a number one hundred. We're number one and you can see there's only four further up than us.'

He checked the office building next door, a deaf receptionist asking him questions through the intercom so that he had to shout his lies to the street. He tried to ignore how stupid he sounded, asking for 100 Brintons Road on a street with five buildings. Tried ignoring the reflection in the glass door that remained firmly shut in his face: four days of growth on his chin, hair uncut in months.

Back in the car he fended off self-hatred. False leads were probably normal; he'd had to check the address; it wasn't his fault. He looked at his phone and wondered whether he should call Natalie. Was still sitting there, staring at the tiny screen, when a text came in from Davie.

I've got exciting news!!!!!! Beer at surf club now? ☺

Murdoch stabbed it angrily away, drove back to Bungaree and found a barber.

34.

The T-Junction Café had seats out the front, but after an hour or so, Murdoch suggested they move inside to the bench of cushions near the window. The sky had stayed blue since the weekend, but something else had changed; maybe the angle of the light or the temperature in the shadows, something which meant there was more winter than summer in the autumn air. Even inside Murdoch felt it and he jigged his legs up and down, rubbing his forearms until Davie begged him to stop.

'Dude, please. What's wrong, are you nervous?'

'I'm fine.'

'You look different.'

'Got a haircut.'

'No, I don't mean that. At least, not just that. You look, well, nervous. Like you used to look when you first got to Montie.'

'When my hair was shorter, you mean?'

Davie rolled his eyes and looked back at his laptop, surfing or googling or whatever it was you did. Murdoch hadn't wanted to bring him at all. He'd tried reminding Davie of how scared he'd been up on the headland. 'Guns,' he said. 'Terrorists.' But Davie was like a kid at Christmastime, worried you were going to open the presents without him.

He'd reminded Murdoch he was the one who had got them off the headland, the one who'd got the rego and now the one who'd got this address. They'd compromised with a deal that they'd each bring a car.

West Crosley wasn't far from the centre of town, but you could see why it had given itself the 'West'. No zombies or graffiti here. The tree-lined streets of West Crosley were populated by men in open-necked shirts and women pushing designer prams. The only traffic was an occasional four-by-four, or a cleaning company van driving from one detached house to another. Davie said you could hear the bored housewives shimmering beside their pools, waiting for a sexy young bloke to come and help them with their sunscreen. Murdoch reminded Davie he wasn't young any more; Davie reminded Murdoch he'd never been sexy.

Number 124 was at the end of Yalta Road, two houses from a T-junction with Malama Avenue. Malama was busier: two lanes of patchy traffic in each direction. Opposite the junction were a bus stop, a café and three shops. Murdoch said it was perfect: they could sit in the café as long as they wanted.

'It's never the ones in the house what spot you,' he explained. 'It's always the neighbours. Some old bird with nothing to do but call the fuzz. Next thing it's a blue flashing light and "Can you explain why you've been here four hours, sir?"'

Davie asked him if he'd got that off a TV show, then blushed and looked away when Murdoch stared at him.

They sat inside the window for hours, Yalta Street quiet beyond the traffic, Davie flirting intermittently with the café-owner so she didn't make them buy too many drinks. Murdoch might as well have been invisible.

'You've got the gift of the gab, d'you know that, Davie? Charm the birds off the trees, you could.'

'Yeah, well, not all of us can be the local hero, can we? Anne Lincoln swooning about us to all and sundry, Natalie Conquest wandering around like a lost puppy. Not to mention Tom Walker happier than he's been in months.'

Murdoch had to force himself not to smile. It *was* like being a hero. The way people in Montauban looked at him – he'd never experienced anything like it before. He took a slug of cold coffee and told Davie he didn't know what he was talking about.

'Dude,' Davie told him. 'Want my advice? Enjoy it while it lasts. There's nothing wrong with being popular. Try being an estate agent … What? What are you looking at?'

It was the sunglasses Murdoch noticed first. Something medical about them, not the kind of thing a woman around here would wear. Only then did he notice her shaved head, its tiny stubble catching the morning sun. She was smaller than he remembered – maybe it was the lack of a gun in her hand – and more feminine. She was in a skirt and heels, a small dog on a lead pulling her along the other side of Malama Avenue. Davie turned to see what he was staring at until Murdoch hissed him back round again.

'Dude, what is it?'

'It's her. Don't move.'

'But—'

'Don't bleeding well move.'

She turned the corner into Yalta Road and, when she got to 124, reached down and picked up the dog, opened the garden gate with her free hand, walked up the path and pressed the buzzer. Just like any other bird in this nice part of town, popping around to visit a friend.

She was inside for less than fifteen minutes, Davie begging to swap places until Murdoch threatened to send him home. When she came out again, she was in the same clothes, but had swapped the dog for an obviously heavy bag, hauling it across Yalta towards a large black Lexus that beeped as she approached. By the time she and the bag were inside the car, Murdoch was halfway to his Golf, leaving Davie with strict instructions to Not Get Noticed.

Murdoch had never followed anyone before, not any further than the nearest dark alley. A thought flickered that this really was like being a detective, but then he forced himself to remember why he was doing it. He focused on the distance between his car and the Lexus and reminded himself it was better to lose her than attract her attention.

At first, it was easier than he'd thought. The Lexus turned onto Malama Avenue, then stayed on roads where there was enough traffic so he could fall back five or six cars before catching up to her up again, closing in and dropping away in an uneven rhythm. He followed her out of West

Crosley and onto the highway. Idled in the slow lane as she went up the hill, then stayed six cars behind as she merged onto the massive freeway.

She was dragging him towards Sydney, both what he'd hoped for and the last thing he wanted, pulling him back across the Hawkesbury and then, as they left the freeway, entangling him in the outskirts of the city. Somewhere north of Lane Cove, so suddenly he almost caught up with her, she stopped and indicated, waiting for a gap in the northbound traffic. Then she turned down one of the leafy roads that fell away from the Pacific Highway. He followed from a distance, nothing between them now, trailing her down avenues of green suburbia, each street steep to the creeks that became the harbour. She turned left and he followed his instincts and drove on past, noting the name of the street and hoping he hadn't lost her. At the next junction he turned too, no idea how parallel the streets might be, then left again and saw the end of the Lexus rolling over a crossroads up ahead. He pulled up there and looked down after it, waited until it had followed a curve out of sight and then turned the Golf that way too.

He was sweating, could smell the nerves on himself, the excitement. He rolled down all the windows so that birdsong mixed with the noise of the engine. This part of town was new to him, but anyone could tell what kind of place it was. Hedges trimmed, pavements swept, nothing under four million dollars. The quiet road straightened and, a hundred metres ahead, the Lexus pulled up to the right-hand kerb. Without indicating he pulled into the next driveway he found, turned off his engine and sat staring at his phone, like he was checking an address or wondering where he was. Somewhere nearby a car door slammed, a dog barked, there were empty seconds and then he heard what sounded like a metal gate opening.

Murdoch leaned out cautiously from the driveway where he had parked. The Lexus stood silent, the skinhead girl nowhere in sight. Back inside the Golf he opened the glovebox, fished out Davie's iPhone and a half roll of masking tape, and took a deep breath.

35

The woman who ran the café was tired of Davie's smile. He'd flirted with her too much, then pulled back when she'd flirted in return. Now, when she asked him if he was all right and he ordered another coffee, she didn't comment, just turned and started making it. He told her he was waiting for his friend to come back and offered to pay for what they'd had so far. It didn't help. When she delivered his new coffee to his table, she walked off to the next task before he could thank her. Feeling himself blushing, Davie dipped a sugar cube into his coffee and stared at the crystals turning brown.

He spent the next hour reading old issues of *Women's Health*, understanding slowly why Bill had insisted they bring two cars: he'd obviously intended all along to leave Davie behind like an idiot. Davie fielded a few work calls, made an appointment for a viewing, was fiddling with Facebook when over the top of his screen he saw movement in Yalta Road. A man in sunglasses, arm in a sling, had come out of 124: a man whose shape he recognised.

The man with the sling walked quickly for a big guy, like he was late for something. By the time Davie had extricated himself from the café – no chit-chat with the tipless payment – and dodged between the cars on Malama Avenue, the other man was at the far end of Yalta Road, his huge frame overtaking an old woman with a tartan trolley. When Davie in turn caught up with her, the big guy was out of sight. Davie stood for a second, wondering what to do, the whine of a wheel on the old lady's trolley the only noise in the street. Then he broke into a jog and ran to the end the road, but he found only an empty crossroads, no way of knowing which way the guy had gone. He took the road to the left, gave up after a hundred metres and came back to the crossroads again.

'You lost, dear?'

It was the old woman with the trolley: the turtle mocking the hare. Davie smiled and said he was fine, thanks. Ran up the road opposite, empty all the way to its end. He was at the crossroads for a third time when his phone rang.

Murdoch walked away from the Lexus and headed the wrong way around the block. He waited ten minutes to be sure he hadn't been followed, which meant he hadn't been seen, then headed back to the Golf. He dialled Davie's work number, no idea if this was going to work, no idea if Davie had even brought that phone out with him. Davie answered on the first ring.

'Where are you, Davie?'

'I'm at the café.'

'You sound out of breath. What you doing?'

'Nothing. What's up? Where did she go?'

'Tell you later. Listen, I need you to do something for me. You know that software you told me about what lets you trace your iPhone?'

'It's an app, it's not like I have to run the software.'

'Whatever. Go on it now and tell me where your iPhone is, yeah?'

'I thought you said you were going to get rid of it.'

'I haven't done it yet. Find it and call me back.'

Murdoch reversed the Golf out of the driveway, drove three blocks down the hill and found a parking space outside a church, signs in red proclaiming the Good News. There were no cigarettes in the car and his fingers grew white on the steering wheel as he waited, forcing himself to listen to the air in the trees around the church, the chirping of the invisible birds. There was no other sound but the hum of the Pacific Highway, a kilometre away up the hill. No foot traffic, no cars, nothing to take his mind off the girl and the Lexus and the heavy-looking bag. After ten minutes, his phone rang.

'Jesus, you took your time.'

'Yeah, well, I had to get back to the … my table. I was in the loo. But it works! The phone's in Mornay Street in Killara.'

'Still? Or has it moved?'

'Oh yeah, look at that, I can see it moving. It's turned right into … er … oh it's just jumped. It's turning onto the Pacific Highway.'

Murdoch used his free hand to start the Golf and pull out onto the street, back the way he'd come. If there was a quicker way to the highway, he didn't know it.

'Bill?'

'Are they going north or south on the highway?'

'South, towards the city. Bill?'

'Call me if that changes. Keep your eye on that screen.'

'Bill, who's got my phone?'

Murdoch dumped the call and accelerated the Golf up the silent street, driving the white line in the middle of the road, telling himself to slow down but refusing to listen, pushing through seventy, eighty clicks an hour. The traffic on the Pacific Highway forced him below the speed limit, but he was in sight of the CBD when Davie phoned again.

'Davie?'

'Bill, who's got my phone? Tell me it's not the skinhead girl with the big gun and the nasty friend. Tell me that.'

'Where is it now?'

'Bill!'

'It's the skinhead girl with the big gun and the nasty friend. But she doesn't know – it's stuck under her car. So you keep telling me where it is and I'll get it back before they find it.'

There was a smarting silence on the other end of the line. Little Davie didn't like playing detectives any more.

'Davie, where's the phone right now?'

'The bridge, the CBD end of the bridge.' Each syllable taut with restraint. 'She's turning left now; she must have taken the Cahill Expressway.'

'Fine. Send me a text message with the address when she stops.'

Like he didn't know where they were going. Like this wasn't confirmation of something too good to be true. When Davie sent him the text he took the long way round, parking outside number 42 like he always used to. Just far enough away to get a good look at who was coming and going, who else might be watching. The Lexus sat illegally parked at the bottom of the Club's steps. The girl with the shaven head didn't like to walk too far.

Macquarie Street was busy, hordes of workers returning to work after an hour of freedom in the Botanic Gardens, groups of them grabbing a late lunch at the pavement cafés, runners picking paths in the crowds. Murdoch walked between the parked cars and the traffic like he was waiting to cross. Not fast, not slow, just the same pace as the suits. Twenty metres away he saw the girl was still with the car, leaning back on its bonnet and talking to someone standing on the steps. Of course, she was just a driver. It was whoever she'd picked up in Killara who didn't like to walk too far. As Murdoch watched, the man on the steps – young and ginger in a good suit – stepped down and took her car keys from her hand, twirled them on his finger and made her laugh.

She turned heads this one: not the kind of girl you normally saw on Macquarie Street; he was surprised the Club stood for it. Arriving at the back of the Lexus, Murdoch looked at his own keys and dropped them. Squatted down like he wanted to pick them up, reached in and ripped Davie's phone harshly off the inside back wheel arch. The whole thing came away in one go, flailing tape and all, and Murdoch remembered a bloke he'd seen on the telly, pulling a crab from the ocean. As he stood again, the skinhead girl stopped laughing. 'Piss off, will ya?' she said to the pale guy holding her keys, and walked past him up the steps and into the Club building. Which left the young guy standing there, open-mouthed, staring at Murdoch over the roof of the Lexus. He still looked too young, still looked like Murdoch at that same age, so many freckles they joined one another.

'You,' said Chaplin. 'Fucking hell, it's you.'

36.

Davie was cold. His window seat in the café had been taken by three plump mothers comparing babies and, to call Murdoch back, he'd had to open his laptop on an outside table. The girl who worked there hated him now and let him sit through the lunch rush unattended; at least he didn't have to drink any more coffee. Ignoring the giggles of three gingham schoolgirls at the bus stop, he sat refreshing his screen, confirming the blue flashing dot was still in Macquarie Street, cursing Murdoch under his breath and wondering why he'd left the house without a jacket. Twenty more cars and he'd go. But the traffic on Malama Avenue had thinned to nothing and, when a bus took away the schoolgirls, a near silence descended. It was broken only by the plinking of a pelican crossing down the road. The only movement in sight was a man progressing slowly up Yalta Road.

The thick-legged postman was about to open the gate to number 124 when Davie reached across him and got it first.

'Oh, sorry, dude, didn't see you there.'

The postman looked at himself, broad in orange safety wear, and looked up again, as if Davie was trying to be funny.

'The wife's always saying I shouldn't read and walk at the same time.' Davie brandished his newspaper. 'You got anything for us?'

The postman said nothing, pulled some envelopes from the pile in his hand and held them out like a challenge.

Davie couldn't face the T-junction café for a third time. Once the postman was out of sight, he walked back that way but then hurried past at the last minute: a busy man who had somewhere better to be. He walked around the block, then back over Malama Avenue. Bill wouldn't like it, but then Bill wasn't here, so he sat in his car looking through the various addressees on the envelopes: Rose Brown; Lachlan Heydos; John Cable. He listened to the quiet, watched the first leaves fall from the trees, realised he was hungry. It was less than twenty minutes before someone pulled up outside the neighbouring house at 120 Yalta Road: a pretty girl with long red hair. Davie waited until she was through her gate before he ran over.

'Hi, excuse me?'

The girl turned cautiously.

'Yes?'

'Is this where Rose and John live? I know it's one of these houses …'

'Not here.'

'Pretty girl with a shaved head?'

The girl was more relaxed now she'd got a good look at him. She rested on one hip and held his eye.

'Yes, I know who they are. But they don't live here; they're at 124. At least, Rose is, no one called John.'

'Did I say John? John's his brother, my mate. I meant Lachlan, sorry. 124, is it?'

She smiled sweetly, said she'd never heard him called Lachlan before. 'We all call him Lachie. I didn't know he had a brother.'

'Well, just goes to show. You think you know people.'

'You staying with them? Going to be round here much?'

'Maybe. Seems like a nice place, friendly locals and all. Not sure whether Lachie would be happy about it, though.'

'You never know,' she said, a twinkle in her eye. 'Let's ask him now.'

He turned to follow her gaze and saw the man in the sling fifty metres down the road, approaching fast, his good arm around the shoulders of a girl. Davie gasped when he saw her, shocked by how grown-up she looked.

Murdoch and Chaplin stared at each other for a long and empty second, the eye of a perfect storm. The city, the violence, the drugs, the money, the suits who knew nothing but funded it all; everything swirled noisily around them while Murdoch thought he should have killed Chaplin when he'd had the chance. Of course, the kid would end up working for the Club – what else was going to happen to him? His clothes had improved, the suit he was wearing actually fit him, but his skin was no better. Nor was the ugly scowl that creased his face as he pulled a phone from his pocket, a gun in a duel, and started punching at the numbers. Murdoch turned and ran, not waiting for a gap in the traffic this time, brakes squealing below frightened faces. He was at the Golf in seconds, had left it unlocked in case the unthinkable happened, and, in a moment, was inside, motor on, car swung into the flow so fast that Chaplin wasn't yet inside the Lexus as he passed.

Murdoch yelled at himself in fury. This was what happened when you were soft on people: this was what you deserved when you broke the rules. The traffic in front of him slowed and twenty metres ahead, he saw the lights near the park turn red, the cars between him and them drawing closer to each other, the other lane also full. He reached down to the handbrake and pulled the steering wheel hard to the right: the move so easy in the movies and so much fun in a stolen car and a car park. It worked well enough now, no fun at all, the scream of the tyres punctuated only by his rear end slamming into the car that until a second ago had been in front of him. Anyone who hadn't seen him had heard him and the whole street turned to stare.

Now he was the storm – he and the Lexus the whirl of violence as Chaplin, in turn, swung the black car into the traffic and Murdoch only just managed to veer around its huge front. In his rear-view mirror, he saw he had some advantage now, the Lexus too long to turn in one go and Chaplin slamming into cars on either side of the street as he forced it round the right way. But Murdoch had gained only thirty metres and no other car was going to pull into that gap. He revved the Golf furiously north, pedestrians on both pavements staring like they were at the Grand Prix, cars in the opposite lane slowing for a look.

The only thing ahead of him was another set of red lights, traffic streaming across the road in both directions. He slowed and edged his way into it, incredulous drivers braking suddenly and rear-ending each other, a blast of horns contributing to the storm, until suddenly he was beyond them and, sharp right, down the ramp to the Eastern Distributor. His mind raced through the options. Airport, motorway, underpass. He pulled into the traffic on the Distributor and was sucked into the huge tunnel beneath the Botanic Gardens, one eye on a chance to jump between lanes, the other on the mirror in case maybe the Lexus hadn't made it through the lights.

It swung in behind him, Chaplin veering into the traffic so suddenly his scrawny silhouette swayed inside the massive car, no more than twenty metres behind the Golf. Murdoch squeezed into a gap in the left-hand lane – more horns – now nine, now ten cars ahead of the Lexus. The Golf was shorter: he had to use that advantage. He swung it right again, into the middle lane, jumped again and had fifty metres of clear tarmac ahead of him. The more dangerously he drove, the more the traffic behind him would slow, and so he shifted lanes twice more. It began to work, Chaplin slipping maybe fifteen or twenty cars back. But he wasn't giving up and the Lexus's headlights flashed in Murdoch's mirror as Chaplin bullied one car after another out of the way. The lanes split and Murdoch pulled up out of the tunnel, only realising his mistake when another set of lights came into view. They were green and he thanked God and watched them turn orange, only four cars between them and him. The first three piled through, but the car in front of Murdoch – a green Fiesta, white hair at the wheel – braked in blind innocence of the trouble behind. Murdoch swerved late onto the pavement around the Fiesta and the lights themselves and out onto the junction with the perpendicular highway. Cars had already started driving through the traffic lights to the left and right of him and they screamed to a halt, more horns and curses chasing him out of the city. He accelerated on through, laughing at his luck, slapping his hands on the steering wheel. There was no way Chaplin could get through. He forced himself to slow down, to concentrate on the new ramp he was driving down, merging back onto the Distributor he should never have left, three lanes of thick traffic heading to the airport. He was still laughing aloud when he heard the siren that had followed him down the ramp, a copper who must have seen him jump the last light. He was at least twenty cars ahead of it, but every one of those cars evaporated in the path of the blue flashing light.

'Sorry,' he said, the sound of his own voice surprising him.

Like he'd learned nothing from what was happening, like he was growing soft to spite himself. He looked ahead, along the middle lane of cars to his left. It wasn't travelling that much slower than him, a thousand commuters desperate to be home, even those who'd noticed the drama racing up beside them refusing to slow down. He chose a Volvo, now fifteen, now ten cars ahead, navy blue, with an empty inside lane beyond it. He slowed slightly, let the Golf drift to the right then pulled hard left on the wheel, the grille ploughing directly into the back half of the other car's side-panelling. The Volvo span so fast its headlight smashed into Murdoch's tail light, a blur of blue metal beside him, left spinning behind as he passed through its arc and into the empty inside lane. Murdoch steered hard to the right and bounced the left-hand doors of the Golf off the protection barrier beside the road, the air thick with the smell and sound of his tyres. Within seconds he was straight again, moving fast up the inside lane.

He knew the Volvo would have spun again and maybe turned onto its roof. He knew the cars behind it would have been unable to brake in time. He didn't let himself think there might have been kids on board. He just shifted lanes again, pushing stubbornly into the traffic that had slowed to see what had happened back there. Only now did he check his mirror to confirm he had closed all three lanes, the Volvo still upright, but it and two other cars facing the wrong way, no direct sight of the blue flashing light. He started to say sorry again, but bit the word off before it could leave his mouth. The rule said you do what you have to do – why was that so fucking difficult to remember these days?

37.

Murdoch took fifteen photos of the Golf before he left it in a dirty suburb beside the airport. The next car he found would have to look like what he'd bought. The one he left behind was beaten into ugly angles: the left-hand doors bent inwards, dark blue scratches across the grille, tyres knocked out of symmetry. Yet another thing he'd taken and ruined. He didn't have time to wipe it down properly, but he cleared out anything which might identify him or Davie. Credit card receipts, addressed envelopes, the small matter of Davie's iPhone. The licence plates he left, the camera in the police car would have captured those, they were no use to him now. His only hope was that no one in Montauban had ever noticed his registration. He thought about Natalie Conquest, staring up the driveway at him all those times and wondered what kind of a hope that was. 'There's only two types of hope,' Maria used to say, 'Bob Hope and No Hope'.

He found a main road lined with shops, the pungent doorways of cheap curry houses reminding him he hadn't eaten all day. He was cold and tired, wanted nothing more than to crawl in somewhere easy and feed himself, but he trudged on until he found a chemist. He bought a blood-pressure pump, then found a dry-cleaners where he begged a wire coat hanger, too tired to make up a reason why. There was a newsagent a little further on, but he wouldn't allow himself cigarettes until later. It was time to be strict with himself, exist solely to get things done. His last purchase was a woolly hat from a Salvation Army store: it hid the stitches and made him look like just another down-and-out in this down-and-out part of town.

It was bright enough when he left the Salvos, only a few cars on the main road with their headlights on, but it was getting colder by the minute. By the time he found the car he needed, he was shivering, rubbing his sleeveless arms like he needed a fix, swearing at himself for not getting a jumper or a jacket when he bought the hat. It wasn't the first silver Golf he found – he'd chosen a common enough car in the first place – but it was the first one that both compared well with the photos on his phone and was on the right kind of street. Half an hour after dark he came back to it. He slid the sleeve of the blood-pressure pump between the driver's door and its frame, pumped it full of air until the two creaked apart, then reached in with the wire coat hanger and unlocked the door. There'd be a more modern way of doing this now, he thought, something to cope with alarms on cars newer than this one. But maybe it was appropriate to be so old-fashioned. Like he was falling backwards through his life: violence, housebreaking, nicking cars he didn't want. Making people hate him again when, in the last few months, he'd got used to something different.

The pub was old-fashioned too, from the days when pubs had carpets, with a ceiling still yellow from when you could smoke. Three guys sat at the bar not talking, taking turns to sip at the schooners in front of them. Two of them had cuts on their faces and the other one looked like he'd supplied them. Murdoch bought four pies and a Coke and took them to a corner table, relaxing only when he looked around and realised he wasn't the most desperate-looking bloke in the place. An old girl came around trying to raise money to feed the cigarette machine or the pokies or maybe even her kids, it wasn't clear, but Murdoch just scowled at her and she shuffled on. Halfway through his second pie, his hands started shaking badly and he spilled hot meat down the front of himself. He held onto the table in front of him, wobbling his Coke till it spilled too, then took some deep breaths and closed his eyes. When he opened them again, suddenly remembering where he was, there was no one looking at him. At nine o'clock Davie called.

'Did you get my phone?'

'Yes, mate, I've got it.'

'Well, I want it back. I'm going to get rid of it myself, thank you very much.'

Davie's rhythm was wrong. He was talking tough, trying to keep a frown in his voice, but, underneath that, he was obviously excited about something. Murdoch asked him if they could speak in the morning, he was kind of in the middle of something right now. He figured if he could sit quietly for a few hours he'd be all right soon enough: he just needed some peace and some food.

'Aw, come on.' said Davie, disappointed. 'Don't you want to know if anyone else came out of 124 Yalta Road?'

Murdoch was too tired to resist. There was a tremor coming up his legs, threatening his gut and making it difficult to think. The yellow light of the pub was fading slightly. He asked Davie what he'd seen.

'Well, first of all nothing, right. Dead boring apart from watching you chase my phone all over the city. Man, you were really bombing it down the Distributor there, you're lucky you didn't have an accident.'

Murdoch let him rattle on, his voice strangely comforting in this wrong part of town, a reminder Montauban was still there.

'Anyway, I was staring at my screen so hard I nearly missed the bloke coming out of 124. It was the same guy who was up at the big house! He had his arm in a sling, but I could tell it was him, same build, same walk, you know? Anyhow, he comes out, turns down the street and disappears. So guess what I did?'

Murdoch let go of the table and pinched the bridge of his nose. A headache had arrived, so intense it couldn't last.

'So then the postie comes along. I can see him coming down the street from the far end, pushing one of those handheld trollies in the garish colours, right. So I pay at the café, yeah? Because I notice you didn't offer. And I wait for just the right moment and I time it perfectly ...'

One of the men at the bar belched loudly and called across to the tired barmaid. She rolled her eyes, leaned down and reached beneath the bar. Immediately, the pub shook with music: coarse drums and a growling guitar distorted by ancient speakers. She reached down again and it grew quieter, the quality of the speakers no better. Maybe Murdoch fainted or fell into a microsleep, there was some kind of gap in his consciousness, but when he came to again, Davie was still talking.

'... so I tell her it's a surprise and she mustn't spoil it and I run off before they can see me.'

'Brilliant, Davie. Well done. Now listen, I've got to go.'

'No, no, you've not heard the best bit! You'll love this.'

'Davie, I'm really tired. I'm probably lost and I just want to sit quietly, know what I mean?'

'Hey, I can turn on my computer and tell you where you are if you want?'

Murdoch sunk his chin to his chest. The contents of the second pie were still there, congealing at the end of a trail of stains. He picked off the biggest piece and ate it. Tuned slowly into Davie again.

'... amazing. So guess who she is?'

'Who who is?'

'The girl with the man from the big house. The man we now know as Lachlan Heydos. He turns up with his arm around her. Guess who she is?'

'I give up.'

'Alycia Thornton! She's not up in Queensland on a school trip at all, she's down here, all cuddled up to our friend with the guns.'

38

Murdoch was at the bottom of a pit, or at least he thought he was. The bottom of a pit wrapped in a rope, tied up in the dark. Then he was walking, dragging the rope behind him as he limped after Georgie Walker, unable to catch up with her. It was dark, but when Georgie turned suddenly, shadow on shadow, the face he saw was Alycia Thornton's. 'Bill,' Alycia said, waving a gun in his face and tugging on the rope now that he wanted to get away. 'You have to wake up, Bill.' Her voice grew louder and deeper, pulling him to wakefulness, the rope now a sheet twisted around his legs. Then his door opened fully, light filled the bedroom, and Davie's words were real and the nightmare left behind.

'Dude, you've got to wake up. It's Natalie. She says she's here on official business. She said to wake you up.'

It was close to midnight, barely an hour after Murdoch had got to bed. He took his time getting his clothes on, telling himself he was fine. Took slow breaths and checked his heartbeat. You could be the best liar in the world, a confidence guy with no record to his name, but someone who knows what they're doing will pick up on your breathing. Or your pupils – but what was he supposed to do, slip on a pair of sunglasses?

He found her in the living room in her work clothes: a black suit and ugly shoes. She turned when she heard him come out of the bedroom – no sign of Davie anywhere – and he remembered how much he liked her eyes when she was scowling.

'Sit down, Bill. I need to ask you a few questions.'

He dropped into the sofa. Compliance first, ignorance second, denial third, fourth and fifth.

''Listen,' he said, 'about the other morning—'

'I'm not here about the other morning, Bill. I'm here because I picked up a report of a PolAcc in Sydney this afternoon. Two city boys chasing a silver Volkswagen Golf, pursuing a known drug dealer by the name of William Murdoch. Thought you might like to talk to me about it?'

'Not me,' he said. 'Definitely not me. I'm presuming he got away, else you wouldn't even be here?'

'Where were you this afternoon?'

'He was with me.'

Davie had been hiding around the corner in the kitchen. Now he stood smiling stupidly with a steaming cup in each hand. Natalie looked at Murdoch, who managed not to stare at Davie.

'I was with Davie,' he said.

'Where? Here?'

'No,' said Davie. 'We went fishing. Why are you asking?'

'Davie!' Natalie, annoyed now. 'Go into your bedroom or something. I need to talk to Bill alone.'

'But we were out fishing all day on Charlie Tamworth's boat. I can prove it. Then we came back here and—'

'Davie, for God's sake!'

Davie did his dumb-boy shrug. He handed them each a coffee and disappeared into his bedroom, like he hadn't a clue what he done wrong, but still knew he deserved sending to bed.

'Bill ...'

Murdoch stood, one hand up to silence her. 'Not here,' he whispered. 'I can tell you what it's about, but not in here.'

He took her outside, down the creaking stairs to the driveway. Like he was trying to get out of Davie's earshot; like it was coincidence he ended up sitting on the bonnet of his clearly undamaged car. If she'd ever taken note of the original Golf's registration plate, he was lost anyway.

'Listen,' he said, lighting a cigarette. 'You remember I was beaten up a few days ago? Remember you couldn't believe it could happen around here?' *Use everything that's true,* said the rule, *use reality to enhance the lie.* 'I told you I didn't know what it was about, but I wasn't being straight up. There are bad people out there who I've crossed, Nat – crossed badly. They need to get me into trouble, need to get me inside. They know what I drive; it's simple enough for them to stage something down in the city and then tell the cops it was me. So this is the truth: Davie and I were out yesterday on his mate's boat. I am not a drug dealer; I am not known to the police. But whoever the police are looking for, it probably is me, if you see what I mean?'

'Right.' She looked doubtful, like she was struggling to understand the implications of this new information. 'And what did you catch?'

'What?'

'What fish did you catch?'

'Oh, nothing. Waste of bleeding time. Burned my neck though, look.'

She didn't look. Instead she took the cigarette from between his fingers, sucked on it and blew smoke into the black air between them. She asked him how Charlie was.

'Who?'

'The guy who owns the boat.'

'He wasn't there.' A blind guess. 'It was just me and Davie.'

The easiest lies are always the ones people want to believe. Murdoch watched Natalie's shoulders drop, watched her take a deep breath like something that had been worrying her had passed.

'Listen, Nat, about the other morning. I'm really sorry.'

She frowned and gave the cigarette back to him. 'This has got nothing to do with the other morning, Bill. Nor the night before. Nothing has, you understand?'

'All the same, I'm sorry. I mean, maybe we could … Oh fuck it, now I look dodgy cos I'm being nice to you. Nothing, forget it.'

'Forget what?'

'Us. Let's forget about the idea of us. Not that we were ever an item, but let's leave it alone, eh? You've got to admit, we're hardly suited.'

She looked away, up at the shack, and he thought she was going to run up the stairs and ask Davie the same questions about the fish and the guy who owned the boat. Instead she sighed and gave him a plastic smile, before walking quickly down to the road. In her black clothes, she was invisible for a second until she crossed under the street lamp at the bottom of the driveway. Murdoch called after her and she turned, her hopeful face yellow in the lamplight.

'What?'

'Davie and I are making real progress. On the case, I mean. I think we're going to find out what's happened to Georgie.'

She nodded once and smiled sadly. 'Good. That's good, Bill.'

Then she continued on and was gone.

165

39

Before he went back to bed, Murdoch told Davie they should go and see the boat; he needed to know what it looked like, in case he had to describe it. It was only early the next morning, when he laid eyes on the thing, that he realised this was actually true.

He'd pictured something with sails, pulling on ropes while Davie watched from the wheel, but Charlie Tamworth's boat was made of tin apparently and looked lighter than the dirty motor that clung to its back. They found it on a trailer in the main car park of a place called Matilda Bay, the kind of town that only comes alive at the weekends: holiday homes and sleepy shops curved around a quiet edge of Broadwater. On an early morning Wednesday, it was deserted except for a few dozen hysterical gulls.

Every other boat in the water was similar to what Murdoch had imagined, masts and wrapped sheets bobbing far from the jetty and making him wonder, the same way he always did, how people got onto them without swimming. Today wasn't the day to find out. He and Davie hooked the trailer up to Davie's Excel, then backed it down a ramp into the water until the boat was floating. Murdoch said he'd wondered what those ramps were for and Davie looked at him strangely, like he didn't know whether to believe him or not.

It took a few goes to start the motor, Davie grimacing and growing red each time he pulled on the cord, while Murdoch hung on for dear life, his knuckles white on the side of the boat. Around them, seaweed and diesel floated on the surface of the stinking water. Closer to the legs of the jetty, sad litter bobbed up and down hopefully, like it was trying to get out to dry land. At last the engine caught and Davie whooped over its racket. They moved a couple of metres and it failed again.

'Seen enough?' said Davie, scowling at Murdoch like it was his fault. 'Can we go back now?'

Murdoch shook his head tightly and Davie sighed and rolled his eyes. He reached down among the empty buckets on the floor and fished out a life jacket, threw it at Murdoch saying he bet he couldn't swim either, and started the motor again.

As they putt-putted slowly away from the shore, then turned towards the open ocean, Murdoch watched the water change colour. Dirty brown in the bay, it was soon green and clear, after that deep and dark. The land was quickly a long way away.

'Where do you want to go then?' said Davie, still sulking.

'How about up to the headland south of Montie? We could have another look at the big house.'

Murdoch wasn't expecting the jolt that came with the roar of the engine. He nearly lost his grip, flailed for a second, and opened his eyes to find Davie laughing at him.

'You're scared, Bill.'

'I'm fine.'

'You ever been in a boat before?'

Murdoch shook his head again and closed his eyes, telling himself to enjoy the salt water in his face. One day soon, if he got this right, he would be on the deck of his yacht. Then he'd learn to swim.

After a while he watched the land drifting past: blocks of green woodland and yellow beach, brown rock and blue water: everything strange from this new angle. The events of the previous day were a dimly lit dream. Davie turned, hair blown across his face, and shouted over his shoulder.

'So what's your take on Alycia then? I can't figure it out.'

'Coincidence?'

'No way. What if she and Georgie used to go up to the house together? Maybe they were being paid to do something?'

Murdoch pretended to think about it. He had to raise his voice twice before Davie could hear him.

'Hookers, you mean? Alycia maybe, but it doesn't fit with what everyone says about Georgie. Is that the headland up there?'

It was more prominent from this side, its southern edge longer and steeper. No trees here – just bare cliffs falling to the sea, a mess of rocks in the breaking waves. No gaps in the rock face either, no hint of how to get down. They motored on, Davie taking the boat wide, saying he didn't know this part of the coast so well, maybe they should head back; no one ever came fishing up here.

'Why not?'

'Dunno. No fish, I guess.'

It was another five minutes before they saw the house. It was even more impressive from the water, a fortress commanding all it could see.

Murdoch studied the cliffs below it, the end of the headland visible only from this angle. Davie cut the motor and they sat there squinting through their sunglasses, the current slowly changing their view. Davie saw it first.

'Hey, check out that little bay – it looks like a smugglers' cove. Looks like it should have a tunnel up to a castle or something.'

It didn't have that, but even from here Murdoch could see it had what he'd guessed it would have: a path, first cut into the rock, then visible in patches as it passed through the treeline. He asked if they could get in any closer.

'Not really.' Davie looked nervous he was going to insist. 'At least not in this thing. If you had a rubber duckie, something flat-bottomed, you could get right up onto the sand, but it's way too risky for us. And anyway, look at that.'

Murdoch turned and thought, at first, Davie was pointing at Montauban. Until then, he'd been concentrating so hard on the cliffs, he'd not realised the little town had come into view. Tucked neatly between the beach and the high wooded ridge, Montie looked like a picture on a postcard, a place you wished you could go. But Davie wasn't pointing at Montauban. He was looking further north, at high-stacked clouds on the horizon.

'Clouds?'

'A storm maybe. Let's go.'

Murdoch shrugged. He'd seen enough.

With the wind behind them, they tore across the waves, but halfway to the entrance to Broadwater, Davie killed the motor again. He gave Murdoch no explanation, just waited until they were steady, then vomited neatly but solidly into the chopping ocean.

'Damn,' he said between wipes of his mouth. 'Every bloody time.'

It wasn't yet eight o'clock when they got back to Montauban, but the morning wanted more from Murdoch. As he and Davie rolled down the hill into town, Tom Walker – school uniform, oversized bag, legs like spaghetti – ran across from the opposite pavement, virtually throwing himself in front of the Excel. Davie braked hard and Murdoch swore violently before winding down his window, swearing again as the winder came off in his hand.

'Hi, Bill!'

'Tom.'

'Can I talk to you?'

'What about?'

Tom looked anxiously over at Davie. 'It's secret.'

Murdoch got out of the car, threw the winder back in on the passenger seat, and watched jealously as the Excel rattled away. He'd caught a chill in the boat, the second in twenty-four hours, and wanted to wrap up warm. To lie on his bed and think about what he'd seen on the headland. Not stand on the pavement under a brooding sky talking to his biggest fan.

'What's up, Tom?'

The kid pressed the back of his hands under his chin and smiled a spangly smile. 'I'm waiting for the bus.'

'Nah, I mean what do you want to talk to me about?'

'Oh. I just wondered if you'd found her yet?'

'Tom, mate, what did I tell you? You shouldn't go hoping for nothing yet. Or nothing ever, actually. And you shouldn't keep asking me every two days.'

Murdoch had raised his voice, but Tom smiled like he'd patted him on the head and told him what a good boy he was. The kid asked if he could help.

'Yeah, mate, you can.' Louder now he couldn't help it. 'You can stop being a pest. Stop asking me how things are going and stop getting me out of cars so I have to walk all the bleeding way home.'

It was a couple of minutes later, after he'd got rid of Tom and was almost at the shops, that his phone buzzed in his pocket. Murdoch fished it out, guilty he'd yelled at the kid on the street and wanting something else to think about. It was a text from Davie:

Don't come home. Police looking for you. Your photo in the papers.

40

The weather Davie had noticed from the boat came ashore at lunchtime, hammering down on the coast with a vengeance. Everyone said it was too violent to last, but they were wrong. It rained all afternoon, darkening the day before nightfall, then raining even harder when the real darkness came.

Shortly after six, a train of football fans arrived at Crosley station. Cheery and loud, singing together and waving their red and green banners, they traipsed along the covered platforms and down the ramps to the street. There, the first of them stopped, looking out at the huge drops exploding on the tarmac and the gutters running full. The crowd backed up behind them, thick as far as the platform, an awkward ripple running through it as Davie, hunched over and hurrying up from the road, pushed through in the opposite direction.

Having found an umbrella in the back of his car, Davie had left the car park protected, he thought, against the rain. But he'd not reckoned with the minefield of watery pavements – his full foot had sunk into a pothole, submerged above the ankle in dirty water. Now, as he pushed through the red and green crowd, his backpack catching on each football fan he passed, his foot squelched irregularly beneath him.

It took him ten minutes to get up to the platform, but at least he could safely say he hadn't been followed. On the drive over, he hadn't been so sure. The early darkness had been a problem: there was no way of telling who was behind the bright headlights in his mirror. But he'd gone twice around every roundabout, taken an hour and a half over a twenty-minute journey.

He found Bill in the filthy waiting room, slouched in the blue light of a graffitied lamp, trying not to look cold. The Englishman's stitches were on full display – the thick thread unruly and puckering the skin near his hairline. He was smoking belligerently, like he'd spent time finding the place on the platform where you were least allowed to do it. Davie sat down opposite him and they watched through the doorless gap as a train arrived three tracks away, filling the platform between them and it with yet more fans, more red and green scarves.

Murdoch nodded towards them. 'S'at all about then?'

His voice was gravel, like he'd had cigarettes for lunch and dinner.

'First game of the season,' Davie told him. 'Someone bought the local club and brought in a few big players. Everyone's wetting themselves about it.'

'Not a fan?'

Davie shrugged. He wasn't in the mood for making small talk about football: he had to do enough of that for work. He pressed his wet foot against the littered floor and watched grey water seep out of the eyelets around his laces.

'Natalie's furious,' he said. 'I've never seen her that angry before, and, dude, trust me, I've seen her angry a lot. She said she could arrest me for aiding and abetting. But get this, what she's really ropeable about is, the reason she came round in the first place last night was so she could arrest you herself. She's blaming you for making her doubt herself, says you've made her look like an idiot. She's got into trouble at work for not reporting your "known whereabouts".'

Bill frowned. 'So it wasn't her what dobbed me in, then?'

'Apparently not.'

'Well, someone did, didn't they?'

'Dude, it could've been anyone. Did you see the paper? It looks like you were caught on a red-light camera. It's clearer of the car than of you really, but you put a silver Golf and the name "Murdoch" together and someone's going to call.'

'Yeah, someone what doesn't like me and knows where I am.'

The crackles of an announcement filled the waiting room around them. A request not to block the ramp, its last words drowned by a squall of rain on the tin roof. Bill asked about the police who'd come to the house. Davie grimaced at the memory.

'Drug squad, they said. The two of them looked like something out of the Channel Seven casting department. The older one was probably an alcoholic; the younger one was polite and about twelve. They kept me there for hours, asked when I'd last seen you and all that. This was after I'd spoken to Nat, so … well, I might have said you forced me to lie about the boat? Sorry.'

Bill didn't seem to be listening. He'd leaned forwards and was staring at his hands. Davie didn't know what else to say, so it was the Englishman, for once, who broke the silence.

'Don't suppose you've got any money you could lend me?'

Davie shrugged the damp bag off his back and held it out until Bill took it cautiously, an expression on his face like he was expecting it to explode.

'What's this?'

'Change of clothes, bathroom stuff, pyjamas. That Sherlock Holmes book you were reading. And six hundred dollars – it's all I could get.'

'Are you nuts, Davie? What if the cops had found you leaving with this?'

'You're welcome. I drove twenty miles out of my way to make sure I wasn't followed.'

The only response to that was smoke from Bill's nose and they sat in silence while Davie asked himself what he'd expected – a medal? He told Bill he didn't have to go.

'There must be some way to get the police to understand you were just trying to find Georgie. Everyone will be so disappointed if you just disappear.'

'Yeah, well, it won't be the first time I've disappointed people.'

'It'll be the first time you've disappointed these people. It's not like …' Davie had promised himself he wouldn't ask. 'I mean, it's not like you're really, well, as bad as the papers are saying. Not unless …?'

Bill stood quickly and crossed to the doorway, flicking his cigarette out across the platform. He spoke as if talking to the rain.

'Davie, mate, that's all right with what you told the cops. But if I promise one day to tell you everything, will you do me a favour? Will you not bad-mouth me to no one what knows me in Montie? Nor let no one else do it neither.'

The question took Davie by surprise. 'Are you on drugs?' he said. 'I wouldn't do that anyway. I'm here, aren't I? You don't need to tell me a thing.'

They were silent for a while, watching the rain lose its strength at last. When Bill spoke again, there was something like a smile in his voice. 'Like you're not curious what this is all about?'

'No, Bill, like I know you'd never tell me.'

The Englishman grunted agreement and Davie found himself smiling. When Bill asked him not to mention anything they had discovered, 'not about the big house neither', he said fine, he'd tell the police nothing more.

'Not just the police, Davie. Them's the least you've got to worry about. I mean no one. Anyone sniffing around your place looking for me, you zip it.'

'Fine. I won't say a word to anyone. Knowing my luck, it would cause me more grief than you anyhow.' Davie realised they were about to say goodbye. 'I suppose there's no point in asking what you're going to do now, where you're going?'

Bill pulled a strange face, like he was trying not to smile. He rubbed his hand over his scalp, scratched his stubble and put a hand up to his stitches. Then, as Davie watched, he walked over to the backpack, lifted it and pulled it over his shoulders. The rain outside was no more than drizzle now, the fans on the opposite platform trudging towards the exit.

'I'm in a bleeding train station,' said Bill. 'I can go where I want, can't I?'

41.

Six days and six nights Murdoch had to wait on the headland. Not bad, considering. Not once he'd got over the electric fear of living in the wild. He'd guessed at fourteen days. At least, he'd hoped it would be no more than that, given that was how long he'd been able to buy supplies for. If he'd known he was going to wait less than a week, he'd have eaten like a king. Bought a six-pack and drunk a beer a day. Instead, he sat in the trees and lived on small portions.

The first two nights were the worst because of the rain. The tent was as easy to put up as the bloke in the shop had promised, but it was a lot less waterproof than he'd said. Every few hours, Murdoch had to bail it out, using his plastic cup to scoop up water that was redder than brown from the leeches he'd pulled off his shins and ankles, leaving the little wounds free-flowing through the night. But even without the rain, Murdoch would have stayed awake.

The previous time he'd been to the headland, when he and Davie had waited on the other side of the big house, Davie had been able to explain what all the night noises were. A wombat snuffling through the undergrowth, possums chattering overhead, birds, bats, lizards, echidnas; all of them harmless, unless you were an insect. 'You should hear koalas mating,' Davie had said, cheerful in the dark, 'sounds like the beast of Hades.' Murdoch didn't know and didn't want to know what the beast of Hades was, and he didn't hear anything at all that loud, but, through the tapping of rain on canvas, he did hear what sounded like snakes, spiders, centipedes. Human footsteps. He missed and envied his little Beretta, tucked safe and warm under Davie's bed. At least, that's where he'd left it. He tried to read his Sherlock Holmes; tried to remember the last time he'd been so scared for so long. Reminded himself he was never going back to that.

On the third day the weather passed, leaving an innocent blue sky behind. Murdoch pulled his sleeping mat out of the tent and dozed in dappled-green sunlight, a million leaves shimmering above him. He allowed himself an hour, then another, then stretched and got up and went to work.

The following days blurred and merged as he planned and practised and perfected how to get his hands on what was rightfully his. Mornings and afternoons, he timed himself walking down the path and back up again, timed himself carrying out his plan and his contingency plans and the back-up plans to the contingency plans. It was time to start obeying all the rules again. He made himself shave every day and, from halfway through the week, even walked down to the little cove he and Davie had seen from the boat to bathe from head to toe. He took his feet off the sandy floor, laid his head back and let the ripples wash over him. Dunked himself and ran out again: cold and clear-minded and fearless.

He explored, remembering how from a distance the headland was nothing but green, as if all the thick canopy across it was a single plant clinging to the rock and protecting everything below. One day he stumbled onto a view of Montauban, not quite as neat as the view from the boat, but beautiful all the same: the lagoon stretching behind the beach like an open invitation. He knew it would be the last time he saw the little town and somehow this affected him more than the idea of what he was planning to do. He studied the view of the town carefully for over an hour, thinking of all the people there, what they thought of him. It reminded him of when he'd studied life going on in the apartments behind his warehouse. Except, now, of course, he had broken in and did know what made people tick.

He went back to the view every day after that. During the bake of the afternoons, as he smoked in the shade and felt the wound on his forehead healing, he stared at the view for hours. He thought of Tom Walker and how the kid would react to the news Murdoch wasn't the hero he'd hoped for. The names anyone in Montauban would call him. Anne Lincoln in the general store; the bartender at the surf club whose name he could never remember. Natalie. He thought about how they had looked at him.

Each evening, in the dying hours of twilight, he lay on his sleeping bag and ate from cans. Watched the trees around him bristle with birds – most of them with names he hadn't yet learned, others he wasn't sure of. Maybe mynas, perhaps parakeets? A gold-arsed thing Davie had once pointed out. He learned their calls and how to spot them in the canopy. How to lie so still they would land around him and peck nervously at his crumbs, heads twitching, aware of their vulnerability but unable to resist the prize. Bush-turkeys scratched their way past and, one morning, there were three birds beside him with ridiculous tails, their voices robotic and unnatural.

From the clifftop, he saw dolphins and, just once, a cruising shadow he took to be a shark. Other than that, the ocean was empty but for the tiny ships on its curving horizon. High overhead, silent planes passed by as irrelevant to him as the stars. After dark, he tried to learn the constellations, but, after those first fearful nights, he couldn't stay awake past sunset, sleeping deep and long and without dreams.

On the seventh night, they came.

42.

In the days after Bill's 'disappearance', Davie avoided the Montie shops almost as much as he avoided Natalie. He wasn't nervous about defending the Englishman's reputation – he'd practised some phrases in front of the mirror – but he didn't want to look like he'd been duped along with the rest of them.

Maybe no one else in town had ever stopped thinking of Davie as anything but the local boy who blew his lucky breaks, but, to a degree, at least in recent weeks, Davie himself had done so. Surprised by the extent of his own bravery, he had allowed himself daydreams of D. Simms, Private Investigator, of lecturing internationally on the small local case that led to all his later successes. Or maybe Simms & Murdoch, a desk each in an office in Sydney, their names in an arc on a smoked-glass window. Now, the naivety of his ambitions embarrassed him.

So he bought his newspaper in Kildare, hid in a café there to read it and watch the rain outside, went out in Montie only to show houses and, as briefly as possible, to open the office and sort through the mail. The only person he couldn't avoid was Brian Blowell.

They'd called him 'Blow-Hole' at school. He'd been short and fat and bad at sports. Later, during those teenage years where everyone in Montie ended up dating for a week or two, Davie had gone out with his sister, Leanne. The family moved away before Davie started singing – the dad was in the army or something – and Blow-Hole and Leanne became vaguely remembered faces on old school photos. Davie hadn't thought of them in years. Then, the day after Bill was in the papers, PC Blowell had been stationed outside Davie's house, one of three police officers watching the place on rotating shifts. Davie had no idea why they were there. In case Murdoch forgot what a policeman was and walked up to the house and let himself in?

Blow-Hole must have done something right because he always got the day shifts. Always got to roll down his window and say good morning to Davie when he left for work; in the afternoons, to comment on how lucky he was being an estate agent, getting home before dark. Davie told himself Blowell wasn't being ironic – at least, not intentionally. Not sneering that, after all the years of teasing, and then the years of watching Davie on TV, here he was, Brian Blowell, in uniform and important, while Davie still lived in his ex-wife's house. No. It was just that Blowell was so small-town minded that he genuinely thought getting home before dark was about as good as life could get.

'Evening,' Blowell said to him on the third day, when he arrived home at a quarter to four. It was the first dry day since Blowell had got there, the first day the constable could haul his soft frame out of his car and sit on the bonnet to enjoy the heat. Davie didn't tell him Murdoch had often sat in the same spot. 'How was work then, Davie? Sell any houses?'

There was still something about him that you wanted to tease. Like he was so stupid he deserved it. Like houses were something you just went out and sold like apples.

'It was boring,' said Davie.

'More boring than sitting outside someone else's house for seven hours?'

'Probably not. Just a bit more difficult.'

'Any gossip?'

Davie was halfway up the stairs by now. He knew full well anyone else would just carry on up and shut the door on Blowell's teeth-grinding friendliness. To remind him he was still Blow-Hole and always would be. But, unfortunately, Davie wasn't anyone else. He turned and leaned on the bannister, the middle steps creaking beneath him. 'No, afraid not. How about you, any gossip yourself?'

'Well, half of Montie's suddenly decided to walk along this street. A few of them asked after you. Anne Lincoln stopped for a chat and said to give her a call. All of them wondered if we'd found him yet, if it was really true, if the papers had got it right.'

Davie asked what Anne Lincoln had had to say – he hadn't faced her yet. Blowell shrugged.

'Not much, which, as far as I remember, is a change. You hear about what happened in the surf club on Sunday? Apparently, Jackson Harper was sounding off about your friend, saying good riddance to nosey bastards and all that. So Anne asks him outright if he'd been the one who called the police. Jackson says, 'I wasn't there, I only heard this.' Jackson says he never called the police on no one in his life. So Anne told him, well, he better sit down and shut up or the favour might not be returned. What do you think that meant?'

There was a gleam in the policeman's eye. The Harpers supplied half the weed this side of Bungaree and everyone knew it. Davie shrugged and then, seeing Blowell ready to start up again, sat down on the creaking steps to listen.

'It's funny you know, I haven't lived here since I was a kid – we're over at Sacramento now – but I reckon everyone I spoke to today, I

177

remember. Or I remember their parents. Makes you feel bloody old when you're talking to some hot girl and you realise you were in the same class as her dad. If it had been the weekend, I reckon some of them would've been tourists having a nosey, but they was all locals and I remember them all. All but two of them. Two blokes turned up just after lunchtime, said they were mates of your friend Murdoch. I was having a pee round the back – hope you don't mind – and I think I surprised them a bit when I came out. Said they were old colleagues of his, hadn't seen him in a while but heard he was living here. Big blokes they were, not exactly friendly looking.'

He stopped and, sheltering his eyes, watched a sea eagle high over the lagoon. Seeing his opportunity, Davie stood suddenly and headed up the stairs. He had the door open before he turned back again. Blowell was in the exact same position: still smiling, squinting patiently from under his hand.

'Why are you telling me this?' said Davie. 'What are you saying?'

The sea eagle was out of sight, but Blowell was still staring after it and the clear air it left over the lagoon. He stayed like that as he spoke.

'There was a bank job over in Crosley. All hands on deck. Me and the boys have been called off this job and hauled over there. I'm finishing in half an hour and then that's it. You can come and go without us boring you.' Now, at last, he turned back, his smile barely different than before. 'You got anywhere you want to stay for a few days?'

'Do I need to?'

'Not necessarily. But contact us if you hear anything. Check before you open the door, maybe.'

And that was it. No further advice, no special number to call to have helicopters over the house in minutes. Just a friendly goodbye and a reminder to call Anne Lincoln.

43.

Murdoch heard them approaching from a distance. Birdsong was loud to him by then; a breeze in dry leaves a riot. There had been the occasional hum of a distant boat, but otherwise traffic was forgotten. In the middle of the night, when two heavy cars laboured up through the woodland on the other side of the big house and rolled across the gravel in front of it, he could almost feel them in the ground.

He'd pitched his tent about hundred metres behind the house, which meant thirty metres below it, the ground falling away fast, the path yet to start hairpinning down the cliffs. Following the rules, he'd planned for the worst, camping out of sight in case anyone came up or down the path without him hearing them. The idea seemed strange now under the rumble of the cars' engines, but it meant he could leave the tent where it stood. He found the small rock he had chosen days before and scrabbled down with it from the ledge where he had slept for almost a week. Halfway to the path, he remembered the boot polish and balaclava.

He went back for them, swearing at himself as he shoved them into his pockets, and was almost back down at the path when the ground below him – not ten feet from where he stood – was flooded with light. The section of the path where he had planned to wait was brighter still: a harsh white light, unnatural, and then gone. He took four steps backwards, dropped the rock and crouched beneath a sharp-leafed bush to wait for the light to come again. When it did, it was in the same position. Not a searchlight then, but a signal. Something quick moved through the undergrowth away from him, but he remained still, covering his eyes with both hands. Even like this he could sense the light flashing regularly on and off, brightening his vision from dark black to light black, filling the end of the headland until at last it must have got an answer.

Murdoch waited for another minute, then lifted his fingers slowly, the night now lit by no more than a small moon, low above the trees. He scrabbled around until he found the rock, pulled the polish and the balaclava from his pockets, then continued on down towards the path again. Plan B. He'd wait at the last curve above the cove, where the path flattened out. There were no trees there, but there was a huge boulder easy enough to climb, flat enough to lie on and survey the path below. He trotted down to it, struggling to make himself move slowly, and found it darker than he remembered, the holes and curves he needed to climb it invisible in the night. He told himself it didn't matter – knowing they were there was enough. When he smashed his knee into the unforgiving sandstone and twisted a wrist finding the position he'd practised, he told himself it could hurt later.

He'd been there for no more than five minutes before voices and footsteps approached from the house above. They grew louder and then muffled again as the switchback in the path faced them across the cliff. At no point could their owners shine a torch down and see him – he'd tried it night after night – but he felt vulnerable all the same: a spider on a wide flat floor. It suddenly occurred to him they might have dogs and he cursed himself for not thinking of that before. Now it was too late: there was no way he could move anywhere but onto the path below them.

He heard a hum from the water, distant, but steadily growing. Then, to his right, lights appeared surprisingly high above the ground, approaching the upper end of the section of path he could see. Patches of air were suddenly bright as the torches turned, one after the other. Beneath them, just shadows at first, then a silhouette, then teeth, as someone cracked a joke and several of them laughed, and Murdoch understood they were head torches. The people wearing them walked mostly with their heads down, careful not to trip, their lights chasing each other across the rocky ground, until there was another joke and the people laughed again and their torches lit the sky.

None of them were wearing boot polish or balaclavas, just random black clothes and a gun across the back, no doubt the same AKs he'd seen last time on Lachlan and Rose in the house. These two now came into view, bickering quietly, so that there were six in total: five men and one woman. Six where he'd hoped for four, all of them with unmasked faces. No luck for Murdoch tonight.

Before the Zodiac arrived at the shore, there was another signal from the house. A confirmation it was safe to approach, perhaps? Maybe a guide on where to point the boat? Or maybe not, as the response was a tiny light on the horizon, a star twinkling in the corner of your eye. Five slow flashes from, what Murdoch guessed, was a container ship. The voices passed below him, reached the sand and stopped, the hum from the dinghy clearer now. Murdoch imagined them peering out to see if they could spot it, shining their torches to guide it in.

He had forgotten the smell of fear on himself, forgotten the horror of waiting. Running and fighting were smoothed by adrenalin: you didn't think until it was over. Waiting felt close to the opposite: the mind focused on bodily functions. Murdoch had counted to a hundred and eighty when he heard the flat-bottomed boat pull into the shore.

New voices, deeper accents, the wake of the dinghy catching up and splashing onto the rocks. At this point in the plan he was supposed to stand up and look down at them, work out how many bags were to be carried, how many trips up the hill, but he couldn't bring himself to do it. Couldn't stand and stare down with no cover when any one of them might look up and pour light onto him. He swore and forced his legs to move, forced himself to do what he had to do, because that was the rule: that was how you survived. His trainers were silent on the rock, but his knees creaked slightly as he raised out of a squat, his stomach growling at full volume.

The scene below him was timeless. Shadows knee-deep in the water were passing heavy things out of the boat – moonlight catching pale features. They could have been holding lanterns, heaving brandy, a masted ship creaking in the background. The bags were standing in a row on the sand, but they were too dark and close to each other to count. Twelve maybe? Then one of the figures in the water turned and the light of his head torch flashed across the beach as he walked over to count them. Boxes, black boxes with handles, not bags. Fourteen of them and, now, four more placed beside those. Then a bottle was passed around, something friendly said, then said again more loudly until it was given up on. Murdoch lay back down on the rock, feeling like a man who had fallen from a great height, unable to move and waiting for pain.

Eighteen boxes, six people: two boxes per journey. One and a half journeys. The rule said to think, think hard and calculate, not guess. The steady hum from the dinghy burst back into noise as it backed itself out of the bay. Eighteen boxes, six people; depends on how many boxes they take each time. They seemed to be having a similar conversation down on the sand. Discussing, deciding, disagreeing. He couldn't hear everything but 'three each' and 'trips' came up to him. More laughter, a loud 'fuck off' in Rose's voice. A breeze came across the ocean and the trees further up the path shivered, the moon now hidden behind them. *Calculate.*

He heard footsteps and voices again, more tread on the steps, more breath in the voices. He raised his head and saw them carrying one box in each hand – all but Lachlan, who had one arm still out of action – moving slowly, some stopping every so often to get their breath. The last one passed and disappeared around the corner, then the voices were above him and there was nothing but the sound of waves against the sharp rocks below.

The temptation to do nothing was difficult to resist. Worse still, the temptation to think he should have brought a boat or should have got a gun – nothing useful. He scrabbled down from the top of the rock and waited behind it, out of view of the path. An owl flew out low from the cliff above him, hovered full of feathers to catch something in the air, then disappeared back into the trees. A minute later, it did it again. Murdoch caught himself watching it, thinking how strange it was to see an owl, unable to think at all about what he was about to do.

Footsteps and voices were coming back down from the house. There were two of them: Rose and Lachlan, their head torches spoiling the dark as they squabbled along the path.

'Because I said so, Rose. Why does everything have to be such a drama?'

'It just doesn't make sense. I don't see the sense of it.'

The other four must have held back, keen to stay out of this one. The first of them – a burly man with a wide-kneed walk – only appeared when Lachlan and Rose were already returning from the beach: one box each this time, twisting out of the burly man's way as they passed. Then the path was empty, a long wait before the next man arrived, an even bigger gap after him. By the time the sixth mule appeared – a soft-chinned man with no neck – the other five had already picked up one or two boxes from the beach, reappeared on the section of the path Murdoch could see, and disappeared up towards the house. Murdoch let the last man pass in the direction of the water. Let him disappear from view, then eventually reappear, the box leaning him to one side as he struggled up the slope with heavy breath, his head torch lighting the rocks beside him more than the path at his feet. When he had taken three steps beyond the boulder, Murdoch stepped out, raised the small rock he had chosen and brought it down with all his force onto the other man's skull.

Now he calculated again. If he caught up too close, the guy in front might say something that needed a response. If he was too far back, they would all be turned and looking when he arrived. If he ran or moved too fast or too slow at any point, he would attract their attention. The only thing to do was whatever the fat man lying at the bottom of the path would have done. Maybe he should go back and ask him. He caught up slowly to the guy ahead so that they came around a huge gum tree and into the garden of the big house with about ten metres between them. Murdoch could see no more than a yellow patch of ground ahead of him. There was no way of knowing who was watching him from the dark – if anyone inside the house was looking out at this unfamiliar mule.

He followed the light of the guy ahead along the side of the building – the side where he had fought with Lachlan Heydos almost two weeks before – around to the gravel driveway, where two muscular black Range Rovers sat silently waiting. The hatch and rear passenger door on the driver's side of one of them was open, its inside light tiny in the night. Someone was bending over into the rear of the car, sorting through the boxes that had been carelessly thrown inside. Murdoch watched as the guy ahead of him added to the pile, then turned and trudged towards the house. Presumably the others had done the same.

'Mate,' said the guy leaning into the car, squinting towards Murdoch as he held up a hand to shield his eyes, 'do us a favour and help me sort these out, will ya? They're gunna fly all over the shop like this. And turn your bloody light off, you're blinding me.'

Murdoch nodded, walked forward and added his boxes to the others in the back of the Range Rover. Then he reached up and turned off his torch. He bent and started sorting the boxes in the same way the leaning man had been doing: pushing them close beside each other so they wouldn't topple when the car took a corner, moving slowly as his eyes adjusted to the weaker light. From where he was standing he couldn't see if the keys were in the ignition or not. He stood and went around to the front of the vehicle. Opened the driver's door and saw them hanging there.

'What you doing?' said the other man, peering over the driver's headrest towards him.

'Look at this,' said Murdoch.

'What?'

'Come and look at this.'

The guy swore, straightened and walked around the open door to the front of the car.

'Hang on,' he said when he got there, 'who the fuck are you?'

Murdoch punched him hard in the throat, stamping on him as soon as he hit the ground. Then he stepped over him as he lay clawing at his neck, gasping for air in curdled breaths, kicking at the ground and sending up sprays of gravel. Counting out loud, Murdoch leaned over – one, one thousand, two, one thousand – and closed the car's back door; then – five, one thousand, six, one thousand – he lowered the hatch closed too. Still counting in slow seconds, he straddled the man on the ground and wrestled the sub-machine gun from his back. There was a yell from the house. Murdoch leaned on the bonnet, took off the safety catch and poured two rounds into the side of the other vehicle. Its engine started screaming out steam and the whole thing tilted slowly towards him. The round of fire was echoed within the minute by a rapid pounding from the house. But by then – fifty-three, one thousand, fifty-four, one thousand – Murdoch and the Range Rover were at the top of the track leading down to the road. The rear windows blew out behind him, beads of glass rattling into the back of the driver's seat and headrest, clattering against the inside of the windscreen. Harmless noises until he felt the pain in his arm, the damp growing beneath his sleeve. Seventy-eight, one thousand, seventy-nine, one thousand. He bumped down the track just as he had with Davie, the lights of the Range Rover making ghouls of the trees, a potential marksman around every corner waiting to fire into the windscreen.

The trees were thick here, the moon meaningless and forgotten, Murdoch the only noise and light in the world. If they shot at the car now, it would be over quickly. But the shot never came and, for a second, he was tempted to believe this whole thing might work. He hit the side of his head with the palm of his hand, swearing at himself not to relax, not to let the universe trick him into thinking he'd got away with a thing. The scrub grew thinner and he pulled over, took the keys with him and pulled glass from his arm as he walked the last hundred metres to the bottom of the track, his head torch bright above him again. They wouldn't have given up – they would be running down after him in fear of their own lives. He had four minutes, maybe five. Around the last corner he found a third Range Rover, identically black, its driver out with his gun ready, uncertain how to react to what he was hearing through his earpiece.

'Again!' he was yelling at it, pushing it closer into his head. 'Say that again?'

Murdoch signalled to him. 'Come on,' he said. 'We've got him. Bring the others.'

He turned and walked back around the turn in the track, the lookout running and catching him in seconds.

'What others?' he said. 'Who the fuck are you?'

Murdoch used the butt of the Kalashnikov on him, hoping vaguely he hadn't killed him. He ran back down to the lookout vehicle, but found it locked. Ran back to the lookout himself, who lay still but breathing. The keys were in his pocket. Murdoch threw them into the dark scrub – ninety-nine, one thousand, one hundred, one thousand – climbed back into the car he'd taken and bumped the last one hundred metres down to the road.

There were voices somewhere up the hill behind him, then a burst of gunfire. But it was distant – soft pops in the night, a long shot. He turned onto the road and drove down the way he'd driven with Davie, towards a car he'd taken the week before and parked carefully out of sight. An hour later he was on the freeway, a greater fortune in his possession than even he had ever dreamed of. Heading steadily north to cities where nobody knew him.

44.

Davie bought a lock and spent an afternoon fitting it to the front door, the sun warm on the little platform at the top of the stairs. When he'd finished, it looked like a child had done it – the screws wouldn't go all the way in and he'd splintered the edge of the doorframe – but it held. The rest of the house looked less secure. He remembered Murdoch's concern when he'd first arrived, his sudden anger one day when he'd realised there was no lock on the door.

That night, Davie phoned Natalie, leaving three voicemails until she called back full of concern, then seemingly disappointed when he told her what was so urgent. She told him she was busy on a case in Crosley, told him not to worry if he'd not done anything else wrong. She didn't tell him to stop being such a baby, but he could hear she wanted to. Then, just before bed, he took a call from Hannah – never a pleasant experience. He reassured her no one had questioned her judgement, nor thought she was implicated,

185

nor suspected she knew of Murdoch's past. The police had questioned her, of course, and she had – she stressed this – told them the truth. The entire call lasted four minutes. After that there was no one else to talk to, no one else who might magically suggest he stay with them for a while.

For the first time in years, he didn't sleep a wink. He heard noises where there was silence, got up every time a car passed along Montagne Road, stared at his ceiling until it softened into light. The next night he stayed in one of the houses he was trying to sell – an empty four-bedder up near Pacifico Road whose owners were overseas. It didn't help. An unfamiliar and empty house had far more opportunities for frightening noises but without the comfort of the fridge or the television. He dragged himself home the following evening and slept for twelve hours. After that, he thought, if they were going to come, whoever they were, then let them. As long as they believed he didn't know where Bill had gone. As long as they didn't torture him to death out of spite.

Thursday lunchtime, Davie bumped into Anne Lincoln in the chip shop. She tore herself away from the grubby television to stand too close to him, tapping him on the chest with a long purple nail for added emphasis.

'You didn't call me. I distinctly told that Blowell boy to ask you to call me.'

'I've been very busy—'

'Well, enough of that, come here.'

She gestured him outside, following him through the ribbon curtain and into the ocean breeze. They'd had less chance of being overheard inside the shop, but Davie didn't feel like contradicting her.

'Listen,' she said in a conspiratorial half-whisper. 'Two blokes were in the shop looking for Bill. Blow-Hole told me that they were at the house too.'

'Yes, he told me.'

'Oh. Well, then.' Anne straightened suddenly, adjusting the handbag hanging from her shoulder, as if Davie had made a fool of her. 'Well, I thought you should know. I didn't tell them a thing, of course. They didn't seem the kind of blokes I imagined Bill would want to know. I don't care what the papers say about him; he's just a bit rough around the edges, that's all. I wouldn't believe he was a drug dealer if Jesus told me.'

After that, the day got slowly worse. Davie's regional boss, Jacqui Russell – a gum-chewing sixty-year-old who wore her skirts too short – made a surprise visit to the office. She interrogated him about sales she felt were moving too slowly and then, perched on the desk at eye-level, listened on loudspeaker as he took a call telling him his latest deal had fallen through. Five minutes after leaving, she reappeared to find him phoning the Kildare branch to warn them she was on the way.

He stayed in the office until after eight that night, starting reports he'd told Jacqui were almost finished, working on rentals he hadn't looked at in months. Years before, there had been days like this when he'd planned on calling Jacqui the following morning and telling her what to do with the job. Now he was beyond pretending he'd ever do it. Instead he locked up efficiently and walked slowly home in the dark, imagining the better answers he could have given to Jacqui's questions.

The night was perfectly still, the bush black and silent around him, his footsteps the only sound. It was only when he reached the streetlamp at the bottom of his driveway that he realised it was the first time he'd walked home alone in the dark since he and Murdoch had been attacked. The day had been so bad, he'd forgotten to be afraid – wasn't that great news? Up in the house, he opened a beer and crashed onto the sofa with his suit still on, flicked on the television and found the channel most likely to numb his mind. A film he'd seen before, with adverts every two minutes.

He woke in the cold, but it wasn't the cold that had woken him. He knew something was wrong and then remembered Jacqui and the afternoon he'd had – the opposite of waking from a bad dream. On the television, a bear in a clown suit was dancing to tinny pop music, garish graphics in the background like a headache on the screen. He found the remote control among the spilled chips beside him and muted it, then heard again the noise that had woken him. There was something in the grass behind the house, outside the spare room where Bill used to sleep. Davie sat up suddenly, dislodging the beer bottle wedged in his crotch so that it fell to the floor with a clunk. Beer foamed onto the carpet, tinged blue in the light from the television screen.

'It's a possum.'

Davie said it out loud. Repeated it, told himself to listen next for the scratching of claws on the roof. Dragging himself upright, he stepped over the spilled beer and headed for the bathroom. In the dark, he urinated loudly into the water of the toilet to be sure he wasn't missing the bowl, wondering what time it was and why he was so scared. There was another noise, similar to the first but far louder, so close he thought at first it was in the bathroom with him. A scuffle, feet unsteady on the grassy bank outside the wood of the bathroom wall. *It's a possum*, he told himself again. *It's a bloody possum.* But he found himself unwilling to flush the toilet when he'd finished, unwilling to make any noise at all. He crept to the bathroom door and looked across the living room, the flickering television screen the only light, the whole space flashing blue and grey as the pictures changed.

On the coffee table in front of the sofa were the remains of his chip packet, a few magazines and his phone. He started towards it, thinking he'd hear the clatter of the claws soon and all would be fine, but instead he heard another noise. Footsteps on the stairs outside, the creak of the middle five steps. Davie backed into the bathroom again, telling himself he'd locked the front door. He'd been distracted, had wanted nothing but beer and the sofa, but, surely, he'd locked the front door? He was shaking, shivering the bathroom door against him so that it, in turn, worried the loose door frame. *Now*, he said to himself, *walk across and get your phone now. Lock the door on the way.* But there was another creak from outside and he knew whoever it was, was at the top of the stairs. He managed a step out of the bathroom and had managed to push himself twenty centimetres further on, when the front door handle started to turn. Then, as Davie watched, the door slowly opened, the night air creeping into the shack.

'Bleeding hell!' Murdoch slammed the door closed behind him, his other hand over his heart. 'Jesus, Davie, you frightened the fucking life outta me. What you doing creeping around in the dark like that?'

45.

Somewhere north of Crosley they were backburning the forest. Murdoch could smell it, light and bitter in the air buffeting through the car window. When the road climbed out of the autumn shadows he could see smoke low over the trees. He was driving slowly, looking into the fields beside him, surprised he'd not noticed the landscape last time he was here. Beyond the rolling pasture, the land fell away, dim woodland around hidden creeks. It would have been safer to steal another car, just one more in a long list, but he'd found himself reluctant to do it. Reluctant too to ask Davie if he could borrow his Hyundai, thinking Davie's refusal would embarrass them both. But Davie had said yes immediately – he'd do anything he could to help.

'I thought you were gone for good,' he'd said late the night before, both of them too wired to sleep. 'I was beginning to think what Natalie had said was true. That you were just a crook on the run from the mob, taking us all for a ride.'

Murdoch had replied quickly, adrenalin still coursing through his veins, the arguments in his head so overplayed that the words tumbled out with no thought for how much Davie did or didn't know. 'Well, if I'd done a runner, she'd of been right, wouldn't she? I'd of still been a crook, no better than the animals. But I'm here, aren't I? Risking my neck for people what I don't owe nothing to. Show me a crook who'd ever do that!'

The vehemence of his words had stunned Davie into silence.

In the early hours, they moved Murdoch into the house near Pacifico Road where Davie had slept earlier in the week. Two journeys of food and candles and everything from Murdoch's room. Clothes, four books of Sherlock Holmes, an old portable CD player and a mix of CDs. Murdoch had even retrieved his Beretta from under Davie's bed, Davie looking on wide-eyed. Reviewing at it all, piled in the corner of an empty bedroom, Murdoch decided that next time he went north – all the way this time, to turn his buried treasure into money – he'd burn everything he'd ever owned. Davie, clearly enjoying himself, said he'd tell the police he'd thrown it all out in anger. It was late when they started and by the time they finished, mist was rising off the lagoon, mingling with early birdsong.

Six hours later, Murdoch found the car park outside Saint Cecilia's Grammar School for Girls busier than the last time he'd had been there: every space taken so he had to park on the verge at the top of the long driveway. The netball courts were deserted, but, on the fields below them, a crowd of adults stretched thin along two sides of a soccer game. Their shouts carried up on the breeze – angry or encouraging, it was impossible to tell.

Murdoch was halfway across the car park when a sharp alarm sounded. He ducked instinctively, then watched through the windows of an old Holden as the school emptied girls onto the pathways and playgrounds.

They shouted and laughed, formed pairs and gathered in huddles to speak about one another. Murdoch realised slowly how he must look. He forced himself upright again and pressed on towards the main building. Unlike the last time he'd been at the school, today someone was behind the reception desk: a thin-lipped woman with powdery skin, who smiled sweetly and asked if she could help.

'Mr Smith for Troy McLaren. He's expecting me.'

'Of course.'

She stood and smoothed her skirt, then disappeared silently down the corridor towards McLaren's office. McLaren appeared less than thirty seconds later. Murdoch had forgotten how young he was, the pale eyes, the blond beard: an image from a religious book they'd used at Cookham Wood.

'Mr Smith, let's go outside.'

'I thought we could sit in your office?'

But McLaren had put his arm through Murdoch's, like he'd spent too much time in the company of schoolgirls, and was pulling on it firmly. 'No, Mr Smith, it'll be safer out here. The receptionist said you wanted to see me?'

'What's the rush, McLaren, where are we going?'

McLaren, still pulling firmly, dropped to a whisper. 'The receptionist told me that Bill Murdoch, the one the police are after, was standing in our reception area asking for me. I imagine that same receptionist is now on the phone to the police.'

They were outside the building by now, McLaren guiding him sharp left along a path between squared-off hedges. Murdoch pulled his arm free but followed the teacher closely. They came out beside some tennis courts: three games of doubles behind a wire fence – slow games no one was interested in winning.

'You're not safe here,' said McLaren. 'You really should go.'

'I need to ask you some more questions about Georgie Walker. I reckon I'm close to finding her.'

McLaren looked confused, no sign of the confidence he'd shown the previous time they'd met. 'The police said you'd never had any interest in the case. I'm sorry, I have to admit I didn't question them on that. I assumed—'

'Look, McLaren, last time I was here you said you reckoned I'd done time. Well, bang on, I did. And I've done some pretty nasty shit since then too. But I'm not like that really, I'm not just a crook.'

'No, you're a private detective.'

McLaren said it with a smile, like it was a secret of theirs. Murdoch looked at his feet, tennis balls pockmarking the silence. 'Well, maybe if I solve this I will be.'

Looking up, he found McLaren was smiling still, slowly shaking his head. 'Do you remember I told you, you should be proud of yourself? I remember saying it and you didn't ask why.'

'I knew what you meant.'

'Did you, I wonder? What did you come here to ask me today?'

'It's Alycia Thornton. I need to know how well she got on with Georgie. Were they really good friends? Even at the end, just before Georgie disappeared?'

'Alycia? God, she upset so many girls who thought she was their friend, it's difficult to remember. But, no, I don't think she and Georgie ever fell out. In fact, from memory it was the opposite. They were as thick as thieves. I used to see them whispering in the corridors just the two of them. I remember being slightly worried for Georgie, I think I told you. Alycia could be a bit of a turncoat and not the best influence. We all felt so protective of Georgie, she was so timid; we didn't want her falling in with the wrong crowd. God, I sound like my grandmother. Now, listen, you really should go.'

'Georgie wasn't scared of her, then?'

'What? Scared? Er, I don't think so. I never saw anything to make me think that.'

Murdoch swore and immediately apologised for it. Like McLaren was the mother superior or something. 'What about drugs? Do you reckon either of the girls were doing drugs?'

McLaren seemed to struggle with the idea before giving it serious thought: a man used to defending the school's reputation.

'I don't think so,' he said at last. 'No, nothing much, anyway. Really, Bill, I think you should get going.'

'Last thing before I do. Don't tell the police I was asking about Alycia. If what I think is right, she's in real trouble. There are these people, if they think she's a threat—'

McLaren held up his hand. 'Don't tell me any more. Get going. But, Bill, you can't stay around here and keep out of trouble for long, you know that. If you're going to find out what's happened to Georgie, you need to do it fast.'

That afternoon, Murdoch visited another school. It was further from Montauban than Saint Cecilia's, in more or less the opposite direction. Its buildings were older, Victorian or something, the playgrounds hemmed in by spiked metal fences in case the boys tried to escape. Murdoch parked outside the front, like he was a parent waiting for a Hunter or an Oscar or a Cooper. But when he looked at the real parents parked beside him, good-looking women for the most part, every one of them staring at a phone, he realised Davie's shabby pink Excel stood out too clearly from the Audis, Beamers and Volvos. Waiting at the gates, unshaven, with a huge plaster on his head, he might not stand out any less, but it was better than his only other plan: hiding around a corner halfway to the bus stop.

He was ready for the bell this time, knew to wait through the minute-long pause until the concrete behind the railings was flooded with children, a thousand shoes trampling the faded white lines, a dozen cars coming to life behind him. What he hadn't expected was girls. He'd forgotten schools could be mixed and, for some reason, as he watched pleated gingham dresses run among the grey shorts and jumpers, he found he couldn't help but smile. It was like a school on the telly.

The crowd in the playground thinned quickly, the kids with waiting parents running straight to them, those with a bus to catch heading out the gates and down the street. The bus-stop kids walked in gaggles of three and four, pushing and laughing at each other, some of them gathered around tiny screens. Others, alone, walked faster, and one of these was Tom Walker.

He trudged fast with his head down, passing within metres of Murdoch, mumbling slightly like he was talking to the pavement or arguing with himself about how the day had been. Murdoch crossed the road, busy with four-by-fours pulling out from the kerb, and followed Tom from the far side. He let the kid get a few hundred metres from the school gates, then jogged between cars over the road again, calling Tom's name as he approached. He had no plan for what to do if the kid screamed or called for help.

Tom didn't break from his daydreams until Murdoch was on the pavement beside him. He turned slowly and squinted up, examining Murdoch's face through the week-long beard, recognising him slowly. He pressed the backs of his hands to his face, obviously trying to remember what he was supposed to do.

'Tom, I need to ask you a question. It's about Georgie; it's important.'

Murdoch had expected the wide-eyed fear Tom had shown him on the beach, a tearful collapse to walk quickly away from. Instead he got a distrustful sulk.

'They said you were a bad man.'

'Yeah, I know.'

'Dad said if we ever saw you we should call the police again. He said you never cared about finding Georgie.'

Murdoch knew what Paul Walker thought of him. Davie had said Georgie's father had been angrier than anyone when the police had come looking for him. Walker had shouted down the phone at Hannah, apparently telling her what he thought of her for exposing Tom to a charlatan and a common criminal, at that. Murdoch couldn't blame him. That's how he'd thought himself until recently. That was why he was back, to prove it wasn't true. He squatted down to Tom's eye level.

'Yeah, but we know that's not right, don't we Tom? Cos I'm risking my neck here trying to find her. I could easily of run away. Well, I did run away, but I came back so I could find her. So I can't be that bad.'

A group of kids walking to the bus stop caught up with them, split to pass and merged again further down the pavement. None of them looked back or bent into fervent whispers.

'I never told them,' said Tom. He was grinding his heel into the tarmac of the pavement, trying to be angry still.

'Never told them what, mate?'

'About you pushing that boy off the roof.'

'Right. Well, that's good. Nor anything else?'

'Like what?'

'Yeah, nothing. Listen, Tom, I need you to think hard. I need you to think about Georgie just before she disappeared. Was she different at all? Did she seem a bit dreamy, or sad sometimes and happy sometimes, or did she want to sleep a lot?'

'Do you mean was she on drugs?'

Murdoch laughed until he noticed Tom frowning. He apologised, scratched his beard and said, yes, that's exactly what he meant. Tom shook his floppy hair. No, she wasn't on drugs. They learned about it in school and Georgie said drugs were stupid. She said if Tom ever did them she'd find out and she'd kill him.

'Are you going to go to prison again?'

'Not if I can help it, mate. Now listen, I need to ask you about Alycia.'

'Dad said you were going to prison.'

More kids were arriving from the school – the main crowd now. A few said hello to Tom as they passed, but the kid ignored them, looking up to Murdoch for reassurance. Murdoch had no idea if kids read the papers, if his face had been on the telly.

'Tom, listen. What about Alycia? Did they fight at all?'

'Not really.'

'Not really?'

'I mean, not at all. I think Georgie was scared to.'

Murdoch bit his lip, careful with a calm reaction. They were surrounded by kids now, two boulders in a stream of giggles, shouts and uniforms.

'Scared? How do you know?'

'Well, you know. When Alycia came round, Georgie would pull a face, like she didn't want to see her, but then she'd go downstairs and be really nice to her. Sometimes she'd pretend to not be there when Alycia phoned, but then she'd get really worried if she thought Alycia might find out and she'd phone her straight back. She'd say, "Tom's so stupid, he didn't know I was in." But I did know, it's just she told me to pretend she wasn't. It was like Alycia was something special. She …'

The colour drained from Tom's face. Murdoch twisted on his haunches to follow the kid's open-mouthed stare, through the short crowd passing around them and into the traffic-jam beyond. There, not four metres away, a police car was idling, two bored uniforms in the front. The nearer of the two turned and looked at them, raised his hands and wiggled his fingers at Tom.

Murdoch turned slowly back. 'Tom, they're not here for me, it's OK. Tom. Tom! Look at me.'

Tom turned and frowned at him, tears threatening his eyes. 'I don't want you to go to prison.'

'Well, then, you have to be cool, mate. You have to not let the policeman see you crying. What you doing tomorrow? Tell me about that.'

'It's Saturday.'

'That's right, so what you going to do?'

'We've got to do gardening. We've got to deadhead the roses and prune the red robin we put in after Georgie went away. You have to cut it back to make it grow red again. Then we have to mow the lawn.'

'And do you like gardening?'

The floppy-haired shake again. 'It's boring and it makes you dirty. It sucks.'

'And what about Sunday? What you doing then?'

Murdoch could see the police car had moved on, Tom's relief like a mirror. He asked the kid a few more meaningless questions, checked he'd pulled himself together. 'OK, mate, I'm going to go now.'

'Do you think—?'

Murdoch watched him remembering not to ask. Watched him blush and smile his spangly smile instead. He stood, told Tom he was a good boy, and ruffled his hair, then walked slowly away.

46.

It was weeks before Murdoch understood the value of his two school visits. Two nights after, when he and Davie made their discovery, he worried they had been a waste. Troy McLaren and Tom Walker had, he thought then, told him next to nothing and, in return, he'd let everyone know he was still around. Shown himself in public, when the information he and Davie needed was back in the empty house all the time.

It was a freak weekend of heat and everyone knew it: two thirty-degree days from nowhere, beaches thronged as everyone charged their batteries for winter. Everyone but Murdoch. He hid in the house and sweltered, smoking for hours on the bathroom floor to avoid the smoke-alarms and enjoy the cool of the tiles. McLaren, he knew, had been right: he couldn't stay safe around here for long. It was time to go. So what if he'd failed to find Georgie Walker, hadn't he at least tried? Hadn't he at least proved something to himself? The idea that he'd failed to prove it to many other people curdled in his cigarette smoke. But tough. It was time to go and unbury his treasure, head north properly and turn it into money.

He was fiddling with the portable CD player he'd brought from Sydney, a sick old dog that refused to die, when Davie arrived dressed in tired work clothes, laptop bag in one hand, pizza box in the other.

'You should buy an iPhone,' Davie told him, watching Murdoch struggle to get any sound from the machine. 'You can download music these days.'

Catching the look on Murdoch's face, he retreated into the kitchen.

Their conversation that night was as stale as the pizza. After the week on the headland, then days alone in the empty house, Murdoch was used to his own silence again. He wanted to plan, to decide when and how to disappear for good. Davie wanted to talk about the case. He asked again about Murdoch's conversations with McLaren and Tom, threw around theories of who had done what and why.

'Maybe we should just confront Alycia,' he said, mouth full of pizza, crumbs spraying onto the bare floorboards between them. 'Scare her with what we know about Lachlan Heydos. Threaten to tell her parents.'

'Yeah, mate, great idea. Except, one: I don't get the impression Alycia gives a shit about what her parents do or don't know. Two: since when was a girl ever turned off a bloke just because he's bad? And, three: in case you've forgotten, we do not want Heydos and his mates catching on that we know anything about them. So, basically, brilliant.'

Which at least stopped Davie talking for a minute. Instead, he swallowed his mouthful then stood and picked up the pizza box, ignoring Murdoch's attempt to reach for the last slice. Murdoch watching him fussing around the room, mumbling under his breath like an old woman, stuffing their rubbish into the bin liner he'd brought. Then he tried to get the CD player working. It had grown dark while they were eating, until the only light in the room was a stretched orange oblong from the streetlamp outside. Murdoch watched Davie drag the CD player into the lamplight, heard him press the clunky button to open the lid. Looked at him squatting there so long, head down and silent, that he thought he was going to have to apologise. He couldn't exactly go and buy pizza himself.

'What's this?' Davie was holding up the CD, tilting it in the faint light to read what was written on it. 'Where did you get this from, Bill?'

Murdoch shrugged. 'Dunno, in the pile. What's wrong with it? It might be one of Georgie's.'

Davie handed it over. Its label was a plain bronze circle. Someone had written *Heydos* and a six-figure number on it in thick marker pen.

'What the hell?'

Davie looked at him. 'It's a date. It's the day before Georgie went missing.'

Murdoch cleaned the disc on his jumper, checked it for scratches and tried it again, but still the stereo refused to work, fussy about what it played. He tried another CD from the pile and the empty room echoed to girly pop. Then Davie slapped his head and went to find his laptop bag.

'Maybe it's not music,' he said.

They moved into the back kitchen in case anyone saw the light of the computer screen, but when Davie inserted the disc into the little tray that popped out of the laptop's side, its screen went black again and left them in a darkness so intense they could barely see each other. They waited in silence, the only noise the whirring of the disc drive. After a few seconds, white letters appeared in the bottom left-hand corner of the screen. A sequence of numbers and letters followed by the name *Georgie Heydos* and the same date they'd found written on the disc.

'Georgie Heydos?'

They both said it and, as if it was some magic password, grey lines appeared on the screen, individual and crackling, then merging to form an image. It was difficult to identify at first, like a bad map or maybe an alien on its back. Then Murdoch saw the hands.

'Is that—?'

'It's a scan,' said Davie. 'That's a foetus.'

Davie reached out of the darkness to touch the screen, a gesture Murdoch understood but didn't copy. The half-formed baby ignored them, its tiny heart pumping strangely fast, its huge empty eyes closed in peace.

'Georgie was pregnant,' said Davie.

And, again, they spoke together, the explanation suddenly obvious.

'With Lachlan Heydos's baby.'

47.

The name of the café in Crosley General Hospital was Patience, obviously thought up by someone who'd experienced the service there. Separated from the hospital's reception area by a huge plate of dirty glass, it was little more than a row of moulded seats and tables, half the surfaces uncleared. Apart from Murdoch – hood up, with his back to the reception area – and Davie, the only person in the café was a buck-toothed volunteer at the counter, poking slowly through coins like he'd never seen any before. Murdoch sat staring up at a television hanging from a corner of the ceiling. The news was showing the fallout from a terrorist attack or a riot or an earthquake somewhere – surging crowds lifting stretchers of the injured. It wasn't pleasant viewing, but it was better than checking with Davie every two minutes that no one was near who might recognise him.

'Jesus, he said, 'last bleeding thing you'd want if a bomb fell on you is a thousand people shoving you around on a stretcher.'

Across the table, Davie was fidgeting glumly. He spoke like he hadn't heard what Murdoch had said.

'Man, I hate the smell of these places.'

'What? Burnt coffee?'

No, said Davie, he didn't mean burnt coffee. He meant that distinct smell you got in hospitals. That unique blend of disinfectant and ill-health; you knew with your eyes closed you were surrounded by sick people. 'Just to think that this whole building is full of injury and disease. And all those white coats. Doesn't it give you the creeps?'

Not really. It reminded Murdoch of being in the prison infirmary, nurses who'd sit and talk, even if you didn't need anything. He blinked the memory away.

'What creeps me out, Davie, is half of bleeding Crosley walking past and only one of them needing to spot me. This was a stupid idea, we should go.'

'I told you not to come.'

Murdoch looked back at the television screen, pulling his hood tighter. He wasn't going to sit in that house all day trusting Davie Simms to be subtle.

'What did we agree before we sat down, Bill?'

'Oh great, here we go.'

'What did we agree?'

'About what, mate?'

'You know about what.'

'So, if I know, why do I have to say it?'

'Same reason I had to repeat your plan at the big house like three times.'

'Yeah, and look how that worked out.'

'What did we agree, Bill?'

Murdoch gave him a sour stare. 'We agreed to let you do the talking this time. But if you're going to do it, Davie, why don't you get a move on so I can get out of here?'

'OK.' Davie gave a sudden smile, all disease and disinfectant forgotten as he started manoeuvring himself out from under the plastic table. 'Come on then.'

Head down, Murdoch followed him out of the café and over to the main reception desk. The receptionists, he saw from a few metres away, were changing shifts, a fatter woman taking over from the cute young one who'd refused to help when he'd approached the desk earlier.

The older receptionist wasn't that fat, not by local standards, but she wasn't a good-looking woman. It was like someone had picked her features without checking they matched each other. Her skin, her hair, her teeth – none of it helped. Murdoch noticed his own mood and reminded himself to keep his mouth shut. He stood behind Davie, who was waiting shyly away from the counter until the new receptionist noticed him and beckoned him forward.

'Hi,' he said, hands politely on the counter. 'My name's Davie and I wonder if you can help me?'

The woman behind the counter looked at him closely, then broke into a gappy smile. 'You're him, aren't you?'

'Well, I don't know. What do you mean?'

'You are! You're Davie Wonder, aren't you? Oh my God, I used to love you. I knew you lived up around here somewhere. Get it? "Up around here"?'

Murdoch had no idea why this was funny, but Davie laughed.

'Busted,' he said. 'I didn't think anyone remembered that one any more.'

'Oh you're kidding, of course they do.' She started singing quietly, like it was a language they weren't supposed to share, '*Up around here, everybody knows me, but nobody knows me but you.* I saw you at the State Theatre. God, that must have been, how long ago? 2001 or 2002?'

'2003.'

'Was it? I'm surprised you remember. You must have played much bigger places than that in your day. Ooh, I mean, not that this isn't your day.' She started wringing her hands, desperate to escape the minefield she'd stumbled into, flabby elbows threatening a pot of pens near the edge of her desk. 'You're still touring, I bet. All the big ones from those days are.'

Davie put her out of her misery. 'Yeah, it's tempting. But it would interfere too much with my new work. Not always too good to be recognised you see.'

He was leaning forwards in a half-whisper. Not many people should know this, but she was all right, he could trust her. She bent in too so there were only centimetres between their faces.

'Why? What do you do now?'

Davie took out a business card and slid it across the counter. Murdoch stepped forwards and just had time to read *Davie Simms, Detection Services* before the receptionist grabbed it eagerly.

'Er, Davie, mate ...'

'This is my partner.'

'Partner?' The receptionist was distraught, struggling to keep it hidden behind her smile.

'Business partner,' said Davie. 'Not ...'

And they laughed again in that language they shared.

She gave them the works after that, gave Davie the works. Murdoch wished he could always be so invisible. Her name was Shannon and she put the disc Davie handed over into her computer and showed them, showed Davie, how the code beneath Georgie Heydos's name showed not only the hospital where the scan had been done but the identity of the nurse who'd done it. She looked up both on a register and wrote *St Harriet's* and *Melanie Howell* on her pad. Then, with a wink that would have struggled on a prettier woman, she phoned a contact at St Harriet's and got not only Nurse Howell's shift register but also her mobile number. Murdoch reckoned Davie could have asked for Howell's bank details at that stage and the receptionist would have risked her job to get them. A queue had built up behind them, five or six people straining to hear what was taking so long, but the receptionist didn't care. It took another ten minutes and an autograph to say goodbye.

As they crossed the overlit car park – the sun and the hospital windows in harsh competition – Murdoch squinted painfully. He'd left his sunglasses in the car and had to hold up a hand up against the brightness as he trotted to keep up with Davie's triumphant pace.

'Nice work, Davie.'

'Thanks.'

'So you really were something then.'

'Once upon a time.'

'So what happened to all the money?'

Davie stopped and turned. 'Shut up, Bill. I thought you were a crook. What happened to all your money, eh?'

'Whoa, mate, easy. I didn't realise it was such a sore point. Sorry. Jesus.'

'Yeah, well.'

Davie turned and started walking again, Murdoch winding between the cars behind him.

'Davie, mate, seriously, that was good. You're better at the chat than me, I'll give you that. Surprised you don't use that Davie Wonder stuff all the time.'

'It only works if they were teenagers in the early noughties.'

'In Australia.'

Davie turned again, his frown vicious until he saw Murdoch's smirk.

'And the States, you arsehole.'

48

Murdoch told himself there was no point in avoiding prison just so he could sit in an empty house all day. Like that explained why he had to go to St Harriet's and meet Melanie Howell. He told himself he'd leave soon enough, get away to where he wasn't known. Just not now, not when they'd nearly found Georgie and everyone in Montauban might remember him as a hero. Davie told him he was nuts, reminded him of the risk he was taking, like Murdoch might have forgotten. They argued as far as the freeway, but then Davie turned left instead of right and that was that. They were both going to Sydney.

St Harriet's, deep in darkest Darlinghurst, was a very different hospital from Crosley General: smaller, grubbier, with a metal door to the needle exchange. But, as Davie pointed out, it still had that same horrible smell. The reception area was painfully lit, depressing on such a sunny day, the whole thing like a stage. There was a minor skirmish going on as they arrived, two security guards holding down a meth head and waiting for the police to arrive. Davie asked Murdoch if he wanted to wait in the car – he could come and get him when Melanie Howell arrived – but Murdoch shook his head, pulled up his hood and headed for the corner.

Nurse Howell had been grudging when they'd phoned from the car. Murdoch had said 'detective' and he could tell she'd heard 'police'. Still, she saw no way she could help. He'd persisted, tried being nice like Davie would, and eventually she'd agreed to see them when she finished her shift.

The seats in the St Harriet's reception area were made for something but it wasn't comfort. Davie sat opposite him again, fidgeting and shifting his arse around, tapping his knees until he spotted a paper and lost himself in its crossword. Murdoch bit his nails and resisted standing to pace up and down, listening instead to an old couple whose seats were welded to the back of his own. 'It's like an airport,' the woman said, in a thick Westie accent. 'Nobody wants to be here.' Then she gasped and Murdoch turned to look at what she'd seen.

Four young men were carrying a fifth through the sliding door to the street, blood dripping thickly across the tile floor. The meth head had been swept out of the way minutes before and now these men were the centre of attention, nurses and a doctor appearing from nowhere, the reception area silent and staring. Murdoch knew one of the four blokes – didn't know his name, but knew who he was – and he stood as slowly as he could, his stomach cramping as he told Davie in a whisper they had to go.

'Could Detective William Murdoch please report to the reception desk.'

The tannoy was modern and clear, tiny speakers in every corner, but no one looked around to see what a detective looked like. The man with the blood, the raised voices between his friends and the nurses, were far more interesting.

Davie came back from the reception desk with a tightly welded woman in a black polo neck and jeans, grey hair pulled back in a firm bun. He introduced Murdoch as his partner and told her they only needed a few minutes of her time. Asked if there was somewhere more private they could sit and talk.

'Not really,' said Howell, uninterested rather than challenging. Then, like she was commenting on the weather, 'You don't look like police officers.'

'Undercover,' said Davie. 'So we'll take that as a compliment.'

A blasting siren arrived outside and the sliding door to the daylight opened again. They all turned to look, but no one came in and the door slid closed again, the tarmac outside vaguely reflecting red and blue, red and blue. Murdoch suggested they sit down, but Nurse Howell said she'd rather stand, thank you. Stand with her back to the door, that was, so Murdoch had no choice but to face the world as he explained about Georgie Walker – the scan they'd found, the code.

'My God,' she said. 'Do you know how many women I scan every day? You can't seriously expect me to remember one from two years ago!'

Murdoch handed over the photographs of Georgie, watched Howell flipping through them as he spoke.

'She'd of been scared.'

'They're all scared,' said Howell, 'especially the young ones.'

She'd stopped shuffling the photographs and was looking at one at arm's length. If she needed glasses, she was too vain to wear them. 'No idea, sorry.'

'Yes, you do,' said Murdoch. 'You recognise her. You saw her in the papers days after you did her scan. And, just in case you're not aware, withholding evidence regarding a missing person case is a criminal offence and, if we discover that's what you're doing, you will be prosecuted. You might not go to prison, sweetheart, but you will lose your job.'

Suddenly the welding wasn't so tight, at least not in her face. Howell flushed red, put her hand up to her hair and discovered every strand was in place. 'How ...?' she said. 'How dare ...?' But there was nothing in her voice but fear.

'Listen,' said Davie. 'I can imagine confidentiality is vital in a job like yours. I don't know, but I'm thinking a lot of girls only come here because they know they can trust this place to keep their secrets. Am I right?'

She nodded tightly, looking at him hard, as if by ignoring Murdoch she could make him disappear. When she spoke again, there was a quaver in her voice, fear still, or anger, it was difficult to say. 'There are girls from certain backgrounds whose lives I can put in danger. Do you understand that?'

'This isn't the case here,' said Davie. 'This girl has already disappeared. Something bad has already happened to her and anything you can tell us might still save her life.'

Now she sat. They towered over her for a second and then awkwardly took seats either side of her. The guy with the bloodied head had disappeared through two swinging doors, his four friends left to sit and look around the waiting room. Murdoch looked at the floor and listened to Howell talk to Davie.

'This girl here told me she was twenty and married.' She hesitated, then plunged on. 'She was terrified, absolutely terrified. And then she was missing.' She ruffled through the photographs again. 'I presumed she'd run away. How do you know she didn't run away? Am I going to get in trouble?'

Davie only answered the last question. No, he said, not now she'd helped them. He asked if Georgie had said where she might go. Anything, any clues, any more words Howell could remember? Did she see a man with the girl? Howell shook her head, straight fingers over her mouth and nose. 'Poor love,' was all she said. 'Poor little kid.'

49.

On the way back to Montauban, Murdoch let Davie rattle off theories about what it all meant and where Lachlan Heydos might be hiding Georgie and the baby. But he knew they were just that: theories with no basis in anything. The investigation had progressed all right, but the chances of it progressing further any time soon were slim. Unless, of course, Heydos arrived in a puff of smoke, managed not to recognise Murdoch and told them where Georgie and the baby were and what Alycia Thornton had to do with anything. As for Alycia answering for herself, she and her entire family had disappeared on holiday.

'Camping,' the neighbours told Davie, when Murdoch sent him door to door that afternoon. 'Lake Nura, they go every year.'

But the slim chances of progress in finding Georgie were the least of Murdoch's fears. The sight of the man he knew in St Harriet's had shaken him. Murdoch had never had claustrophobia in his life, more like the opposite when he got out of jail after his first long stretch, but, returning to the house from the visit to St Harriet's, everything seemed suddenly close and heavy. Later that evening, he woke from a nap to find the bare walls looming over him, tilting in at the edge of his vision. When he heard the front door open and slam, he jumped up without thinking and made for the nearest window. He was fiddling it open when Davie appeared in the bedroom doorway.

'Dude, what's up? You look dreadful.'

'Nothing, feeling sick. I'll be fine. I just need five minutes.'

He was right. He was fine, he did just need five minutes. But only because by then he'd made a decision.

After pizza, he packed Davie off home early with an excuse he needed to be alone for a bit. Then he packed everything else. At nine o'clock he left the house, a bag over his shoulder, and went looking for a car. The nights were cooler now, the streets of Montauban quieter than ever. There was a sweet smell in the air, the same smell he'd noticed in Walker's garden what felt like months before. He still didn't know what it was. Climbing the steps between the steep streets, he turned and saw a fat full moon reflected in the lagoon, its perfect circle spotlighting three floating shapes. He stared at them until he saw they were swans, necks turned and hidden under their broad black wings. Taking a deep breath, he pushed on, losing himself in the high maze, further up the hill again until, on the highest street, he found something suitable. An old Nissan outside a house with cobwebs across the path, clearly no one home.

He got into the car easily enough, then walked away, watching from a hundred yards to check no one had heard. Nothing. Just the gums creaking, the soft and distant boom of the ocean, countless rustles and snaps that no longer frightened him. A life he'd only recently discovered and already had to leave. He thought of the few foster homes he'd liked as a kid, how even there he'd fucked things up.

Halfway back to the Nissan, he heard the clicking footsteps of a woman approaching, her intermittent speech clearly one half of a conversation. He stood back from the road to let her pass, invisible in the heavy shadows, and slowly recognised the voice of Alycia Thornton. Not such a coincidence, he realised – he was in Pacifico Road, only a few houses away from where she and her parents lived. She came slowly into view, teetering on high heels, a shadow moving among shadows, the only light from the phone in her hand. She was putting on a voice that reminded him of Cynthia and the receptionist in George Street a hundred years before: a smooth invitation.

'No, I'm telling you, baby, there's no one home. No, they all went in the end. Exactly. That's what I thought. I'll see you in ten minutes.'

Murdoch watched Alycia let herself into her parents' house, then carried on to the Nissan and threw his bag inside. He climbed in, leaned forwards and reached under the steering wheel. A quarter of an hour later he was still there, engine off, window down. At last he heard a car climbing the hill, heard it change gear and turn, until its headlights were bright in the Nissan's mirrors. He pressed the side of his face into his bag, the lights of the other car bright beside him and then bright again as it reversed and parked. Engine off, lights out, door pressed quietly shut and then a muted beep as the whole thing locked. Murdoch sat up and watched in the wing mirror as Lachlan Heydos, one arm in a sling, crossed from the Lexus to the little walkway that joined the road to number thirty-four. He was halfway across, avoiding the bike that had never been moved, when the front door opened, bright in the dark night, to reveal Alycia Thornton in her underwear. She pulled Lachlan Heydos in by his good arm and let the door swing slowly closed again.

And Murdoch was supposed to just drive away?

The door onto the back deck was open, the breeze worrying the curtains in and out. Murdoch stood there, catching his breath, the clamber up the stilts from the steep ground below harder than he had thought. He was sweating and his holster had rubbed a blister across his left ribs, but all of that seemed unimportant and far away. Important was in the house.

Inside, the ground floor was as messy as he remembered it. Picking a careful path between furniture and toys, it was easy to convince himself the only other people in the house were upstairs. Easier still to find the right bedroom; other than the high moon through dirty windows, the only light in the house was a thin strip of yellow under and around a door. From beyond it came breath and gentle moans, then a muted giggle. Murdoch checked the other bedrooms were empty and returned to the one with the light. Taking the Beretta from its holster, he used it to push the door slowly open and stood there for a moment, watching Heydos's pale buttocks pressing between Alycia's legs. Her bra and his sling were curled intimately with a sheet on the floor.

'Don't mind me,' said Murdoch.

Alycia was inconsolable until she could cover herself. She didn't scream particularly, was more concerned at contorting herself away from his stare. Heydos said nothing the whole time, just sat at the bottom of the bed with his hands over himself, staring at the Beretta.

'You'll notice it's cocked,' Murdoch told him.

He reached down, rescued the sheet from the floor and threw it to Alycia, who pulled it up to her chin shivering, like it was the cold she was trying to escape.

'Yeah, don't mind me. I've just come to ask a few questions and then I'll be on my way. Seeing as we're all cosy here together. Alycia, you first. Did you know Georgie was pregnant?'

He could see her choosing which role to play. Haughty mistress, innocent foreigner, poor little schoolgirl. She shook her head, eyes wide, and Murdoch took two steps across the room and slapped her hard across the face. Heydos stood suddenly, paler than he'd been before, and Murdoch held the Beretta out to his face.

'Go on, mate, make me. You know I want to.'

Heydos sat again, looked down and remembered he wasn't completely naked. He peeled the condom off and threw it into the corner.

'Bit late for that, mate. Now Alycia, shall we try again? Did you know Georgie was pregnant?'

She was crying, hands over her eyes, but she nodded hard.

'And do you know who the father of the baby was? Sorry, didn't catch that, darlin'. Do you know who the fucking father was?'

She looked up, mascara everywhere. Shook her head, then screamed as he took a step towards her again, speaking as fast as she knew how.

'He was older. He was older than us and had a lovely car. I don't know cars; Georgie didn't know what it was called. It was black. A lovely big black car. I never saw him. He wasn't from around here but he came up from Sydney a lot, they met when she was working in the café. She wouldn't even tell me his name or where they went. Said she wasn't supposed to. They had sex, she wasn't sure about it at first, but she liked him so much. She wanted to go away with him. He didn't want to but she said she was going away anyway. He had big feet. Please, please that's all I know.'

'Would you like me to tell you his name?'

Murdoch had managed to keep his voice calmer than he felt, but Alycia seemed too scared to answer either way, unsure which response might lead to another slap. She sat there, wet and blotchy, and staring in silence, sucking at the air between them in tiny irregular gasps. Murdoch repeated the question slowly – did she want to know the father's name? – and Alycia nodded as much as she dared.

'His name was Lachlan Heydos. They were sleeping together. You didn't know that?'

Murdoch didn't know what he expected but he didn't expect her to laugh. She managed it somehow, all the frightening contempt of a woman laughing at a man.

'That's rubbish. Lachie's not been here since after Georgie disappeared. I met him …'

She caught the blankness of shock on Heydos's face, every muscle in her own twitching as it fought against the truth. 'Lachie? Lachie, you said—'

'I didn't know she was pregnant.'

Now she screamed. She kicked hard and got herself standing in the corner, the bed pushing out from the wall and the sheet twisting between her thighs. She was level with the shelves above the bed, knocking against them so old paperbacks and a mug tumbled to the mattress.

'No!' she screamed. 'No!!!'

She reached down, grabbed the mug and threw it with all her force at Murdoch. It caught him on the forehead, solid and sharp – just a mug, but painful enough that he stumbled backwards through the open door. He uncocked the revolver and put his hand up to his stitches, pulling it away again to stare at the blood at his fingers. A movement made him look up and he saw Heydos coming at him, his fist filling his vision. Then they were on the ground, grappling on the narrow landing floor, punches constrained by the railing and walls. The last thing Murdoch remembered was pinning Heydos to the ground. Which left Alycia behind him. Whatever she hit him with, it was large and heavy and blunt.

50.

Something was badly wrong. At first there was just that and blackness. Then there were nightmares, disjointed half-scenes one after the other, none of them frightening enough to wake him but all of them deeply wrong. They weighed him down and held him, pinned him until his discomfort became pain and he was almost conscious. It was his own voice that woke him in the end: a dull moan of protest against the restriction and the hurt and the wrong.

Murdoch opened his eyes, one eye, and didn't know where he was. A bare room, angles in the dark, a narrow high window. When he woke again it was daytime, cold light pushing through the glass which ran along the top of the opposite wall, bars casting shadows diagonally down into the room. He moved his head and saw his feet, beyond them a uniform reading a paper. The uniform turned a page and the noise of it echoed lightly against the empty walls and floor. Then he turned another page and, glancing up, saw Murdoch was awake. They looked at each other in silence for a while, until the police officer stood, crossed the room with the paper trailing in one hand and pressed a button on the wall. All without a break of eye contact. Returning to his chair, the officer sat, the newspaper no longer interesting him. He stared at Murdoch until Murdoch realised he was scared. Scared of an injured man secured to a bed by thick leather straps, handcuffed to the rails, in case his middle name was Houdini.

There were noises outside and a door opened somewhere out of Murdoch's sight. A woman greeted him by name and asked if he could hear her. She came into view, young and Indian, white coat and a tiny torch in her hand. She repeated the question. He nodded slowly, painfully, and as a reward she shone the torch into his eye. She reached up and adjusted something above his head, her breasts firm against the bland white of her coat. He closed his eyes and was lost again.

Her name was Doctor Rai. She came twice a day, sometimes with nurses to whom she gave instructions. She asked him how he felt and if he was experiencing pain. If he could tell her his name, his age, where he came from. He wanted to stay there forever with this gentle dark woman, but she left him most of the time with the uniforms. Constable McEwan, who'd been a copper forever; Constable Riley, who'd seen him wake up; Constable Brown, who looked about twelve: a roster he couldn't keep track of. It was Constable McEwan who told him what had been done. A broken jaw, dislocated shoulder, six broken ribs, something McEwan couldn't pronounce, snapped metatarsal, liver and kidneys badly bruised, fractured kneecaps and internal bleeding.

'My eye?'

Salvageable apparently, but he'd have to ask the doctor. Murdoch asked for a mirror, but McEwan knew his job.

'Ask the doctor,' he said.

Murdoch slept often and spoke little. He knew speech would bring different people, men with questions and threats. But after ten days there was no more delaying and he spent two hours with Detective Inspector Bad Cop and Detective Sergeant Good Cop, who didn't go away any happier than they'd arrived.

On day twelve Davie came, flustered in his work suit. Flowers, a card, a huge bowl of fruit, all taken from him by Constable Riley and passed out to whoever was guarding the door. Davie sat beside the bed with a face that made Murdoch want to punch him.

'Thanks for coming.'

'Are you kidding? I've been trying to get in here for ages. They're treating you like some kind of serial killer. What happened?'

'I went to see Alycia. Heydos was there …'

Only then did he realise Heydos hadn't done this alone. The drugs were slowing his thinking. Heydos had called people and Murdoch wondered why they hadn't killed him. How they knew to send him to hell instead.

'My God,' said Davie. 'We need to tell the police everything we know.'

Constable Riley, reading beneath the window, looked up at this until, bored with the ensuing silence, he gave up and went back to the paper, pretending not to listen. Davie repeated what he'd said more quietly until Murdoch's feverish whispering interrupted him.

'Listen to me, Davie. You don't tell no one nothing, you understand? You don't know nothing about Alycia or the big house nor nothing. We was flatmates, that's all, you got it?'

He didn't get it. Murdoch struggled against the straps, twisting his wrist into the leather so he could grab Davie's fingers. 'What have you said? Who have you spoken to?'

Davie pulled his hand away. 'No one. I haven't spoken to anyone. I just think—'

'Davie, you say nothing. You got it?'

Davie nodded slowly and used his other hand to rub the pain from his fingers. They sat in silence for a while, the only noise the rustle of Riley's paper.

'Here, Davie, have you noticed? This place don't smell like a hospital.'

Davie didn't look up. He was pinching the bridge of his nose. 'Yes, it does. You just can't smell it because you've got tubes stuck up your nostrils. It smells exactly the way these places always smell.'

He looked up and Murdoch smiled at him, pulled a conversation out of him bit by bit. News of Montauban, what people were saying, what the papers were calling him now. Then he saw Riley check his watch and he twisted to grab Davie's fingers again.

'One more thing, mate. Don't come here again, you understand?'

No one else came either, weeks of just him and the constables. Then, on the morning of his transfer, he had two visits in quick succession, difficult to say which was worse.

Earlier, an argument between doctors and police had been lost and won somewhere and he was no longer bound to the bed, not that it did him much good – he struggled to walk to the toilet without crying out in pain. On the morning of his transfer, the high window showed empty blue, the sky cleared by a wind he could hear whispering softly, so he knew there must be she-oaks nearby. He sat on the side of his bed listening, willing himself to stop and get dressed instead, but it was the loud unlocking of the door that interrupted his thoughts. It swung slightly open, obscuring whoever was on the outside, and his guard, Constable Brown that day, was called out, leaving him alone in the room for the first time since he'd regained consciousness.

He pushed himself off the edge of the bed, the demeaning hospital gown riding up and open behind him. Then the door opened again and Harris from the Club walked in, heavy in a dark suit and leaning on his cane. Murdoch took a step back and steadied himself against the bed. Looked around quickly, like anything that might be used as a weapon hadn't been removed long before. Harris smiled his big rich smile and said nothing, just pulled the metal chair Brown had been sitting on noisily across the floor. Murdoch had remembered Harris as looking tired. Now he thought the light on the night of Maria's death had been kind. There was something wrong with the man. Too much good living or too much bad, Murdoch recognised a man in pain. And yet, Harris's eyes sparkled.

'Look at the state of you, Bill.'

Murdoch looked down at his gown as if he'd not noticed it before. 'I can get changed, but you're stuck looking like that for life.'

'Always the funny man, aren't you, Bill? Always the witty and biting line. Trouble is, I don't know whether you've noticed, but no one's laughing any more.' He raised his cane and let it drop heavily onto the bed, two inches short of Murdoch's left knee. 'And while I appreciate your need not to appear frightened right now, you might want to watch your mouth. The terms of my visit do not allow me to kill you, but some further injury is probably permitted.'

'I'm quaking in my boots.'

'The funny thing is, Bill, you really are. Now that you know I know where you are, you must be shitting yourself. But I've come to tell you not to worry. We're not going to do anything to you yet. You see, I'm a great believer in delayed gratification and I'm well aware that the day I have you tortured to death, I will no longer be able to look forward to it. Also, if we do it here no one will see and, as you know, crowd control is an important part of the Club's work. No matter how much you suffer it would be a bit of a waste if there were no witnesses. And then …'

'Is this going to go on for long? I've got a massage at four.'

But Harris knew Murdoch wanted him angry. He paused for barely a second before continuing. 'And then my colleagues on the supply side believe there is another reason. They believe you will gladly give up what you stole from them for the peace and quiet of death after what they have planned for you inside. But I disagree. I know a stubborn bastard when I see one. So we've made a gentleman's agreement. If you haven't told them anything within two months, I'm allowed to do what I want with you.'

'Anything else?'

Harris glanced at his watch and grimaced slightly, annoyed at last or maybe in pain. He stood with difficulty and smoothed the dark fabric of his trousers.

'Bill, Bill, Bill,' he said, shaking his head and dragging the chair to where he'd found it. 'When I last spoke to you, I said next time I saw you you'd be a dead man. I'm not upset that I was wrong. But soon, very soon, Bill, you will be.'

He leaned on his cane back across the floor and Murdoch smiled and turned away like he couldn't care less. But the sound of the door closing made him jump and turn, one arm up in defence before he realised he was alone in the room again.

51

Two hours later and he was still lying on the bed in his hospital gown. There was some delay, Constable Brown told him, it would be after lunch before they could move him. Murdoch didn't care. Maybe by then he'd be able to dress himself. He'd tried twice since Harris had left, but an insistent shaking had overtaken him, his fingers unable to settle. He didn't feel like asking Brown for a hand. There was no reason to think the young constable knew why he'd been called away, but that didn't make it any less forgivable. They ignored each other, Brown deep in some manual, while Murdoch lay on the bed staring at the sunlight that stretched across the wall too high to reach. It was, he'd realised over the recent weeks, like being at the bottom of a pit.

When the door opened again he thought it was lunch: another opportunity to guess what the shapes on the plate were supposed to be. Instead it was Natalie, looking her best. Hair down, casual T-shirt, tight jeans and a frown. She gave Brown a discreet nod and he stood and left again – always happy to escape from Murdoch, little Constable Brown. Then Natalie turned and looked at Murdoch properly.

'Oh my God, Bill.'

Murdoch thought of Alycia, her only concern to cover herself with the sheet. He turned his head away so he couldn't see Natalie staring at his injuries. Felt the bed dip as she sat down, felt her hand on his arm, a tiny squeeze that hurt.

'I'm sorry,' he said, rubbing his eye.

'I bet you are.'

'Nah, I mean sorry to you, Nat. Really sorry. I've got good at saying that word in the last few weeks – fuck knows, I never said it much before then. But I mean it, I'm sorry. I didn't mean to make you look bad.'

She leant back trying to catch his eye, but he wasn't ready to look at her yet. He swung his legs painfully off the other side of the bed and sat so they were back to back. Listened to Natalie sigh slowly.

'I saw your record from the UK.'

'Nat, please …'

'Why did you have to lie to me, Bill? Why couldn't you have told me you'd been in prison?'

'I told you I'd had a few run-ins with the law.'

'Oh please. Bank robbery with manslaughter, assault, twenty-odd years in one prison or another. "A few run-ins with the law" is a lie.'

'I didn't want you thinking I was like that, did I? An ex-con up the coast on the make.'

She didn't respond to that, at least not as far as Murdoch could tell through the mattress between them. He looked at his legs, as pale and scarred as the floor below.

'Jesus Christ, Bill.' Now the mattress wobbled. 'When I think of all the times I tried to help you. How, every time you were so rude to me; how I always came back in case it had been my fault.'

'Don't, Nat, please.'

She started to say something new but stopped, the silence so long this time that when the bed bounced suddenly, he'd thought she'd decided to leave. But then she started again, her voice louder so he knew she was facing the gap in the back of his gown.

'Why did you even come back, Bill? Why didn't you just stay away and leave us all alone?'

'I don't know.' He did know. 'I just ... I didn't want everyone in Montauban thinking I was some crook what didn't care about Georgie. Didn't want you thinking that neither.'

'Why not? Since when do you care what anyone in Montie thinks of you?'

He shook his head and heard someone with his voice saying, 'Ever since they started thinking good things about me. I just wanted to prove them right. Prove I'm better than ... I dunno.'

'And that was worth risking your life for that? Really?'

He shrugged, hoisted himself to his feet, coughed and confessed he couldn't get his clothes on. Natalie appeared in front of him, a strange twist on her lips.

'Underpants?'

On the floor where he'd left them in frustration. She found them and pulled them over his ankles, then halfway up his thighs until he said he could manage the rest himself.

'Trousers?'

The same procedure, one leg after the other while he half sat on the bed, except he needed her to do up the buttons. The smell of her made him want to cry. He bit his bottom lip and nodded over to his shirt. She was doing the buttons on that – a wife sending her husband to execution – when she seemed to remember why she was there.

'Let me help you, Bill.'

'You're nearly done.'

'No, I mean help you out of this mess. They're going to throw the book at you. Breaking and entering, dealing, assault. All that shit with the car in Sydney.'

'I'm sorry.'

'I don't want you to be sorry; I want you to let me help you. I know you know stuff and I'm pretty sure, if you told me everything, I could find someone high up enough to make a deal.'

Too late, he caught himself shaking his head. Natalie dropped her hands and took a step back, that frown he liked creasing her brow.

'You're joking, right?'

'I can't, Nat.'

'Why can't you? Not because you don't know anything? Not because there's nothing I can do?'

He looked down and shook his head again. Held out his hand to her, looked up at it hanging there, useless. Natalie's face was red.

'Oh, let me guess! It's because your stupid criminal code won't let you talk to the police?'

'Nah, nah, that's not it. It's cos there's nothing to tell. I mean … Georgie was pregnant, did you know that?'

'What? No, I didn't know that …'

'We found the scan. She was sleeping with, I mean, I dunno, some local lad. I think she ran away.'

'You're so full of shit, Bill, do you know that?'

'What? What do you mean?'

'I mean you know full well that's not the kind of information I'm looking for. I mean you've got some of the nastiest people in the state looking for you. Some very choice types who contacted me, of all people, to see what I know. I mean my boss has been getting calls from extremely dodgy solicitors claiming their clients have got enough on you to see you go down for twelve to twenty. I mean, Bill, that you have an opportunity to end all of this, to stop being a criminal. What did you say just now? That you wanted everyone in Montauban to think you were more than a crook? To think that you're something better? So be something better and tell me what you know about the people who did this to you. Help me make a deal.'

'I don't know nothing.'

'Oh for God' sake! You know plenty. Last time I saw you, you told me you'd crossed some bad people in Sydney. I believed you, at least about that. It's the reason I didn't arrest you there and then. I thought maybe … The point is, Bill, I still do believe you. Except now I think those bad people are very organised and very powerful. And I also believe that if you told me all about them, I could keep you from spending the next decade in prison.'

He realised she'd rehearsed the words and wanted to be angry with her about it. Wanted to accuse her of using him for her own ambition. But when he spoke again, all he heard in his voice was weakness.

'I can't, Nat. Don't you know what that would make me?'

She moved away, putting distance between them so she could shout through it. 'You said you wanted to prove what you are. *This* is what you are proving. Right here, right now – that you're a crook.'

He stood and hobbled towards her, meaning to hold her, but she moved away. Turned to the corner, her hands in her hair. 'I thought I, at least, knew you a little bit.'

'You do know me.'

She shook her head, still not looking at him. 'They're going to kill you in there, Bill.'

'They'll try.'

'Oh stop being so fucking macho. They will and you know it.'

'So get me somewhere safe.'

'Didn't I just offer to do that? Didn't I just give you a way out? But give me one good reason why anyone in the force is going to lift a finger to help you, when you won't do anything to help us?'

'To stop me getting killed?'

Now she looked at him, suddenly calm. 'I can't.'

Over the previous weeks he'd given in. Accepted what was coming for him. It had been more comfortable that way, better than clutching at straws like this. But Natalie was here now: he had to try. 'Why can't you tell

217

whoever needs to know that someone inside's going to do me harm? Tell them my life's in danger.'

Natalie rolled her eyes, blinking to keep them dry.

'Don't you think I've already tried that?' she snapped. 'Don't you think I've already tried everything?'

52.

Time bent and stretched. Murdoch's weeks in hospital – a lazy weekend; his first days in Glenburn – six months of hell. Winter had kicked in since he'd left Montauban, a biting cold more keenly felt because of the warmth it had replaced. Unlike any prison he'd seen in England, the older cells in Glenburn – of which his was one – had no glass in the windows. With no fat on his body, he shivered and suffered through the nights. Murdoch's cellmate, Jones, an old lifer who knew no better, told him he'd soon get used to it. But even Jones cursed every morning when he had to run the hot tap over his carton of milk before he could drink from it.

Apart from the lack of glass, their cell was pretty much the same as any other Murdoch had known. A door onto the walkway, two beds, two cupboards, a toilet and a sink. Nowhere to curl up and be left alone to die. It was overlit, these places always were, the effect heightened by the prison greens everyone was forced to wear. Despite the light, daytimes Murdoch mostly slept.

'You need to get to the gym,' Jones told him halfway through the first week. 'You behave right, when you're well enough, they'll let you play sport. Keep yourself busy, mate, until your trial comes around.'

Murdoch said yeah, thanks, and rolled over to face the wall.

'Basketball,' Jones went on. 'That's the big thing. They've got a team here in a local league; other teams come in and play against them. Big deal in here; you could try that.'

Murdoch stubbed out his cigarette on the floor under the bed, pulled up his blanket and went back to sleep.

It was surprisingly easy to exist without actually living when all you were waiting for was death. To force yourself off the bed when ordered to eat in the canteen or stand in the exercise yard. To wash as little as you could get away with. To let your cellmate talk without putting your hands over your ears. Being still injured helped somehow: an excuse Murdoch could wallow in. Ten days he existed this way, awaiting the inevitable, until even Jones gave up sharing the gossip of bets on the basketball, or who'd arrived in the supermax next door, and who was due for a fall. It was on day eleven that Murdoch woke up.

If he'd had his wits about him, if he'd cared about surviving before then, he'd have seen it coming from a mile away. He'd lost all sense of time by then, but it must have been evening because they were being walked down for dinner. Glenburn was an old jail: four storeys of cells built around a huge central hall, iron walkways joining the cells, iron stairs joining the walkways, an iron fog of noise so you had to shout to make yourself heard. Above, five storeys up from the ground floor, thick glass panels in the roof had once been the only source of light. Now they were supported by electrics on each floor: dim yellow bulbs behind frosted security glass welded to the wall. After the overlit cell, it always took Murdoch a while for his eyes to adjust – men in greens filing along the walkways and down the stairs like dots on a dimly lit screen. On this day, he was still blinking, halfway to the first set of stairs, when the bloke three ahead of him dropped to a squat. The guy in front of Murdoch tutted. He was a young Aboriginal guy, lanky, six foot and then some. In a different life, he'd have played AFL. In front of him was a skinhead with scars across his head.

'Come on, mate,' said the skinhead to the guy squatting in front of him. 'Whatcha doing?'

The guy who'd been squatting stood and turned in one move. He was thickset with a monobrow – Greek or something. A broad flat nose and dark skin, a tattoo beside one eye. 'What's it to you, Marshall?'

The skinhead retreated slightly, hands up to pacify. He backed into the lanky indigenous bloke behind him, who in turn bumped backwards into Murdoch. Murdoch stood his ground, looking past the other two at the big guy with the tattoo.

'What you fucking looking at?'

Before Murdoch had a chance to answer, the screw behind yelled at them to get a move on. The monobrow turned and they were all walking again, the skinhead keeping a safe distance back. Twice more the monobrow dropped to tie a shoelace that wasn't there and twice more they all stopped, silent but for the lanky young guy, who was tapping his hands against his thighs, drumming to a song in his head. They were halfway down the last set of stairs, prisoners and staff milling on the ground floor below them, when the monobrow stopped for a third time. He didn't squat – it would have been impossible on the steep staircase – instead, he just stood and waited.

Murdoch never saw the prisoner who pushed into him from behind, then held fast onto the rails so that five of them were crowded onto the bottom twelve steps. And later he couldn't remember what had made him look down. Maybe he'd got used to walking around like that, head bent and eyes on the ground. Either way, he had a clear view through the wrought ironwork beneath his feet and saw exactly what happened next. A pale prisoner with a lantern jaw and scraggy blond hair matting into dreadlocks walked quickly across the concrete floor below them, at the last minute producing a pair of short-handled wire-cutters from his sleeve. Reaching through the steps below Murdoch, he snipped the right Achilles tendon of the young Aboriginal guy. They all heard it snap – then heard nothing but the kid screaming as he fell, taking the skinhead with him. The two of them landed in a writhing mess, the Greek monobrow having stepped out of the way.

'When we say lose,' said the monobrow, one foot on the young man's pain-stretched face, 'we mean "lose".'

The man behind Murdoch laughed. 'He'll have long enough to think about that one.'

The monobrow looked up and noticed Murdoch, who had by now reached the bottom step.

'You got a problem?'

'Nothing to do with me,' said Murdoch.

And he walked off – just another animal.

That night he didn't sleep. He'd forgotten how efficient prison violence was. How tidy and contained – everything over and everyone gone before anyone knew what had happened. Aggro on the outside was different: badly planned – if planned at all– messy and difficult to hide. Inevitably this made him think of what had happened in Montauban and what might have happened to Georgie Walker.

He lay staring at the darkness, listening to Jones snoring and looking at what had happened over the previous months. From a distance, he could see who was afraid of who and why that might make sense. He thought of conversations he'd had – everything clearer to him now that he was so far from it. He remembered everything little Tom Walker had told him, Georgie's CDs, how Alycia knew Georgie was pregnant and why she might know that. The memories made him question things he'd not questioned before and think over comments and gestures he'd not noticed at the time: a treasure trove of details. Apparently unrelated things: like how he had wanted sunglasses on the night Natalie had visited him in Davie's shack. How Tom was so scared his dad might get knocked down too. He started with a 'what if' and when that didn't work, he tried another. Then a third, until slowly, slowly, slowly, things began to make sense. He tested his logic and found the testing made it stronger. Argued with himself until he knew he was right. Eventually, by the time dirty daylight began seeping into the cell, he realised he knew exactly where Georgie Walker was.

53.

Organising a phone in Glenburn was no easier than in any other prison in the world. The authorities wanted notice, wanted reasons, wanted to make you wait. Murdoch was told it would be two days before he could expect to get his welfare officer's approval; even then it would be a twelve-minute slot with a signed understanding they could listen in as much they wanted. It was a long two days. His senses had been asleep till now, like they had shut down in defence against the violence he was expecting. Now they made up for lost time. Now he could smell Jones's farts, smell the stench of five hundred men locked in together. Now his eyelids were no good against the harsh light and his cell shrank, his bed no longer a refuge, the constant echoes from other cells impossible to ignore. Even the exercise yard grew claustrophobic, the wires between the buildings a barrier between him and the sky.

Worse was the fear. All his life Murdoch had avoided authority, walked slowly the other way when a uniform appeared. Now he hovered within sight of the guards, a frightened child clinging to a teacher's skirt. He slept badly at night; didn't sleep at all during the day. He remembered the young indigenous guy's Achilles heel and trod carefully wherever he walked. Smoked alone in the common areas, his back to the wall, every movement catching his eye.

The phones were at the end of a low-ceilinged corridor, past a small window where they checked who you were and made you sign again. It was empty when Murdoch arrived and was handed over, very quiet after the echoing iron hall. The guard behind the glass called himself McKinnon. He was a big bloke, wrinkled and greying, not a bad one as screws went, giving the basic respect as long as it was returned. He looked Murdoch up on a list.

'Yeah, not good news. We've tried reaching the party concerned ...' he consulted the list again, '... Natalie Conquest ... but she's not answering.'

'I thought you guys booked it in with her?'

'That we did, mate. And, yes, before you ask, we told her it was important. Always so important. Listen, Murdoch, we'll keep trying every five minutes, but if she doesn't pick up in twenty, you'll be bumped. Sorry about that.'

'Bumped?'

'Till we find you another slot. There's one coming up on Monday next week.'

Murdoch forced out some thanks, keen to keep McKinnon onside. At the other end of the corridor, up towards the main hall, two other prisoners had appeared. One of them was the Greek with the tattoo.

Murdoch leaned against the wall opposite McKinnon's window and pulled out his cigarettes. 'You got a light, McKinnon?'

'Not here,' said the guard without looking up from his paperwork.

'Scuse me?'

'You can't smoke down here, Murdoch. Games room or back in your cell. Wait until someone comes to get you, then I'll send someone up if your call gets through.'

Murdoch had forgotten this. The self-restraint required, all the little prisons inside the bigger one. He pocketed the cigarettes again and waited for a guard to take him back to his cell.

Jones wasn't there. Nothing unusual in that, but Murdoch should have turned around as soon as he saw it. Instead, he looked around to see where he'd left his lighter. He was looking under his bed when he heard an alarm somewhere, shouting and running, doors slamming shut. He stood quickly, but before he was fully up, four huge prisoners he'd not seen before were in the cell with him. They were a mixed bunch, one Islander, two white and one Aboriginal, and he knew this wasn't a random attack – a race hit in revenge for another somewhere. Any one of them could have held him down; four of them did so quickly and quietly, the rustling of their greens and the squeaking of Murdoch's bed the only sound as a fat hand covered his mouth. His wrists and elbows, ankles and knees were pinned into the bed, the pain from his injuries unable to compete with his fear. Then a fifth man entered the cell.

It was the blond guy with the lantern jaw and the half-formed dreadlocks. Murdoch knew his name was Saville. During the previous days, talk at the canteen tables had been about nothing but what he'd done to the young basketball player; his name whispered in fear. He was pale with brown eyes, skin mottled with moles. Taller than he'd looked from the staircase, thin, but carrying a belly, like all he'd ever drunk was beer. He had a twitch, a little jerk that kept pulling his chin sharply to the left as he spoke.

'Hello, Billy-boy. You've been upsetting the wrong people, mate. Spent a fortune they have, organising something to keep the guards busy so we can have a little talk. Hope you don't talk too easy though, because—'

Saville looked sharply at the huge Islander on Murdoch's left leg. 'What you say, Jerro?'

The prisoner he was looking at twitched with fear, driving Murdoch's barely healed knee further into the mattress. The other three looked down at their knuckles.

'I didn't say anything, Sav,' said the Islander. 'Honest, I didn't.'

'Yeah, well, make sure you don't.'

Saville stood silently for a second. He seemed to have forgotten what he'd been saying. He rubbed his chin and produced a scalpel from nowhere before speaking again. 'So, Billy. The guys would like to know what you've done with their stuff. What do you say? Please say no. Please tell me to fuck off. Then I get to try something I've always been curious about.'

He reached down and wielded the scalpel close to Murdoch's eye. Moved it lower and Murdoch felt it enter his cheek, felt it cut through the resistance of his flesh and move towards his chin, the pain not as bad as the knowledge of damage being done. He closed his eyes, tried to calm the tremors that were shaking his body. 'Look at that,' he heard Saville say. 'I said look at that!'

Murdoch opened his eyes to find Saville close to him still, dangling a wispy piece of skin three inches from his nose.

'It's called "flaying",' he said. 'You can skin someone to death, apparently. Always wanted to try it. But I reckon we can start somewhere more interesting than your face, don't you? Unzip him.'

The prisoner called Jerro used one hand to open the Velcro at Murdoch's crotch. Then, with an expression of disgust, he reached in and pulled Murdoch out of his underpants. Murdoch didn't want to struggle, but the urge to protect himself was too strong. He thrashed as hard as he could, but the four men on his limbs just pushed him harder into the mattress. Saville let out a feminine giggle that filled the cell, then bent over Murdoch's exposed parts with the scalpel. There was a noise from out on the walkway – three sharp whistles, a pause then another three. Saville swore and stood quickly. The other four prisoners released their grip and clambered off Murdoch, the bed creaking loudly in protest. A pushing flurry of green and they'd disappeared from the cell. Murdoch lay gasping for second before reaching down and tucking himself back into his pants. He was still struggling with the Velcro, fingers like feathers, when a guard appeared in the doorway.

'What's going in here? Saville, what you doing here?'

'It's nothing,' said Murdoch. 'I scratched myself; Saville's looking at it for me.'

Saville smiled, the scalpel nowhere in sight, and shrugged his shoulders.

The guard looked back and forth between them, not believing a word of it. He was on the point of saying so but then just sighed and shook his head. 'Murdoch,' he said. 'Your call got answered. Get down to the phones now if you don't want to lose it.'

54

They put him in a windowless room in a building an hour and a half from Glenburn. Brought him in the back way, through a fire door and down a featureless corridor to this: a room that could be anywhere in the public service. Anywhere that needed a two-way mirror. A bare bulb hung over the coffee-stained table and weak plastic chairs; the only other feature an old-fashioned radiator, bolted to the floor, drip marks visible in its thick green paint. The smell of the radiator, of its heat, filled the room, the air above it burning like a barely veiled threat.

They gave him tea and cigarettes and then, as a second thought, metallic tap water in a Styrofoam cup that had been used at least once before. Then they let him wait. Impossible to know if this was police inefficiency or part of the game, a reminder he was theirs not the other way around. Two hours, three cups of tea – no pretence they weren't watching from behind the mirror – and no real response to his request to turn down the heating. Eventually, the door opened again and he turned to see Natalie, clean and stunning in a white shirt and jeans, hair loose in a way he knew she never wore to work. She smiled like she was shy, shut the door quietly behind her, and sat down opposite him.

'Hello, Bill.'

'DC Conquest.'

She looked at the bandage that covered his right cheek.

'How are you?'

'Holding up. How are you, love?'

'I'm well. It's good to see you, Bill, really good.'

'Is this how you really want to play this?'

That frown. That quizzical little frown. He didn't know she could do it at will.

'What do you mean?'

'Nat, I'm here to tell you whatever it is I need to tell you so I can get the hell out of Glenburn and find Georgie Walker. There are at least three people on the other side of that glass watching how you do it. Now, I don't want to make you look bad in front of your superior officers, really, I don't, darlin', but I don't think the fresh lipstick approach is gonna work. This is what I think you should do. I think you should go back there and get in here the person what can make the decisions. I don't want you running back and forth, being the injured go-between, talking about "them" as something different from the two of us until you've bled me dry. I've been there and done that, darlin', and I'll beat you at your own game. And that's not what I want. I'm here to make a deal, Nat, and, with respect, a DC doesn't have the authority I need.'

She took that pretty well. Sat back in her chair smiling at him, not giving up yet, but unable to control the flush in her cheeks, the nervous quiver of her top lip. Murdoch looked at his hands; he'd meant it to come out nicer. The door behind him opened and he turned to see a short, grey-haired woman, manila file in hand, entering the room. She had shiny dark eyes and a nervous energy barely contained by her expensive suit. She was like a bird – alert and hungry.

'Detective Chief Inspector Warren,' she chirped. No hand offered to shake. 'Thank you, Conquest, I'll take it from here.'

'Nah,' said Murdoch. 'She stays. I know what I just said, but … I need her here for this.'

The two women looked as confused as he felt, but he had no answers for them on that score; no idea why it was true. Warren sat and opened her file, the table tilting as she leaned on it, spilling some of Murdoch's tea. She read out the date and time, the names of the people present. Made a note with her expensive pen, a scratching so tiny it was difficult to believe it could be of any use. Then she looked up at him. Those beady bird-like eyes were curious but no more than that.

'When you spoke to DC Conquest on the phone, you said you would come here on the understanding that, with the right information in our hands, we could let you walk today. I have to tell you now, Bill, that is extremely unlikely. But stranger things have happened. So, what do you have to tell us?'

As little as possible. 'Well, like I said to Nat, I can tell you where to find Georgie Walker and who's responsible. But I want to be there when you confront him. You can keep me under supervision all you want, but I want to be there, understand?'

Warren put her pen down carefully on the table between them, then picked it up quickly again when it started to roll towards the small pool of tea. 'This isn't some Hollywood movie,' she said. 'We don't let people charged with serious crimes run around so they can play heroics.'

'Serious crimes?'

Warren referred to the file. 'Breaking and entering, illegal possession of a firearm, assault, drug supply, operating as a private investigator without an appropriate licence. Should I go on?'

'Serious crimes? Don't make me laugh. You wouldn't be here today if you thought that. You know I'm inside for nothing and you also know you've got an unsolved missing person's case on your files. I solve that for you and you look good, so don't come all high and mighty talking "serious crimes" to me, Detective Superintendent.'

Warren started to correct him and then realised he'd promoted her deliberately. She smiled a smile that broke into a little laugh and turned to Natalie. 'Goodness, Conquest, who did you tell him I am?'

'I'm not sure I did, ma'am.' Natalie smiled too – a real smile this time, nothing kind about it. 'DCI Warren is from the Organised Crime squad,' she said. 'Nobody connected to the Georgie Walker case knows you're here.'

Murdoch frowned, took a sip of his cold tea, and lit a cigarette he didn't want.

'No missing person case is going to get you out of Glenburn,' Warren said slowly. 'Are you deluded? My heart goes out to that poor girl's family, it really does, and I think it's wonderful that you've shown a genuine interest in finding her. But, come on, Bill, let's not waste my time. As I said, there is a possibility you can walk today, but I need an awful lot on the table to make that happen.'

Still he denied it, like he'd denied it every time he got caught. Refusing to believe there wasn't some way out, listening to the voice that said it would all be all right. Like his soul couldn't believe in the life it had been given. He told Warren he didn't know what she wanted.

'I think you do, Bill. We want the Club, just the same way they want you. What few leads we have into them tell us you're the hot topic on their agenda. A bit more digging and it turns out you were, briefly at least, one of their very best. So, we want their full MO. Names, dates, times. We want to know when it's coming in and where and how the distribution works. Everything, Murdoch, or you're going back to Glenburn to await your trial.'

She smiled kindly as she said it, like she was doling out some unpleasant but necessary medicine. Ash fell from his cigarette into the pool of tea on the table and he found he was shaking his head.

'I don't ... I've never ...'

He turned away from the two women and found a worse sight. Himself in the mirror, beaten up, in a white prison visiting suit across the table from the cops. He closed his eyes and shook his head. 'I can't.'

'Why not?' The hoarseness in Natalie's voice cracked the air around them. 'Because of your stupid criminal code; the law you grew up by? But what about *you*, Bill? What about what *you* want? You told me you wanted to get out, be better than the animals. But you never will, don't you realise that? You're never going to be any different from the rest of them.' She stood, her chair scolding the floor as it pushed back from the table. 'And what's really sad is that you know it's true. You know you could be better than them just by talking to us. But instead your trapped by *their* stupid rules.'

Warren looked at Natalie with the same calm expression she'd assumed since entering the room. Murdoch wanted her to interrupt, to tell Natalie to sit down and shut up, but Warren waited in silence with slightly raised eyebrows to see what else she had to say.

'And you know what?' Natalie went on. 'This is it! This is your big chance to leave the animals behind, to get the hell out forever. To prove, not to me and not to them, but to *yourself* that you really are different. And what do you say? You say "Eugh, I can't."'

Her last three words mimicked a pathetic little child and he found himself thinking of Tom: the trusting look on the boy's face when Murdoch had last seen him in his stupid school uniform. Warren coughed and gave a little nod, some tiny signal in police-ese that Natalie should leave now. Murdoch looked away to the wall with the mirror, but even there Natalie had second-guessed him – her reflection locked eyes with him, long seconds of contempt before she turned and quietly left the room.

She knew her stuff, DCI Warren. Once she and Murdoch were alone together, she sat slouched in her chair, like she was equally defeated by Natalie's outburst, the choices on the table. After a few minutes, she reached across and shuffled a cigarette from Murdoch's packet, lit it and smoked dejectedly. She said nothing, expected nothing, was nothing. There was not one ounce of triumph in the woman. Not when he started talking and not even when he signed the first piece of paper six hours later.

55.

THREE INMATES RECAPTURED AFTER JAILBREAK FROM GLENBURN

Sydney Morning Herald

8 July, BOMBALA — Three inmates who escaped from Glenburn jail in southern New South Wales have been recaptured after a high-speed chase which left a police officer hurt.

Officers say the three men car-jacked an elderly couple after failing to show up for roll-call on Friday.

The couple were confronted by the men outside a business on the corner of Bridge Street and Napier Street and threatened with a screwdriver.

Officers in Bombala spotted the car on Friday night and pursued it, but the prisoners jumped out near Cathcart and fled into the State forest.

Police found the three escapees on Saturday after launching a manhunt, using officers, a helicopter and a dog unit. A fourth man, William James Murdoch, is yet to be recaptured. Police warn that Murdoch, who is awaiting trial on drug and violence offences, should not be approached.

A police spokesman was unable to provide any further details. Officials say an officer suffered a shoulder injury in a crash during the pursuit.

56

They made him walk down the echoing stairwell, through the damp garden and up the stairs next door five times. Each time he came back, someone new had turned up. A technician for this, an expert in that, someone just assigned to the case. Eventually Natalie, who Murdoch had insisted on being there, had to press herself into a corner to keep out of the way. It was a dull room with fancy plasterwork on the high ceiling cut off by a modern wall. Half of someone's bedroom once. An office more recently, until the police had moved in. Thick curtains were drawn against the dawn, but the beginnings of rush hour rumbled up from the street and vibrated against the thin glass. Somewhere out there, people were leading normal lives.

There were seven of them in the room by the end, perched on various pieces of furniture, scribbling notes or turning knobs, trying to look like they weren't just waiting. None of them looked like coppers. The technicians probably weren't, but most of the rest had to be. Two at the back, Rutherford and Hanson, looked like heavies from the other side: short hair and scars, not an inch of neck between them – Murdoch would never have known. They stood and examined him shamelessly as a young bloke with bad breath and pens in his breast pocket fiddled with the wires under Murdoch's shirt. The young bloke asked him to turn around, then to raise his arms. So there he was – half-naked and strung like a puppet, when DCI Warren walked through the door in her smart black suit.

'Morning, team. Morning, Murdoch. Ready for the wedding?'

She was excited, her beady little eyes alive. If this went well she would shine: another victory in a no doubt stellar career. If it went badly, well, what was one more dead crook? Warren clicked her expensive pen, found a spare square metre by the window and started the briefing. Like anyone in the room hadn't heard it a hundred times before.

'The target normally arrives at 7.30 a.m. His friend goes off and parks the car, grabs them some coffees, has a quick dart – round trip about fifteen minutes. We'll intercept him,' she nodded at Rutherford and Hanson, 'but as soon as the target suspects Mr Murdoch is here on anything other than a personal vendetta, he'll clam up. He's not stupid. So Murdoch, you've got fifteen minutes. And remember—'

'Prosecutable evidence,' said Murdoch. 'You said. Several times.'

Warren smiled at him while everyone else stared at the floor. 'Which means nothing vague,' she said. 'We're going after the murder charge, but anything on the trafficking is a bonus. Of course, if you're stamping on his head at the time, it won't stand up in court; please try and remember that.'

She glanced at her watch and asked around the room to check everyone was clear on their roles. Once that was done, there were three empty minutes, Murdoch's stomach playing a symphony of its own. He couldn't remember why he'd wanted Natalie there; now he found he couldn't look at her. Then, suddenly, it was time for him to go next door again.

The office looked exactly the same as the last time he'd been there. Heavy furniture on tiny legs, thick green curtains pooling on the floor, studded sofas either side of the fireplace. Even the globe by the window was still open, glasses and heavy decanters reflecting the dull morning light. It was like none of the previous nine months had happened; like Maria was about to arrive, insist he have a drink and pat the sofa next to her. The lack of change unnerved him, like you could set anyone on the Club and it wouldn't make a difference. He thought about Harvey Clarke; about if the journalist had called in senior police at all, or if the first copper he'd spoken to had called the Club. He shook the idea away – the police the only thing between him and death right now – and concentrated on his surroundings again. The office was cold: the huge windows that baked it and the waiting room in summer provided no insulation in the winter. And it smelled different. When Maria was alive, furniture polish and her perfume had hung in the air. Now it was stale cigars.

Murdoch wanted to be sitting with a casual cigarette when Harris arrived. Behind the desk or in the huge wing chair just inside the door. He wanted to let out a cool line like, 'You look tired, Harris, you should take a holiday,' and watch Harris spin round and wonder how the hell he'd got in. But that wouldn't disarm him. So after he'd walked around the room for a few minutes, run his hands over the satin walls and felt the plush velvet of the curtains, he stood beside the door and waited. Breathed slowly and looked at the dimly lit office, wondering if he shouldn't have accepted Harris's offer all those months earlier.

At first, everything went to plan. Harris arrived at seven thirty-two, the creaking cage elevator signalling his approach. He was halfway into the office, door handle in one hand, cane in the other, when Murdoch simply stepped forward, reached his two hands inside Harris's jacket, unclipped his holster and pulled out the Glock he'd used to shoot Maria. Just like that – smooth as you like. He threw the pistol behind him so it clattered noisily across the floorboards and onto a rug, then used both hands again to pull Harris into the room. That bit wasn't so easy. Harris might need a stick to walk, but his upper body was still strong. As Murdoch got rid of the revolver, he'd let go of his cane and was pulling the door closed between them, breathing in heavy grunts. Murdoch threw himself into the closing space just in time, the edge of the door banging painfully against his spine and the back of his head. He had to put two solid kicks into Harris's bad leg before the big man went down. Even then he fought back, swearing loudly and throwing dangerous punches as Murdoch dragged him into the office by the back of his collar. Halfway to the sofas, Harris's phone fell from his pocket. Murdoch kicked it under a table, but not before he'd noticed the time that flashed as it came to life. Seven thirty-six. Nine minutes until Harris got suspicious that Hussein hadn't arrived.

It was seven thirty-eight before they were in a position to talk. Harris looked like the walking dead: shadows like bruises under his eyes and a grey tint to his skin. He sat on the floor, propped up against the end of a sofa, rubbing the leg Murdoch had kicked and breathing heavily. Murdoch walked over to the Glock, unclipped the cartridge and slid it into his pocket. Maybe the coppers could prove it was from the same gun that had killed Maria.

'Now that this is empty,' he said, 'maybe we can talk like grown-ups. I want a deal.'

Harris pushed his fingers through his thick hair, rubbed his chin with the back of his hand, checked his watch.

'Expecting someone?' said Murdoch.

Harris looked up and grimaced. He wiped his chin again. 'Unfortunately, not. You've got me all to yourself this time. You've got balls coming back here, Bill, I'll give you that. When I heard you'd got out of Glenburn – and please tell me how you did that – I thought it was the last we'd see of you. I underestimated you.'

'So, a deal?'

Harris coughed out a laugh. 'Jesus, Bill, you'll keep. You *should* work for me, do you know that? With your bloody-mindedness and your obvious talents, I reckon you'd go far.'

'I said I wanted a deal.'

Harris sighed and dropped his head – a man so tired he'd do anything to be left alone. After a slow minute, he raised his eyes. 'What kind of a deal would that be?'

'You take the Club and your suppliers off my back and I give you your delivery. Then I disappear and it's all over. I don't want to go out the same way as Maria.'

Harris pulled a face like he was thinking about it. Slowly. He reached out and flattened the rug beside him, pulled his shirt and jacket straight. 'The delivery's nothing to do with me,' he said at last. 'As for the Club, I'm not sure there's anything I can do.'

Murdoch waited for him to go on, but that was it. No counter-offer, no bargaining. An ornate clock above the fireplace said it was seven forty-six.

'Weird being in here without Maria,' said Murdoch. 'I still think of it as her office. You're probably regretting it now, knocking her off before finding a replacement. Having to do all the dirty work yourself.'

'It's not too late for you to take the job,' said Harris. 'Running away from us will be tough, but stay here and add value and all this could be yours. We could set you up no problem …'

He continued talking, explaining how it would work, but Murdoch wasn't listening. He could see Harris's phone flashing again, shaking itself silently under the table by the door. If Harris turned, he'd see it. Murdoch walked to the other end of the office and leaned against the huge desk.

'How do I know you won't finish me off like you did Maria?'

Before Harris could answer, the door from the waiting room opened. It was still dark in the office and Murdoch presumed the silhouette in the doorway was one of the heavies who'd intercepted Hussein – that the idiots had come too soon. Then he watched as the silhouette set down two coffees on the floor and stood again with a revolver in its hand. It took a step forward and Murdoch saw it was Ibrahim Hussein himself.

57

They put him on the sofa facing the door: the one where Maria had first told him about Harris and the changes at the Club. Hussein perched on the arm, uncomfortable in his smart suit, holding the revolver on Murdoch while Harris, refusing any help, pulled himself up to his feet. It was a slow and painful process. The big man was hurting, wheezing as he dragged himself from sofa arm to tabletop to chair back until he could bend and pick up his cane. Even then he forced himself on, over to his Glock and, after a brief search, the cartridge Murdoch had let slip from his pocket behind the cushion of the wing chair. Then back again, tapping hard on the rugs, before collapsing into the sofa opposite Murdoch and Hussein.

'You all right, boss?'

Hussein was watching Harris carefully, leaning towards him as far as his jacket would allow, his eyes intense – a hand grenade in a well-made suit. Murdoch had watched him growing steadily angrier as Harris struggled around the room. Now Hussein was breathing heavily through his nose, his gun unlocked, his thumb itching at the safety catch. Harris waved the question away, then cut the wave short to pinch the bridge of his nose.

'Bill, Bill, Bill,' he said, still out of breath. 'Did you really think you'd get away with coming into my office and telling me what to do?'

'Let me look after him, boss.' Hussein gestured at Murdoch with his gun. 'You needs to rest up.'

Harris shook his head slowly, looked up, and smiled his big rich smile. He checked the clip on the Glock's magazine and weighed the gun in his hand.

'No thanks, Ibby. He's mine. Killing Maria was work for me – it was a shot in the back she deserved. The Club shifts eighty per cent of Sydney's narcotics – did you know that, Murdoch? We can't have someone running it like a mothers' group. But killing you is going to be fun.'

The force of the bullet knocked Hussein backwards off the arm of the sofa and through the narrow glass table behind it – a violence of noise that filled the room and ended with the thump of Hussein's head hitting the floor. Murdoch flinched, then stared at Harris who in turn was staring at the pistol in his hand. Behind him a heavily padded marksman filled the doorway to the waiting room. Murdoch rolled himself backwards over the sofa – a slower, more cumbersome version of Hussein's trajectory – and shouted, 'Harris has a gun.' But the marksman had already seen it. There was another dull thud followed by a long slow groan from Harris. Then the room was full of voices, two of them on top of Hussein, yelling at Murdoch to stay down, stay down. But there was no need. Hussein had lost his gun in the fall and was moaning softly, bleeding heavily from one shoulder and the side of his head. On the other side of the sofa, Murdoch heard Harris being read his rights.

Once the room was secured, they let him go to the bathroom. Warren was strutting around like a peacock, congratulating everyone and inspecting the office. When Murdoch told her where he was going she laughed; yes, they'd all heard his stomach rumbling down the wire. In the marble en-suite, he stripped off his shirt and unpeeled the contraption from his skin. Rolled it into a tight ball and buried it in his underwear. Later, when one of the heavies asked him for it, Murdoch said he'd given it to the technician with the pens. After that, they forgot to ask him again.

58.

It was Rutherford and Hanson who drove him to the safe house. Rutherford and Hanson, who'd been supposed to intercept Hussein. They drove him south-west of Sydney, pretty much in the direction of Glenburn. The two of them broad-shouldered in the front; Murdoch alone on the huge back seat like a kid being taken to school. Did he want any music? No, he didn't.

Rutherford, the younger and more senior of the two, turned back from the front seat with a sincere frown. 'Mate, I have to apologise again. Really. That was not supposed to happen.'

Murdoch scowled at him. 'So your boss and all your colleagues keep telling me. But you know what? I kind of knew that already. I was listening to the briefings and I was the one what ended up with that gorilla waving his gun in my face. What's the matter? You worried you wouldn't get a murder charge unless you got to witness one?'

'No, of course not. You know that's not true. We ... well, as a result of human error ...'

'It was my fault,' said Hanson from the driver's seat, glancing into the rear-view mirror to catch Murdoch's eye. 'He changed from his normal route. The sarge spotted it, but my radio was off.'

He didn't look particularly upset about it. Rutherford mumbled another apology and turned back in his seat. Murdoch stared at the back of their buzzcut heads, the outskirts of Sydney flying past, fields and warehouses and hills mixed in with the sprawl. Relaxation and relief collapsed into sleep.

He woke up a few minutes before they parked in front of a pale brick house, as featureless as every other house in the flat streets around it, all of them built in the previous two years. It was detached but only just, built to the very edges of its plot, more thought given to a driveway than a garden. Hanson opened the garage door with a remote control and they all stayed in the car until it had closed again.

'You don't need to worry,' said Rutherford, once they were in the bare kitchen that adjoined the garage. 'No one will find you here. And even if they did, we'd look after you.'

He tapped the firearm on his right hip and gave a reassuring smile. Like that little thing would be any protection against the kind of armoury the Club would bring.

There were no more than the bare essentials in the house. A freezer full of ready-made meals, sleeping bags on bare mattresses in the bedrooms, brand new sofas and a television with three channels. Hanson switched on the football and swore when he saw the score. Stood close to the screen, staring at it like no one else might want to watch. Murdoch asked how long they were there for.

'No idea,' said Rutherford. He was in the kitchen opening one cupboard after another. 'Few days, maybe?'

'What are we waiting for?'

'Instructions. I don't know more than that, mate. But we'll be here with you the whole time.'

'Just so as you're not the only one pissed off by the entire experience,' said Hanson, before cursing again as another try was scored.

After one day, the house smelled of the three of them. Murdoch struggled to sit, every chair uncomfortable, every hour ticking slowly past.

236

Natalie had shown him the article describing his escape from prison, planted in the paper for Harris. 'Nice job,' he'd told her, thinking: *too nice.* Someone up on the Central Coast would be more worried by it than Harris had been – someone already at work to cover his tracks. He doubted DCI Warren would prioritise the search for Georgie Walker over tying up the loose ends of her own case.

On that first evening, Hanson came in from the end of the football to find Murdoch kneeling on the surface beside the kitchen sink, examining the lock on a window that overlooked the garden.

'Don't worry. No one's going to get in here without us knowing about it. We'll do our job.'

Murdoch climbed down and faced the detective. 'You don't sound too happy about that.'

Hanson shrugged and turned to the fridge. They'd picked up some beers on the way down – it was against the rules, but what the hell. When Hanson turned back, Murdoch was still looking at him.

'Do we have a problem, Hanson?'

'You don't want me to answer that, mate.'

'Oh, I think I do. Mate. You see, I've been banged up with more blokes than you can imagine and I know it's best to get any shit out on the table straight away. What's the problem?'

'OK.' Hanson took the top off his beer and threw it clattering into the metal sink. 'I don't like grasses. Stupid, ain't it? You'd think anyone on the force would be grateful. Glad there's people like you with no values at all so we get to catch the rest of the scum. But funnily enough, it doesn't work that way. I don't like you, Murdoch.'

'Don't worry about it, Hanson. It works the other way too. Grasses are scum, sure. But nothing's worse than a bent copper.'

Hanson started a question, but Rutherford, who'd muted the television, called in loudly from the living room. He wanted to talk to Hanson. In here. Now.

The front door was bolted top and bottom, fastened by a Chubb and two noisy chains. There were patio doors between the living room and the garden, but these were locked with a key Murdoch had never seen. Same story with his bedroom window, which looked out over the front driveway.

The downstairs bathroom had no window at all, but upstairs was a small one that opened. Standing on the toilet seat, Murdoch could see a highway running across the bare green escarpment that held in the estate – a thousand cars an hour on the way to somewhere better. There'd be a town nearby, factories and a Westfield, but between the house and the highway were only undergrown gardens, toddlers, bored dogs and low wooden fences baked pale by the sun. The kind of place he'd spend the rest of his life in, if the system got its way. He wondered what the suicide rate was. How many bodies were hanging in those pink-brick boxes, still waiting to be found.

That night, Rutherford found him in the kitchen watching a cup rotate in the microwave. 'Bloody hell, Murdoch, you frightened the life out of me. It's two o'clock in the morning.'

'Hanson doesn't seem too bothered.'

'Yeah, well, fortunately one of us is a light sleeper. You all right?'

'Not exactly dreaming sweet dreams.'

'Want to talk about it?'

Rutherford still felt guilty about what had happened in Macquarie Street; not a bad bloke for a cop.

'No,' said Murdoch. 'I just always need a drink in the night.'

The microwave pinged and he took out the milk. Forced a smile and said good night.

The next night they met at the top of the stairs. Rutherford gave him a sleepy smile and went back to bed without a word.

The night after that he didn't even get up when he heard Murdoch moving around downstairs.

59.

The store on Bridge Street looked more like a sex shop than anything else. Its huge plate glass window was papered black on the inside so that if you walked past, you saw nothing but your own reflection. The woodwork – door, window frames, panelling – was all black too. There was a black buzzer for whoever wanted in to communicate with those on the inside and a tiny camera allowing those on the inside to have a good look at whoever wanted in. So maybe not a sex shop, after all.

It sat in the northern end of the Sydney CBD, squeezed between a computer store and a solicitor's office, in one of those little terraces that somehow survived when all the glass towers went in. Murdoch had noticed it on his first week with the Club. He'd asked Maria what it was all about.

'Clever, isn't it, my dear?' she'd said. 'It's pretending to be anonymous, but not so anonymous you don't notice it. It's saying, "Look at me, I'm invisible."'

'It says it sells spyware.'

'It does. Big business, keeping an eye on each other. We use it all the time.'

Which was the problem that now faced Murdoch. Getting away from the safe house had been easy enough – one more stolen car and a promise to himself it would be the last. Forcing himself into Sydney CBD with a brand-new price on his head had been more difficult. Stepping foot into this shop, used 'all the time' by the Club, was proving almost impossible. It was too cold to gather his courage in the street – he'd left the safe house in the T-shirt they'd arrested him in – so he sat in the huge glass foyer of the office tower across the road, a building he used to sell in when he was wearing better clothes. He ignored the late office workers trotting past, sucked on a coffee, and focused on the shop until he'd run out of excuses.

Inside the door from the street was a narrow flight of stairs down to the basement: a long narrow room with a blood-red carpet. Light from tiny bulbs on tracks glinted off the glass cases and made everything look expensive. The guy behind the counter was clearly ex-police – standard issue, stamped with whatever it was about coppers that only Rutherford and Hanson had managed to avoid. A face that had seen it all. He had vague shadows under his eyes, wrinkles of tiredness, and didn't look like he was enjoying running a business as much as he had hoped. He was talking quietly with a man whose back was turned to Murdoch, the two of them leaning over a catalogue.

'I won't be a moment, sir,' said the shopkeeper.

Or, *'Don't stand there and listen to our conversation.'*

Murdoch wandered past rows of hanging binoculars, rubber torches, a small display of body armour, all the way to a cabinet of cameras at the back of the store. There was no exit there. He drummed his fingers on the top of the glass cabinet and looked at the prices of the tiny machines inside.

'Yes, sir?'

Murdoch hadn't heard the other customer leave, but he was now alone with the shopkeeper. Then the door at the top of the stairs slammed and Murdoch failed to hide the effect on his nerves. He ran his hand across his unshaven chin and wondered what he must look like. He strolled over to the counter.

'You were looking for something, sir?'

'Yeah. I've got this microphone and I need something what can record off it.'

He took the tangled wire from his pocket and laid it in front of the ex-cop, who picked it up and inspected it carefully, like this was a normal request.

'Nice piece. Top of the range. Shouldn't be a problem at all.'

He came around from behind his counter and guided Murdoch to a series of shelves on the other side of the room. He'd started describing the different devices available, the range of costs and advantages of each, when a series of short sharp buzzes filled the shop. The ex-cop excused himself and went to look at a screen beneath the counter. He pressed a button near it and the sounds of the street came down the stairs, followed by a pair of heavy feet. They brought into the basement a small blond man who, upon seeing Murdoch, stood and stared. Murdoch stared back.

'What is it?' said the shopkeeper.

'Morning, Joe,' said the blond man, remembering why he'd come. 'You want a coffee?'

'I'm with a customer.'

'Don't mind me,' said Murdoch. 'I'll be gone by the time he gets back.'

The man at the bottom of the stairs looked at Murdoch again, a second longer than necessary, then looked back to the ex-cop with a raised eyebrow.

'Coffee?'

Murdoch remembered who the blond man was. An old customer of his from the office tower across the road. No reason he shouldn't still be a customer of the Club. No reason he shouldn't have been offered a reward for making a call if he ever saw Murdoch again. The ex-cop ordered a flat white and within a minute they were alone in the shop again, the door at the top of the stairs slamming on the street noise.

'You was saying transmitting to a remote recorder is better?'

The shopkeeper took him through what they had in stock, starting into detailed descriptions which Murdoch interrupted with brief questions until he quickly picked one and insisted it was the one he wanted. When the ex-cop started saying what a good choice it was, Murdoch carried it to the counter himself and took out the credit card he'd borrowed from Hanson. The two detectives would have found him gone by now and probably checked their wallets, but Murdoch had replaced Hanson's card with a similar-looking one he'd swiped from the guy who'd wired him up. Hanson wouldn't notice until he tried to use it.

'And I'll need your ID,' said the shopkeeper.

'Why's that then?'

'It's policy.'

'Is this your shop?'

'Yes, sir.'

'So it's your policy.'

'Yes, sir, that's my policy.'

'You got any stock that's not shifting?'

'Excuse me?'

'What have you got on your shelves what's been here so long you reckon you're going to have to take a bath on it?'

The man behind the counter was about to say something, but then he looked past Murdoch at the shelves on the other side of the room. He rubbed the back of his neck before making up his mind.

'The body armour.'

'How much does that go for then?'

'That's three grand's worth over there.'

Murdoch looked over at it. Counted silently to five and said he'd take it all. The ex-cop swiped the card through the machine – over four thousand dollars in one purchase – and they both watched in silence as the machine spoke to the bank.

60

The payphone sat in a row of five in a pedestrianised high street somewhere north of Chatswood. It took Murdoch almost two hours to find it, driving around streets he didn't know, blinded by a low winter sun that did nothing to warm the day. When he'd been a kid, there had been things called phone boxes where you could hear and make yourself heard. Now he had to shiver over a dirty mouthpiece in a street full of lunchtime shoppers, every one of them turning to look at a full-grown man who didn't own a mobile phone. He left a message on Davie's iPhone, the machine crunching mercilessly through his coins, then tried to remember the name of the estate agents where Davie worked.

'You gunna be long?' A homeless woman, startling blue eyes way back behind her skin, scowled at him from the phone next to his. 'This one don't work.'

Murdoch ignored her and fed in his last coins: no choice but to try Davie's mobile again. Davie answered on the first ring.

'Davie, it's me.'

'Bill! Dude! Oh God, I'm so sorry I haven't visited; it's just I couldn't find where you were for ages and then Glenburn's miles away ...'

'Davie, it's fine. Listen up, I'm out.'

'You're what? How ... I mean ...What?'

'Davie, shut up and listen. I need to ask you a favour. We need to meet as soon as possible.'

There was a tiny silence on the line – not even a crackle audible over the sounds of the street. Murdoch stuck the receiver between his ear and his shoulder and tried to rub the cold out of his arms. A few metres away, a spruiker was setting up a speaker outside a clothes shop.

'When you say "out", you mean they let you out, right?'

'Davie, I'm on a payphone; I've not got any more coins so you've got to shut up and listen.'

'Oh well, you haven't lost your charm, I see.'

The phone clicked and the line went dead. Murdoch closed his eyes and took a deep breath. Listened to the spruiker testing her microphone, the volume so high you couldn't understand her words.

'You need more money!' the homeless woman shouted at him. 'More coins!'

She shuffled closer until he could smell the dried urine and alcohol on her. He smiled and asked if she had any.

'Any what?'

The spruiker beside them turned off her speaker and disappeared into the clothes store.

'Do you have any coins?' shouted Murdoch.

The homeless woman opened her toothless mouth, put her head back and let out a screeching laugh that turned every head in the street. 'You asking me for money?' she howled. 'Kinell, mate, you must be fackin desperate.'

Murdoch got to Montauban shortly after dark. He'd toyed with the idea of taking one last walk – on the beach or up the steep streets in the bowl of the hill, smelling the air and the ocean again – cleansing himself of Glenburn. It was the cold more than the risk that stopped him. He'd had the car heater on all the way from Sydney, blasting the chill from his bones, but as soon as he parked in the overgrown darkness and looked up at the stilt house the car started cooling around him. He didn't want to get out and into the freezing air again.

He sat there for half an hour in the dark, checking his theories and plans, listening to the wind in the casuarinas, watching Davie's silhouette move back and forth between the living room and the kitchen. Now and then someone would walk past the car, out with the dog or coming back from the shops, through the pool of light cast by the streetlamp at the bottom of Davie's driveway and on into the dark again. Murdoch recognised every one of them, even those he couldn't name. If any of them spotted him, the whole town would soon know he was there.

The time for his meeting with Davie came and went, but Davie continued moving slowly around his shack, like being late was an art form that needed perfecting. It was only when Murdoch was looking up from his watch for the fourth time, swearing slowly under his breath, that he saw the lights in the house go out one by one. He wound down his window and heard the front door slam, and, a second later, the familiar creak of the middle steps. Then Davie appeared below the streetlamp, a bag slung over his right shoulder. He looked up and down the street, turned sharply to the right and disappeared into the darkness. Murdoch gave him three minutes. Timed it by his watch – no other way to resist the temptation of going straight after him. But no one was following Davie; no one in those three minutes anyway.

The air outside the car was even colder than he'd expected. There was a wind coming off the lagoon and through the trees that bit right to the bone. Murdoch stood for a few seconds, rubbing his arms in the dark and wondering if he should run up to the stilt house and nick something. Or maybe just get into his old bed and stay there forever. He heard footsteps running from the direction of the shops, looked around and realised this was pretty much the spot where they had been attacked a few months before. He swore at the memory, at the footsteps and the cold, and set off after Davie. But he'd left it too late. The footsteps were close behind him now and as he passed through the pool of light at the bottom of Davie's driveway, he heard a familiar voice.

'Oh it's Bill! Bill, wait for me!'

Tom Walker – dressed for a trip to the North Pole. A thick jacket two sizes too large, a pink woolly hat with a pom-pom, a bright orange scarf. Mittens probably joined by a piece of string inside his sleeves. He was out of breath from his running, steam pulsing from his mouth, but he managed a last sprint and threw himself at Murdoch. Held him so tight his words muffled into Murdoch's stomach.

'Dad said you were in prison! He said we'd never see you again!'

Murdoch peeled the kid off and squatted down to his level if only to shut him up. The kid went to hug him again, padded arms around his neck, then stood wide-eyed when Murdoch forced him back.

'Yeah, Tom, listen. What you up to? Why you out?'

'Swimming was cancelled. Mrs McGrath brought me back to Montie. I was running because it's cold.'

'And where you going now?'

'Home. Do you want to come?'

'No. What I want is a favour. I need some help on the case. Do you reckon your dad would miss you if you helped me out for an hour?'

Tom took a step back, terrified by the idea, struggling with the right thing to do. Murdoch thought for a second he was going to cry, but instead the kid unburied his watch from a sleeve and a mitten and held it to catch the light from the streetlamp. Murdoch could see him counting, lips calculating slowly.

'No!' Tom said slowly, still unsure if he dared do this. 'Swimming doesn't finish normally until eight o'clock and then we have to drive back to Montie and then it takes me ten minutes to walk home from Mrs McGrath's so we've got … one hour and thirty-two minutes.'

He stared wide-eyed at Murdoch, unable to believe he was on such an adventure.

'Nice one, mate. And do you reckon you could help me?'

Again a few seconds to think about it, then the pink pom-pom nodded slowly.

'OK, this is what you have to do. Go up there to Davie's house and wait inside to see who comes in. You'll have to hide so no one sees you. Stay there until, er, eight fifteen and then, if no one's there, you can go home. Do you reckon you could do that? Later on, you can tell me what you saw. What do you think?'

Murdoch never got a response. Tom turned, ran up the driveway as fast as he could, padded arms out beside him like a toddler, and disappeared towards the house. A second later, Murdoch heard the middle stairs creak, then the front door slam. Davie still didn't lock the bleeding thing.

61.

Murdoch heard Davie before he saw him. Stomping the cold from his feet, flapping his arms in his puffer-jacket, whistling to kill the boredom. He hung back for a second to watch him, trees creaking above in time to the wind, leaves and twigs falling like rain. It wasn't too late to find another way. But the cold forced him forwards and he called Davie's name as loudly as he dared, signalling to him to come out of the light. Once again, he was hugged by padded arms, asked unnecessary questions.

'Jesus, Bill, aren't you freezing? Here, put this on. I brought you a bag of clothes too.'

Davie peeled off his jacket and handed it to Murdoch, who in return handed him the plastic bag he'd brought from the car.

'Clothes?' said Murdoch.

'Well, I'm guessing you're on the run again.'

Murdoch didn't answer that. Instead he zipped himself into the warm jacket and pointed at the items Davie pulled from the plastic bag.

'That's the receiver; that's the recorder. You just plug that wire into that hole and listen through that earpiece thing. But we need to test it.'

'Where do you want me to record you from? It's freezing out here.'

'There's a car outside your place what I borrowed. How about we bring it back here and you sit in that?'

'Borrowed? I thought you weren't going to "borrow" any more cars?'

'Or stay out here in the cold if you thinks that's a better idea.'

They tested it for twenty minutes. Davie in the car; Davie outside the car; Murdoch walking two hundred metres away, whispering to himself and talking at full volume, counting slowly all the way. Davie reckoned he could hear every word, even through the jacket, and when they rewound the tape, it proved him right. Every tiny murmur was there, from one to four hundred and four, loud in the darkness of the stolen car. Murdoch told Davie how he'd diverted Tom, something of how he'd got out of Glenburn, a little of what had happened since then. He said he wanted one more smoke and then, after Davie had sworn he wouldn't come in or call the police no matter what happened, not until they had a confession, they sat in silence for a while, the orange end of Murdoch's cigarette the only light.

'I just want to say,' said Davie, winding down the window, 'for the record, I don't think you should do this.'

'Yeah, mate, you kind of did that a few times already.'

'Why don't I go in?'

'Not happening.'

'Or why don't we let the police handle it?'

'Oh yeah, cos that's worked really well so far.'

'Bill, if what you've just told me is true, you're a free man. You can walk away from this. You can clear off and disappear. But what if you're wrong? You go in there and things get nasty, they'll throw you back inside.'

246

At first Murdoch didn't have an answer for this, but before he'd finished his cigarette, it came to him. 'When you say "a free man", Davie, you mean not locked up in jail. But there's blokes I've met on the inside what are loads freer than I'd be if I scarpered now. I want to be …'

But he didn't have the words for that. Nothing that didn't sound stupid. He took a last drag and, stubbing the fag end out in the ashtray, said it was time to go.

62.

Walking quietly into the room, Murdoch remembered the pictures he'd cut out and stuck on the noticeboard in his shack on the warehouse roof. He couldn't name the details he'd liked in them, but he knew they were here too: his dream house come to life. There was a soft glow to the space, warm light from lamps at the ends of each sofa. A fire burning in the hearth. Even the soundtrack was perfect: a choir of monks chanting slowly through the speakers. Paul Walker sat on the sofa to the right of the fireplace, his back to the French doors. He was wearing jeans and a thick cream cardigan, Ugg slippers on his feet. No sunglasses for once and Murdoch saw he had deep brown eyes. He was staring into space, listening to the music like he was waiting for someone. The sight of him sitting there, calm and patient and utterly in control, made the hairs stand up on the back of Murdoch's neck, but when he spoke, Walker jumped, clearly startled.

'Bill, my God! What the hell are you doing here?'

'The door was unlocked. Can I come in? No, don't stand up.'

He said it firmly enough for Walker to comply. The older man lowered himself back into the sofa, his body a different shape from a minute before. Back rigid, hands pressing into the firm cushion either side of him, limbs alert and angular. Murdoch sat on the opposite sofa and they faced each other across the coffee table – kings on a chessboard.

'You frightened me, Bill.'

'I'm sure I did, Paul. I'm sure I frightened you the very first time I walked into this room.'

Walker looked down at his hands and started to speak, but Murdoch interrupted him. 'You know, Paul – or, maybe, you don't know –

but when I first met you, I really looked up to you. I had this idea of what life should be like and I thought you'd got it. I really admired you for it. This house, for example. Just the atmosphere in here,' he took in a deep breath through his nose, 'it smells so rich and comfortable.'

The fire cracked, a spark hitting the fireguard, and Walker flinched. He looked at the door to the hallway. The monks on the stereo had finished singing and the silence was broken only by the crackle of the fire and the ticking of a carriage clock on the mantelpiece.

'But then,' said Murdoch, 'then I found out it's not the smell of rich and comfortable. It's the smell of White Satin room scent what costs forty dollars down at Kildare shops. Which kind of sums it up really, don't it?'

'Bill, I don't know what you're talking about. You're frightening me.'

'It's just another thing what you can buy, innit? It don't mean nothing. Don't mean this is a happy family home or nothing like that.'

'Bill, you should go. I know you've been in trouble with the police and I'm sorry for that—'

'You should be, Paul. You really should. The thing is though, you're not. In fact, I reckon when I started getting into trouble with the law, that was the first time you relaxed in months. You probably thought it saved you the bother of having to get me into trouble yourself. But the thing is, Paul, me being in trouble ended up with me being thrown back in the clink. And there's one thing to be said for being inside – it gives you time to think. Would you like to know what I thought about, Paul?'

Murdoch heard the anger in his voice and forced himself to breathe. There was no need to rush this. 'I said, would you like to know what I thought about, Paul?'

Walker shook his head slowly.

'What I thought about was everything what happened to me in this town. Everything people said; everything people was worried about. Take Tom, for example. Cracking little lad, not as thick as he seems. He'd get that from you, the smarts. But you know the one thing he's terrified of, that kid?'

'Everything,' said Walker bitterly. 'He's terrified of everything.'

'But most of all he's terrified of you, Paul. I saw it the first time I was in this room, but I didn't think nothing of it. And you know what?

Georgie was terrified of you, too. Everyone talks about how timid and shy she was, when, really, she was just scared. She caught Tom following her once, following her somewhere where bad people was, and all she said was "Don't tell Dad." Not "Don't tell no one else," not "Don't tell no one at all." No, it was just "Don't tell Dad." Like she was more afraid of you than any of the thugs she'd got involved with. And everyone says how protective she was of Tom. I thought they meant at school, but they went to different schools, didn't they? So what did that mean then? Protecting Tom from what? I reckon it was you, Paul. Still, lots of kids are frightened of their strict parents. Doesn't mean you're a bad man or nothing, does it?'

Walker had started rubbing his temples with two fingers of each hand, his brown eyes staring and unfocused.

'You listening, Paul?'

'Yes, I'm listening. No, it doesn't mean I'm a bad man. What's this all about, Bill?'

Murdoch ignored the question. Ignored how confused Walker genuinely seemed.

'What is weird, though, is something what you said to me. You said – do you remember Paul? – you said, "I heard that two guys had a go at you." Remember that, when I got damaged down the road? Do you remember?'

Walker frowned, lost and frightened. A madman was in his living room and he didn't know how to react.

'Well, Paul, the weird thing about that is hardly no one knew there was two of them. Hannah didn't know. Only Davie and Natalie and I know neither of them told you. So how come you knew it? Weird, innit? Unless of course you was the one what paid 'em. You being the one what wanted me to piss off. Anyhow, it got me thinking about other things what people said. Like Tom telling me that you'd said if either of you ever saw me, you'd call the police again. Why "again", Paul? Unless it was you what called them the first time? Doesn't prove anything; maybe you did call them, that's what you're going to say, innit? Why shouldn't you? But wait, there's other stuff. Like when you told me you'd listened to all Georgie's CDs all the way through cos you was thinking along the same lines as me. But that was a lie. Because if you had of done, you'd have made damn sure I didn't take them

CDs away, cos you'd of known one of them was a DVD with Georgie's ultrasound on it.'

'Her ultrasound? What do you mean? What did she—? Are you telling me she was *pregnant*?! Don't be ridiculous. She wasn't like that; she was a good girl.'

Walker's pupils had dilated and the colour had drained from his face. Murdoch realised with horror that you couldn't fake that. He blinked the thought away and pushed on regardless.

'And that's the other thing, Paul. You always talk about her in the past tense. You always have done, ever since we first met. I'm surprised because you're really clever, so I'd of thought you'd catch yourself doing that. But no one's perfect.'

Walker flushed and stood suddenly, held back only by the coffee table.

'How dare you? How dare you walk into my house, tell me Georgie was pregnant and imply I'm somehow involved in her disappearance? Get out! You disgust me!'

He turned and took a step towards the hallway, but Murdoch was there before him. Walker's voice filled the room. 'Get out of my way! Get out of my house!'

'But, Paul, what about the best bit? What about the biggest lie of all? What about the red robin?'

Walker took a step backwards. His eyes were wide and, for the first time, Murdoch recognised the features he'd learned from photos of Georgie. Their eyes were the same. 'What are you talking about?' he whispered.

'The red robin, Paul. You told me you planted it a few days before Georgie disappeared. But Tom very clearly remembers planting it with you the day *after* she was last seen. Now why would you lie about that? Why would you lie about a freshly dug bed in your garden the day after your daughter disappeared? Would it be the same reason you told the police you were with your kids the night your wife, Sarah, died? When, in fact, you left Georgie babysitting Tom? Georgie, who was so terrified of you that she never contradicted that fact. So terrified of you, that she chose Alycia Thornton, of all fucking people, rather than you to tell she had a boyfriend? I'm guessing it's your temper that's the problem, Paul. I'm guessing that's why you killed your wife. And then,' Murdoch refused to think of Walker's

250

earlier surprise, 'why you killed Georgie when you found out she was pregnant.'

'You will leave this house now!' Walker pushed past Murdoch, spittle flying from his mouth. 'I've had enough of your sick fantasies; you're an animal. I'm going to call the police.'

Murdoch let him get into the hallway. Then he leaned back and put a solid donkey-kick into his kidneys. The older man fell heavily, his back arching mid-air and staying that way as he writhed on the black-and-white tiles. Murdoch reached down, undid Walker's belt, pulled it from its loops and used it to tie his hands behind his back. It wasn't easy. Walker realised what he was doing and started to resist, hands and legs flailing in all directions. A small wooden table beside them toppled over – a figurine of a shepherdess – falling and smashing on the floor. Murdoch had to punch Walker twice before he could still the man enough to tie him up. Then he walked to the kitchen to find a knife.

'You scum,' Walker screamed after him. 'You criminal scum. Your type, you come in here; this is my—'

Murdoch heard him stop at the same time as he heard the front door opening. He ran back to the hallway and stood there, knife in hand, and watched Natalie Conquest let herself in.

63.

At first Murdoch did what she told him to do. He put the knife on the floor and kicked it past Walker, who lay silent and wide-eyed, no sign of anger in him now. Then he stood back as Natalie approached and untied Walker's hands, her own hands shaking hard, struggling with the belt as she kept her eyes firmly fixed on Murdoch. She helped Walker to his feet – a weak old man attacked in his home – then fished out her mobile phone and called triple zero. Walker looked in the huge mirror that hung beside the door to the living room, cautiously touching the swelling around his eyes where Murdoch had punched him. He flattened his hair and coughed weakly until Natalie interrupted her call and told him to go upstairs and clean himself up. Which left her and Murdoch facing each other in the narrow hallway beside the stairs.

'Yes,' she said to the phone. 'I'll hold.'

Murdoch bent down and picked up the small table, started gathering the pieces of the smashed figurine.

'Please don't touch anything,' said Natalie. 'This is a crime scene.'

The scuffle with Walker had made Murdoch sweat in Davie's jacket and, standing up again under the weight of Natalie's frown, he felt suddenly claustrophobic. He fiddled with the jacket's zip, but it wouldn't move. Looking up, he found Natalie shaking her head at him – a kid she no longer had patience with. He gave up on the zip and frowned back at her.

'Please tell me you're calling for help to arrest Walker, Nat? After everything I told you and DCI Warren? I don't know why you've not done it yet.'

'No, you idiot. I'm calling for help to arrest you. I heard you'd done a runner and I came here straightaway, praying you didn't actually believe that nonsense you fed us at the station. I honestly thought I could stop you doing something stupid, but, for some reason, I'm still underestimating your abilities in that department. What are you *doing*, Bill? Why are you so determined to get thrown back in jail?'

'For fuck's sake, Nat, didn't you hear a thing I told you about him? Paul Walker killed Georgie – and probably her mother too!'

Natalie glanced up the stairs and whispered furiously. 'All DCI Warren and I heard were unsubstantiated allegations based on evidence so weak, I wouldn't even call it circumstantial. The police investigated Walker when Georgie first went missing; he was our prime suspect, I told you that.'

'So you did think he'd done her in, then?'

'We thought maybe he had, but we found nothing to corroborate that. Besides, he had no motive to kill her. And as far as Sarah's death was concerned, Georgie confirmed she was with him and Tom that night—'

'But he wasn't, I told you Tom confirmed he wasn't! And besides, like I said, I know where Georgie's body is; we just need Walker to confirm it was him what killed her.'

Natalie looked at him differently then. Shaking her head, like he was beyond help. 'Bill, I know this means a lot to you. And I know you once said you were more jealous of Paul Walker than anyone in the world, but …'

She frowned at what she heard from her mobile phone. Then she held it out towards him, a high-pitched whine from the speaker quickly replaced by a persistent crackle.

'Are you wearing something, Bill? Have you got a wire on? Oh my God, you have to be joking.'

She took a quick step back, like she was suddenly uncertain what else he was capable of. They both heard the bathroom door and Walker's slow feet on the stairs. Natalie looked up and, as she did so, Murdoch pushed her hard, then ran back as fast as he could to the kitchen. Before opening the door to the garden, he paused to hit all the switches on the back wall, the patio and the lawn lighting up in strange angles and patches of sickly green. He could hear Natalie coming after him, shouting his name furiously. He ignored her, stumbling more than running across the half-lit patio and down the crooked stone steps to the lawn.

On his knees beside the young red hedge, he looked up and saw her standing on the terrace, arms crossed and weight on one hip, in that frustrated pose she'd struck the first time they met. She was shouting at him still as he looked around in the dim shadows for something to dig with, yelling at him as he gave up and buried his bare hands in the cold earth beneath the hedge. He'd been digging for less than a minute, huge handfuls of dirt thrown across the floodlit lawn, when Natalie's voice was drowned out by another.

'Leave her alone, you scum!'

Walker's words bellowed through the cold night air. He pushed heavily past Natalie and took the steps to the lawn two at a time, breath visible in the lights from the house.

'Get your filthy criminal hands away from her.'

He must have picked up a rock on the way, or brought something heavy from the house, because the next thing Murdoch knew was darkness.

He wasn't out for long, not fully. But it took him a few seconds to remember where he was and what was wrong. There had been a fight; there still was a fight – he could hear it close behind him. He was lying in cold dirt, his head under a hedge, its new leaves shining scarlet where they caught the lights from the house, like they were bleeding too. Pushing himself onto his side, the pain immeasurable, he saw two figures struggling on the lawn beside him – Natalie and Walker grappling in a muted dance. Natalie had her arm around Walker's neck, pulling him hard from behind and struggling to keep her feet on the ground. Then, as Murdoch struggled to push himself up, Walker bent suddenly, using his weight and throwing Natalie over his shoulder and onto the lawn. She landed badly, two metres from Murdoch's feet, her full back thumping against the cold ground. She lay there shocked, her arms flailing beside her, her mouth wide and pulling hard on the freezing air, creaking it slowly back into her lungs. Walker kicked her hard in the side of the head, then came around and straddled her, sitting heavily on her stomach, his hands around her neck. Murdoch found he couldn't stand – the effort of sitting had made him vomit slightly, the acid from his stomach mixing with soil from the garden bed. Standing would involve his feet, which were too far away.

'Is that what did you to Georgie?' he managed. 'Is that how you killed your daughter because she'd got herself pregnant?'

Walker turned, his eyes catching the lights above the lawn, his breath heavy and steaming. His grey hair was sticking up again, but otherwise he seemed calm, a man working hard in his garden. He let go of Natalie's neck and left her limp in the grass, dead or alive it was impossible to tell, stood slowly and walked towards Murdoch, towering above him, his silhouette darker than the star-littered sky.

'I'm not going to kill her,' he said. 'You are. You're the kind of scum who'd do that. You slept with her, after all; did you think I didn't know? And now you come breaking into my house, attacking me, killing the police officer who came to my rescue.'

'You don't have to kill her.' Murdoch's voice sounded distant to his own ears. 'Just move Georgie's body tonight. No one will believe I killed Natalie.'

'Yes, they will. They'll believe anything of an animal like you. They'll think the only mistake they made was letting you out of a cage. There's a thing you don't get, Murdoch. People like us, good hard-working people, we're better than scum like you. We deserve our lives and you deserve to be locked up.'

Murdoch tried to push himself to his feet, but Walker was on him. He tried to throw a punch but, without a hand to hold himself up, he fell backwards through the hedge. He could smell the sweet scent he'd first noticed in the garden with Tom and, even now, a part of his brain managed to wonder what it was. Walker's shadow came through the hedge and he felt a knee on his chest, strong hands struggling to find his neck.

'You're the animal,' said Murdoch, too weak to fight back. 'You've got a nice house and a big car, but you're the criminal. You killed Georgie. I'm not—'

But Walker had him by the throat. 'That was an accident,' he spat, his full weight tight around Murdoch's neck. 'I can't be blamed for that. She knew my temper but she wouldn't shut up hinting about Sarah; where I was that night. Then she said if I stopped her from leaving she'd go to the police—' Murdoch felt the fingers around his neck grow weak and loosen. When he opened his eyes, Walker's hands were over his own face. 'I didn't know she was pregnant,' he moaned into them, like he was praying for the pregnancy to be true. 'I never meant to hurt her. I couldn't hurt my little girl.' His silhouette jolted against the inky sky, and a howling sob came through his fingers, steaming in the sharp cold of the night. Murdoch tried to roll away from under his weight, but he was still too weak. He pushed against Walker's knee with both hands, but the only result was yet more pain in the back of his head. 'Sorry,' sobbed Walker. 'I'm so sorry.'

He leant forward again, blocking out the stars and the lights from the house. Murdoch's vision was going again; then there were other shadows blocking out the sky – figures and faint blue flashes in the stars behind Walker. Murdoch felt the man's hands placed more carefully around his neck, his own flailing fists useless against Walker's longer arms. Walker's thumbs tracked across his throat, a doctor looking for a lump, until they found the Adam's apple. 'Sorry, Georgie darling.' Walker's tears fell on Murdoch's face. 'Sorry, my baby.'

Maybe he said more, but Murdoch couldn't hear. The only thing in his ears was the booming of his own heart and the words he'd wanted to say: *I'm not an animal. I'm not an animal. I'm not an animal any more.* And then, listening to those words himself, he relaxed and let the darkness take him.

CENTRAL COAST ARCHITECT PLEADS GUILTY TO THIRD MURDER

Sydney Morning Herald

10 December, SYDNEY — A 52-year-old man pleaded guilty today to murdering his wife, almost ten years after she died. Paul Walker of Montauban, NSW, entered his plea in the Supreme Court via video link from prison.

Last month, Walker was also charged with the murders of Georgina Walker, his daughter, and William Murdoch, an investigator employed by his wife's family to solve his daughter's disappearance.

Police had previously investigated the successful architect and failed to find any evidence he was involved in his daughter's disappearance. The death of his wife, Sarah Walker, had been thought to be the result of hit-and-run, but police reopened the case when they found the body of seventeen-year-old Georgina Walker in the garden of the family home.

Sarah Walker's sister, Hannah Simms, claims she had always suspected her brother-in-law and had hired investigator William Murdoch to prove his guilt. Mr Walker is charged with strangling Murdoch to death.

'At last, we're getting closer to justice for Sarah and Georgie,' said Simms. 'I have lost a sister and a much-loved niece, but maybe now I can move on. I wish I could thank Bill Murdoch for what he's done for my family.'

A motive for the murders has not yet been publicly confirmed.

Walker will be sentenced in July.

There never really was a funeral, but, after the fuss from the trials died down, Hannah Simms organised a private memorial service. It was late January, the hottest day in New South Wales for four years – children kept indoors and the landscape wilted at the edges. Davie was late, of course. He'd spent longer at the beach than he'd meant to, reluctant to leave the water on such a glorious day. He pulled up outside the chapel in a messy spray of gravel, then sat there for a second enjoying the shade, composing himself before he went in. He'd driven past this place a thousand times and never given it a second thought other than to use the flower stall at the gates when he'd forgotten someone's birthday. The cemetery was on the winding Crown Road between Crosley and Montauban, only the gates and the flower place visible when you passed. It turned out you had to drive through five minutes of gravestones before you reached the chapel itself.

Davie had imagined something older, more like a church, not this functional red-brick building. Something with a steeple would have been more comforting. He stood in the shade of the awning over the smoked-glass doors and looked out at the baking cemetery. It was deserted but for a distant groundsman taking a smoko under a tree; too hot a day for laying flowers on a grave – hot enough to remind you of nothing but hell. He heard music start up inside the chapel, voices singing out of tune, grimaced and decided to wait another minute before going inside. The cars arranged on the gravel told him who was waiting for him: Hannah and Tom, Natalie, Anne Lincoln.

Hannah had insisted on the memorial being invitation-only. Otherwise, she'd said, tutting and sighing, half of Montie would turn up, subtly asking for details and – she wouldn't be surprised – taking photos. The secrecy explained Anne Lincoln's presence. Nothing could stop her from finding out anything local, but she could keep things quiet if she was on the inside of them. The car closest to the chapel was the only one he didn't recognise. A sleek Mercedes with the roof down, two white leather seats confident of the weather. Davie stared at it, unable to believe it belonged to the chaplain. Then, curious about who owned it as much as anything else, he took a deep breath and walked inside.

Hannah glared at him as he chose a pew. Tom smiled. Natalie rolled her eyes. Anne Lincoln ignored him, belting out the hymn two tones flat, no need to read the words. Davie picked up the hymn sheet and sang along half-heartedly, wondering what was bothering him so much. He looked up at the stained-glass windows, religious without reference to a specific creed, and tried not to think of the large bead of sweat crawling slowly down his spine. There had been an acrid smell outside: the dirty afterthought of something recently done there. On the last line of the hymn, he realised what it was and a huge smile broke across his face. When the music ended he didn't sit, but turned instead and walked quickly back to the glass doors. He could feel, actually *feel*, Hannah glaring at his back as the chaplain or priest or whatever he was coughed awkwardly and said, 'We are here to remember Georgina Walker.'

The glare from the white marble headstones was difficult to bear, even after Davie had retrieved his sunglasses from the Excel. Walking slowly in the suffocating heat, he stuck to the road that wound up away from the chapel, jacket over one shoulder, his footsteps eerie in the middle of the day. The figure he'd seen from the shade of the awning – the man he'd taken to be a groundsman – had moved on and it took Davie ten minutes to find him, resting against a family monument in the shade of the trees that bordered the cemetery. He was smoking the end of the cigarette Davie had smelled by the door to the chapel. His eyes were closed, like he was resting or praying or half-asleep. Davie was almost upon him, sweat slathering his shirt to his back, trousers sticking to his legs, when the man heard him, opened his eyes and slowly smiled. Davie smiled back.

'Aren't you supposed to be dead?'

'That's what this place is for, innit? Dead people?'

Bill stubbed his cigarette out carefully and put it into a plastic container he'd produced from the pocket of his shorts, his watch glinting heavily in the sunlight.

'What about the witness protection program?' said Davie. 'All those people who're not supposed to know you're alive?'

'Pleased to see you too, mate.'

He took a step forwards and they shook hands awkwardly for a moment until Davie pulled him into a hug.

'Bleeding hell,' said the Englishman. 'You feel like you just got out the shower.' He pushed Davie away, then held him at arm's length to look him up and down. 'You've put on weight.'

'I mean it, Bill. It's dangerous for you to be here.'

'Nah, you read the wrong papers, mate. My old gang's done. A bunch of Russians with big money moved in. The territory's all broken up, Lebs, Sudanese, Chinese, they're all at it. Everyone who wants me dead is dead themselves, or not in a position to do much about it. My lot's boss, bloke called Harris, copped it with a heart attack during his trial. You might of seen that in the papers?'

Davie shook his head slowly. He leaned against the monument, feeling the heat in his head. A new hymn floated up from the chapel, the voices tinny and too few.

'So what *are* you doing here?

'I've got some business to attend to. And besides, I wanted to see you lot, didn't I? Check in with the old crowd. Thought it might be nice to see how Tom's grown.'

'That might not be a good idea.'

'He knows I'm alive, don't he?'

'Yeah, it's just he's … well …'

Davie struggled to find the right words.

'And then I thought I might have a look at Montie. Thought you might buy me a beer; we could talk about old times. Only one mind, I'm driving.'

'I'm guessing that's your Merc down there?'

Bill smiled and rubbed his palm across the top of his head. 'You like it?'

'Tell me you didn't "borrow" it.'

'Me? Nick a car? Oh no, mate. As of a little while now, I am straighty-one-eighty. I even pay taxes; daylight bleeding robbery that is. No, I bought it fair and square.'

They sat in silence for a while, Davie wanting to ask where Bill had found the money for that, but knowing he'd get no answer. Or, if he was honest, not wanting the answer, in case it broke the spell of the moment. There was no birdsong, no traffic on the winding road from Crosley, and after a while, no music from the service. It was too hot for noise. Soon, there

259

was movement down at the chapel, tiny figures in black in the shade of the awning.

'Come on,' said Bill, suddenly. 'Let's go and say hello.'

'Yeah, dude, I'm not sure that's a good idea.'

But his friend was gone, the heat not bothering him at all, jogging quickly, in as straight a line as the headstones would allow, down towards the red-brick building.

Murdoch stopped when he saw Anne Lincoln was one of the figures by the door. She was the only one there who didn't know he was alive and, while he planned to let everyone know in time, turning up in the middle of a funeral wasn't the way to do it. He waited by a headstone as she hugged each of the others, crossed to her van and crunched it across the gravel. When it had disappeared round a bend in the driveway, he started walking again. He was fifty metres from the awning when Hannah, chatting to the chaplain, looked up and saw him.

She was out of breath when she reached him, her smile a strain in the baking day. She was wearing a thin black dress, sensible heels scratched by the gravel. Her blonde hair was long now, no sign of the glasses he'd last seen her in, but she still looked a mouse. That pale skin, the faint pinkness around the eyes, those teeth about to bite. She reached up and kissed him on the cheek – a gesture he'd not expected – then put her arm through his and led him along the path that wound through overgrown grasses towards the back of the chapel. She told him he was looking well for a dead man.

'Not so bad yourself, darlin'. Where you taking me?'

'I wanted to talk to you, Bill.'

'Funny that, I wanted to talk to you too.'

She stopped and looked up to him, her pale eyes blinking against the bright sky. She glanced quickly back over her shoulder, then said, 'With me? What about?'

'You knew, didn't you?'

'Knew what?'

'You knew about me the first time you met me. You knew what I was and that's why you sent me up here, innit?'

She let go of his arm and gave a thin smile. Walked on so he had to walk too if he wanted to hear the answer. The path grew narrower and they had to continue one behind the other – Hannah Simms telling him the truth over her shoulder.

'It does get frustrating when we see people so obviously profiting from crime. This may surprise you, Bill, but I'm a keen advocate for the legalisation of drugs. Then we can tax them – imagine what we could do for public education, hospitals and the like. Unfortunately, though, we mostly have to pretend we believe in the fronts you people put forward. Yours was terrible. A private detective! Half the reason I gave you the case was to watch you squirm your way out of it. You should have told me you were a cage fighter or something.'

He laughed and she asked what was funny.

'Someone else suggested that at the time. And I reckon you knew about Paul Walker too, and about what he'd done to Sarah. Or at least had your suspicions. I wish you'd of told me; it might of saved me some bother.'

'If I'd told you, you'd have just agreed with me and told me it couldn't be proven. I'd kind of resolved myself to the fact you'd do something similar anyway, find some excuse. But then you really started investigating and finding things out. I was impressed, wondered if I'd got the wrong idea about you. I didn't realise you'd be such a bulldog, so English and determined.' She laughed at the idea. 'Listen, Bill …'

'But why did you keep me on? Once I'd found a bit of stuff out, why didn't you get a real detective?'

They'd reached the end of the path, a locked gate to a fenced-off area behind the chapel, lawnmowers and a cement mixer visible through wooden slats. Hannah turned back towards him, then looked at her shoes as she started to speak. His turn to walk, hers to keep up.

'I was frustrated the police hadn't found anything. I thought maybe you wouldn't feel the need to … Well, you know. Can we slow down?'

'You thought I'd be all right to break the law to get to the truth?'

'Maybe, yes. Listen, Bill, slow down. Before we go back, there's something you should know. It's about Tom.'

They were within sight of the awning again and Murdoch saw the kid as Hannah said his name. He was standing beside Natalie, impossibly tall, the kid he'd known stretched by a foot or more. He and Natalie were looking in all directions, probably wondering what had happened to

261

Hannah. Natalie turned towards the cars as Tom stepped out into the sunlight and looked directly down the path towards them.

'Hello, trouble,' said Murdoch.

Tom flushed and his mouth fell open. Without hesitation, he broke into a run, coming down the path so fast Murdoch braced himself for the hug.

'Oh no,' said Hannah. 'Tom—'

But Tom was already upon them, his first punch catching Murdoch neatly between the legs. Murdoch wheezed and fell into a foetal position, dirt on his face as Tom kicked him weakly in the ribs. Then the kid fell to his knees and started peppering Murdoch's head with punches.

'You pig!' he screamed, his voice breaking in fury. 'I hate you. You said you'd never let anything happen to my dad. You said you'd push them off the roof. It's you they should push ...'

The punches stopped and Murdoch looked up from the pain in his stomach to see Davie dragging Tom backwards along the path, the kid kicking and screaming still, his face red and covered in tears. Murdoch heard Hannah's voice behind him.

'I'm so sorry, Bill. It's my fault as much as yours. I mean ... it's neither. I'm so sorry.'

She stepped over him and he watched the back of her run down the path towards Davie and the still-screaming Tom. Watched the three of them wrestle around the corner and slowly out of view.

Natalie was only slightly more pleased to see him. 'You're supposed to be dead,' she said. 'Not wandering around ten minutes from the scene of the crime.' Since he'd last seen her, she'd picked up a tiny scar on her eyebrow; if anything, it made her frown more appealing. They were sheltering in the shade of the awning again, Davie hovering awkwardly between them, the noise of Hannah's car fading in the distance. Murdoch was dusting the dirt off his shorts, checking his watch for scratches. He looked up and caught her eye.

'Yeah, go on darlin', tell me you're not pleased to see me.'

'I'm not pleased to see you, Bill. Have you any idea how much it costs to put people into the program? We've spent a lot of money trying to keep you dead. Alive. You know what I mean.'

'And it worked, didn't it? Here I am, alive and kicking. Job done. Davie and I are heading back to Montie for a beer. You want to come?'

'You are joking. You know everyone there thinks you're dead!'

'I'll just tell Anne Lincoln,' said Davie. 'Then everyone will know before Monday.'

'Why are you encouraging him, Davie? Hasn't he caused enough trouble?'

'No, Natalie, he helped us out. He solved two crimes. Or have you forgotten?'

She swore, said she needed some water and slammed through the glass doors into the chapel. Murdoch grunted a little laugh and nodded at the two cars parked on the gravel.

'You giving her a lift then?' he said to Davie.

'Oh damn, I can't. I've got to get back to Montie for three; Hannah was supposed to drive her back to Crosley. I guess she forgot in the … you know. Hang on, I'll give her my keys and you can give me a lift.'

They were reversing onto the driveway, Davie playing with every knob on the dashboard, when Natalie re-emerged from the chapel. She'd washed her face, wet hair clinging to her forehead and dripping onto her black dress. Murdoch looked away, but she called out to them and jogged across the gravel.

'Listen,' she said, one hand on Murdoch's arm, her voice barely audible over the rumble of the engine. 'I never said it.' She struggled to say it now. 'Thank you. Thank you for everything, Bill. But,' a harsh finger in his face, 'you listen to me, you put one foot wrong and I'll be on your back, you got that?'

She didn't wait for an answer. Just turned and crunched back to Davie's car.

Halfway to Montauban Murdoch pulled up between two yellowing paddocks that fell gently out of view. He said he reckoned it was the only place you could see the lagoon from the Crown Road; said he'd always wanted to stop and admire the view.

'Don't mind, do you?'

Davie checked his watch and grimaced. 'I've got a meeting at three. It won't take long and then we can go for that beer, but I can't miss it.'

'You'll be all right.'

Murdoch got out of the car and walked over to the paddock fence. Next thing he knew, Davie was leaning on it beside him.

'Why did you come back, Bill? Business, you said?'

'Yeah, well. That and something some bloke told me. He said it's friends what make you rich. Years ago this was, and I laughed at him. "It's money what makes you rich," I said. But ... yeah, I dunno.'

'I'm sorry about Tom,' Davie said after a while. 'I tried to warn you.'

'Yeah, well, next time try a bit harder. Wouldn't have thought the kid had it in him. I won't walk straight for weeks.'

'You all right?'

Murdoch squinted up at the sky. 'About Tom? Course. Everything I've been through, I can cope with some kid not liking me.'

He gave Davie a look meant to be convincing, took another drag, and snapped on a smile. 'What about you then, Davie Wonder? How's the real estate business? You sold anything recently?'

Davie blushed and found a stone to kick at.

'I did actually, my biggest ever commission. It was ... It was Paul Walker's house, actually. It wasn't easy either. I could have sold tickets to all the people who wanted to see the garden, but, of course, none of them wanted to live there. Ended up selling it to a cashed-up buyer interstate. Bought it sight-unseen and took all the furniture too. Probably some foreigner or someone who doesn't read the papers.' He checked his watch. 'Actually, Bill, we should go. That's who I'm meeting at three. I've got to give him the keys.'

'You got them on you?'

'Yes. Why?'

'Just hand them over then, mate. Then we can go for that beer.'

The End

CLASS ACT

Because there's no such thing as a happy ending…

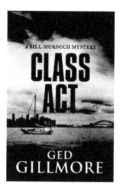

Can a man who's lived a life of crime ever escape his past?
The world's most reluctant private investigator is about to find out…

Former bad boy turned local hero, Bill Murdoch, should be happy with his little piece of paradise. After all, he's got the fancy car and the big house by the beach. The only trouble is he's slowly suffocating in small town life.

So when Murdoch is hired to investigate who framed wealthy businessman, James Harte, for murder, he jumps at the chance. Going undercover amongst the jet set, Murdoch is quickly drawn into an exciting world of yachts, horse racing and glitzy parties. But soon Murdoch's shady past looks set to catch up with him and when he falls for Harte's beautiful wife, Amanda, things take a deadly turn.

Class Act is the gripping new murder mystery from Ged Gillmore. A perfect piece of modern Australian noir, it will grab you and keep you guessing until the very last line.

Coming January 2018

For news on upcoming books, please visit www.gedgillmore.com

Printed in Great Britain
by Amazon

80720485R00161